The Elusive:
Four Romances

Also By This Writer

Awareness Alone penetrates to the heart of experience, the eternal dance of absolute awareness. Grasping that it is all we can ever be, beyond endless becoming born of desire and fear, we discover the miracle of our own borderless freedom.

The Wandering   Distanced from partner Marsha and her daughter Matty by physical and psychic wanderings into geographic places, historical scenes, other lives... the narrator Blank dances solo with his unavoidable other, claiming to alert her to opaque parts of his nature and to her own: on clinging and running, victim and perpetrator, freedom and fundamentalism, splitting and taking responsibility... and on Samsara, the trivial endless recurrence. *The Wandering* is Blank's ruminating travelogue, tainted-love diary, mythic karmic romance, meditation on being and becoming, conscience and commitment.

The Labyrinth: Tales of Entanglement, Escape
Don't Worry About a Thing   The meditator Dust is steered into community work by the Divinology Church, where like Dante in infernal circles he trawls people's rubbish in aberrant and miserifying scenes. With sainted girlfriend Blue Wendy and ascetic Anna Rex, underhinged by his Employer's spidery cult, we trace a satire on Dust's fabulations with the need to evolve, with the problem of who and how to be.   **Chaos**   Lean the journalist claims he is terminally ill. 'I spent a career conjuring stories for public consumption: now the parasites eat me'. The unruly girl Dora Jarr worms in. Her mission? To skewer corruption in 'the business of nano-genetics'. Trash novella, rant, love-lust letter, apologia - Lean's diarybook seeks a balm of chaos under tyranny of order. Who can live without narratival dreams? 'I'll be tragic hero in my last whodunnit.'   **The Labyrinth** At the heart of a Labyrinth, incarcerated by a Beast, is the goddess-temptress Conscience. In a Stalinist prison Drilov the clerk pens prisoners' confessions. The last, within a fundamentalist materialist machine where victim and perpetrator dance, is his own. In a brave future country, Dreeley the storyteller takes to the road with 'Dionysus' in search of an elusive woman. His goal? To deconstruct history and karma, snuff the beast of inconsequence, unravel the knot of death, surrender to immaterial sky.

Heartland: An Australian Idyll   Our Aussie democracy 'binds us as one', but who'll blow the whistle on myths and rorts of the lucky country - our fair-go hard-yakka dreamtime multiculture of aspirational lifters and bogan leaners in a hearty-grim hot utopia built on sand, we affable understated competitive Aussie nuts? Not to mention the new totalitarian yellow peril... It's election time and the silos square off - Superbia heartland high rollers, shadowy media influencers and coming leftie (female) heroes - in a fight between selfism and mutuality for the soul of the nation.

Total Drama (Macmillan Education Australia, 2010) investigates the dynamics of interpersonal encounters and the core ingredients of drama through original scripts and exercises.

THE ELUSIVE

FOUR ROMANCES

NICHOLAS FROST

For purchasing information, go to:
www.mouthsofillusion.com / nfrost@odp.com.au

Cover design by Alicia Grady, Struck By Violet www.struckbyviolet.com

Typeset by BookPOD

ISBN: 978-0-6450137-6-4 (pbk) 978-0-6450137-7-1(e-book)

NATIONAL LIBRARY OF AUSTRALIA

A catalogue record for this book is available from the National Library of Australia

Contents

THE ELUSIVE

THE ADVENTURES OF SALLY BANG

NICHOLAS FROST

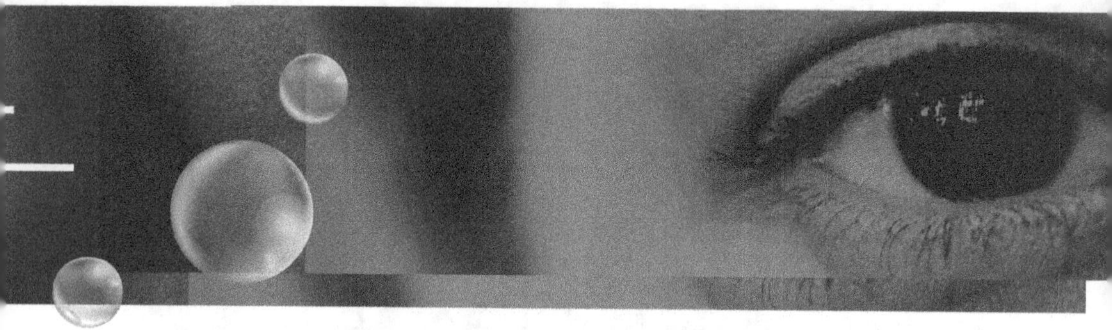

THE ADVENTURES OF SALLY BANG

A book's going round about ME, says Sally Bang to anyone who'll listen, and a Ghost is writing it all down! Who is he but? Sal meets Won the Korean and life gets a groove on: co-starring in aristocrat Tiffany Haigh's soapy dramas, falling on face with love interest Jean Paul (no issue he's 28), weirdness in the Brunswick underland, sex shock at a peace retreat, olds and enemies tearing at our anti-heroine's sense of self and an explosive reckoning in the outback wild. What's gained and lost in growing up? Whose story is it anyway? At sixteen there is insight and beauty that never come again. And inside every adult is a need to get it back.

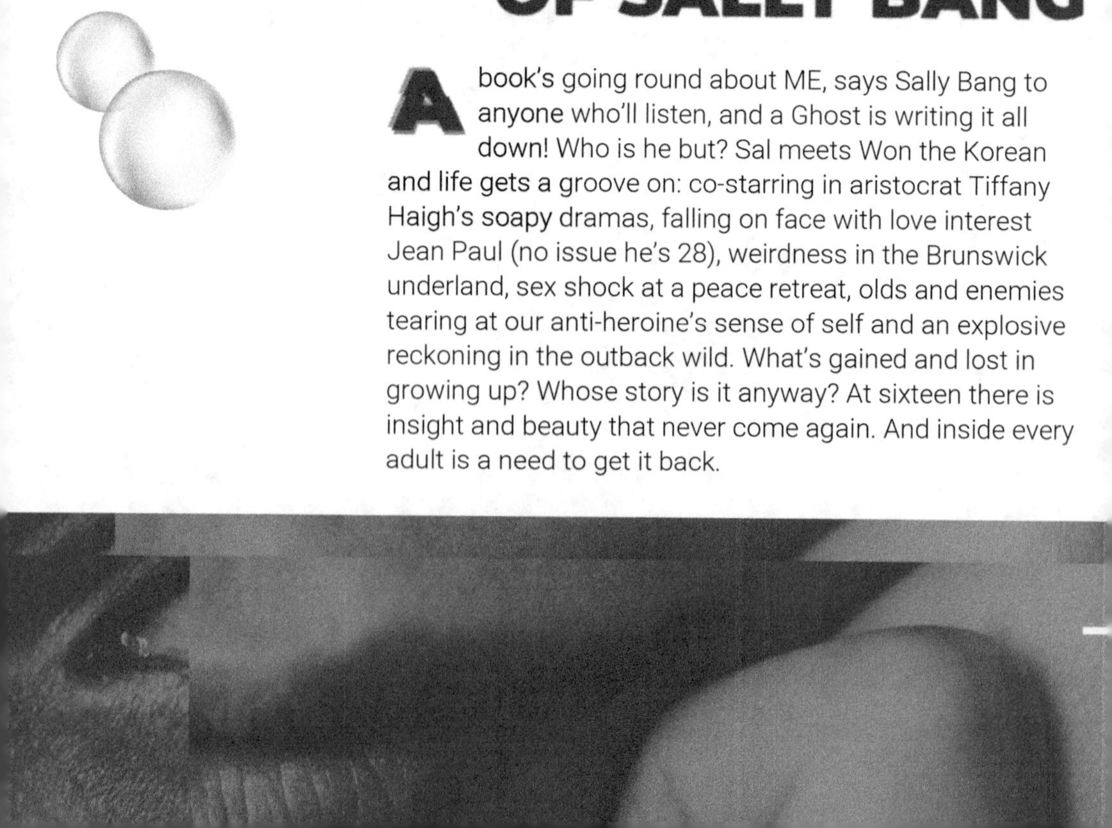

A book's going round about ME, says Sally Bang to anyone who'll listen. It's called

The Adventures of Sally Bang!

Sally Bang, aged 15.7, has a crush on boys. Totally random, but girls are capable of crazy things. Boys come in all shapes and sizes, Sally knows. Here's a sample: her little brat bro has a mate called Johnson Toast, who has a famous fat big sister called Finger Lickin'. Meet her shortly. Toast's thin mate is Juice Nick. Sally has a couple of dreams. In one, Johnson turns up on his bike at lunchtime when she's wagging school. Parents are at work or something, Sally's feelin' sick and J's come to comfort. Except, like all 14-year-old boys he smells and has nothing to say that girls want to hear. His opening line is: 'You sick?' Sally switches to Juice Nick. He is as thin as a straw and intellectual. She meets him at the door. There's a bit where he sidles in and says 'Cool'. His best line is 'Cool'. Sally dreams he may be deep but he isn't. Sal wants hot so that's that. What now? I wish i was at university, says Sal. Then i can do a lot of drugs make out and go on fully sick demos.

Animal Road

Sally's next dream is she joins a commie cell of cool young ones who all live together in a big flat in town, and they do drugs and have arguments and stuff. The ingrates are called: Finger Lickin', Kar-en, The Eye, Tall Uncle Bill (American weird guy) and The Terrorist.

Sal dreams to be going out with The Terrorist (aka The Arab Guy) who lives in the attic or basement or garden shed. No beard cool accent and got bombed eh. Cool bananas. At the table in the kitchen at Animal Road they all like hang for breakfast.

Finger Lickin' (Johnson Toast's fat sister) is sitting there taking up space 'cos it's her fat flat, and at Uni she's famous for being fat and sitting round in the caf making comments like who fucken keeps emptying the fridge?

and As I'm hip and portly I'm gonna be a journalist and report war stuff from the safety of my armchair. Sal doesn't react to her at all.

In comes Kar-en (pronounced Ker-ENN) who told Sal to read a book called Anna Kerrenina. Was she in South Park? asked clever Sal. Sal's impressed by Kar-en, who knows a frig of a lot. She's up for some intellectual biffo today, Sal can tell.

Next, in strolls The Eye. The Eye is a member of the *why?* generation, naughtily says Finger Lickin'. Sal notices he's pushing 30 (or 300) and has no hair to speak of. Eye is fully interested in himself as far as Sal can tell. That's good so am I. The guy could be a creepy homo but probably nah. He's sure creepy-deadly when Finger's around. He has a glass eyeball but no-one can ever tell which one it is. Finger reckons they're both glass but she's fat sarcasm personified. Eye confides this to spectator Sal. Finger takes up 2 chairs on the east wall as usual and holds court. Eye gives Finger the eye and Finger gives Eye the finger. The old greeting comrades. Fing' opens with: Who fucken keeps emptying… Wasn't me, says Eye, quick as anything. As you know, I eat no *fatty* food. Sal notes how slim he is. Could he have a dong bigger than The Terrorist? How do I check? Umm, I know. He and the T. are gaylords doing it in the basement and I Insta their dongs yeah! Sally imagines. Finger Lickin' is pounding at him this morning. *So it's the dick-tatorship of the prowler-tariat? Brave nerd world?* Yo. Philosophy for breakfast. Sal's way out of her depth. Kar-en to the rescue: Marx is irrelevant to late capitalist consumer culture 'cause he's a dead twat with a beard… and er he's dead. Finger: Kar-en's been on Wikipedia again. Eye: Our fresh young schoolie visitor full of dreams (mostly wet) doesn't care to hear such 'sallies'! (Uh? Someone says he studies Eng. Lit).

K: Bollocks. She's a rat in wolf's clothing. But listen, does my curvy butt look cute in these tight jeans? K. says this to Eye but Sal gets she aims to wind up fat Finger. Kar-en is what Sal wants to be right now. No-one pisses on or off Kar-en, the girl who kicked the hornet's nest! She'll be an activist wikileaker and rescue dudes in Libya and be bisexual wherever she wants. Kick-arse Kar-en!

But Finger farts and they all faint. Merely on cue! she claims. Loud and proud to please the crowd and top o' the mornin' to ye all. Eye makes for the door with his bowl of Special K and scummy skim milk. - Don't she just conjure up those curvy chicks in the Special K. ads? Glossy glass apartments, fresh and regular. Yum, he smirks. I'm obsessed with toilets, Sal chips in. Non sequitur. Everybody looks at her as if a turd got dropped among the teacups.

- Sally's just a bunch of dreams and none of 'em come true, says Finger Lickin' fatly. My bro Johnson was in a TV ad for jocks, little Sally. Well hung I reckon! She arches her eyebrow in an arch way she's practised. Who reacts? Nobody.
- I prefer brains but, says Sal.
- You'd like Juice Nick then
- How'd she get inside my dream? Sal thinks. This fat troll has power over me.

Kar-en, who gets slimmer and cleverer by degrees sums up: Sally Bang will 'kick arse someday'. Sal agrees with this. Sal is gonna be sexy famous on youtube witty meany-poos whenever she wants and hot and In A Band and stuff. And be a girl terrorist and die famous in a desert and whatever! Er, Sal agrees with bits of that too.

Enter The Terrorist. He's a Muslim and he comes in Laden with watermelons, bomb-making materials and last night's felafel. He stuffs them in the Bin.
- Do we haf toast orr some such?
Sal loves this guy. He says what he says.
- You're up early for a fanatical suicide bomber!
Finger's tactful best. (Sal longs to speak up) Shut up! Yes we have toast. Shall I butter it for you?
- We don't butter people up here, snaps Finger.
Eye sticks his head back in.
- Fatso *is* toast. My special cupboard, mate. Help yerself.

Sal compares these boys for size. Which is more slim more cool more foreign less gay? Hmm. The Eye is baldy-buddhist up himself and cooly ironic. The T's a black-haired Muzzo and he's my yummy boy. The broody Islamist chews his toast. There's always a hiatus when a Muslim is in the room. Is he a commy like us? Is he even a student?

Finger in piratical voice: - Arre you one of uss?
Eye: - He's my refugee. (Eye *is* gay)
Finger: - No-one should be a tenth-class citizen 'cause of his religion
Eye: - Fat girls want sex as well!
Muslim bungs in his earbud and mutes the lot of them.
Sal is somehow not pleased with this arrangement this crowd this breakfast banter. Today Sal is suffering from a talentless *ghost writer*.
- Where's Captain Thik, your Garfieldy flat cat? she absurdly asks.
- In the oven, says Kar-en. Which reminds me. It's Sal's birthday! (It isn't) Sal, how coolly are you dressed today! How emo grungy gothy waify punky chic! Are we 14 or 15?
Sal plays along: - Today I'm 19 and I'm coming to your cool party.
- No longer an *oik*, says Finger sweetly.
- You wish, says Kar-en.

Sal is hurt by Kar-en's wit. Has she no tact? A girl of 15 always wants to be 19. How cold are *you*, Miz Russian Novel? Sal dreams suddenly of exiting this cell-load of cretins. She dreams of better people better role models better planets better songs to sing. But where?

Her Arab Guy heard it all. - It eez your beerthday? When I vas 15 I dreamed better life, bekoming doktor. My country is bombed by American dicktators and my parents are kill-ed and my child dreams seem broken. I flee to Infidel West alone, hidden in container where I suffocate with 300 sad souls. But I am alife, my friends. I haf life and love! (with my little Sally Bung Bung this day of Rumadun, Inshallah)

- Blimey, says the Eye, completely sucked in.

Sal definitely made up the bit in brackets. But this is *love*, the strong silent type! She extends a tentative mitt toward her Muzzy but he's stuck his earbud in his earhole again. How so? Is her dark lover but an arrogant chatterbox? More complicated than you think, says a little voice.

Punishment of languishing dreams circles our 15.7 year-old. Sal moves off and out into the proletarian daylight. Stiff wind blows from the north. Cold Animal Road turns into Smith Street. *Who am I really really?* thinks Sally Bang.

The Grim Pill's Progress

This night Sal heads for some acid party she heard about from Kar-en. But K's not there yet. Sal's never been to an A. party before, but like a donkey at the door they give her a sugar lump. Half an hour later she's off her tree under a picture of green tropics on a red wall. A large-headed boy looms, wearing bow tie striped trousers. OMG it's that Gregory guy.

- Greetings. *Windsor Gregorian.* He presents his card which says GENIUS.
- 'Zat your name?
- I'm Windsor Gregorian. The genius you all require
- No flies on you bro
- It's true my life is exemplary. I d-decided at age 6 to be the b-boffin I am. One excels at most things but is s-somewhat ig-ignorant of g-girls
- Sure talk good
- Are you 'high'?
- Dunno. The room's moving
- I'm here to observe animal behaviour. On assignment from G-Government. G-girls included!
- F-Fark, says Sal.
- What are you 'f-feeling' now? Windsor has his little red book out, and a sharp pencil.
- I'm walking in a rice field. Green trees rake the blood sky I'm a survivor. Scarecrow turns her ragged face to me. I run to help. She's a yellow girl and fly's blood on her face the helicopters rumble it's Vietnam Juba Juba go the blades. Rice field waves in bloody sun. BANG! She's going down the kids are running. BLAM! ...i told you red. i mean she's *dead*
- F-fascinating! says Gregorian, scribbling. His bow tie's a helicopter blade.

7

The scene alters. Windsor ain't there no more. Sal feels cold and faint. She's sitting in a group. Kar-en seems to be talking. Has a hammer and sickle on her T-shirt. We are enduring Doctor Zhivago. Her red hair flows like za Volga. She's off her face and they all stare and stare.

- Kom-rades! Kill the fascist Guv'ment right? You say I'm Kommie, man? I'm Fundamentalista. I suicide yorr baby. Gimme voordka. Faark! Izlaam iz where its at! My boyfriend is bad dude from da dezert. He's ay bomber, maan!

And much much more. Reality's unintelligible red walls roll out and in. People turn to green ghosts. Outside, Sal is fully sick and her bowel's unstable. Later she thinks: I'm just a tragic poet on acid, where do i get off? She's definitely outside. Cars rock and roll down a street. Is K. doing my Terrorist? I'm 15, out of my league. That Vietnam thingy in Mod. Hist. must of freaked me out today. She notices there're high heels on her feet. Step on a crack, marry a rat. Feel totally soiled. This day will have to end Downtown. I wannabe the pure clean girl on Special K in my classy glass apartment in TV world and it's always happy brekky time and i get to go toilet prop'ly... We'll crash Oggy's Bar then. Sal stumbles away.

A Tiff with Tiffany and Co

OMG. Tiffany my upper class bitch sort-of friend is coming this way with Rude Boy and Lotta BS! Quick, call somebody. *Bleeep...*
- Ullo it's me The Eye hi hi
- *It's Sal.* (hiss) *Say something now!*
- Err, tis EYE, the narrator in your head
- *Say my cousin died*
- Your cousin died?
- *Omigod.* (loud) *My cousin died? What? How?*
- Err, nuclear war? Tsunami? Road crash?
- *Road crash? Oh crap! That's so baaad*
- Who's with you?
- *Blood and everythink? I feel fully sick*
- Where are you?
- *Oggy's!* (hiss) *Rude boy and Tiff and BS are here!*

- Yay! Who?
- *My EX! Urr you're my boyfriend right now. Say 'Babe'!*
- Okay Babe. Oink
- *I'm comin' to your place.* (loud) *My cuzin died in a crash! Pick me up at Oggy's Babe. I need you NOW!*
- Yawn. Byeee. (CLICK)

Her people are staring in unsubtle ways.
- Aw hi Rude. Tiff. Lotta. I'm so freaked
Tiffany: - Sal darling. Have a coffee? (Tiffany's invariably polite)
- Nah. My cousin died
Rudi: - Buh bummer!
Tiffany, who is in the know about Rudi and Sal's *recent one-nighter*, winks at Sal and asks Rude 'if he fixed his stutter yet'.
Rudi: - Huh? Huh? W-what you guys w-winking at?
- My cousin died, stutter boy! There's blood on the street. Her face is a tomato. The ambulance is *there*. It's horrid. My family's dying and I'm standing talkin' to you!
Lotta: - How d'you know all that?
- Er, they said it on my phone and stuff.

Tiff, Rude and Lotta BS look at each other. They know Sal has had a tiff, is generally rude and is full of BS. So they smile. Well screw them. Now Sal is running. Not to Animal road. Not to the bloody crash site. Not to her family to cry and mourn. In circles. Where is she running to?

BLANK! Her GHOST WRITER makes his entrance. Say a big hi to your ghost writer guys. Let's see. Your parents are Alicia and Ron Bang of Fitzroy Vic. Your mum was Alicia Mary Connaught, exotic milkmaid of Ireland (not). Your dad was probably Ronald Bang, butcher of Melbourne. They claimed to fall in love and settled in this fair city 16 years back. You were more or less an accident. Grew up like the weeds. Had no cousin by the way. You went to one school then another then another till you arrived at the one you're at. Lot of schools! There was one dark teacher you liked once. Had a black earring. He felt illegal, said things to you, had dark opinions. People dislike you, laugh at your silly sally name. Was there ever a spotty guy behind the bike sheds?

- Yeah, Johnson Toast whatever
- Then came Rude Boy with his stutter we presume?
- Fuck yeah
- That all?
- So what? You making a list, ghost writer? That's all past now. It's called childhood. Now I'm here. Always said I'd check out early. (Boo hoo) And who'd notice?

Sitting Duck

4 hours later, the bench in the park is cutting into her back. One duck has been floating back and forth on her greasy pond for 4 hours. Now 'Bazzy' arrives. To feed his duck.

- Arrr, how're you?
Sal sees it's time to go.
- Nah, stay there. Oil feed me duck Maddie
- Your duck
- Every ole trooper has 'is duck.
She looks at him. - Maybe I could be your duck. (Sal has no idea why she said this)
He raises an eyebrow. - What you call yerself?
- Sally Bang
- Orr right 'Sally Bang'. Me I'm Bazzy. Feed 'er this... He pulls out a greenish loaf.
- Whole thing?
(Guffaws) - If yer like
- Duck 'll sink
- You're sharp. The others 'll gather round though. They're in the bushes. Maddie's their front man
- Entrepreneurial ducks?
- Uh?
- Clever ducks?
- Yeah.

Several clouds pass. The naked trees round the lake stir a little. Sal stares like Narcissus into the water. Those ducks have drifted away, full of greenish bread. Bazzy says:

- Where's yer home?
- I live in a glass apartment in the sky. 28th floor
- That right? You goin' there?
- Yup. Nope. Going to my friends. There's Eye and Finger Lickin' (she's not my friend) and the Terrorist (he's a refugee and cool as) and Karen, she's a commie but not Russian and another weird guy Uncle Bill or something. They live at Animal Road.

Sal is surprised she remembered all her details.

- Animal Road? Never 'eard of it
- Oh yeah big old flat in the city. Finger's fat as, but I won't ever be fat like her. She puts people down tho'
- D'you put people down?
- Whatever
- Listen Missy. What're you, 14?
- 15 and three-quarters
- Yer parents?
- They're like, dead
- No kiddin'
- Dead as. So dead. Me, I'm dead

(Doubtful pause) - Nah.

Sal totters away at this point then stops. Bazzy is eyeing her. She wilts a bit.

- Okay, not dead but they're old as
- You're a good 'un, you are
- Like my girly stories?
- Nop bad. Bit far-fetched. Siddown. I'll tell ya one.

Moi dad was in Nam, that's Veet Nam. Got captured by the Cong, that's Veet Cong. Them yellers worked 'im to the bone. Was thin as a stick mate, but he 'ad this doc who got them Veets to let 'im rest in camp on bad days. Saved 'is life did Doc Thieu. Other blokes fried in the jungle. Skellies they were. Tropical lurgies the works. S' what ya call dead. Livin' dead. Them commies don't care. Matter of honour, supposed to die for yer country. Screw that. No 'ucken use dead mate. Got on home, not in a body bag.

11

Couldn't settle. No decent job. Was a bum. Gov'ment bum! Wife never stuck around. Me neever. Think *you* got problems. Uh? You listenin'?
Sal slowly surfaces out of the deep well of Bazzy's world.
- Uh, yup! No use dead… Cool story dude. Depressing good.
She's inclined to believe some of it. He's obviously practised it.
- Think I'll go now. You here every day?
- Ev'ry day. Rain or shine
- Say 'lo to Maggie duck
- Will do
- Don't let her get fat and sink.

Stuck back at home, Sal thinks of her apartment in the sky. Not the commie terrorist one, the Special K one where she's always *alone*. Sal looks in a mirror in her parents' bedroom. They're out (of this story). Better steal some dough for rip-dirty noo jeans, thinks Sal. Or I could be honest. Work or something. Nah I'm a student. Don't do work. She rummages in the drawers. There's a stripey scarf. She wraps it absently about her. Men have real odd bits in their drawers… washers holy sox stone age condoms old spice maltese coin 1953. No dough though. Sal sucks her stomach. Am I fat yet? If I am I'll be past caring. I'll be meany-poos like Finger Lickin'. 'Hey Kerr-en. My butt's bigger n' your brain definitely. Why pose as a Kommie? All that went out with Putin. Still trying to bang Arab Boy 'cos he loves Allaaaah? They don't do sex stuff!' Finger's jealous but Sal is not. *Because the M. will turn his face to her one day in the red desert her bleached hair silhouetted in the sun's halo they'll kiss once and she'll step into the void scarfed like a bedouin on the Lonely Road to Libya and he at last will notice the Girl from the West who made a sacrifice boys like him could never dream of…* Good dream Sal. Then BANG! Oop, someone. BRO probably. Yurk. She spots Juice Nick's pointy head pass her window. He spots her too and actually winks. Next thing he's in the door. Hull-oo?

- Hey Sal. Fifteen today
- Yeah? Here's a medal
(Pinteresque pause) - Sooo… umm… Johnson's not here
- My bro is

- He's in the toilet. (Cavernous pause) - D'you um, like me? (The guy's a smooth romantic)
- Uh, I'm with a Uni guy
- You? (Palatial pause) Reckon I'd be real good
(Presidential pause) - So you got a rubber?
- Uhhh... I got a pencil...?
Sal starts to scream with laughter to let out some tension. A *pencil!*
- All right. Ferget it
- No no! I really like intellectuals and nerds.
She grabs him by the neck and starts to pash him but Juice Nick's disconcerted and Bro walks in. *Aw shit what's this?*
- Get orf, says Juice.
- I love you, honest! says Sal.
- Get a room, says bro.

A Room of One's Own

A woman needs a room of her own, preferably with a view. Or a basement in a seedy part of town. Who has one? She asks the Commie. Kar-en tells.

- Go see my 'Ex'. Corporal Punishment. Real name Ned Corporal. His dad was a general in the navy or admiral in the air force whatever. He's a sucker for 'lil sucks like you.

I'll beat on Kar-en one day, thinks Sal. But today she does as she's told. Finds an address in the Seedy BD. Corp Punishment is there. Comes to the door.
- Yeah?
- Hi, I'm a schoolie who wants to hang with druggies and deadbeats in a basement. Kar-en knows me
- And you're - ?
- Sally Bang
- Okay 'Sally Bang'. You got dough or dope?
- Nope, nope
- You can earn it. Come at six. Two doors down. The Basement.
She hangs in the 7 eleven and goes at 6. Corp is not there. A guy says:

- Corp's not here. Go sit with that Asiatic chick.

There is a girl disposed on a rug in back of the room. Low green light haloes her still form, reposed in semi-lotus. Sal sits. The Asian stares ahead. Imperial silence reigns. Then:
- What iss your name?
- Sal. (She suddenly thinks, this is a temple!)
- I am Won
- You are One what?
- Won iss my name. You are Sall. Sall - Won.

Doesn't mince words! But her eyes are inscrutably present, unreadably sad. And there's no curious smell of opium pervading the bluish-green gloom. No yellow-eyed monkeys skitter on the dark rafters. Won lowers her oval head in contemplation. Sal wonders.
- Are you...?
- I am a daughter of the old east. And my people were of Pyongyang. Not servants. For generations we lived in consummate luxury and ease. Yet we practised discipline. My father taught me stillness. And taught me self-defence. To enter the silos of the lower worlds, the sties of ignorance, the chambers of the living dead, I came to this country of the West. Now I worship the feet of the gods of disgrace.
Sal is amazed and stirred by this holy speech. - But...
- Be still. They come.
The door flings open. Corporal Punishment is there with two boys. The city belches through the doorway.
- Take yer pick, he says audibly.
Won stands in a single move. - Both. At once. She! will go home.
Won speaks it like holy writ. Corp looks worried. Sal sees he's pissed. The boys behind look in, squinting.
- Farrr out, says one. - Aziatic!

Sal crawls behind Won, courage gone. The boys shuffle shamble forward. One puts his hand on Won's navel. She lets him do it. The other tweaks her slight right breast. Again she forbears. They come in closer. Won closes her eyes, parts her lips. Sal is in the corner. The boys fiddle with their flies

14

and Won starts to hum or moan. *Nnnnn…* It's getting hotter. Won's eyes flick open. *Now!* The Asiatic brings Boy One's head down so his mouth is close to her crotch. *Nnnn…* Next thing, she swipes a blow to his head! He goes sideways! But the other guy is right on her… he's pinning her. Sal gulps at the dazed guy. Won lets the on-top guy do his angry angry thing and just as he's getting in the swing Won kicks him hard right in the nuts and he rolls over with a howling bark! She stands up.
- So sorry! Let's go.

Won has her hand, is leading her out and down a laneway. This is easily the most grown-up scene Sal ever witnessed. But Won seems (nearly) calm. They enter a café, sit at a booth. Won orders tea for both. Sal looks in awe at the Asian. She's made in my image! (Sal has yet no idea how) Next, Corp. Punishment comes barrelling in. Plants himself.

- We see how you got yer shitty name, says Sal.
- Nah nah it was all wrong look they're good guys it's their first time I swear they liked her shit I got the dough from 'em they would've paid shit take it dude here sorry sorry… Is she for *real*?
- Too real for you mate. Shall we take his money?
Won smiles a smile.
- Yess, you take it. All for you.
Stupid Corp. is sent packing. And Sal feels good for the first time in weeks.
- Money, she says. Monee…
Stashes it in her pants. - I think I'll go to the loo right now.
She has no trouble going this time. She returns. But the Asiatic is nowhere to be seen.

Soul Food

Despite her relentless drive to the bottom, Sal has to admit her Asia-girl role model is superior. Won won her over. And Kar-en who sent her to that basement? K. is therefore a bitch no question. And Fat Finger is like no role model at all. But cocky Sal is drawn back to the weirdos at Animal Road. Hip and portly Finger Lickin' is in her usual spot.

- I just knocked off a whole Kentucky Freud chicken. Finger-lickin' guuud. Now for these donuts

(Sal) - Are you truly obnoxious?

- You like it

(Contrary) - Nope

- You think it's a girl's world

- S' my world

- Think you're in control, Sally Bang?

- Are you *really* flip about everything?

- Yup. 'Cept what I'm not flip about

- Which is?

- Food, nosh, grub and food. Truth about me is I always lie. Keeps the flies off

- So you're lying now?

- Yup. Nope. (Fing' is rummaging in her donut bag) You see Sally B, despite all the madness squalor adversity of the world, there is nothing nada niente too doo. Take this iced donut. All fat on the outside, empty in the middle. I eat fat and emptiness.

Sal didn't know fat people could be poetic. Finger is repulsively impressive.

- Know why I'll never marry a bloke get a kid live in the burbs do the mortgage life-insurance schoolie PTA life-work career balance skincare medicare vote green make the scene eat-a-bean thingy?

- Umm…

- 'Cos I got a brain

- And I don't?

- Shouldn't you be at skool?

- Urrr. What school did you go to?

- I was dux of Bumfuck High

- So what *happened*?

- Grrr. You're so sassy clever, teenager. Wadda you come here for anyway?

- I like animals

- You met Won then?

- You *know* her? (All of a sudden Sal feels soiled)

- Ooh. I know something the teeny tot doesn't. Kar-en and me set it up! Some animals huh?

(Shock) - The basement thing?

Finger bats her eyelids. - Ain't we nice?

Too embarrassing! Sal sees it's time to slink away. Down the hallway's a door she's never been into. It's ajar.

- Yo there!

(Pause) - Me?

- Step in! (Some kind of American)

Sal, dressed in red socks soiled up schooly skirt two-buck vinyl jacket neck bandana doc martins assorted thicky rings fingerless lacy green gloves holy knees shoddy eye pencil top knot sprouted from side of head - hesitates.

- Whoa! Who's the *Doll?*

Carefully nurtured self-esteem in short supply right now, Sal pouts.

- You wish

- K. and Finger told me 'bout you. Smoke?

The American appears to possess a large sculpted cigarette in the shape of a funnel. The room smells illegal.

- 'Kay

- I'm Tall Uncle Bill. TUB for short. Knock yerself out

Sal sucks. The pot is hot. Don't cough!

- You look like a chick with a brain. You do poetry?

Sal drags again. Still no cough. Smoke seeps out her ears.

- Nope. (Hold breath) - 'm writing a novel, me (grunt)

- I have a Plath poem to screw your mind. (Sal lets out her luunng-ful. They burn in hell) This is *Plath,* baby. Dame's a stone genius. Killed herself, stuck her kids in an oven.

Sal slumps onto a green divan littered with butts and books.

- Ugh I'm screwed.

Sal overdid it a bit. Her mind goes on safari. - How did... Fat Finger... Kar-en... Won... in the basement... Those guys? Where is Won... the cafe...

Tall Uncle Bill's in front, shaking her.

- Hey you, wake up!

- Ugh... ugh... no poetry

- Get up. Walk about. Drink this. Don't hoik on my floor. Outside! He marches her out into the night. Street lamps rock and roll down the treeless avenue. Tall Bill guy's talking. A taxi slows. Sal is on her knees, throws up. Taxi pulls away sharply. Sal observes the contents glumly. Tall says:

- You ain't eaten. This way.

Like a doe-eyed lover, Sal totters along with her new Uncle Billee. In a booth at Bilbo's she sits, kind of content at last.

- Had the munchies, doll. Horse tranquilliser's wearing off
- That big joint?
- Yup, sorry. Time to say your real name
- Sally Bang
- I believe you. Finger claimed you were somebody else
- She's all crap. I liked the food but. (Dough-eyed Sal feels mellow now) Actually *like* food though it don't like me. Chocolate milk and kebabs yay. Raisin cookies
(Bill) - Cold fried egg 'n gravy ice cream yumm
- Butter cookies my mum made
- Baked seaweed and sprout milkshake. Double yum
- Shut up you. And gingerbread men smarties cream-soda milk bottles jet planes jaffas cherry ripes
- Love ya stomach. What are you, six?
- I wannabe six. Curled up at home… in winter… with my Teevee
- With your familee? Well, you apparently have parents. And clearly not anorexic. Tick
- No family no parents
- It's ok. I don't talk to mine either. Mind you, they're underground
- Why's no-one believe me when I say I have no parents!
- I believe that you say you have no parents
- Screw YOU
- I bought you dinner? Hello?
- I guess. Keep yer pecker in yer pocket
- And now we're going to a club
- What club?
- *The* club, Sally Bang!

10 mins later we're at HOT ROXX on ---- street next to ---- underneath the ----.

Sal shouts: - This like a basement?

- Wassamatter, gotta thing about basements?

- I'm epileptic

- Cool! The strobe 'll wipe you out

(Sal peers in) - Then I'm a psycho killer!

- What?

- *Psycho-killerr! Na Na Nah Nah!* Sal is in, past the Tongan bouncer.

Danse Macabre

It's jam-packed for a Tuesday. The 6 foot 4 hook-nosed yankee swaggers through a sunken room of Talking Heads. Punters seem to grock him. Sal feels the horse tranquilliser ain't worn off. Heavy club groove clouts her with a body punch. Uuuaaah! She's the sudden middle of a bouncy jiggling human whirlpool. So this is what you want, little girl! Frenetic electricated tragic ragdoll Sal the gal is dancing! Limbs and heads loll in all directions. Ain't cool or hip or anything, but crafty sexy Sal comprehends well, all there is to know 'bout heaven and hell. Mad bodies jerk, strobes finger up your soft white parts, sharky boys confer with rolling eyes. Seduce me! I ain't no con, fifteen forever *yeah.* Yer a foxy fiction Sal and that's a fact. Sweaty dudes all get in step, paw your nubile instrument, breathe your pheromone scent! Which one'll play the snake-like gentleman? The night is Young and Love is in the Air. Fifteen's fifteen forever WOO HOO yeaaaahh!

* * * *

Your eyes are open. Fuck knows where you are. Torn curtains flip lazily in a frame. Glamour of night tips itself in the bin of morning. What's this? Semi-clothed, seems your softy bottom bit isn't. A door stands ajar to a room. Toilet flush. Who dat? Boy in a doorway. No reassurance. Bottom half clothed. And the back of his head. Yo, Jewy Guy.

- Hi how're you? I'm Bibi from the club? I leave now. Call me? Or maybe no. Take some dollars, here. Where do you live? Er that's my shirt. It's eight, I go to Synagogue. Here are your clothes. I folded them. Your name again? Or no don't say. Maybe G dash D will make us pay! Ha ha. Steal our self-respect away. So. You're beautiful nice (oy vay). Have a fine day.

Bye bye Bibi Bibi goodbye. Rack off religious boys. Shit in yer guilty nest 'n spread it round. Truth is dirty. Not my scene. Signs of disrepute all about. Her phone discarded on floor is bleeding texts: mother father mother mother Bill… Unknown. This last one: *Is these your phon? I went to call you but your not at hom. I want to see you.* Aha the Terrorist! (doesn't have a name) Text to mother dear (who doesn't exist): *I said I'd sleep at Tiffany's place chill be cool!!! Be home after school. Sorry sorry* - Out of here. Where the bleep *is* this? Schoolie skirt, a nasty tear. Shove it on, not convincing! No schoolbag books or toothbrush. Ugh I stink. But it's all *experience*. 'S what I want. Don't remember a thing. Experience is a bore. Or the bore is me? Deepy shit for Wednesday. Better go school… no bus pass! thank you Fate. Text my girlfriend. *Hey Tiff, said I wuz with yu last nite if mother calls!!! Can u tell teachers I'm away? Sick today luv Sal.* Tiffany 'll get it, she sees right through me. Oh CRAP she sees right through me.'

'Cause Tiffanee will ever bee successful lawyer dux of uni women's hero governor general perfect girly TIFFANY HAIGH who marries into Murdoch's millions crap! no cellulite no mutton shanks no body odour there, she'll own Australian Vanity Fair the four-car driveway Toorak house of gated splendour not a louse in sight 'cept *me* her pampered doll or dog from school she keeps to show her famous friends the TRENDS, the Sallies of the modern age the haute pretence the decadence the titivating vio-lence the punky party culture-vulture dolled in black, no self-esteem but faking cool - just like she used to be at school…

Finger Lickin' would approve *that* shitty speech, thinks Sal. Unfair to Tiff? Prob'ly. But I don't feel like sub-tle right now. Better crawl back to Animal Road.

Virgin Heaven

Onward and down. At Animal Rd The Terrorist's out. The Eye is there though. Asks her in. Sal is casual as you like.

\- You met my mate Tall Uncle Bill?

\- I guess

\- Blew your head off with some weed I gave him?

\- I guess

\- He's wondering where you are, parental-like…

\- I guess

\- And now I 'guess' you're needing (wait for it) The Terrorist?

(Discovered. Curses) - No wayy

\- Word o' warning, says the Eye (of Sauron). Not a puristic Son of The Faith for nothing you know

\- Huh?

\- He'll force you into servitude of Karmic Debt. Listen: *'Cleave ye to he who hath not ploughed his field, discarding him who hath'*

\- Ya lost me

\- I'm but a metaphysic riddler. The guy gets a kick from racking up WESTERN dolls. Won't do sex, commitment only - on *your* part. Sex is evil, purity is 'Islamic'. You commit, he dumps! and moves right along. Religious arrogant. You're his type

\- I get it. You want me

\- Did I say it?

\- Where is he?

\- No idea

\- Where, fuck it?

(Lightly) - At mosque. On Medley Road. (She leaves, he calls out) - I may not have his BODY but I've a kindly hand! I plough no fields but I'm a goodly man. You could do worse!

But our Sal is gone gone.

\- Out of here! Right, Medley Road… m-e-d-l-e-e? Third right second left on Turnbull? Right left right left what? That guy told me right on Turnb… YOU TELL ME. Quick march Sally Bang left right. Sal sits on her bog haunches in the street, all pissed off. People notice. Sacks of hair holey

knees ringy fingers. Ugh what a pest. Suddenly *there he is* the other side of the street, walking away. Hey! she shouts. He sees her, strikes a POSE. She runs across. *Er… Hi.* She realises he has no name she knows about.
- So er, you're… I'm -
- I text you and you come. Simple, no?
- Nnnn?
- Come to mosque. But wait outside. Women outside
- Mmmm.
- One block no problem, he announces. He smoothly strides. She tries not to jog two paces behind in an undignified manner. *You have never been to Mosque…* More a pronouncement than a question. Everything with a small smile. She dodges dustbins. He strides.
- Now I go in. Pray to Allah. You wait twenty minutes. Then we relax. Sorry to rush
- No, no worries. I'll wait.

He fingers her blossomy cheek and goes. This is quite sufficient for 20 minutes. Virgin Sal communes with Allah. Next thing he's back, and with a male friend or two. Introduces 'The Sally'. They actually shake hands. Everyone is cool. They walk a little. *Three* hot dark-haired men. Here's the park. Conversation, cool smiles. Arabic, English. Sal does not participate. At last, the others glance to Arab boy and take their leave. *Inshallah we shall meet again.* Smooth, ceremonial.

- My Great Friends.
He claims.
- Ooh, the lake.
Sal recognises it. There's wee Maddie duck. Inshallah no Bazzy though!
- Ha ha, I know that duck. It's Maddie. (This is super-childish)
He turns to her. - Let me tell you my name
- Don't. (Sal surprises herself) Save it.
The middle-eastern looks her over.
- I like you lots, he says. (Sal feels theatrically dizzy) But you don't yet know me. I will tell you
- I heard your breakfast speech at Animal Road

- That speech was for the cynics and politicals. I have sense of humour, no?
- Oh
- Your friend Kar-en is quite the 'comic communist'
- Says she is
- I see she is not real

(Talk about *me,* not about K!) - Uh… what do you think about *her?*
- She is - *was* - too 'demanding'
- It's over then?

Sal wants to know how where when Kar-en and her Arab DID IT. But he knows it, and a boy like him would never tell. Even if he never did it. Right now she'd be happy to drag him into bushes *grab his black head shove his tongue into her hot c -* …But err crap he's talking again.
- Yorr life is like how do you say… 'breakfast of a dog'. Let me advise. Sit. (The bench) Your women here are somehow…'liberated' but they have no sense.

But Sal's imagination, liberated, dwells on sense. The mouth is smooth and wide the nose is prominent the hair cropped neat and black the torso full in ways she cruelly cannot countenance; fitted shirt and curvy slacks below (no bulge), the hands a smooth unwrinkled flow of wise demeanour promising all the heavy mm-massage of a muzlim mann.

- My country is not perfect I agree. Far too dirty, but you see I wish a woman to be super clean, to worship me.

Sal's eyebrows go up. (He's super-arrogant. Like me!)
- I know I know, my words are controversial. But I am honest, no? And you like it maybe? A woman shall be free, for in our faith we truly say: 'Be modern, respect the other, believe in each to each'. And that is how you worship me.

Now Sal, if she'd been just a wee bit older, would have sniffed the big fat rat. But Sal has promises to keep and miles to go before she sleeps.
- Sure. I agree. Girl or boy on top. We can choose
- You do not misunderstand? (says the Musselman) I like you much. I like your crey-zy clothes, your crey-zy looks!

Sal fifteen is keen to fall into a bottomless well wherein sunlight cannot dwell.

- Now. We share my music, no?
- Er okay, cool
- One earbud for you, one for me. So
- What music's this?
- A love song from my country
- Got any *Bolt in the Brain*?
- Nooo. Concentrate on sacred music of love.

So they sat together on the bench and entered Virgin Heaven. Sal failed to notice old Bazzy with his mouldy bread come sallying by, stop and grunt at them… then pass beyond, his mouldy sack in his veiny old mitt, to feed a sitting duck adrift upon the mirror pond.

Submission

A novelistic pause of several months pushes our story on. The proverbial Moving Finger writes, but it's the travail of a Ghost Writer, not Sally Bang! It hardly need be said though: he keeps well out of her way.

Sally Bang, aged 16.25, has finally submitted to Arab Boy. Here's a terrorist of unusual ilk. 'Kind but firm', he has her on a dog lead. A boy of prim hot principle and passionate pebbly heart, he's everything booky muzlim boys are cracked up to be in western parts. Sal as we know is somewhere to the left of Boadicaa Empress Wu and Raging Bull, but inexplicably she finds irresistible his subtle sadism, bondage of benign brutality; and though Sal has had to get her kicks elsewhere by now (the onanistic cow) once in a while he lets her touch, and she falls for it 'cos she fell for him sooo much. Like a kid in candy-store heaven she likes a hell-ride. 5 timeza day the Prayer. But *you* do not participate. I study now, you WAIT. You cover up; in time we shall discern your virgin underage body. I dress you as my own (and you will never be my own) or else you will not meet my parents! In the streets of the west Sally Bang goes in hijab e'en unto the gates of school, where seeing her coming Rude Boy and Lotta BS set up a howling like the Muezzin. *Sa-lleee the slave girrl!* But Sal don't care, she loves a dare. You see, her nest of brackish hair - it's gone! Cut off by the Muzzo's sister, Sal open-mouthed at her own daring. We won't quite quote what her momma said: something about being dead. Sal is really not past caring, but sure wants to get to be. Anyhow, now she has to cover her head. In class she's like Mohammed's wife, smuggy centre of it all. Then Holy Month: no food from dawn to close of day! But she is faithful, she who quaffs no Special K no chocolate milk kebabs or raisin cookies jaffas smarties cherry ripes. And sex denial, ghastly trial, will against will! The moving finger writes, horrid lack of post-school delights, 1001 unenchanted nights. Spiritless days with Muzzie Joe, his golden rule of stifling all that's hip and boho, his smug satisfaction at her passive inaction. But our Sally reads alone in magazines: the fate of women who cook and clean in far Afghanistan. Unheralded lives, the thrill of passive lack. The lack! I *shall* deny my dreams, sings Sally Bang, while her ador-ed faithful man delights in studious learning, sucks up his future prospects of earning. For such is his manly right. Inshallah shallah hu akbar.

Let it be said: no-one, no-one, in Sal's other life (including her ghost writer) approves one skerrick of this. But Sal smells victory in contrariness: she's sixteen after all. She's the pain-in-the-arse surly Eve after the Fall. But life and fiction 'll have their span, will surely unravel her contrary plan; with her meek annoyingly-folded hands, her softly pallid mocking cheek, her fake expression: subservient, bland…

Party Party Party

Word one day mysteriously reaches Sally that Red Kar-en is gonna host the mother of all parties at Animal Road. 'Commie fascist fundamentalista corporate Pigs! she cries. Come celebrate Uni summer break-up! Dress code: Wildly Uptight.'

Hmmmmm. Now child of sixteen summers Sal decides she might be ripe for a sea change. Her hair's a pretty crop by now and she could mock up Proletarian Chic - red leather red wig red fishnets steel-cap doc martins yadda… turn up as a Commie and startle her old cold mentor. Makes a change from Wimpy Fundamentalist in a Sack. But what to do about Arab

Boy? His exams are upon him, so invite him for a laugh? He started out back there at Animal Road. Sure, he shuns the place now. But what's it to me? Time to spread my angel wings. And the fag end of our love affair? Let us see if we can stub it.

- Tarik. There's a party on at Ani -
- I know this. They invited me (Invited him not me? Weirdos)
- Will we go?
- I have exams. We will not go
- I'd like to go. May I? (bat eyelids on cue)
- My sweet Sally, you will not. They are not such good people I think
- They're okay, they don't stink
- I tell you: idle women, drugs and hippie men will help you not at all
- I'll represent *you*, like a faithful wife
- You could not represent me in my life
- Why don't I ask your sister, then?
- Garani does not mix with Western men
- Are you certain? I observe she's no longer getting her Whey with that Kurd
- You are absurd. They will be married. Have you not heard?
- She dumped the hijab on the street. I'd say she's voting with her feet. I saw her with a western bloke
- You think this Islam is a joke?
- I think it passed its use-by date
- You're sounding like a whore of late!
- We haven't done it since Ramadan!
- I'm not a pimp, I am a Man!
- Okay… I take it you're not going. I'll go with Garani then. Ciao baby.

Mission *accomplished*. Go Sal! But why'd that gang not invite me direct? I'm hip. Or guess they think I'm hitched. Okay this is all my fat fault. Of course I was always fundamentally anti-fundamentalist. Guess I've really grown up. Ah, I do embarrass me sometimes. Allow me to shed a miniscule tear.

* * * *

26

One hears on the grapevine Sal is so antsy she's gonna let Johnson Toast give her a poke!

- What?

- Betcha

- Get back in your coffin box, Ghost Writer! I'm handling my sex life from here on in

- Don't say that. I'm managing your life

- I'm living it, old fart. Who d'you think you're messing with?

- When there was but one set of footprints in the sand my child, that was when I carried you

- Bollocks to your religious babble

- Thought you liked religion

- I liked religious HUNKS

- No joy there

- Rub it in, jerk

- Older and wiser? Learnt our lesson, have we?

- I learn no lessons. I'm Sally Bang!

- Yip de doodle, all grown up

- Right. I'll outfox you, ghost boy! I'll get real clever, ree-al unpredictable. Won't see me for dust. Kiss my butt, ghostie

- Mmmm, if you insist.

* * * *

The day of the party dawned bright and clear. Tall Uncle Bill had made a Spotify party-pod and lovingly rolled many big spliffs. I'll huff and I'll poff and I'll blow your heads off! he cackled jauntily. The Eye had carefully polished his best eyeball and was practising popping it in and out to entertain the guests, including his dear Finger Lickin' who practised balancing donuts on her middle finger and presenting them to her friend. She sat in her favoured spot, bum torturing two chairs. Kar-en, the leader of the busy team, had thrown lots of the furniture into the front garden so there was more room for 'dancing and political rave-ups led by me. I shall go as Bin Laden channelling Gaga', she squealed delightedly. I even rehearsed a little speech, though when I get really pissed I'll improvise!

No-one could wait for *this* treat. Least of all our dear friend Finger. She who by tradition contributed jack shit to the fevered preparations watched fascinated as Uncle Bill cooked up a big storm of chilli spaghetti in a ten gallon drum-sized pot. I can heat it up later, he exclaimed jocularly. I put in 138 chillis! Or was it E tabs? I forget! he grinned roguishly, and Finger batted her eyelids demurely.

Now Kar-en consulted her A-list excitedly: Hmm. There's Psycho Jaxi (our DJ). Marcus Factor (well-hung, filthy rich, mine). Cute Adelaide (blondie little bimbo. Is she 14 yet?) Fierce ManGinas (transvestite band). Shawaz Yafanni (Libyan belly dancer). The B-list: Windsor Gregorian (dickhead, worth a laugh). Corporal Punishment, my Ex (dickhead, not worth a laugh). Sally Bang plus Arab plus Sister (they won't come). Banjo Baloney (smelly old poet hanger-on). Sundry Uni boys I invite to torture with my wit and curvy butt. Besides, they bring booze. Hangers-on, rent-a-crowd etc. Should be around 300. Or 3000. No sweat and screw the neighbours. Or better still, invite 'em. More booze. Masterstroke! Tick!

All was in readiness in the great house. The evening hour was at hand. A pause and hush fell over the land.

And who should turn up at 6.30 but potty Windsor Gregorian, card-carrying genius.
- Party starts at 9, Windy, says K.
- Oh, ay don't maynd
- Talk to yourself then. Not in Sanskrit.
Finger spots him. - Hey Greggo. Got a pill for you
- No, no. Merely here to observe. Came as Kevin Rudd you see? (striped shirt bow tie)
- Too dull for you, mate. Here, pop this
- Don't mahnd if ah doo
- Now we can be entertained till the others arrive, says Finger.

A bit later, huge-headed Windsor is getting talkative in the kitchen. - *The thing about g-girls you see, j-jezebels, is they are fundamentally insecu-are. Need to be pampered and new-aunced. According to MY research it's clair they won't respect us chaps if they view us as fuhhndamentally air-nimals. Air-nimals. Simply meat for sex etceterahh. End fethermore... What do ah say? Aah say...* Finger and K. can't get a word in edgewise and are getting jack of him. Solution? Drop a bigger pill and bellow him down.

On cue at 9, half the grungy world turns up at Animal Road. For some reason everyone brings hard liquor. This will evidently be no sprightly lightly gathering of scintillating wit and chardonnay, instead a heavy downerish shit-show of dark-clad studes and clods grungeing and boinging about in sweaty upper rooms. Bill's podcast already veers teeth-rattlingly dark and loud, and the neighbours' fingers are twitching for the first police call. Spewing into the street are lines of cokey blokey boofheads (Uni's out after all) plus their alco-poppy dancy babes with skirts around their ears mouthing wankerish blaa each to each in universal Galah. They're scarce aware of the Animal Road epicentre, yet animals all are determined to become.

Sal rocks up with Garani (sister-muzzo) who's bought a leather one-piece somewhere north of skanky, even Sal is popping her eyes. Holy cow, I wanna feel her clite! I'd be lezzo for her! Garani is newly-liberated, the Kurd boy's history. So where's the drugs? I wanna get *laid.* Sal agrees *no limit,* for many grotty doings will be done tonight. Now Psycho Jaxi's doin' his Dee Jay thing, Kar-en leads boinging in the upper rooms, fat Finger's lickin' in the kitchen, slutty Fierce ManGinas jiving on the lawn. Shawaz Yafanni (belly dancer) is showing *hers* - and grungy kids are pointing chucking money laughing and tinkling clink of breaking bottles howls of Faaark! as Eye removes his eye again, the crowd is rolling mad and drunk and clunk! some Jill assaults the pavement with her head. She barfed on Jack? And Yaaaay! as our Garani does the panties-down atop the garden fence. *If only holy joe bro could see me dance!* she screams. Upstairs Marcus Factor's holding court. Ya big cigar! Well-hung you are! says K, her commie pose forgotten. I'm porky pig! You want me, dig? They're on the floor the horizontal tango-bango! Psycho Jaxi revs it up the people howl with new delight beneath the swingeing of the light. Kar-en has found her lover boy! Roll up roll up Cute Adelaide the copy-catty schoolie queen the blondie bimbo (green as slime) now tries her luck:

gimme a fuck! And several boys oblige. At once a scrum ensues, a bog of heavy shoes. No limits! shouts Corp. Punishment (who slunk in here few minutes back with hordes of louts, some yellow, black). He wants a Time! We want some Crime! Yeah fucken oaf hey baby here's my trouser-snake come get me! But it's *Sal* - don't fricken mess with *me* shit-face to face with Corporal P! He backs away the foaming loon back to his mates across the room. *And Sally sees a basement room, sees Won the oriental goddess loom, green as Buddha in the gloom. She wants to cry or maybe die - which of you pricks can tell me why?!* Her voice is drowned in Sodom's Hall, but dear old Windsor hears her call: Dear Sally here I am your f-faithful knight I do believe. Your eyes are bright! She grabs Gregorian by his ample head. The gaping windowsill makes their bed. She pashes and claws and bites his lip. Poor Windsor tries to wriggle but her grip! She won't let go she won't let go they roll and rock - then sailing outward into space they crash like stones onto the fetid lawn below. Some craggy bottle spears a hole in Windsor's back. Windsor stares aloft. His eyes are bulging. Blood is oozing from a crack. For several seconds nothing moves, then someone screams and people scatter. Sally stiffens. Nightmare dreams are closing in. Her leg is lead. Windsor is twisted under her head. He doesn't breathe he seems to be dead.

Then cops and medics are there. Red light splatters the night. The party people hang in huddles. Nobody dares to shout. The night descends into fag-end chaos. Sergeant Harmer picks two bodies apart. The girl's concussed. Put her there. Get oxygen. This guy's deceased. Put him in the ambulance (get a priest). Sal is only vaguely aware. Alien faces leer and loom. She recognises no-one in the gloom. The thudding groove has stopped, the blood-beat in her head has not. Now she feels a mask upon her face. And that is the end of this night of grace.

Aftermath

Sally's ghost writer is suitably shocked and outfoxed, and our heroine awakes in her home bed the midday after. Mother demands to know Facts, and so do the cops. But she's not saying anything at all. Why bother? Better to *die.*

Many times she drifts away, away. ...In a far-off desert she meets Won by a roadside. Won the Korean is beautiful. Her oval head glows in Libyan sun. Orange sands bow to the sky's blue begging bowl. Won wants to speak to her. The river wants to flow but no oasis yet... Won is there again. *All shall be vanquished,* she intones. *You love me. You are me. Kiss me, and I shall remain. In Old Shanghai we'll meet again...*

On waking, Sally makes no sense of this. Except, she has a feeling Won has stirred her soul, that Won is a kind of problem-sister of the mind. *Anyway, I don't want no boys,* she said. (*Won is her alter-ego! - ED)

Following recovery, Sal is absolutely grounded. Weeks are lost to bad TV and burly cops coming round to interview. The parents pick their distance. What to do? In the absence of a better melodrama, Sal practises her answers in the stately monotone of the tragic dispossessed. *Yes, it's true I was drinking. A terrible accident. No, no-one else involved but me. I saw it all.* Such youthy honesty, the cop's impressed! But on it drags. Now looms a Court Inquest. What the hell is that? Sal is kind of depressed. Meanwhile word has spread about at school (tho' mum's the word) and schoolies love to torture. You might think Sal would win some kudos and mystique, but too many revenging oiks want a piece of her arse. This is why superior martyrs like her despise skool at the best of times. Lotta BS and Rude Boy lead the charge, but Tiffany's more circumspect and 'distantly supportive' as only head-girly aristocrats can be. But in truth our Sally's stately doe-eyed martyrdom is grinding to its rest. Sal's no great martyr, unlike Won, and soon the old impatience and cute ironic cutty lip are back. Fuelled no doubt by Rude Boy's spastic stutter and Lotta BS' fatuous brain of butter. Yes, positivity's in short supply but so is stimulation. And who can keep a subversive spirit tied to guilt for evermore? 16.25 years old my life is over? The gods say NO. So Sal's young spirit is ultimately revived by her own fading interest in being nice, plus an awful lot of crummy TV and Manga comics. In fact life is so jolly rotten, Windsor Gregorian is near forgotten.

The Inquest

So. Demurely clad in natty ankle-boots green tights red lace-up bodice tartan skirt a mere 2 tongue studs and a lick of Addams Family - Sal trots into court all too ready to kick the hornets' nest. It's not that Sal is especially brave, but simply inclined to misbehave. Protected by youth's blythe insouciant ignorance, Sal cultivates a cutesy cutting cool designed to beguile the average adult fool. We understand! It's truly hard for you to dwell on others' grief. But the Gregorians' lawyer carries a different brief.

- Hello Sally
- Hi there
- My name is Miles Vane SC, representing the family of Windsor Gregorian. You are Sally ---- *Bang, aged 16, of Fitzroy? (* Sal doesn't want her middle name published - ED)
- You're on the money
- I beg your pardon?
- Yes Sir
- You knew Windsor Gregorian, didn't you?
- How d'you mean I *knew* him?
- He was your friend
- Not really
- An acquaintance then?
- Hardly. That's the point, isn't it?
- You knew him to talk to though?
- Oh yeah. Everybody did
- What do you mean by that?
- He's pretty famous
- Famous how?
- Spotty ties, stripy trousers, big head, genius so he said. Not my style or anything, but
- Did you like him?
- Er, sure. I mean he was okay. Can I say something?
- Go ahead
- I was like really sorry to hear about his dying and everything
- But you were there

- Oh, yeah
- And you are sorry?
- Shit yeah. I mean yeah
(Pregnant pause) - Let's keep this simple, shall we? He fell from an upstairs window with you on top of him. Am I correct?
- Ye-up. Correct. Sort of. Well actually, umm...
- It's a tragic event. Would you agree?
- Ye-up. I felt bad about it
- Do you still feel bad about it?
(Pause) - I guess.
(Pregnanter pause) - O-kay... Now tell us in your own words, how you came to be on a window ledge with the deceased
- Was I on a window ledge?
- According to four witnesses
- Like who? (Sal has conveniently forgotten the police evidence)
- Mr Marcus Factor, Mr Simon Jaxi (known to you as Psycho Jaxi, I believe), Ms Corinne (known as 'Cute') Adelaide, and Mr Ned Corporal
- Who can trust those guys?
- What are you saying?
- In my own words?
- Yes please
- Cute was getting gang-banged. Factor was doing the horizontal tango. Jax was off his hip-hoppy face and Corporal is a pimp who hates me
- That's all interesting. You were on the window ledge
- Says who?
- *I* say you were (Objection here)
- You're bullying me
- I withdraw that. But you had Mr Gregorian by the hair and you were biting his mouth
- No, that's not -
- And he tried to pull away but you wouldn't let go. You caused him to fall four metres onto the ground below where he was impaled on a bottle and died.
(Objection!)
- I didn't know there was a bottle there! So he died. I know he died

- *Why* did he die?
- You said it just then
- Was it an accident?
- Wadda *you* think, wise guy
- I really don't know.
(Objection! Sustained!)
- Wadda you say I killed him? I murdered him? Is that it?
- *How* did he fall?
- He *fell*. Shit happens. We were all gone. Gone - you know what that means? We were shit-faced, including him. He was pilled up. Raving loony tried to kiss my face. The fucking loony said he liked me. That fucking toolhead has no girlfriend so he hooks into me! That's what you get when you try to hit on me! You fucking DIE!
(Large pause) - No further questions at this time, your honour
- We'll adjourn, says the Judge.

Well, that went well. Sal has the stray feeling she has exposed herself in public. She tells her ghost writer later, how she *'felt like she started to rise up out of a deep well... it felt like anything was possible'*. A weird euphoria crept over her skin for a minute or two, she said. Which then replaced itself with some kind of cold feeling. Like dread.

Sal avoids her parents and puts down her head. Driving home though, she thaws out in the back seat of the car. *They let me off then?* Neither parent says a thing.

Psychology

Pretty much by the end of her first court-ordered session with the psychotherapist Bilk, Sal has decided to attach herself to him. Bilk is a big course-shaven Germanic teddybear guy with curly black hair (which Sal approves) and little round specs. Plus his mouth hangs open slightly when he listens, his jaw moves sideways when he talks and his special thing is to fold his fatty arms and sniff. Sal 'll take him seriously precisely because she doesn't have to and there are no consequences. Forget what the judges parents care workers and other uptights have to say. This guy's a very serious loser! I'll try to hug him after our talk, she resolves. Bilk's office, disorganised in a hopeless sort of way, smells largely of old sandwiches. There's a stunted cactus in a pool of water on the sill (a gesture to the desert of laneways outside) but Bilk never looks out of his greasy windows, he's intent on inner worlds. He has no wife to speak of. Has a reputation though. In nanoseconds upon arrival Sally takes this all in, smiles an imperial smile, settles cross-legged in the centre of Bilk's green floppy couch, rolls a ciggy (which art she hath but lately taken up) and says:

- Like your office, Doc.
Doc frowns. It wouldn't occur to him to play the adult.
- I do not
- Not married, Doc?
- Not right now
- No girlfriend?
- No girlfriend
- Here we are then
- Here we are
- Wanna puff?
- Tobacco, yah?
- Yeah! (She knows he's never puffed it) Your cactus needs some water
- That is so (Irony is lost)
- You like Fitzroy? (She knows he wouldn't know)
- I think so, yah
- Are you from Germany? Seig Heil
- I vass from Germany, yah
- How come you treat little girls?
- You are little girl?
- I'm a *tiny* little girl (She flutters her eyelashes)
- Do you haf a problem?
- Yes Daddy. (She bites her lip. Can he take it?)
- Should I help you?
- *Please* help me
- Okay. Don't worry. (Yesss, he can take it! Sal is elated)

PAUSE.

(Sal) - Zo. I ask za questions

- Very good

(Sal enthroned, sucks her thin little durry) - Are you like… gay?

- I think I am not

- You like girls then

- Girls are… interesting

- We can be little psychos

- You like zat, yah?

(Her eyes narrow) - Me ask the questions

- Good

- You met a little girl like me before?

(Pauses to consider) - I sink so

- Bullshitter (He's in a corner...)

- Okay. Screw you.

Yaayy! Sal is happy. She settles in for Session One.

* * * *

Over their weeks together, Sal is developing some theories about *older men,* since Bilk has divulged his life story (under interrogation) including some dodgy but juicy info from the time he started going to Uni parties in Germany. Sal learns that Bilk underwent the desperate agonies that non-popular adolescents do, and that he 'truly liked' a girl called Traudl who was 17. Sal learns he used to dress in unconventional (even clownish) attire (striped shirts, bow ties for instance) and tried and tried to impress Traudl with his one true weapon: his unique brain (and studied nonchalance). But Professor Bang does not hesitate to warn him of his fatal error: he liked the wrong girl, and boys like him spend years of fumbled effort liking wrong girls. As soon as they learn to *give up,* then girls start liking them (despite no action in the trouser dept.). Bilk is well impressed with this advice. He 'had no idea' the conversation would take these turns, and now maybe even *he* can get a real girlfriend. But neither of them are fools, and the ghost of Windsor Gregorian slips quietly through the conversation. Sal is tranquil. She wonders how Windsor may have turned out had he lived, like Bilk perhaps? And Bilk ever so nonchalantly concurs this may be so.

And so their session weeks go fruitfully by. Bilk is happy too, for Sally lets him be the manchild that he is. She tends to feed him chews and Manga comics, which he'll read with the comic held to his face, his goggle-glasses steaming as he sniffs and pouts like a teutonic seal and mouths to himself the steamy plots. And Sally stretches out upon the green divan with her phone and her ciggy and regards him and dreams. Gentleness reigns in their room for half an hour. At last the ritual complete, she comes to him and puts her head in his lap. He is obliged to stroke her (now green-purple) head, and at length she kisses a finger, pops it to his lips and off she goes. Same time next week…

You'll say it makes no sense for a teen's world to mix with an adult's. But an adult with no sense of being one (like Bilk) where there's no desperate hidden bullshit power game and he never wants respect, is quite a catch. Likely he's trying to work out what respect *is*. Childhood happened and (being timid) he never worked it out. The kid inside never left. To his eyes, all are people-souls and age is nonsense. His absent self-regarding bubble is what Sally craves. Though Bilk suspects his life is one long silly fiction, gormless gesture in a desert of fictional time, he recognises Sally as a girl he'd have liked to meet, and do romance with. And old old Sal wants to be in a zone of comfy love - just the once, without the threat.

For a brief span Sal's world's an easier place, and others start to notice. Sal's mother stops her worried nagging for a short season, and Sal accords her likewise a tiny speck of respect. The dad, home from brutal butchering will even mute his brutal soporific TV, offer the girl a grunt of hello and pass the time of day. Sally's adults almost exist.

Adulter Notions

But folks, mid-16 is an age of revolution-enlightenment that bristles with lightning speed. You'd easily miss these incomprehensible kids making their mad doodle-scribbles in the margins of old people's settled histories.

And so the fond affair with Bilk the Psych is now but a lotus-eating interlude… in the rush to adulter notions.

Old Sal is finally getting tuned into 'politics'. No surprise you'll say, but now it dawns the world is complex and absurd in subtler ways than self-consumed fifteen ever could see. Sal's eye for a phoney grows keener as well. Kar-en her commie redhead role model of yesteryear now channels 'hot environmentalist man-eater'. Kar-en is a noise unto herself, the 'fucking fundamentalist' - all curvy butt and lip. Still, her noisy friends and causes can be *tempting*. Besides, all the spunky boys on campus know Kar-en. *Worth following?*

Animal Road, now a legendary grungy shrine following 'The Gregorian Incident', still sports Fat Finger Lickin' holding court in its kitchen. Sal observes the Finger with keener eyes. There's youthy pathos inside all that fat, and those rougy jowly cheeks and gap of a mouth dispensing ironic doom for all who make the pilgrimage, let Fat Finger sharpen the only weapon she has: her tongue. In fact the legend in her own kitchen is anaesthetising a young Eng. Lit specimen as we speak.

- I don't *read*. Why would I read a book? (A lie, she reads everything) I want experience! Writers are jerk-offs trying to squeeze your mind into their own box (so to speak). You think a fact is a fact? Fact is fiction by fecked-up people fooling themselves they can make a measly mark in a desert of human wank! (*ghost writers take note) …What *about* Freud? That mysogynist Beardo bottled women like insects in a jar for calling out *male* hysterias…

And so on. *Worth following?*

- '*Don't* (comes a voice). Too sad. Finger is the world's spinster who'll never face the horrid confines of her own fat frame of reference but will defend it to the death against all comers, read men.'

Thus observes the all-seeing Eye, who evidently still holds a flag for Sal or he wouldn't have bothered with this longish sentence. Sal takes seriously his one-eyed vision, though never his beanpole body. So it's Exit The Finger, spat out by callow youth. *Kar-en it is, then.*

- Wanna Tarot reading? says Eye in his best voice.
- Or show me your crystal eyeball, she says.

Now that Sal 16.35 has taken her mental finger out of her mouth, she's up for this or that.

The Eye's den is a ramshackle annex, scene of many a grandiose self-promotion. Sal in stripy tights pleated skirt fairy jacket and booties... sits neatly sweetly in Eye's best chair and rolls a ciggy in her fingers. *Shoot,* she says, torturing him in ways only boys could know. The Eye is known as a professorially vain poseur who uses his physical disadvantages (bony angular sunken chest no crotch interest) in gestures of self-deprecation to win over impressionable young girls and get them in the sack. Trouble is, he knows Sal is light years past this game. She knows he knows, and still he can't help himself. He's a studiedly ironic thin loser-crock in love with Sal. She kind of likes him in a repulsed sort of way. Possibly she feels sorry for him. She bides her time in his gloomy room.

- *O-kaaay.* This is a Celtic Cross, right? This is where you're AT. Your 'now' problem is: The High Priestess is crossed with the Empress over the Eight of Swords. Basically it says you're a hot narcissist Harpie who wants to be famous and obnoxious but poses as blindly suicidal yet secretly loves home and hearth curled up with her man-god, represented here by The Fool, who you worship uncomprehendingly like a good Muslim girlie wife or a fuzzy German shrink's little protégé
- You made that last bit up, did you not?

Eye tries to twinkle his good eye.

- I guess. You're part of the family, Sal. We worry 'bout you.

Sal rearranges her bottom.

- No need. Listen Eyeball. I'll take you on. But only once. That's it. So you won't be jealous
- Beg your pardon?
- I'll go to bed with you once
- Er now Sally dear, you really shouldn't -

- Cut the crap. Lock the door.

And he does it. Stares at her. Looks hopeless. Sal is discovering Girl Power! Her breath starts to rise.

- *Come here.*

He pads over. Gulps.

- *Drop the pants now.*

He does it. She slides her stripy tights off in the chair.

- *Down here, baby.*

He kneels. She spreads her legs out over the chair arms. He's red in the face.

- *Don't let your eye pop out.*

She pulls him onto her and she comes in about 24 seconds. Next she pushes him backwards hard on the mangy rug and reverse-straddles him. He is pretty much overwhelmed. As the *coup de grace* she takes him in her mouth his head bangs on the floor everything is quick. Swallow that's it.

After a moment or two she gives him a kiss on the nose and stands up. One leg either side offers a worm's eye view. He gulps. So does she, actually.

- Where'd that come from?
- Dunno. But my old ghost writer will be pleased.

* * * *

Is she right? Ghostie wishes he was young again. Or wishes *she* was young again.

- Suck on it, ghostie. Bang is out of her box and the big world better beware
- I worry for your welfare Sal. Be warned though, I'm not beyond a bit of told-you-so cynic *schadenfreude*. See below.

Phoney Precocious

Yo there, young Sally Bang 16.5. I see your latest pose is to winter alone in Old Shanghai (famously bland Smith Street café) wagging school eating grass soup reading Kerouac Kafka Castaneda or is it Chompsky (chomp chomp)? No such luck. It's Manga Comic number 4002. Today, Asiatic heroine abandoned by family boo hoo faces Dark Worlds yet meets mystery friend who helps her win against all odds and she never gets poked.

- Poked? I believe the generic term is assailed, assaulted, harassed…

Whatever. Schoolgirl you technically are, but embarrassing Alma Mater's barely mentioned despite its cooool mantras neatly nuanced for tomorrow's up-grown trendies like New Sally Bang. *The young are adults too! Empower yourself. Live the dream!* Hey, are we quite as original as we thought we were? (Sure are, dad) Could we possibly be a product of something deeper than our own ego? Not a more nano-nuanced self-regarding product-conscious youthy girlpower new-age missy was born in the year of the raspberry 2--- in the icky city of Melbourne. (*'Uck off, ghost writer*) Today we're digesting totally better books notions nutrients, o cultivated Fitzroy MeToo activist playing hard to get round campus. (Ain't we supposed to be at skool?) Hail the macro soul foodie whose body's a temple (like Won) and life's no more a constipated schooly homey bore. No uptight sicky tummy or dodgy bowel, we changed all that. Eat Special K shit feng shui, chew with care have a regular day! Remember Finger Lickin' and her donuts? She was right: candy sugar outside, void in the middle. Watch the trap New Sally. At 16.5 you wanna gobble the future and it's *lonely.* Can't blame you for that. There's a rollicking white energy welling up and its outrider is LUCIFER. All unfathomably big and real. Don't want no deep space, no loneliness. Every damn thing gotta be swallowed NOW. Oh but what is it? And who to do it *with?*

Down Smith Street past Old Shanghai an oval-headed Oriental passes by and is gone… By chance young Sal looked up and saw. OMG. It's Won.

Won! Radical not crazy, wise not fake, void not avoiding, simple not artful, meaningful not mouthful, hard to get never playing hard to get… her *problem sister.* Now we see why Sal hung out in Old Shanghai. She's waited for her would-be lover all along. A glance to Mirror on the Wall to check her late identities are there, and Sally hastens out into the beckoning air.

Yin and Yang

- Oh Won! Hello Won? Won!
Won is intent on the journey of a thousand miles. Twenty hurrying steps
and Sal is at her shoulder.

- O Sally Bang! I did not see! How your face has changed. Is it older
than before? Your clothes, so sexy young, what do you sell? We met in
basement, yes, that time I was a whore. A boy was killed? So sad. And yes,
I live still in the silos of the lower hells. I meet some clients *today.* Come
with me! Are you afraid? So good! You like my dress? Oriental girls must
seek to impress. Businessmen, consumers yes. Oh, some city tower, all
steel and glass. Definitely not in our class.

A downtown tram deposits them at ----- Tower. They whoosh in a lift to
the eighteenth floor. Padded corridor, apartment four, a heavy darkwood
door. A silken hostess opens... and wondrous Won and Sal step into
glossy glassy space. Dude, the roof of the city! Three oriental men in
chairs turn complaisantly to look. 'This is my friend, she comes to learn
our ways.' The Orientals stare then smile, exchanging glances. Apparently
the sight of Sal entrances. Sal whose dress code luck would have it (pouty
emo black + pink with natty Jappy pigtails) could possibly posture in this
decadent den as 'titivating treat for oriental businessmen'. Cutey Jappy
schoolgirl fantasy! And she's *white.* They appreciate the clever joke. Won
commands new respect.

And though Sal smells the clash of worlds, despite a gulping moment as
they entered, Won in charge makes Sal feel oddly at peace, as if her void
were filled by silky folds of strange release. Won had said: *Though sky may
fall, we shall laugh at them all!*

Won advises in a whisper. These men will drink and eat, we entertain
their lotus feet. Enter an inner room with crimson dragons, deep green
walls and black divans. The parties sit in grave conclave, the silken hostess
now dismissed.

- Whah is your name? says 1 (he seems pretty young) in oriental tongue.

- My name is Sally
- SA-REE? blurts out 2. (He's older, fatter, sweaty-sweaty) - This one for *me*
- I doubt Sa-lee will waste her time on you, says 3, who seems to speak the eenglish perfectly.

Now drinking starts in earnest, just the men. The females pour, and pour again. They practise Zen! But Sally is an actor too; she'll foot it with these Boss boys from Guangzhou. Now Won assumes the lead. How animated she becomes, applauding all her clients' bawdier utterings. A quip, a grin: Won is eerily practised in the Game of Sin.

Says 1: - Your frien', she talk as well?
- Beg yours? Sal answers. But Won in natty pidgin English says: 'My frien' is daughter rich Australian! He own two shipyard! Sallee Bang, famous in Land of Australee. She study economic master degree. Top of class (she no take it up the arse) and top of Universitee.

Sal sagely nods amid a flurry of translated Oriental for 2's benefit. He pitches in: Oh oh, Bang Bang? (He starts a shoot-em-up routine) You rike Cowboy Western, Sarree Bang!

And the beef-boy grabs at her. They roll to the floor. The guy's gurgling. Sally cool as custard flips him on his gut and straddles his head. A little curtsey. The men applaud, find this super sexee. 2 bangs the floor submissively. You fukme fukme? Now Fatgut's up and circling Sumo Sumo! Sal leaps on his back, n' rides Cowboy Cowboy! Won copies, straddles baby 1 while 3 applauds superiorly from the mat. And now he ponces up and pours expensive whisky over them all. Sal's gallant Horseman beats him back! They crash to the divan. Won grabs a bottle, sprays them all; 1 gets behind, shoves her into the maul. The five of them, all sweat and skin are set to scale the heights of Sin. 2 yanks his trouser down while 3 takes 'missy' from behind. Won steps in but's undermined! Probing hands, he grabs her tit, wants a lick. Won's too quick and bites him, 3 keels back, hits the mat like lead. Now baby 1 tries sitting on *his* head, then: Hey Sarree BANG you dead! But Sal's got in his trousers, grabs his dick! He howls, while Ugly 2 staggers sidewise, feelin' sick. Won steps in, aims a kick, table slaps him like a brick. And Sally laughing like a child, clutches her handle! - 1's eyeballs pop, and Won is giggling fit to drop. Poor 1 released at last, the chicks collapse in a tangled pile. Feckless feller just got the joke. He clumps to a sit, tries to smile.

A scene of devastation greets our friends. Surely time to make amends: Won the mocking mother hen feeds the bottle to her boozy Boys - who dared to think for all their drink and stink that they'd be big boss men in their Little Boy den. The doubtless duo step to the bathroom. Sal sees Won is relieved to have protected her protégé.

- This is how, my Sally, we avoid to have sex relations with such men. And funny for you, victim of your dick trick is, how you say, 'batting for other team!'
- Should be 'gay' then, not sad
- You dress as boy next time?
- Next time? How many times 've you been here?
- This is my third
- And last, I presume.

After freshening up like flowers, our girls are off. Arising ghost-like from within, the silken hostess hands an envelope, and they solemnly depart in peace. But the woman eyes them narrowly (ruefully?) as they slip like giggling schoolies through the darkwood door. So glad to have flouted just one time the old profession's oldest law... that it's *they* who should have finished as victims, spreadeagled out upon a greasy floor.

Girl Outside

The spectacular re-entry of Won into her world has flung up a mysterious mirror. Shreds of doubt now sully Sally's headlong assault on the world, for Won is somehow beyond, unimagined, fitting not at all the postures and poses of Sal's studied socio-sexual self. Won has travelled roads within that Sal has never seen, and deeply, it scares her. And to be sure, late that day her Oriental sister slips away. Bereft, our Sally tries to self-assure they'll meet again. But sister Won is gone, and Sal must deny once more the loneness of it all.

The Activist

I am Sally Bang! Lazy exemplar of a surface generation, loyal to nothing (save Won), sniffing winds of fad and fashion at quantum speed, wanting the THING before it happened, gobbing life's troughs and troubles (if only we could grock what they hell they are). Study up the road less travelled, masticate the psycho babble (which ghost writer needs to unravel). 'If i wuz actually honest, my problem is 'how do i have it all without really DOING IT? Sidestep shortcut bin and edit, grock it all before i know it, pluck a rose and never grow it, pick muh nose and never blow it. Rebels without a cause? Tomorrow's crashing bores. Leftie Sister in lock-step to a righter world! Yay, how do i swap conformist for Uber cool? Uuuh what am i: media savvy or media fodder? Tick the box to save the abos, dodge da crime but do the time, risk unscathed, commit uncommitted, sin all undefiled, taste eternity still a child, be as i am yet change forever, sacrifice yet forfeit never. Slack lives matter. Gotta abort a world too fast for wannabes like me! With lilywhite hands let me clutch at a gone future, linger with the lazy, posture with the absurd, dance the stoopid dance of irony, drink draughts of dead decadence since it's all shit and nothing's left for ME TO DO'.

Sixteen is such a simple age.

On the *other hand* I just bumped into Red Kar-en on campus! She and those cock-hot brainy boys that hang round her are making a kickarse speech to a crowd right as we speak.

- *Lissen up, people.* Those meathead politicos wanna spout their oldie crap that Our Future hangs on their next military kill fest in Muzzostan! Our Aussie roight to kill as many towelheads as we want! Rather eat Funnelwebs than vote Liberal right? And since fighting for peace is like fuckin' for virginity aaand it'll be a great day when the air force has to hold a cake bake to buy a new fighter jet etcetera blaaaaaa… so we the Yoof declare political shit stirring shall not vanish from This Land our Land of better Broadband! Now gather sons and daughters of the west for Bread and Freedom! Join the Stolen Generation Land Rights For Transgender Whales Global Warmin' Slack Lives Matter Me Too Demo right now right on YEAH.

- Now THAT sounds cool as! and so original. I'll just text the olds I'm doing a Year 11 political science study tour of the citee. Yay.

Down at the river a largish mob is milling about waiting for someone to shepherd them baaaaa in the right direction and teach them the slogan of the day. Looks like Red Kar-en has sufficient balls and chutzpah for this task along with Mincemeat and Poodle, two subtle sophomores who follow her every move (view's better from behind). K's red river hair and curvy butt are the goods as she stands like Lenin on a council bin and wields the deadly megaphone.

'Ooo-kaayyy! Shudduuupp!! Thenk you. I'm Kar-en your organiser today. And I say we march down t' the Casino and show them Liberal mutherfocker fleabags with all their moolah that we don't bankroll no new war in Muzzostan. An' our ANZAC diggers don't wannit either! Baaaaaa! goes the crowd. *1-2-3-4! We don't want yer phoney war! 2-4-6-8! Lib. high rollers masturbate!* the flock repeats with glee. At this moment a solid contingent of constabulary hovers into view south of the river, fans out over the bridge and forms a line. Drivers are flagged to a standstill. Sal who's just stuffed her schoolie uniform in a binliner, now in new-activist kit of black on black, finds herself alarmingly near the front of the crowd pressing onto the bridge. She for some unholy reason finds herself unable to chant their holy song. Not so the mob, ramming forward like lambs to a slaughter. The parties are face to face, everyone stops, the noise dies down a bit. Sal feels slightly stupid facing burly coppers with batons. Suddenly recollects an earlier encounter with such types after she and a fat boy fell out of a window. Red Kar-en is nowhere to be seen. Now from the back her mega voice screams: *Down with Piiiggs!* This seems to be a signal for the Blue Team. They surge. Sal is caught by the hair dragged forward through the line and out to the rear, an extension of a stout female constable's arm. The blue team is now pushed back and waves of activists crash through. Sal breaks free minus a handful of hair (didn't need it anyway) and starts to run. Yow, it stings up there on 'er head. Starts to feel hot. Female Lezzo cop comes at her. Sal is by the bridge railing. The press is pushing. Suddenly, what the fuck? She climbs on the railing. Lezzo grabs at her, Sal kicks, cop falls back clutching face. Sal feels sorry for that. Someone grabs her skirt, yanks it free. Sal is teetering… and she's sailing outward into space! Fuck me, the river! She flaps her arms the water seethes up in her face, she's under! Shit it's cold muddy slick in my mouth can't *breathe*, winded can't breathe can't breathe. Ugh I'm here, I'm up. OMG! Boots off, get 'em off. Start swimming. Go!

Sal is under the bridge, reaches the shore wall, hangs on. It's slightly dark. She seems alone. Hold on now. All still. Voices far away… Water laps her up against a bollard thingy. 'Tween the legs… she fits round it nicely. Up and down the water laps. Just wait just wait… and… *oh man oh man… come on come oonnn… Oooooops!* The water pushes sweetly up and under. She holds the moment close.

A shout. We're coming down! She's yanked all clammy up the bank by some *guy* into a pack of students. She starts to scream with laughter, no particular reason. The guy pulls her aside. Here, take my jacket. She puts it on, covers her rear. Her skirt is gone. What happened to you? *It's a story,* she says. Hurry along the embankment, legs naked. Across a railway yard. He has a car. She slips in back. There's camera gear. You from the press? Keep yer head down he says. He drives hard out of town into the burbs. She sits up. And there he is. And he is like… *beautiful.*
The fellow smiles.
- Well well. And who the hell are you?
- I'm Sally Bang, she says.

* * * *

What's a Ghost Writer to do with all this? Our chick's big sally into activism is a lazily convenient emotional gap filler with no particular point except presenting the middle finger to authority plus sublimating rebellion against parental nests in general. Pah! To have a decent *cause* might lend some respectability and let us deny the pesky childishness. But what? Let wiser heads decide, young lady. Meanwhile, I advise you to watch out for *that dude.*

- So far so boring, ghostie! I'm a stoopid kid? I'll do the stupid option then, and bollocks to you. Now back to the *god* who pulled me out of the river.

Jean Paul

- Actually noticed you at Uni and again before the demo
- So you know who I am?
- Yeah, I'm a bit of a watcher. Look like you haven't done this sort of guff before
- How can you tell?
- Trying to look cool and confident, not succeeding
- You see me kick that fanny cop in the face?
- No, thank goodness
- See me jump in the river?
- Nope
- Swim under the bridge?
- Saw you hanging about down there. Doing what exactly?
- Enjoying a private moment
- Mmm-hmmm. (Pause. They look at each other) Looked like a drowned rat
- Come off it
- What's your issue, Sally?
- Nothin'. (Pause) So you saw nothing?
- My girlfriend's got some clothes in here. Why don't you take your pick
- Your girlfriend
- Yup. She won't mind
- Where are we again?
- St Kilda
- Dude, I get it. …So how's about this one?
- Pretty short, but nice. Take the top. Yup, put it on. How about these heels? Yep. Everything seems to suit you

- I'm her size then
- Looks like it. (He surveys her) Let me take some photos.

Later that day Jean Paul (for that is his name) conducts her back to Fitzroy. He seems not a bit concerned that she never quizzed him on why he plucked her out of the crowd. Asks questions about her parents though, some of them pointed - and she finds herself answering in a quasi-mature patter. She makes sure to invent a boyfriend who she refers to at her convenience. The embarrassing subject of school doesn't seem to bother him either. In fact he's matter of fact, not to say sure of himself. She has the vague feeling he knows things about her she doesn't.

But sometimes a girl just wants to be where she is. Without knowing any damn thing at all.

Dad's Brainwave

Sal's old man has had a rare brainwave while hacking up his chops. - I'll get my girl a job with the Lard Boys in their chippy down the street. Might smarten 'er up a bit. She can learn the ropes (and later come flog flesh for me of a Sad'dy). Despite expecting a battering from said obtuse offspring, Dad finds Sal unphased when he puts the plan over dinns. Sal's not your natural macrobiotic despite her weedy cleansing diets. Besides (she calculates with lightning speed) Lard Bros is in the Brunswick strip - always a good lurk. I can even slip in and hang with Pil and Pol (the Bottle Twins who live above the bottle-o). Thursdy, Fridy, 4 till 8? No wuckers dad. Yeah I know it, 'cross from Horgan's Hotel! Little bro rolls his eyes. Sal kicks him under the table. Her Mother cherishes vaguely higher dreams for her only daughter, but aireth them not on this occasion. Dull Dad, since he has few elevated daughter visions (he doesn't know her) seems satisfied... Sal knows the Alt-music set-up at Horgans is supposed to be where it's at. All these underground grunge bands in the Bottom Bar channelling Kurt Cobain and Velvet Underground without knowing them personally. Bolt in the Brain and Barf Boys for instance. Even Fat Finger's bottom has been seen to grace the B. Bar of an evening. The lonely fat girl with the lippy lip sometimes needs to eviscerate things in public.

Pesky Ghost Writer is back:

- Sal will not admit her relentless odyssey to the core of the social scene makes her more and more conscious of her limits. And picky, introverted, not to say hypersensitive limits they are. Sal's not really the crowdy type despite her obsession with the ins and outs of 'The Scene'. True, she's not so self-conscious that she can't toss off her assigned social role with extrovert swagger. But which is it? Does lazy childish 16 year-old Sal quietly want to be *defined* by the people she pursues? Err... basically you're complicated
- *Just for you, Ghostie*
- Despite Action Girl's obsessive need to taste it all, she seems to want to play ultra-sophisto non-attached voyeur. There's a snobby superiority denied here somewhere
- *Double complicated*
- Ah! You want to stay a child. It's not about growing up at all
- *That'd get your goat, wouldn't it, oldie?*
- Come on. You're not that self-aware, you're just young and silly-sally
- *What are you, my DAD? Who are you to say the young don't get it? Your position, Ghostie, is all Decline. You wanna get it all back by using me. Well then shut up, listen and LEARN*
- Whooo! You can be my action girl
- *Pervert.*

The Lower Depths

Come Thurs'dy Sal heads on down to Lard Bros. establishment in Brunswick. The proprietors of this salubrious grease outlet will let you know in Greek (sorry Macedonian) why they serve the finest battered seafood this side of Bass Strait. Sal suffers to learn the delicate art of slipping fillets into a vat without sustaining a burn to the wrist, watched by Lard Junior (otherwise known as SpottyCock) whose expression confirms some mothers do have 'em. Sal affects dainty detachment at the new cultural experience. Thanks to the kindly attentions of Lard 1 (fondly known as Alexander the Greek) and Lard 2 (known as Zorba the Macedonian) Sal soon surprises herself, collecting money (pocketing a bit) and wrapping greasy mounds with faint relish. Spotty is assigned to the perimeter (as usual) as his dad and uncle court their new daughter. (No-one really knows how SpottyCock got his name, but there's a rumour Lard 1 was a chicken farmer who named the boy after his favourite rooster.) It's unexpectedly soothing being down and out among the working class, and Sal can take a mental holiday as well as check out the crowd on the Street - her real purpose. Until schoolies Rude Boy and Lotta BS sail in to leer at Sal in her purply-green pigtails behind the counter. Rude Boy orders a 'Big Sausage and Sauce' with a porky grin. Sal feigns fey disgust but keen-eyed Lotta knows better. Since she's acquainted with SpottyCock (to put down), and since it is her local, BS informs the Younger Lard that 'Rude and Sal are going out'. Sal, disconcerted by this invasion from the schoolie world, quietly asks Lotta to fuck off. Keen-eared Spotty on cue repeats the charge:

- Dad, Uncle! Sally said Fuck Off to a customer! Dad, Uncle! Sally said -
- Shut up. I didn't. Lotta's a friend of mine
- ZbottyKock! Zhut yorr mouth! Gett out off here! You are zuch ay rude boy - zuch ay dizappointment to yorr uncle and me. You will never make potato-chip prroprietor! Unlike Zally here' (etc).

Lard Junior slides down the back toilet to have a wank, telling Sal to 'just you wait'. Lotta and Rude Boy sidle out with ironic smirks (and sauce) all over their faces and Sal knows tomorrow the whole school will hear she is the Darling of the Greek (sorry Macedonian) fish shop in B. Street and going steady with a kid who's got a SPOTTY COCK (and beats the sausage).

Around 8 on her 2nd night (Fry'dy) after half the district has been loaded with Eff n' Chips, Sal starts to feel the grinding spiritual poverty of this humble profession. The stoic faces of the kindly Lard Bros. whose destiny it is to serve the human mass forever amid a foreign world of latte cafes and chi-chi boutiques, make her simultaneously sorry and disgusted. But at that moment Pil and Pol Bottle signal her from the front window, and she's ready to get the hell out.

- 'Zee you negz week', call out benign Lards 1 and 2.

Running down the street with Pil and Pol, Sal is ready for a Night. Pil and Pol always have PLANS - and they're always subversive. These denizens of the Proletariat, working class scrubbers who go to Sal's old school (the one she last left) recognise her as a fellow troublemaker. The brother and sister Twins refer only to each other, as if telepathically, so that no-one ever thinks of them apart as individuals. This accords them a sort of demonic energy that attracts impressionable souls like Sally Bang. Up in their tatty room above the bottle shop a block away, the threesome sit in oiky conclave on the floor and suck on weed cigarettes. Tonight we're doing a Banksy! announces Pil. Huh? says Sal, whose cultural education has not so far extended to the legendary graffitist. Don't worry, says Pol. I never heard of him either till Pil read a book and's been raving like a loon for the whole week about Banksy Banksy! You're a doodler right? says Pil. 'S all you ever did in Art class. Sal reflects that this is indeed so: she used to start at one corner of a page and fill it in with weird shapes until hours later a sort of stream-of-consciousness gunge would emerge that allowed her to regard herself as a neglected genius of heroic complexity and subtlety. Pil now pulls from a smelly sack a series of cutout patterns on cardboard that show he's mastered the use of the machete. He has also managed to purloin quite a lot of spray cans in different colours, namely green. Announces he: We're going to improve the environment. Be eco-warriors! We trace these shapes in unexpected places and then the cops chase us but never catch us and we get famous. But no-one'll know who we are if we don't get caught, says Pol, who (as a girl) is more practical. So what? We'll be famous, persists not-too-bright Pil. And how do we improve the environment if we scribble all over it? adds naughty Sally. This starts a Punch and Judy show of insults which Sal realises the twins resort to with no other frame of reference other than their bubble universe, which serves to leave other mortals out of the frame completely. After Sal has extricated Pol's head from a bin where Pil has shoved it, and suggests they start out on their expedition, Pil poutingly agrees to take charge since girls haven't a fuckin' clue about expeditions. Pil now produces his piece de resistance, some balaclavas for their heads which immediately make them look like the IRA and which Pol points out will make them sitting ducks in a neighbourhood of latte outlets and chi-chi boutiques. We're gonna be on roofs and stuff! Not on the street! protests Pil. Pol: What's the use of roofs? No-one will see our graffiti on a roof! - Unless they're in a police helicopter, observes Sal helpfully.

Now Sal is told to shut up. And she begins to fade… The weed they are sucking in is pretty suspect, and anyway she is tired from her muscular stint as a working girl. That familiar paranoidy feeling where every emotion is amplified, and the voice of conscience in her head starts to prattle and the world seems frighteningly absurd and distant as if she has no role any more in familiar mankind… starts to take her over.

But the inseparable Twinz are now in action mode. Pol produces some unusual-looking pills, slips a couple in Sal's mouth, kisses her mouth in front of Pil, then swallows her own. What's this? Sal asks vaguely. Sshh! You'll see, says Pol. Next they climb all three out the back window of the upper room onto the corrugated roof, one of a row above shops and offices and warehouses that spread chaotic across the neighbourhood. They proceed in a noisy stumble across the sloping roofs. It's 10 o'clock and the streets are still busy. It now starts to rain and surfaces are getting slippery. Pil at one point shows daring generalship as he balances on a parapet like a loon and howls to the street below. Heads turn. Pol pulls him back and they crash into a drain. Sal grazes her knee and blood starts to trickle. Presently all start to feel a new feeling, as if things are getting luminous, and the heartbeat seems to increase. Now Pil leads them onto the ledge of a factory wall 3 floors up. Sal feels greasy pigeon shit under her hand and there's a moment where she is about to fall back into space but Pol grabs her and pushes her into the wall. Her nose hits wet brick and she stalls. Window light blares at them across a laneway. They must surely be seen. Pol whispers furiously to keep on. Sal reaches, finds a windowsill. Her hands are tingling. She is paralysed. Pol suddenly pushes her through the window frame and she lands inside a room on a wooden floor… Pol follows immediately, landing with a clunk that echoes about. Sal feels sick, but Pol grabs her arm and pulls her behind a steel pylon. The dust makes her cough. Pol sticks a mitt over her mouth. They crouch there. Pil is nowhere to be seen. The distant street booms, and drunk voices leer up from the laneway below. Shafts of light poke about the room from windows opposite.

Sal feels spooky. But Pol is up and checking the space. It is a wide empty cavern supported by pylons with a dusty wood floor. Through a far wall comes the sound of a thudding beat. A club no doubt. A door in the same wall reveals a staircase. Pol pulls her back. *Not yet,* she says. Everything's in weird motion. Sal feels Pol pulling her out to the middle. Next, Pol is giggling and pulling at Sal's belt. Oh no she wants me to *strip*. Sal hesitates - then lets Pol pull her jeans down. She shrieks and starts to pull at Pol's jeans. They get tangled up, almost fall, but in a moment they are standing there staring at each other. And Sal realises she never let any girl be with her like this, anywhere, ever. Not even in the change room at the pool. Pol now ceases laughing and her stare gets intense. Sal notices she is very wiry and not too sexy with her thinnish legs roundy eyes spiky hair tattoo - and Brazilian. Sal feels a sudden need to run about the cavernous hall. She runs to where the beat is and starts to jive. In the lightbeams leering from windows across the street she sees her trail on the dust-matted floor. She feels an unknown total coolness on her unclothed skin... But Pol is there and claps an arm about her neck. Sal is pushed to the wall, feels her spine against brick. Pol plasters her lips with her tongue. Seems to wanna prove a thing. Sal wants to slide away but Pol crushes against her. Pol is breathing in her ear and pushing fingers into Sal's vagina. They slide to the floor. Sal gets a splinter in her backside. Her hand is shovelled between the girl's legs. Their heels scuff at the floor. Sal suffocated, manages to prise herself away a bit... Then Pol pushes her roughly back. Stands, runs off.

Sal is naked in the grime. Her buttock stings. She sees Pol squatted at the far end. After a pause she goes to her. Pol has evidently found an old drink bottle and is finishing a *job*. She looks up and her eyes are hollow glassy. Sal doesn't know her. The girl moans and stretches out on the hard dust floor. The bottle rolls.

In time, she starts to cry. Sal crouches by, smooths the spiked hair... and feels she knows why Pol has to dare everything, win everything, make every scene, do it all. But Sal doesn't really see that Pol needs to defy her lifelong locked embrace with her twin, that Pol has only extreme thoughts born in a vortex of rivalry, and needs to be a better girl than Pil can let her be. And *he* takes his sister for granted because he can't live without her. Her acts are the violent acts of a girl who doesn't know how to be a girl but only partner to a violent boy. For what haven't they done and committed together in their tense solitude? Both are wannabe victims of an eyeless family without promise, grinding out a life above their bottle-o in a grubby suburb of Australia.

At any rate Sal feels sorry. Mother Superior, she wants to nurse. Pol sucks at her mouth and Sal suffers dessicated lips and tongue. She cradles, Pol sucks at her breast awhile. This is quite pleasantly unusual. By and by it gets chilly and Pol wonders aloud where her brother might be. She waits for Pol to urinate in a corner. They put on clothes and head for the door in the wall. It leads down a stair to a door that enters the club. They step into pounding limelight and a hundred glances. Feeling underage they slip down to the street. Pol agitated wants to find her boy. Sal lets her run off. Then she walks away in a vague direction of home.

I guess one is not a lesbian. Tick. Fact is, she feels somewhat older... like a warrior returned from the fray. And none too clean.

Ideal Girl

At the late night café by the furniture factory sits Nev Budge on a milk crate in his overalls with his arm stump and his glass, which is half empty of something or other. Nutty Nev-ull he's derisively known by all, who never sat anywhere else or did anything else 'cos his arm got mangled in a machine at the sheltered workshop ten years back. Nev spots his girl, calls out.

- Ay Sal
- Ay Nev. (Sal pulls up a crate)
- Bin workin'?
- Yeah. Chippy down at the Strip (Sal slips easily into the vernacular)
- Them Lard boys eh?

- Yup
- Cool job eh?
- Could be worse
- Reckon I need a job eh
- You're all right, Nev
- Oi was a Joi-ner
- Yeah, everybody knows
- Lost me arm eh
- Yeah Nev. But you got a second one
- Fucken gone eh
- What is?
- Me arm. I was gonna be a joi-ner
- You were, mate
- I was brainy mate
- Hey Nev. Guess what I did tonight?
- You was at the chippy
- After. Me and my girlfriend Pol got naked in a big factory and ran round screaming and laughing
(He looks at her) - Yer a bit of a girl, Sal
- 'Reckon (smiles)
- You n' me could do a thing or two
- I reckon
- Next weekend eh? You n' me?
- Sure thing, Nev.
She smiles into his eyes. He puts a hand on her leg. She pats it. He takes her hand and smooches it. She rubs his cheek. She gets up.
- See ya round.
But he holds her round the waist and nestles his head to her shoulder. She holds his head tenderly. Pause. Some guys turn to look. She gives them the finger. Soon, she goes.
- See ya, Sal
- See ya, Nev
- I'll get me job back. Just for you. Gonna be a joi-ner
- Sure you will, Nev.

Sal heads home. Feels a bit cleaner. With nutty Nev, she can be his ideal girl.

What is it with Tiffany Haigh?

…Sal wonders, as she fingers a gilded invitation to Tiffany Haigh's birthday party. Her seventeenth.

Why do I always feel like being unfair to Tiffany when I know I've no particular cause to be? She's unclassifiably frigging normal, everybody's ideal girl in a middle-class without being condescending, upper-class without being weird sort of way. And mummy's a Successful Lawyer and daddy's a Fund Manager and brother's a Clone of daddy and she's the Clone of Mummy even tho she knows and jokes about it… and she's *so aware* of her opportunities in life and how we need to give to charities in Timor and she *doesn't* think it's a mistake being sent to a non-private progressive school for senior years 'cos her parents are so enlightened and don't want her to be cut off from the real world. How wise how true. The world is indeed full of nasty little secrets and Tiffany badly needs to get her share. Anyway, I'll mix with her Toorak crowd just like I did every birthday since we were 13 and tried to practise being Yunga Dolts. And I'll eat her canapés supplied by auntie's catering firm and schmooze with her future fund manager male friends who'll all wanna marry her at some stage and her girly girlfriends who'll never be jealous. All of us nattering cleverly round a grown-up mahogany table with grown-up drinks while I pout and make monosyllabic remarks just apposite enough to maintain the company's soiled curiosity in me…

What the hell *is* it with Tiffany Haigh?

…Sal wonders, as she fingers the gilded invitation to Tiffany's birthday party. Her seventeenth. Oooh, RSVP. Intimate affair, 12 people only. Couldn't she have asked me at school? Using her mouth? I get the old feeling Tiff is avoiding things in her perfect life and can't decide whether to take me into her confidence. Do I want her to? 'Course. She knows too well I love a dirty bit o' this and that. Better not trust me then, though

I'm her token wacky buddy and she can't get away with treating me in the usual caringly-standoffish comradely-aloof conspiratorially perfumed way she reserves for everybody else. She knows I know aristo girls like her (who don't put out) put out the excuse that they're brought up to be 'polite' boo hoo, and she suspects I might just *get* what the hell goes on 'in private' with her (if it ever goes on). It's not about details, it's *astrology*. I just see through her. Perfect basis for friendship.

BUT NOW today she rings out of the blue and wants to talk about *private stuff* but can't be sure I'll take her seriously 'cause of my working class aloofness which she knows is a game 'cause maybe I wanna be in her upper class Toorak set. No way! Oh, but inverse snobbery prevails with *you* Sally, and now you see why I maybe kept my distance a teensy bit (and now I feel we should've had more intimate tete-a-tetes in my bedroom in our earlier years). But why do you insist on being so cuttingly ironic when you know it's only fair to be *normal* and sort out *issues* in sensible ways like we were taught? You think I deep down don't want to be sensible? But I *do* darling. You think I'm stuffy but I just don't make a fuss. Your tryhard route is definitely hiding inadequacies. And don't be defensive! If I'm being pushy and self-centred I feel I have a right to be for once. Anyway, you know I'm fond of you so come to my place we'll have a swim in my indoor pool and watch movies in my cinema and then I can unload about… something. Oh my god why am I telling you? There's this 28 year-old boy who has turned my life upside down and now I can't concentrate at school and we're going into final year and I've never been so stressed, I can't face my own birthday party and I want to *die*. I think I'm totally in love with this guy. His name is *Jean Paul*.

- Whaaaatt?!!

- And there's something else as well but I can't say it. Oh fuck. I never say fuck but I'm saying it. Talk to me Sally. Just come to my house and *talk* to me.

* * * *

For the first time in the history of Australia barring state occasions Tiffany Haigh is not at school next day. And Sal in her gum-chewing way decides about period 2 to get the hell over there after school and check out this unbelievable soap opera. And no, it could not possibly be the same Jean Paul who fished her out of the river at the demo and quietly hit her with the *love brick*. But of course she knows it surely is.

So on this cold day Fate creeps up and taps Sally Bang on the shoulder. And despite her being the privileged recipient of great tidings, she has to run to the bathroom a heap of times.

When she gets to the big Toorak gate through security up the stairs and into the Balcony Bedroom she's no longer in schoolie uniform you can be sure of that. Tiffany is lying in state, suffering from an unnamed condition which baffles mummy who texted her at 12.13 pm between divorce cases. Tiffy in her neglige smiles the wan smile of a lover who wants to die. Whose life is over at any rate. Sal will hide her consternation behind the actor's mask: concerned friend, deeply humbly honoured to receive tidings of great import.

- So you're preggers
- How do you know *that?*
- You told me
- I don't believe I did
- Who's the guy?
- His name is Jean Paul as I told you
- French is he?
- I believe his ancestors were, yes
- You missed the Othello test. Must be serious
- Sally, don't make fun or I won't talk to you
- I think you spilled the beans already. Is he a good lay?
- Sally! I'm in trouble!
- All right sweetie. I've got a feeling I've seen this guy round anyway
- How could you?
- At the school gates
- He never came to the school gates. Do you think I'm crazy?

- Tall, slim, small light beard, ear-stud, Yin-Yangy thingy round his wrist?
- How do you know all that?
- I asked around
- What?
- Calm down. …You should be slightly more careful.
Pause. Tiffany looks at Sally with baleful eyes.
- Come and lie next to me. I need you
- No worries. (Yay, I got away with *that!*)
Sal props herself in line with Tiff.
- Do take the boots off
- Sorry
- They're nice though. You're good at fashion
- Ta
- You're so together. So normal
- Me?
- In a way. You know things, you see things. (She starts to cry. Sal cuddles up, kisses her)
- Come on now Tiffy. Kids are starving in Timor
- I know. I should be sensible
- But you haven't been, have you? (Tiff cries again) But it's good. *Be* the fool. *Do* the wrong thing. Just pick the right guy.
Tiff looks at her.
- What do you know about him?
- Nothing… much. I can see he's not right for you
- Why is he not right for me? (Tiff becomes stern) Why is he not right?
- He doesn't fit into Toorak?
- But he does. He's perfect. He fits in with everything
- Have mummy and daddy seen him?
- You're being hard on me
- Does he love you?
- Yes…
- Did he tell you that? (Pause) So he hasn't. Clue number one.

Sally is surprised at how calculating she is being. It's moments like these that reveal our nature to ourselves. And wonder of wonders, even enlightened Tiffany Haigh can't talk to her wonderful parents about everything.

- So tell me about you and him
- Secret? Just you and me?
- Sure thing.

Tiff snuggles up real close. Sal is aware of her sweet subtle scent, bob of blondy hair framing those fine cheeks, those elegant lips.

- I was at a gallery opening with my mum. He was there taking photographs of the minor celebs, or so he said. He seemed, I don't know, kind of self-contained. Cool, sexy, magnetic, whatever. I was in the short champagne dress, you know the one, and he complimented me. And why not? I look hot in it. He was smooth. But deep. Seems to be always thinking about something but he was still there with *me* you know, as if he took me seriously. I like to be taken seriously, Sal. (I know you do, darling) And he asked me out. Like there and then. Mum was somewhere else. Fuck, I felt weird! I said: *Why?* Sally, why would I say why? ('Cos you're a schoolgirl?) I was a stupid little *idiot*. Then I said like: Okay. Okay! He had me. It's not supposed to *happen* like that. Oh my god, I was gone
- When was this?
- Six weeks ago. He took me home in a battered old car he drove. (I was surprised he drove that, I have to say) And mum didn't mind a bit. Apparently he'd already worked on *her*. Besides, she's a sucker for boys like him. She just batted her eyelids. She's supposed to protect me! (For god's sake Tiff, she's an older version of you!) Anyway, he showed me photos at his flat at St Kilda and we had wine and we had this weird talk about spirituality and Buddhism of all things blaa blaa. And then I asked him to stop talking. (Why?) Because I was totally soaked down below! And... oh my *god*, you can imagine the rest.

Sal wasn't sure she wanted to imagine the rest. Or whether to get sordid detail from the horse's mouth. She felt weirdly possessive of Jean Paul, like she owned him and hated him at the same time. And hated Tiff for knowing him. And hated him for being such a schmoozer. And hated him more for being someone who matters to *herself*. And suddenly hated being in this bed with Tiffany. But Tiff held her very close.

- Darling. I want you to take a *message* to him. Because I refuse to talk to him. I can't even text him. You know I'm not even seventeen. I want him like fucking anything... *but I'm going to dump him.* Today. This is the worst day of my life. There's no going back. He'll understand you. He might even like you. Watch out for him! I've been seeing him for six weeks and I don't know who I am any more. I am totally lost, totally confused. Don't try to handle him, Sally. He's a demon, a spiritual beautiful demon. You will fail. Just give him my message and go.

So this is her plan! (*Is it? - GW*) I underestimated the beautiful bitch. She wants to see if I get a come-uppance as well! Tiffany freaking Haigh knows I can't resist a challenge. How much of her story is bullshit then?

- So you *are* pregnant?
- I'm sure I am, darling. I did a test kit thingy
- How many times?
- Darling, I did it, all right!
- Does he know?
- Doesn't know anything - yet
(Pause) - Okay. Okay. I'll help. Don't worry, I'll do it. But you owe me, okay? (Sal *is* crazy)
- Oh Sally (now comes her best bit) you're wonderful. As soon as you've done it I'm going to tell mummy everything. I knew you and me were close. We don't *need* boys, do we? Actually?

This is where Tiff kisses her on the mouth. For just a little too long. Sal is not a fool and kisses back with a hint of tongue. See if Tiff has any guts. If she has, it'll improve her story when she gossips it to her adoring friends in a frozen future time. Sal slips her hand onto Tiff's sweet light breast. Tiff flutters her eyes. Now the hand slips down to her pussy region. Tiff's smile drains away but her eyes widen and her lips part. What now hey? Breath mingling, they search each other's gaze. And Tiff suddenly recollects she's human frailty personified and she goes limp in Sally's embrace. Ha!

The scene is over. Sal gets up and puts on her boots. Tiff lies still on the bed, looking strangely at her.

- Are you gonna get a termination?

And Tiff starts to cry. Again.

Later Sal will reflect that the saga likely has some grains of truth, but that Tiffany Haigh could never play the warrior-explorer she assumes Sal to be. Tiff will look jealously down on her from a height for evermore, and that's why Tiff will keep her as friend and invite her to all her parties for evermore. Our Tiffany at 17 craves to know there's more than the safe little gilded world she could never bear to step out of - for a child in a gilded cage is mother to a woman who looks back and wonders: *if only.*

Sal heads on home via several cafes and the park. Feeling like - she doesn't know what. That's it. Depressed.

To flee or not to flee - that is the question

Sal got the good mark in the Othello test. 17 out of 20. 'Write an apology for Iago'. She can relate to the slimy guy somehow. 'O is a Tool (she visualises his black tool) tho' I feel sorry for him. And his wife Da Moaner reminds me of Tiff on her death bed for some reason.' Truth is, Sal at school is no great hit. She's acceptable in English or Mod History without doing any work, does her avant-gardey bits in Art without being able to draw a stroke but is saved (curiously) by Religious Studies which trawls through Faiths of the World in a vaguely provocative manner for a 16 yr. old iconoclast without a cause. In the supermarkets of faith, the Eastern goods seem more on the money (so to speak). Sal tends to dwell on Won - and her romantic imaginations are stirred by Buddhism's or Sufism's inscrutable mysteries. Naturally the privations of eternity don't appeal, just the results. Sal likes the idea of lonely deserts mountains ruinous temples... their solemn solidity sits beyond the twitchings of this corny life. Blissful cave, windblown plain, silken lake astride high deserts, gnarled tree silhouette swaying in the white Andes. *Go quietly 'midst the noise and haste and remember what peace there may be in silence...* 'Desiderata. I read that. That's how my leaving dream can be: the silent spiritual has no humans in it! Exit this shit world. *So what* if I've a snobby superior-complex like Ghostie says? This news junk daily babble is a phoney farce compared to silent prairie spaces of Eternity. To be free and alone. These posers who claim to live 'spiritually' in the middle of this mess are full-on fakes. But I wanna drink the disgusting world *as well*. No I fucken *don't*. Shit!' Sal is creepily amazed at the cynic clarity of her own thoughts. And where does this feeling come from, this tingling sense of bigger destiny, fully formed in her skin?

Forget it. At sixteen nothing's practical. The world's still too majorly entertaining! This free-for-all circus of manners and madness and ins and outs, this soil and muck and farcical fuck this Sodom Gomorrah Fool's Paradise freak show vanity fair multi-fantastic human dream! There's even something cool about my trudgy grudgy daily grind, my growing up and out to meet the solid world, its pavements shops its people poor its buildings fog and chilly winter mornings and the dog. And comfy clothes and drink n' food and TV prattle toast and beer and screw-you sneer and all the human scrabble and each new year. Life! This is it! I wanna BE, love the sea, have random parties (won't you be with me?) and feeling lost and feeling free I'm sixteen gotta touch the wind my face like sultry lace and *Jean Paul* in his banger waiting at the gate we'll surf the roads the thudding bass let's go let's freak let's do the race! I gotta live and breathe and cry, get born forever don't care why. I don't care what or who or how! I wanna EAT it *Now Now Now.*

The Lower Lower Depths

Next week it's back to the chippy in grungy Brunswick. Sal hasn't called up Jean Paul (except in dreams) and Tiff is silent tragic on the phone. The Brothers Lard with hairy reassuring wrists serenade Sally over vats and sweat on high, and loser SpottyCock is plotting things to make them all *die*. To this end he ingratiates himself with Pil Bottle (not Pol) who really can't stand Spotty but is in for a dare because local drug dude Bin Fang (oooh) has hired our Spot' to do some 'chemical shit'. And Pil is in on principle. Pil by the way fell on some drunks in the alley last week doing his Banksy routine. They kicked some of his teeth out. Now he has to eat humble pie through a straw till he gets 'em replaced. Faithful Pol nurses him, but he with gritty gravity brushes sister off and plots revenge on all mankind.

Past midnight in the kitchen at the back of Lard Brothers, SpottyCock and Pil are making something filthy bubble in some tubes. Lard Bros are home snoozing Macedonian dreams in their suburban beds. Sal and Pol have sneaked in in their 4-inch heels to watch, following several hours of booze and Karaoke at Horgans Upstairs. They're dressed as sluts since it's the only get-up that passes the bouncer in the absence of 20 bucks. Not their real nature of course. This act in fact wins them free drinks from dumb punters who mistake their obnoxious cacklings for sexual interest. Turns out their duet *I Will Survive* won the night's Worst Rendition Award.

Spotty in his dad's big chef's hat seems well cooked, doing his ceremonial stir of the vat when Sal lurches in, and toothless Pil holding a big spoon peers at instructions on a bottle of drain cleaner. A Frankenstein smell pervades the room and seeps into the front chippy. But SpottyCock's in charge. His greasy neck runs in little rivulets under his black hair and his yellow eyes suggest he tasted the evil P. For the benefit of the sluts Spotty barks an order at Pil, who wild-eyed in the manner of a lunatic swivels and knocks a beaker of steaming muck off the bench. It oozes across the floor and Pol and Sal leap onto chairs with a howl. Pol's greasy burger shoots out of its bag and lands in the vat with a heavy plop. Sal considers this beyond hilarious and screams out, whilst a vaporous discharge ascends to assail the nostrils of our lunatic band. Now Spotty's mobile bleeps. As he reaches for it he slips on the tiles, his elbow comes down on the Bunsen burner and it tips on the floor. A wave of blue flame erupts across the kitchen and Pil is caught, his leg in its path. He howls to the night and blunders into the chippy. Just at that moment there's a banging on the glass street door. A burly constable is framed in the neon doorway. Sal and Pol perched on the bench in their tiny skirts watch SpottyCock crash to the back passage, wrenge open the door and lurch off into the night. An Asiatic voice jabbers from his mobile that floats like a turd across the floor. Pol steps into the glimmering wash of flame, grabs the phone in her fingers. Come on! Sal slips sideways and her flimsy heel collects the apparatus. There's a ghastly hiss. She totters down the passage after

Pol pursued by a crackle and then the BANG of explosion. Smoke starts to billow out as they stumble over rubbish in the yard. Sal loses a heel and they fall over a wall and stagger squealing down the lane. Out in the street lights flood their eyes. They pick their way through the late crowd to the shopfront door. It's blown clean through and glass is scattered on the pavement. A bleeding cop is shouting to people to stay back. There's a body in the doorway crawling into the street. It's Pil. Pol feels the mobile in her hand, the voice still yabbering. She thrusts it away and starts towards him. But Sal sober now, yanks her back. They fall headlong in a gutter. Pol is shouting but Sal shoves her away up the street. They're totally soiled and shoeless. The cop sees them. They run like hell for two hundred yards and are away gone.

Whew. All this is a heaving brew of hysterical funny awful, but then a sort of slow nutty shock sets in. Still the night's nowhere near over. Pol has to find the Hospital blaaa and shoves Sal in to check if Pil's there and yeeeah… he's not dead just lacerated. Who are *you* anyway? A friend, and no my sister won't come in she's drunk. Yes we're keeping him overnight for toxic testing blaaa. NO Pol! you can't go home 'cos the cops might come round. My place. Honey I'm as munted as you are! …Hi mum yeah sorry bit drunk can she sleep here? No we had a quiet night but Pol's allergic to cheeseballs and vodka combination yeah unbelievable, had it since childhood but forgot 'cos it's her birthday. What new shoes you bought me? Um, an Asian guy stole them off me. I'll get a new pair! I know its 3 am we got *lost* no don't wake dad we'll sleep top-and-tail no we *don't* need new sheets FUCK can we all just go to BED NOW?

The local radio has cool terror reports next day. Says the police are 'continuing their enquiries'. It's Saturday so Dad is at his butcher's and Sal (bleary) goes there after Pol shot through to find Pil who will by now have concocted a likely story about being a 'Hinnocent bystander near the door Offisser when said blast took place' etc. Sal offers to help grateful Dad chop chops and serve his customers, and by the way drops a hint that Lard Bros. might be *closing* for a while and yeah they're heading back to Macedonia, so she heard on the grapevine. More and more lies. Sal in full damage-control mode is surprised how good she is at those.

* * * *

[*Enter a sensible grown-up voice.]
- How many exaggerated bloody scenes are we going to have about you fooling with sex terror drugs and rock and roll?
- You like it
- Serious?
- Don't pout or I'll get a new ghost writer
- You don't see the art that goes into this
- Your life was over at 17 and you wanna use me. Loser
- You dunno diddly squat about life beyond your precocious ego!
(Little smile) - What's 'precocious' mean, daddy?
- Sod off
- Don't get mad, ghostie. You know you need me
- This is a game to you
- A game? I have to live every second. I have to grow up
- Got that right
- Didn't get the irony?
- Got it. Calm down. Carry on growing then. You've got a way to go
- Might never go there
- Wassat mean?
- Find out, old wannabe
- That a threat?
- Bloody parent types always wanna make ya sensible
- Why do kids always talk in clichés? So conservative
- You want what I'm gonna be. 'Cos you never had a Time
- I know things you don't, baby. And I know what you need!
- I don't give a rat's what you think I need
- Hmm… So we're a Team then?
- Yeah Ghostie boy. Now shut it and write what I want. And I'll feed you a Mars Bar.

Teen Ruminations (Mills and Boon)

Sal is under big pressure in the matter of Jean Paul, so has the demonic idea of inviting him to Tiffany's 17th at Swaggers Bar. Guest appearance!

That'd make lucky thirteen. Truth is, Sal is afraid of Jean Paul and it occurs to her Tiffany is as well. Amazingly, Sal doesn't doubt she can really be his girl, and says to herself she doesn't fear Tiff as a rival. But with him everything's so weird and special that a frigging *ceremony* is required. This gatecrash idea would let me play heroine in a neutral space. Too effing complicated to meet him alone. Couldn't handle the *importance* (*haven't the guts you mean). Nope, that dress-up episode in St Kilda made me feel like SIX, and I wanted to kiss his FEET or something.

Besides… (Demonic voice) he *told* me he had a girlfriend. Whose clothes *fitted me.* Tiffany is my size too, give or take. Ugh, couldn't be her! Yes it could; the demo was only 4 weeks ago. Tiff met him *six.* Hmm, this JP is pretty darn deep. Too deep for me? Oi, why the bleep should he be too deep? (Angelic voice) Don't talk that way, Sally dear. He's your Future! Future what? Lover? Husband? Fellow Traveller? Guru? Father? (Demon) He had sex with *her.* Mind you I would. She's gorgeous in her neaty blondy way. Or maybe she made that up too. Nope, sounded real. But I don't believe the PREGNANCY crap. Can't imagine he does sex. Can't imagine he *doesn't.* Probably he's like, *Tantric.* Bet he gives Sacred Bangs. Me dressed up as his Goddess… fleshy hot photos… now we're talking. Don't go there! Anyway, it'd be a doozy of a night if he turns up. I'll tell Tiff there's a mystery guest arriving late. *This is your Life!* Mystery chair, next to me. Too tough on her? Prob'ly. Mind you, she practically dared me. No, I'll meet him beforehand and errr… Hey! Why's she getting me to do her dirty work? Not yer effing maidservant, stupid tragic. I'll sell him a line: *Tiff is my bestie and she can't see you any more 'like that' 'cause she's not in love with you 'like that' but still wants to be your like 'friend' whereas I Sally am her faithful blaaaa.* Then see what he does. He'll wanna see *me* then. Then I'll err… wing it. Frigging Mills and Boon complicated! (*And boringly pathetic. G.W) Not ready for this guy. But everything else is starting to look *stupid.* Oh what to dooo? I'm such a child.

*- You may act like a child, Sally, but you're a mature woman inside. Be one
- I know. I must
- Meanwhile, you're not the least bit jealous of horrid Tiffany Haigh.

Desperate Diversions

Now that Lard Bros is a contaminated site and no-one (least of all Sal) knows a thing about how it happened, the sad Macedonian bouzouki boys are forced to move to a new temporary chippy blocks away. Not zo bloody good. This takes at least 2 mournful weeks, and Sal helps them move, out of the goodness of her heart. Spotty is looking guilty but still wants to root Sal as if nothing happened. Sal treats him with the contempt he doesn't really deserve since he's just a dumb greek sorry macedonian kid who'll be forced into *crime* to prove to all the world (and Sal) that he's not a dumb greek sorry blaa blaa - kid.

Sal has now graduated to Horgans' Bottom Bar of a Fri'dy Sad'dy (her slutty bottom usually gets her past Izzy Folau the Tongan bouncer) and has struck up acquaintance with a puny redhead Asiatic Rapper and his sultry Latino lead guitarist known as Manitu. These are The Barf Boys. The Eye (from Animal Road), apparently a video genius, dabbles with their backing shots and even squeaks a turntable or two. He's sure pleased to see Sal again, and patronises her with knowing winks which drives her nuts in front of Guitar Man, for whom she keenly wants to be Chief Slut Groupie. Specifically keen in fact since she's in frantic denial over Jean Paul. (The build-up to the BIG PHONE CALL is on. Tiff at school regards her with mistful eyes, and Lotta BS and Rude Boy are starting to suspect something *big* is going down. Worse, those two oiks are not invited to Tiff's notorious she-bang.)

Now Latino Lover Manitu's a slow mover, and likes to get mystical since he's from Peru. His big baleful eyes scan the room as he plies his Axe in penance for being associated with this scrawny asiatic Lead Barfer. - *You fink rap is all 'bout Bling; but you gotta sing sing sing! On da stree' is rea-ry wild; is no prace for Litt-le Chile...* (etceterah) Sal is not a little Chile and couldn't give a shit about Asiatic Rap; neither could the big Peruvian. After the gig Sal drags him out of the club and guides him up a particular alleyway of her choosing, ahem. Then she pushes him to his flat for more. He's like the big Sioux Chief in an alien kidsy world: not the slightest bit emotional about anything, least of all her. And Sal is determined to be the kidsy Fitzroy Kid with giggles and jokes and dribble-drinking on his knee while he's TV surfing. She wishes Pol were here so she can play a better game and turn more tricky tricks. She has coke and snorts it, getting wild and antsy. But it's like cavorting with a tree, he's in a different universe from me. I'm 16 - stupid local Friday girl without no pants on. Who the hell am I? She ends up barfing in the loo. Dismissed, she tumbles through the door he locks without a smile. She slips on stairs and breaks a heel and twists her wrist. At the very bottom of the stair she'll totter homeward. But The Eye accosts her out of nowhere. He's been round the block to find her. She tells him eff off but he takes it well - and calls a taxi, the gent who's always there to help a silly-sally girl from going to hell.

Shit Hits the Fan

Out of the blue on Monday in Art class Sally gets a call from The Man. From *Jean Paul*. By luck or no, Tiffany is in the room. And she, like a wolf in spring, senses something is amiss. Unbelievably, Lotta BS and Rude are present as well. Arresting their oiky conclave at the back they prick up their ears. Tiffany doesn't know where to put herself when Sal throws the whole game and dice away with her big baleful eyes at that sudden Jean Paul voice. Tiff sways in the middle of the room like Anna Karenina, her pinky lovely cheeks turned pale, her lovely hands gone limp. Sal slides behind a computer and fiddles with technology. The relief teacher is ignored. The phone burns in her ear. A school uniform's no garb for this! She's completely thrown for one time in her life.

- Are you Sally?
- Yes. This is Sally
- Can you find me Tiffany please?
- Don't know where she is
- This is not a game
- I... didn't think it was
- Is she in your class? Yes or no?
- Yes. But she's not here... today
- She told me to ring this phone. Her mother said she is there. Put her on.
There's no arguing with this. But Sally tries.

- You see Jean Paul, we we - have a problem, and -
CLICK. The voice is gone.
- Jean Paul?
Sally listens for more. Her ear burns. She is tiny small in her uniform. Knees are shaking, throat is dry. The whole universe can see. Tiffany is wildly staring at her. So she *is* pregnant. The emotional cloud they all denied is about to burst. Everyone heard 'Jean Paul'. The name looms like a claxon in the room. Lotta BS is first.

- Who's Jean Paul?
- *Why didn't you give me the phone?* Tiffany kind of shouts.
- He rang off
- *What the fuck are you thinking?*

A breath-intake goes round the room. Fifteen pairs of eyes exchange glances. No-one ever heard FUCK from Tiffany Haigh. The male relief teacher freezes.

- Give me the telephone.
Sal is frozen.
- *Give it to me Bitch!*
Tiff heads for Sally. Sal thrusts it out at her. She swipes it, heads for the window, raises an arm and hurls it out with a high grunting sound. It is heard shattering against the stone wall opposite. Rude Boy stands bolt upright and instinctively slams the window down. He has an eye for theatre. Now she goes for the door. But self-serving Lotta gets in her way.
- Easy, Tiff. It's all right
- Get away from me! What do you want?
She swivels to face the mass who stare like statues.
- What do any of you fucking want?
The teacher moves. - Just a moment - !
Sal starts forward. A chair whangs her knee and Tiffany Haigh comes at her. Sal is pushed over a bench. Tiff has her by the neck with one hand. *You fucking want him - you have him!* Sal, her back twisted, grips the arm. *But the child is mine! It's mine, you hear. It's mine. It's mine!*
Sal shoves her off and she falls - all willowy like Cate Blanchett - onto the

sharp edge of another bench then onto a chair. She gulps nastily, crashes to the floor.

There is a pause. Then she starts to wail.
Teacher: - Everybody out.
Nobody moves. - Now!

Students shuffle randomly to the door. Lotta's eyes are wide wide and Rude Boy is pumped. Sal kneels beside Tiff, who swings vaguely out at her and crawls away. The teacher pulls Sally up. *Go. Just go...* Bundles her out, locks the glass door to the corridor. Sal and several others watch him kneel under a bench, trying to get Tiff out from under. He is pleading with her. He succeeds after a time. Tiffany sways on his arm as he leads her to the staff annex, waving the gawkers away. The students trawl up the corridor. All eyes glare at Sally.

- No comment, she says. And hastens away.

* * * *

Tiffany Haigh isn't seen for days. Needless to say the 17th Hooley is off the agenda. News of the incident in Year 11 Art 1 roars round the school at TikTok speed. Sal is summoned to the Head the day after. She is told the Haighs have some questions. She stalls on the incident until the Head gets annoyed. That evening she calls the Haigh residence. The lawyer mother answers. She is told Tiffany is in hospital being checked after a blood discharge in the night. It appears to be a miscarriage. Mrs Haigh is at a loss to know who or how the hell she got pregnant but it is definitely a Stain on the Family and everyone is 'extremely angry'. She wants to know exactly what Sally knows - because if they find the boy who did it, there'll be hell to pay. Sal listens to this impassively. She's gone limp by now and offers nothing. How could Tiffany ever think she wanted that child?

Three days later she calls again. Tiffany is there. After some hesitation she takes the phone.
- Yes?

- I'm sorry, Tiff

(Pause) - It's okay. I'm sorry

- Are you hurt bad?

- I'm okay. Just exhausted. My fault really. Miscarriage. For the best really. Stiff upper lip. Embarrassing though. ...S'pose I'm famous?

- Sure are. You'll never be head girl now

- Head slut more like

- No no. Is - um… have you -

- Let's not talk about Him. Not now

- If you say so

- He came to the *house*. This morning. I was alone. Wanted to give me advice

- And?

- Did I *ever* give you his phone number?

- Sure you did

- That's all right then. Mum suspects him. No evidence though. Unless… unless someone…

- Don't worry about it, okay?

(Pause) - I won't, darling. (Pause) Mmm. Thanks for calling

- Sure

- 'Bye for now.

CLICK.

This Jean Paul Thing

So commences the long decline of Tiffany Haigh, which will drag Sally into its clutches no matter how hard she wants to avoid. The day she plucks the courage to call Jean Paul a week later, we learn that Tiff has had a fainting spell on the way home in her father's car and been taken to hospital. But it's not so serious. She's overwrought, the doctor says. Jean Paul without hesitation asks Sal to come to a crowded market in the city, where there's a cafe called *Triangle*. It is inconvenient in all possible ways, but she finds herself running to keep the appointment as if her life depends on it. Sal recognises the battered car across the street and knows she has to enter. Dressed hastily in red jeans, hair in a top knot, pink top, navel exposed under, Sal doesn't feel her best. The face has worry lines only a stranger would notice. Certainly her mother did. Stomach is in knots and she knows this rendezvous will be interrupted by her seeking the ladies room. This annoys her more than she'll admit. For a moment she is sick of sixteen. He's at a booth in the corner, on the phone. She watches dryly. His gestures and manner seem assured. He spots her, signals with a finger to come. She stands formally by the booth. He gives several instructions, puts the phone down and smiles at her through narrow thinking eyes. Sal realises she's wearing Tiffany's Top. Which *he* chose at his house. She reddens.

- Glad you could come, Sal.

He offers a hand. She takes. He asks her to sit. She does, beside him in the smooth booth. No kiss. Sal is flushed and flustered. He surely sees! But what does he care for tinny nuances and little worlds? Yet he *notices*, she is sure. Vertical learning curve, so much to know in an instant. Suddenly Sal realises she's not seen him since their first day. How can this be, so avidly has she formed him in mental detail! With the certainty of the inexperienced she feels he is hers, that she has the right to be where she is. I'm not your average Joanne! (Readers will grock that by now) But she fears a coming drowning, out of depth… and her mood segues to pouty brittleness. It won't serve at this juncture. For Sal suddenly wants to wonder what Tiffany felt, and what she did and what he said to her. She feels Tiff beside her for the first time. Her stomach twists. Yet this guy seems a master at subtlety: he has not the faintest problem putting young girls at his ease. It was the sudden conspiracy of their meeting and flight from the demo that gave her the absurd feeling she was really his. Yet he'd already watched her. And he already knew Tiffany. Spooky! Sal is lonely for an instant. Then the sun comes out. He grasps her hand and says:

- I missed you
- Oh!
- You think that's crazy? Considering
- Considering? (Don't say *Tiffany*. Don't!)
- You're a bit stressed today (He noticed)
- Er yeah, I guess

- I note the top. Suits you
- Oh… How does it suit me? (Sal is surprised she asks)
- You're a girl of particular colours and moods. Pink with red - beautiful.

This seems sufficient to send her into a mini rapture. He takes her top knot, loosens it with professional touch. *That's* it. Next he takes her face between thumb and fingers and massages the eyes and temples. She feels idiotically light. It's a simple communion, like… home. Now she feels the need to return his gesture. But to touch the face seems crazy. She does nothing.

- Nice, she whispers.
He looks with the steady gaze of a mystic.
- You're not Tiffany at all.
She jolts. Looks at him like a baleful deer.
- I'm sorry. Maybe we shouldn't mention
- Okay. (Hollowly, but adulty) No, we can. If *you* want.
He seems to consider. There's a pause. Like all their pauses, she is unable to fill this one.

- Look… (his tone is lightly confessional) Tiffany is a beauty but trapped by upbringing. She claimed she was aware of it and I took her at her word. She asked me to be her lover. I didn't necessarily ask her. I thought, here's a way to bring her to life. Why should her life be set in stone? You know what I'm saying. There's something else and she needs to have it. Forgive me saying this but I don't fool round with just anybody. If I see… potential (he shrugs lightly) I see it. Those eyes, mmm, that fluttery smile. She could go in any direction! Just doesn't know it
- But she's in love with you now.
He considers.
- What can I do about that?
Sal is not sure where to put herself. Feels weirdly defensive for Tiff. And for herself.
- *You* have to deal with it.
This is a very womanly thing for Sal to say. He is moved to glance at her - then drop his eyes. A nod.

- True. True.

Pause. There seems no prospect that he will deal with it.

- I mean she's vulnerable. In Art class when you rang (He stares now. She quails) - I mean she went ballistic. It was horrid actually. I hated it.

A challenge. The atmosphere definitely stiffens. Sal the schoolgirl feels she utterly doesn't belong. He is immobile. Finally she looks out the window. He runs a hand through his hair.

- Let's go for a drive.

In the car Sal can't get anything back. Familiar feelings? None. She sits like a stranger, riding to nowhere, recognising nothing. He doesn't speak, gazes ahead. He's so Older, with his fucking coping skills. Does he really give a rat's? Sal feels the stomach abyss. The elderly car grinds on. I'm *dead*. They pass a beach. Sal suddenly demands to get out. Ladies room, she says. He stops, doesn't look. She runs to a building. Public convenience. Inside, the loos beckon in a line. The end one. Seat is cold. She does nothing. Her knees are shaking. Puts her head down between them. The floor is cracked and blue. She stares. A draft lightly licks her legs. Outer silence begins to impose, minutes go by. A distant rumble. Finally she stands up, rearranges. He must be long gone. She steps out. Indeed the car is gone. Sal walks over to the beach. The greyish day meanders away to the south. No-one around. She stands at the low sea, scans the sheen of the bay. What a fool. Loser! I'm never coming back to this shit... Two gulls strut and eye her sidewise. They wait.

Sally Bang. Not seen again. Mystery disappearance. Windswept shore. No trace. Parental grief. Mass funeral. Great promise. Eulogy. Loss to humankind. We'll miss you.

The gulls are waiting.

I'm cold.

I have nothing to feed you.

Finally she moves off in a northerly direction, her little boots sinking into sand.

Sweet Sixteen

Every emotion for a new lover is hyperbolised, and so it is with Sally. Now begins possibly the drudgiest period of school ever. Not that she remembers how boring it was before. All teachers are a pain in the arse. Tiffany's beauty quietly drains, unseen by others' eyes. As for Sally, she daubs herself with black ornaments and gothy eye shadow. This atmosphere drives normative kidsy kids like Lotta BS and Rude Boy into paroxysms. They're powerless to exploit the fallout from The Art Room Incident or break into its adulty cone of silence. How could they, yet untouched by interfering fingers of the adult world, ever notice that an autumn change has come? And has it come - so early in the spring?

Mature ghost writers want to shout: *It's exaggerated mush, just a phase!* Sensible voices say a wee text exchange with Jean Paul would solve it all. But there's a million nuances in this growing up, crammed in the tiniest possible timeframe, each an exquisite new taste that tortures. *Leave me be!* says Sally Bang.

And so with an eye for drama and for torture, we linger with our heroines in the autumnal depths of sweet sixteen. Heroines plural, for who can fail by now to feel the pathos of our tragical blonde from Toorak? She, beacon of decency, pearly prize, tomorrow's white hope, is a girl who never will be Sally, thank the innocent lord! For there's a time when beauty's so serene, in no-one's imagination can it fade. When the skin of girls is pure ice cream, and their artless eyes stare from a garden glade. What fool would dismiss this Eden as 'passing phase'? For if our life is all mere phases, if we are never *what we are* but dragged on to other phantom versions of what we will *become,* who then can say we ever *were*? In the midst of soulless grasping growing up, let us nurture these our timeless princesses. Oh let them live unsullied 'yond mossy walls in private palaces, and we shall garland them with gift and reputation, disturbing not their flower dreams.

Jean Paul's Dilemma

Don't doubt the enigmatic JP would like to have written the foregoing paragraph, him being a mystic lover and guru. Why be so microscopically interested in girls like Tiffany and Sally as they tilt and feint at adulthood? That cliché 'decisions we make at this hour affect a lifetime' is neither here nor there. Life's ins and outs are not that crucial. So? **Naivety...** We crave the *pivotalness* of this time of youth, yet its impossibleness haunts us. We've no idea where we are or where we came from and everything is *difficult* with no solutions to anything, like a razor's edge: those postures of pain we long to flee from but *never should*. We say we've no energy to flirt with the extreme uncertain, to let it push us or fold us like a river. And our ego is so demanding, desperate to find 'identity'. But what's that? Frozen mask, skeletal chainmail imposing itself on the fluid wind of us, lashing us down in the tempest of adolescence! Oscar Wilde said: life's too too important to be taken seriously... What if we took no position but anarchy? Iconoclasts forever, surrendered to glass gods of chance; bring on the vision of hopeless naivety! **Or... get mature!** Instead we tell ourselves there's a big demanding spirit beyond this vulgar world that's silently hunting our hearts. Like automata we turn to the *serious,* whisper with folded hands to solemn and certain gods under the Buddha stare of destiny whose apron eyes take us for dust. Heads bowed we affect to pray: 'this stupid *maya* is nothing but a dance of figurines in a frightened void, lurch of skeletal lust in gouts of wanting. Ugh. No more to be laughed or wept at in grimace or glee. *Go quietly amid the noise and haste.* Embrace tradition, be serious, stay unfree.

Ghost Writer shreds Jean Paul

- Jean Paul, 28, obsessed with 'spiritual growth', fears his 'discipline' will dump him on a lonely limb. Competitive narcissistic controlled yogi meets sexual charm god. Truth seeker plus guru to girls? Pick on chicks your own age
- (JP) Yep, at my age I feel like something's been lost. But I made a deal with myself: evolve, work at evolving like a painstaking pointillist
- Screw up! Be funny or free or freakishly fat. You shirk the one thing you need. What happened to spontaneity?
- Maybe I did it
- Tiffany Haigh? Bollocks

- I let that fake-innocent siren suck away what I have, a thing I hardly know I have

- Crap. You know your own beauty and mystery; girls can't resist. And the moment you have them, they're lost. Love and beauty find their death the moment they're aware. Will *you* explain it to them? Wanna have your cake and eat it. Predator in your twenties

- A 'ghost writer' calls me predator? I dispense truth as people *want* it

- The truth *you* want, pompous bloodsucker. But just try avoiding Sally Bang. She's impervious to you though she doesn't know it yet. Yeah, she still quails at your awesome calm sad-cool irony, though she sees the arrogance I'll bet. Later, you'll be the one to quail. If she can spit out that Muslim she can deal with you

- It's me who values *her*. But irony is best. Don't dump your guilt on me! You're involved with her

- How many role-models did she trawl through in her rush to maturity? She plays with identities like dolls. We're the latest. One day all she'll need is herself and eternity. Youth's a frantic rush to age. She'll get old soon!

- Okay 'dad'. The rest of your life, you'll be sniffing out the moment when you actually 'felt young'

- It never was! Siren Tiffany who 'tricked you': was she allowed to be young? She'll never be again thanks to you, impregnator, killer. Gorgeous girls at sixteen have something you want, but *you* can never be it, never learn it or keep it. And they wanna love ya. Deal with it

- I'll wallow in narcissism then? Tiffany wanted to grow up fast. Not my fault. You want me to patronise, or help her grow?

- Smartarse dabbler. Don't be responsible, don't have the guts to face your complexes. See if I care

- But you do care, mister ghostie. 'Cause it's your stuff. *You're* writing it and you're jealous. The helpless romantic. Suffer, man.

JP's Likely Story

Jean Paul nearly didn't drive off that day. Sat there in his banger aware he'd pissed her off, surprised she defended her so-called friend. 'Girls are quite madly loyal and principled with each other, I notice. Something I never felt the need to be. Actually she told me to fix my 'guru problem' right there though she didn't know it. Chicks! They're so fucking serious clever with their *intuition*. Wait a minute. I wonder if Sal knew I was talking to Tiffany when she walked in? S'pose I should be ashamed. China doll Tiffany Haigh didn't deserve to be disturbed by me I guess. But those bloody Toorak guardians shouldn't be allowed to totally brainwash her. And it was a love child, and she lost it. Now she'll grow up. Shit, poor girl. Wouldn't get near her now, though I bet she's still in love with me. Okay, better write, keep the relationship 'open'. Let her know I care. Don't I? What if she gets older? When *she's* 28 she won't want the likes of me around. She'll marry a banker. What rhymes with banker? Okay, stay for Sally. She's different, tougher. No you *don't*. Fool, get out of here now!' Vrooomm...

Though we'll say Sal should've been patient with His Lordship, we forget she's the volcanic extremist, and at sixteen this dominates. Extremists want it all. And why not, the argument goes. With nothing to compare with, perfection's the only option. And if not available? Then let me die from a thousand cuts: '...He's sooo different from the Arab. God, that was such crap. How could I be such a child? Won't text him. Feeling tragic. Think I lost his number anyway. Got school work to do (!) Tiffany needs me. Ugh, she looks too fucked up for words. I need my sister Won. What would she do? Kick his nuts! Don't say it, he's a god. And I'm a silly little schoolie loser...' *Etceterahhh.*

Ghosts of the Past

Mother, despite not being an educated woman and being of nervous disposition, sees a thing or two. She hovers about in the back of Sal's life hoping Sal won't make the drastic mistakes she did, and knowing Sal will make them all and more. Alicia Mary Connaught is a fine Irish name, except there's a touch of Spanish in the Alicia. She had an unnamed boyfriend once, when she was 28. Before Ron. He was lively too! Though not reliable. Followed her to Melbourne, all the way from Ireland. Then Ron came along and saw him off with his butcher's knife (not really). So he disappeared... and she was *pregnant*. But she was sure he'd not gone far.

She had the feeling his eyes were still upon her and little Sal when the two of them used to perambulate down to Ronnie's butcher shop…

But we don't look back, we look forward. Mum says to Sally one day with unusual courage: *Darling, if you have a boy then treat him right.* And don't *mope.* And unbelievably Dad chips in with: Yeah girl, can't avoid them blokes for ever. Your mother's sorta roight, but finish yer schooling first. This painful sad advice has Sal tearing up in an alley one day. She never took her parents for anything much, but still (as their only girl) she cares about them in a hard resigned sort of way.

Connections

Re-enter Tall Uncle Bill. Recall her old Yankee mate who seems to know just about every-bodeh and's doin' whatever drugs 're goin' down? Well, he runs into Sal on Smith Street one slow Saturday. Aha! Rangy Bill sees with his eagle eye she's not herself.

- Hey doll, lemme feed you up. Where's a joint?
This time he means a feeding hole. And yes, it's Bilbo's. Serendipity. In they go.
- What's yer poison? Hung over? Bin snortin'? Bin on the 'P' maybe? (Hell, what does he *know*?) Ah see you may be hitten with the LURV drurg! Am ah right?
They scan each other. It's one of them moments when she knows the 20-somethings have been round the block more times than she has.
- Okay Tub. Wadda you know?
- I'm a tall tall mayn. Ah see for mahls
- Knock it off
- Today ah channel Roy Urbison. 'On-ly Yooo…'
Irony clunks.
- Shit, is it that obvious?
- Sho' thing Lil' Doll. The whole world's just starin' at *you.* Lemme buy ya some crappy food. We got lemon sausages and cherry pah.
Sal in black knee-boots blacklace coat black finger gloves black lank hair black eye shadow… looks unprepossessing in a black sort of way.

- Man, you look *black*. Why 'ncha give dat Boy a call? Black lives matter
- What boy?
- That *Jeen-Paul* boy!
She looks up in wonder.
- What the *fuck*?
- That's what *you* need
- How did you… (She shakes her head) - Oh man…
She is exhausted. Silence.
- Go on. Do it
(Now she pouts) - Don't have his number
- Maybe I can help ya there.
He flicks out his phone, scrolls. She stares at him! - 0412 666 666. Easy. Devil's number!
- Oh God.
Big pause. He drops the routine.
- You're some girl, Sal. Don't mind if I say it. My skinny flatmate Eyeball thinks so too (ahem). Now let's feed you up. Then we call the number. I'll set it up. Then you go home and get outa that funeral gear. Then you get your arse round there. Unless he's shot through to Mars or something. Worse things have happened, mind. (She looks at him) In which case you can come home with me and share my cosy bed. Deal?

She smiles for the first time in a hundred years. - Sho' thing, Unca Billy.

The Good Wife

Turns out Jean Paul had dematerialised to lands mystical and rural, and it took another week to track him. Bill helped her out (in more ways than one) but finally she 'had the talk' and told JP she was coming to his place in St Kilda. It's a Sunday. The dude, being a controlled yogi, was still arranging which hairs to leave on his designer stubble when Sal slipped through the back door. Twenty-somethings always need to impress the teens. If he was nervous (and he was, Sal said) he didn't show it. Sal had decided to take control. Somewhere within the week her old determination had seeped back (aided by Bill), and with it her vision of boys as a lesser race. This, fuelled by Tiffany's daily texts and calls in which the stricken girl says nothing coherent at all.

So Sal arrives and kisses him on the mouth abruptly first. Admires his ear stud then roots out his tea collection and makes a pot. But there's no *organic* honey so she simply must slip to the neighbours to ask. Finds a noisy crowd of arty types called the Verbals, stays too long. When she returns he's sitting there wondering. You met my neighbours then? Sure *did*. Then she proceeds to talk expertly about them all and how *interesting* they are. He nods and agrees. She serves him tea oriental-style, precise and neat (where'd you learn that?) then announces she's Hungry. He wants to do it but she says NO, ransacks his cupboards, takes over his kitchen. It's all macrobiotic! she says. No worries, I've seen *worse*. While she concocts her messy lentil veg curry she prattles at speed 'bout all and sundry, including Cool Jazz Gigs she went to with her *best mate* Tall Uncle Bill. Before that she had *another boy* called ummm… Johnson! But he was a Spotty Macedonian Muslim Intellectual with a fat sister called Toast. Ha ha funny eh? Not at all like *you*. He is required to thank her for the victuals which are not too shabby served in his beautiful blue bowls with sticks. Which she handles not well at all. Frig it, she laughs, and gets a spoon for him as well, though not necessary. And by now he's sagely learned to keep schtum and eat his rice and nod and drink his tea, the Buddha with his faithful woman running rings around his house. Shall we go to church? she offers. No I'm serious! There's a nice Catholic one down the street. They're serving god at 4 pm. I like those hymns and things, don't you? Sure do, he says, convinced she's gone quite mad. She chooses his shoes from a rack by the door, straightens his hair and off they go, his arm in her fawning vice grip. She even manages to whistle. The service is odd and goes too long, but surprisingly they enjoy it. The married couple steps outside to take the air. She leads him to the promenade. It's still and cool, the sun is sweet and low. Their shadows reach beyond the world.

And for a moment Sal actually wonders if it could really be like this. Winter romance, rugs and home, he and me… slow-burning love, quiet suburb by the sea. The end of life, the frozen future visioned at its start. Romance of life's Evening, executed exquisitely by the young.

She lets him buy her coffee and cake at a place of her choosing. She likes (she says) to observe the people, passers-by. She talks of higher things, of Michelangelo, and a book by Kerouac which makes her dream of the Road. To get away, be the person you need to be. Don't you think? He agrees. His eyes are misting over now. She secretly sees. She leads him home. She dabbles with his oriental music. Then abruptly says she's off, her *friends* await. She leaves him at the door, and he ironically applauds. She grins in triumph and swings off down his path, sweet backside prominent. She makes sure to say 'bye to those nice Verbals going by. One last glimpse at her from him (she doesn't return it) and Sal is Gone.

* * * *

Back in Tall Uncle Bill's messy bed, and aided by one of his dick-sized mega-joints which nowadays they have no problem knocking off between them, Sal reflects it's been a trying day. Bill's R n' B collection helps put her in her 'funky' mood, but Bill knows only too well her mind's elsewhere. And it's not the weed that's doing it either. Frankly surprised when she lately started turning up at Animal Road again, Bill played along - and got the bonus of massaging a sweet 16 year-old rump at least once or twice. But he's not an idiot, and he questions her about her frigging Yogi quite a bit. She jumps on his cues as well.

- Thing wiv *him* right (lemme suck on that) - is he's not any kind of *boyfriend.* True, I feel like waiting on him like a *geisha* most of the time - he's totally like fucken *controlled* - and he puts up with me! even tho I'm like *ransacking* his house and I'm like paying attention to his frigging *neighbours* more than him - and I'm like talking *all the time* and he like *nods and smiles* and shit (frig that's strong) as if he's frigging *God* - which he *prob'ly is* - and I drag him off to a fucken *church* like we're *married* and he doesn't even bat an eyelid. What? I din't Bogart the joint! Ughh, I'm rooted. Wadda you think, Billy Willy? You gotta nice big dong and everythink, but maybe I'm just like freakin' in love with this GUY! Or is it all *over?* Please tell me it's over. Pleeeease?

- It's not over. Hasn't even started. Shit, you better go home. It's 10 o'clock. Your old lady 'll freak

- She's cool. She was a milk maid of Oirlannd. But my great-grandaddy eez Spaneesh. No bullsheet! Ole!

- Okay cutey, listen to me… Listen! I'm gonna tell him to take you out for the weekend to his country place. Yeah I'm a dickhead, I know it. But you're gonna do this properly.

Flesh and Spirit

Next weekend's the long weekend. The Parents have been assured it's a 'crucial study trip' for the Oriental Religions course. Er, it's called Agni Sanctuary. Only 3 hours drive. Here's the phone number. Yeah mum and dad, all cool. Back on Monday night *late*.

Outa there! Sal is met at a crossroads by Jean Paul in his banger. He looks quizzical when she waves at him, so she leans in grabs his head and gives him a wet smooch. This wins a raised eyebrow. Then it's onto the road west. Will this crock make it? Sal asks. He says no problem and who cares if it doesn't? *That's* the spirit, says Sal. Anything can happen! She notes he's wearing jeans, unusual for him, and a trendy Asian shirt. Too nice, she says. He seems okay. Their vibe is definitely err… better.

So what am I in for? asks Sal. - Hmm. 10 hours a day meditation in a hair shirt, lecture by the Boss, loo-scrubbing and sprout-planting with seaweed and mung beans for dinner then straight to bed women in one dorm men in the other no sex no drugs no rock 'n' roll, says JP with a droll look. Cool, says Sal. D'you bring my whoopee cushion? - Brought you two, he says. - Can't sit still for 10 seconds, she says, but he knows she's joshing. Sal wonders out loud if she's dressed for it but he assures her those ripped-arse jeans are holy enough. Next question: can I sneak out for durry breaks? Probably not. He seems solicitous, she plays the girl. Don't worry darlink. I won't let you down. But how in god's name do I meditate? - Talk to Orwell, he's the man. He sounds weird! she says. Do we sing *Kumbaya?* I can do OM for 48 seconds! Timed it! Wanna listen?

Knock yourself out, he says with narrowed eye. OOOOOOmmmm...
Hey, it's in tune with the car! Check my sexy lotus pose! All tits and arse!

This girly mood continues for the duration, including the comfort stops
wherein she piles the car up with coke and burgers, fries and starbucks,
lollies cookies and shakes. I brought my own money, she beams. Today
he's Dad. She nestles in his lap. He drives along, she wonders what she
might be leaning on. He seems a study of calm. Maybe he's meditatin'. C'n
I drive? she asks as they head down a country road. Aw why not? Your
bomb's as dented as it's gonna get... Yay! I'll take some risks! she says, and
ploughs it in the dirt. He grabs at the wheel, she screams and tumbles in
his lap. He's still unphased! They stop. She runs into the land. The trees are
stark and grand with bark and flowers underfoot. And where's the big bad
wolf? She waits in a dell, he comes at last. She takes his neck and holds her
cheek to his on tippy toe. Her eyes are all aglow. Does he appreciate it all?
Perhaps he's tickled. Who can say?

At 2 o'clock she gets a text from Tiff but doesn't answer it. Tiff wants to see
her. Too bad. They pull in to the Sanctuary. She notes a cool blue Beamer,
parked in front. Yum.

- *Orwell's,* he says.

A session's in progress in the Hall. They slip in the back. JP points and she
sits. Me squaw heap make lotus on mat. Some guy in a toupe is droning
in Tibetan. Gut shows under his shirt. Some baldy japs in yellow sacks
bang on drums and tinkly bells. Smells like a farmyard. Must be incense.
Smoke gets up her nose, she coughs a bit. JP gives her the eye. Law against
coughing? Don't have a fit. He frowns, she settles down. Sounds not bad...
Guess I could handle this kind of fad... Okay, they chanted OM... that's
cool... how long does this go ON? Kinda hungry. Love a drink. Izzat the
ladies room? Is this a bore or what? What's with that guy? Looks kinda
high. Is he on pot? Shuddup city girl, empty your mind! Empty empty
ooooommm. Yay, they finished.

Truth is, the car journey's booming in her ears, and you can see she's having a city-girl culture shock. Hasn't tuned into the retreat's intense cosmic vibe. This will take some hours. In the meantime, her junk-food lunch is starting to repeat. The flesh is willing but the sphincter is weak. She slips away. J. peers at her out of his yoga trance. It's calmer outside. She feels sun on her skin as she heads for a hut marked ladies. Inside a large Russian-looking lady in a sari is having a fag on a bench. She jumps, but Sal says Relax I'm not the KGB. Lady seems grateful. Sal dips into a cubicle. The paper's 13th century and she uses 200 sheets. Very environmental. She's glad there's incense around. Time to get pure, thinks Sal.

Later there's refreshment (*not* hungry, says Sal) and JP points people out in a semi-whisper. They're all on silence today, we will be soon as well. He winks. That'll test you, huh? She shrugs. He frowns again. - Just go with the flow, it's easier. No worries sweetie, she reassures him. JP nods and smiles to several folks, some of them elegant girls in brilliant sari cloths. They're all irksomely serene. Sal hasn't yet succumbed to the self-satisfied smug nirvana of spiritualists en masse. Her ripped jeans feel fairly Rad right now but JP tells her, we'll change you later. She's introduced to a fattish guy in white who scans her penetratingly, touches her hands, says nothing but 'welcome'. The Russki reappears, looking stressed and breathing through her nostrils. People smile indulgently at her. The sharing caring pantomime goes on a while, then tinkling bells announce the session to come.

This time it's the head honcho Orwell, who turns out to be the fat guy in white (he owns the Beamer, right) giving a talk. Sal sits right near the door, and this time J is at the front. He sits up, straight and impenetrable. Our leader exudes an easy wit, compliments the Russian on 'kicking the habit'. Everyone laughs. A silence falls and he begins.

- What is Simplicity? Explain it. Can you do it? Can you touch it, see it, smell it, taste it? Show it to me, show me how it 'works'. And what is 'Truth' where one man's meat is another man's poison and everything is Judgement? What is Acceptance? Can you describe it to me? (*And what is boredom? Can you describe it to me? Shut UP Sal*) You see, they are indescribable, and why? Because we insist on seeing the world as an outward thing. Our senses shoot outward, we interpret this being, this truth, as object. We objectify, we judge, we grab. We live in the difference between *me* and *other*. This is repeated countless times and becomes the habit of mind, of sense, of behaviour. We are automatic beings, caught in the endless cycle of habit, where people are materialised objects. And do we respect? No, they are to be exploited. The truth 'you are me and I am you and we are all together' (thank you John Lennon!) surely is *one* being, one action, one love. But where is respect? We are crazy to judge the other with our clever sense brains. But there's no description outside our ego, outside our need to objectify, create borders, pass judgement…

This surprisingly starts to go in, kind of. But it's a mouthful and (she tells me later) her mind begins to fuse and can take in no more. She closes her eyes and drifts. The sensation is pleasant. The words 'pass judgement'… pass fudgement… pass bludgement… I get it, we do that. Yeah, we judge. Whole world does it. But I don't. Or maybe I do. Wow, what if we never did it? It'd be cool. We'd be free. Do watcha wanna do… just be happeee… I respect you… don't judge me…

Sal claims at this point that she went into some kind of mystic trance. Anyway suddenly she's aware again, the talk is over, people are standing up! Far out, what happened? She spies Jean Paul seated at the front. Seems absorbed. She feels tender, goes and sits by him. He turns to her, nods curtly (no smile) and rises. Oops. She follows him out, two paces behind. Outside she wants to talk but he seems to discourage it. Instead he leads her to the women's dorm, introduces her to an elegant girl dressed in yellow sari with chic blondish hair (she's the only one there) and says: This is my friend Sally. Can you find a suitable dress? The no-name girl says *not a problem Jean* in an English accent. She smiles sweetly at him, and he at her.

Suitably garbed, debutante Sal appears at dinner. JP comes across, scans her and nods. He's not talking at all, so she wanders about the absorbed silent throng. Most are white, comfy middle-classish, thirties and forties. At the buffet a darkish boy, good looking (koori?) catches her eye. What's he doing here? She smiles, pops a lentil thingy on his plate. He pokes his tongue comically. She snorts, stifles a giggle. He frowns and pokes it with a languid finger. She holds her nose. They both burst out and hide their heads. His plate slides. Some weedy slop hits the floor with a plop. Sal can't take this, kneels on the floor in her sari and shakes. He kneels too, looks quizzically up at her, shakes his head like an Indian. After a recovery moment they scoop up the macro mess together. There's a stain on her perfect silky silk. Oops. This little communion goes unnoticed. *I am you. You are me. No judgement. See?*

She doesn't see JP again that day, and surrounded by girls and women including the wheezing Russian, she passes the night. An outside walkabout reveals a moonlit silence. No aboriginal. The ghost gums fret against a blue-black sky. It's chilly. Back in bed she feels for her phone, falls asleep to the thud of Bolt In The Brain.

Next morning Jean Paul is there, waiting when she emerges after a thin shower. She takes his hand and holds on. He frowns, seems slightly agitato. Been up long? she says. Three hours. The boss would like to see you. Orwell, yeah, the guy in white. He usually does. Besides, I brought you so he needs to meet you. I am responsible.

They stand in frosty sun. Sal's feeling undressed. I like the dress, he says.

Truth is, Sal looks fetching in slim blue silk, hair pinned sweetly back. It makes her feel quite feminine, like a Sixties Chile. She can probably get into this spiritual lark. Just schmooze about looking vacant and you'll be jake. No-one bothers you it seems. Mind you, no-one talks. This is a setback. But the winter sun's light on her skin and she's aware of dreamy treetops and the sky. It's kinda nice.
- I'll get some cornflakes, she says.
- If there are any, he replies. But be quick. He's waiting, basically.

A hasty snack, no time for the bathroom. She's led by him to a cabin set apart up a slope behind some trees. The Man is there on a sofa in a sunlit room. An oriental rug is on the floor. *Come in please. Do sit.* J. parks her on the rug facing the Man, then sits in lotus to one side. A silence. Sal has no bearings. Orwell gazes at her a whole minute. She half looks at him, then round about. Now he talks.

- Thank you for your patience, Sally. I am Orwell, the retreat leader. I am glad you have come. Jean Paul tells me this is your first time. (He smiles) He takes you seriously, our Jean Paul! You are fifteen? Sixteen?
Sal's stomach gurgles.
- Sixteen
- This is a very good age. Development is very rapid now. We must assume you are intelligent since Jean Paul brings you. But not experienced, yes? Not at all your fault! But we will help. You heard my talk, I think?
- Er, some of it
- And did you like?
- Yeah, good. Don't judge... we're not objects... avoid nasty body habits. S' what I got from it.
Jean Paul sits rigid. Orwell's eyes narrow.
- Do you think I am judging you now?
- Don't know. Don't know you.
Orwell smiles. He likes a challenge.
- Enlightenment is a huge journey. Most will not seek it. But you will seek it. I congratulate you. Jean Paul has chosen well. But you are ignorant now. I do not mean that in a poor way. It is the human condition. Please do not take this personally, but at this time you are a fool. We have all been that. Allow me to help you. Would you please come closer.

Sal looks at Jean Paul. He nods imperceptibly. She crawls forward. Her sari's tight round the knees and she stumbles into his lap. His hairy thick wrists steady her shoulders. He is perfumed.

- Come close, that's it. Don't be afraid. I intend to open you now. Relax.

Sal is tense perched on her knees. He takes her head in both his hands. She cannot hear so well. He chants some stuff for several minutes. Her knees ache. Then he brings her forehead onto his, and she feels his breathing on her nose. Minutes more of this. Finally he presses his lips to her forehead, says OM, lets her go and leans back. She is suspended in mid-air. She looks at JP. He nods. Orwell seems quite extended by this routine. He sweats slightly, and his chin is lowered to his chest. JP now stands and pulls her gently up.

- Let's go.

They move to the door. Orwell says after them:

- This is very good. Thank you, Sally. Please come back tonight after dinner. Yes? Come alone. I will help you once more.

This is all. And after a pause they step out into the sun.

- You're lucky. He put a lot of energy into you. You should be glad.

JP seems lighter. He squeezes her hand. Sally is bemused, but the morning dew on her feet soon distracts her. She feels uncomfortable. Need the ladies, she says. A few minutes later in the cubicle, Sal reflects. How was that? Actually I felt like some kind of insect in a jar. He must be some kind of a dude though. JP seems to love him. And he did seem relieved. Okay, better play along for JP's sake.

Fact is, this incident shakes her up just a little, and she is not sure how. The vibe in the meditation hall has changed for her. She has the feeling most of the girls around her (they sit in segregated blocs at 45 degrees) have had the treatment from Orwell. They sit with slight forward lean and rapt-intense expression as he talks. She feels embarrassed to be among them. Sal does not focus on the talk at all; it seems to take place somewhere overhead. Instead she gazes at faces in the room. Opposite are the men, with Jean Paul again in front. His form seems somehow fragile here. She feels a tender ache, mixed with consternation. He really is too intense. On the outer sits the dark boy. He looks her way a couple of times with brown liquid eyes. She wants to *touch* him. What is he doing here?

At lunch the English beauty whispers to her Jean for half an hour. Sal doesn't know her name since the girl dressed her yesterday in silence. She took care to say *not a problem Jean* though, I recall. Later JP hurries over.

- Don't forget the meeting with Orwell tonight. Straight after dinner, in case I don't see you.

The afternoon drones on with silent meditation and chanting and what not. Sal for a while gets lost in the chants… almost joins in when the rhythm seems to surge with a force outside the human throng. Later she steps out to fields and woods, a little distracted, her sari covered with a jumper against the late afternoon shadows. The trees sway against the sky. She felt (she said) somewhat 'outside myself, as if I could become the wind'…the feeling that life has its *own* life, utterly separate from she, the little ant. Impersonal. Not scary, strangely comforting. As if she had no more need to tread the human journey, the soap opera of her future.

Later her mobile bleeps again. Tiff. This time the message is long and garbled, accusing her for not calling, railing openly against Jean Paul. Sal now feels a far-off pang of fear, as if there's something splitting her down the middle. A need to run, a need to face? At dinner Sal eats little. The koori boy stands off on his own. He looks mournful. Maybe the chanting got to him… And where is Jean Paul? Nowhere.

Spiritual Rape (*trigger alert)

She steps through the trees, lifting her silk to her knees. Her hair is clipped back sweetly. The door is ajar. Why go in? Because I'm Sally Bang, she says. I'm not afraid of anything. And Jean Paul said I should.

Orwell is there, on the sofa. He beckons. - I'm glad you came. Come close. The perfume's different this time. His eyes are shaded with a lamp. He holds her hands in his, then touches her cheek. Shall we pray? She says okay. She is seated by his bulky form, their knees touching. He murmurs something Indian. He knows how to make a spell, says Sally to herself. Next he pulls her close, whispers a mantra in her ear. Repeats it over. She is dizzy. He is breathing long and slow. If this is it, I'll get out alive, she thinks. No such luck. Next moment he has her on her knees on the mat. And now he presses her backward to the floor. Expects her to lie down. Why does she do so? Is she hypnotised? He lies on her. He is heavy. The hands grip tight. Her arms are pinned at her sides by his. Her legs are together though. She's lying there. She does nothing. He is intoning the moaning mantra with great intensity in her ear. His face is sweating. She stares at a branch, mooned in the window.

At length he stops. He rolls away. She's intact it seems. He breathes beside her. Thank you. I hope I was not heavy. No need to reply. We practise *Tantra*. Have you heard of it? She has now. May I help you? He sits her up. She is disoriented, limp. A silence. He turns to her, breathing through nostrils: This is good for you. You are very good, a controlled girl. Jean Paul has chosen well. Please go now. Om. He is controlling his breath by an effort, it seems. Sal gets up and totters to the door. Before she reaches it, he says: *One thing. Come back.*

And why she does so is beyond the reason. Is it because she really wants to give in to something bigger than herself? Who knows - who fucking cares? I'm angry about this, but she isn't. Not enough. He now drags her down and slides her sari up. The panties come down, he slides on top like a whale, and this time there's no Tantra mate. Just a big pain in her vagina.

* * * *

Later. After he's nursed her and patted her and cleaned her with a cool cloth and even arranged her hairclips and hummed to her (and told her even *his* old habits die hard), she stumbles down the hill, the wind fingering her burning cheeks. Her feet are shod, she has her pants, her sari's clean. What else? Her faithful partner's slumbering! What else? Don't tell a living soul. *Or else.* Sal crawls into Jean Paul's car and goes to sleep. Later she wakes up cold. Finds her dorm bed, pulls the covers over and faces the blackness.

She rises not for breakfast Monday. The cool Anglais regards her with a smile. Are you enjoying your stay?

Go away, she says. Her face looks set. Soon Jean Paul comes looking for her, alerted no doubt by his English consort.

She tells him: wait a sec. Dresses in front of him, into her holy jeans and jumper, then takes her sari and stuffs it under the bed. Then she takes his hand. He resists but she leads him to his car. She pushes him in. Drive, she says. There are no keys. She tells him wait. Walks right into the men's dorm, asks where Jean Paul sleeps, grabs his bag. Several pairs of eyes regard her, not with bliss mind you. Outside, the keys rattle as she thrusts them in his hand. He looks numb. What happened? he says. Fucking drive. They drive. His jaw sets firmer with each passing mile. They're on a rising plateau, woodland all around. Stop! she says. They walk. Her hand grips his. A firmness lacking last night.

He knows there's something big. An understatement! Or no, perhaps a sixteen-tantrum? Too much silence too much seaweed too much English beauty sari competition, too much Guru power! Happened to me once, lost my head when the guru zapped me… This is a *test*. Play it, play it, discipline discipline.

At last, a ridge. Some hanging trees. A lunging view of the vast inward deep of Australia. Sally sits down heavy, propped by a tree. She runs her hands back and forth over the dirt. She looks not up. Then up she looks, head back, into the far plain. He has no idea where to put himself. At last she says:

- Your guru did me in last night
His eyes go hollow.
- What?
- The fat bastard raped me
- No.
She's up on her feet and she charges at him. He falls backward in the dust. A rock grinds at his back. She crushes him. He is winded. She pins him. Her teeth are grinding against his face. Her tears splash across his eyes.
- And you didn't save me. You didn't save me. You threw me in it!
A weeping groan. I hate you. I fucking HATE YOU! This time she grabs his hair with both hands. He holds her wrists but can't stop the tearing. His scalp is burning. Finally she loosens. Her hands drop to her sides. Lies on him, limp as a seal, wet hot cheek sidewise on his face.

He puts his arms over her back and clings. Her breathing slows. Minutes pass. He senses a wind on his forehead. The gums wrestle above him in the sky, make their lonely whisper to his ear. He raises his head. She is spreadeagled in the dirt, toes pointed inward, jeans torn out at her rear. On Him, all over him like a corpse. As if asleep. It is miles down there to her boots.

This is a baby you'll never hold again. Let it last.

Jean Paul feels sorry for himself. Then sorry for her. Precious beautiful. Tough? Fuck me, is she tough! No, unreachable, just like a woman. (Shut up Dylan) Not young. Bold. Older than I can ever be. Poor stupid me. I'm the loser. Sat there in that hall ignoring her. Shame on me. Sweet sweet girl. That Orwell! *Fucking loser!* Ooh I said it. Ugh it hurts. Poor stupid guy! I'll never go back there. Not now. I'll do it on my own. On my own from now on…

She sighs and he rolls her sideways with difficulty. She is like asleep. He cradles her head on his arm. Their forms run together in the leaves. The ghost gums rail the sky. Sunlight makes their bed. His back is killing him.

He just made love to someone for the first time in his life.
Her.

* * * *

Sal opens her eyes. Wind brushes her face. She looks up. No-one. Lowers her head. The leaves nestle her. A little bull ant jerks forward, stops, jerks to the side. Which way? Her body is the great ridge of Australia that he must traverse, her leg is the far mountains, her lap the river valley. Her fingers are the watering hole; her nail, smooth rocks. He basks on them… An instant in everness. His only holiday… Then on and on through caverns in her jumper. Lost.

Later, he is back with snacks from the car. They're two days old but rough enough. Water too. He feeds her. Nothing is said. They walk the rough track down the valley in single file. In the car nothing is said. They pass the Sanctuary on the road. He doesn't stop. By the gate, the koori boy is there. Fails to see them as they pass. It's middle afternoon. As winter evening falls they're back in the city. He takes her to a café. She eats some chips. He eats a couple. Drops her off. She says thank you. See you soon. She steps in, shuts the door to her room. Straight to bed.

Let It Fall Away - A Prayer

Your middle-aged ghost writer needs to meditate on all this. On the things we belong to, cling to... Jean Paul, ever since he got conscious of himself as an individual around fifteen, has felt the need to compete for the damnable male idea of 'spiritualism'. No doubt it comes from deep, from past incarnations, whatever. Purity tops all else, despite the usual loathsome experiments in the fields of sense - always a problem for purity types in spiritual clubs. Tiffany tripped him up, and Sally cornered him.

And Orwell was his antecedent: old Orwell peddling his *Tantra*, nothing but sublimation of his sweaty fear that uncontrolled desire and sex might undercut his brittle middle-aged selfhood. Have to pity that schmuck: let it be a weapon of our freedom from him. 'Purity' abhors the body's karma, while shame begets shame unto the generations. Jean Paul's attaching himself to this perfumed fellow was the result of his need to run from his own beauty. Attraction to sex and feeling, potent because forbidden, created the mess of him mixing with virginal goddess girls. And girls haunt he and Orwell, since that youthful time where they first got aware of their sticky dilemma.

JP is too green to know that it's not necessary to *like* a person who can teach you something. In fact the ones who teach us most are the ones we detest. They're our shadows. If we've the guts to admit this, we can use the Tantra of pain and pleasure to wrestle out our limits and fears. Naturally, gurus like Orwell are mere students who take the guise of master in order to face or avoid facing (always a double-edged sword) the inadequacy they fear. Purity-austerity is their only answer to the fucked up confusion of dealing with *emotion*: caring, needing, vulnerability, weakness, sex, and all the other things that make life on this planet so solid. Even Jesus had a girlfriend. Krishna fell in love with a village girl. In fact he was a bit of a goer, with his flirty flute and his milkmaids in tow.

And now Sally. Why'd she return to relieve the low karma of that sweaty guru all over her bluesilk sari when all the other episodes of our story say she would not and could not? It has to be childy loyalty to her sister Won, who is fanatically loyal to self-effacing female degradation, all for the sake of purity mind you. We know the quick way to self-effacing degradation for women in this world! Perhaps her old man taught her to do it.

Yet submission is complicated. Jean Paul submits to Orwell, thinks he cares for him, knows he doesn't. In fact he fears that the secret contempt with which he holds this clever and manipulative man is contempt for his own 'purity narrative'. Who can cope with self-contempt? JP must thereby conclude he is superior to the world's spiritualisms, a scary thought for a young arrogant who dabbled with 'saintism'. Who ever needs anything but oneself? Are we not borderless infinitude? But we don't trust it or don't want to admit it. We just can't include the astonishing crap of this world in the unending painful pleasurable delight of living and being alive. Young Jean Pauls want to live. They surely do.

And what of Won, the mystic who loves to rub her face in dirt? Who can tell her it's not needed? Not her father, not a thousand years of Oriental tradition. Not the Siddhartha Buddha who saw through all that austerity shit. I predict Sally will never again submit to any face-in-the-mud sex routine. Sal is a child growing up, needing to belong: to Won, to JP, to Bilk, to Orwell, to Daddy whatever. Yet fearing she'll never, she copies Won because Won seems to belong to nowhere. Maybe Sal felt at ease with her because Won lets her be lazy, because she took on Sal's need to be 'a crusader who faced it all'. But one day it will be Sally who gets to the real, and The Korean had better listen up. Sal's only obstacle is the slow tear of time... but let's hope she chews it up and spits it out. Let her be a heroine of youth, working class warrior of failure, loser who wins (or better, winner who knows how to lose), lover of life who needs no other soul.

Meanwhile, what of gilded goddess Tiffany Haigh: she who plays out another mode of JP's need to rise above the lowly? Was she really touched by his attack on moneyed comfort and the mummy-daddy highbrow establishment? Not for her sake did Jean Paul shake her. Disgust drove him, not respect. Tiffany seemed an open window precisely because her die was cast: she lived in a protected garden! Now she's suspicious of her nobleness, now she suspects it's all empty, and she's not ready for anything else. Her madness at the loss of her pregnancy is but a step on the road to a neurosis she hasn't the faintest hope of dealing with now…

And here cometh the homily: Life will be the teacher. All our belongings, desperate as they are, must fall away. Degradation. Dead tradition. Snobbery. Fake loyalty. Austerity. Purity. Submission. Let them fall. At 16, let them fall. At 28 let them fall. In middle age let them fall. For nostalgic ghost writers, let them fall. For sermonising gurus let them fall. For fictional heroines let them fall. Forever let them fall away. Amen.

Last Supper

Back to the cliff face. Tiffany Haigh has resolved to resurrect her 17th party, now to be held Saturday next at Swaggers in the city. Their mutual handsome prince now gone, Tiffany requires Sal to fill her void. Never mind Sally's void. The ashy blonde in her Enchanted Garden never knew what hit her re. Jean Paul. How can she now live? She could turn to people like Sal and in her lofty loss stay soft and longing (the Martyr). Or she could harden up against the world, a manipulative rival apportioning blame (The Witch). Or she could leave this life for good, metaphysically of course (The Seeker). Where are the Elder Guardians of our Precious when she needs them most? One thing Tiff's practised at is masking her feelings from her lessers, except she now makes a point of letting Sal have the lot. But Sal can't mention the wound hacked out of *her* in the name of love and spirit. And what does Tiff know about the state of hers and JP's relationship? Or what does Sal know about the state of Tiffany's joust with JP? Only ghost writers know this. In the meantime Sal will be forced to rescue the Martyr, deal with the Witch. The battle for posturing and feelings rages in Tiffany. Sal is corralled to text-message the entire Upper Set, a chosen Twelve of whom will wait apostle-like on Tiffany. Everybody knows something evil went down (and might yet go down) and 16s want to make it badder still. So in the absence of fact, rumour 'll serve. There's a serious rush to get to this shindig now, and lowly Sal gets pestered by Toorak's elite begging her to reserve a place! She complains to T. (who knows all about it) but Tiff is resolute. The chosen few shall come. Our melodramic set piece is heralded two days prior when Sal gets a call, late. Tiff coldly announces she went to Jean Paul at his house. There was an altercation and he refused point blank to explain why he 'left her' and she considers this the pinnacle of heartlessness and he's an utter chauvinist, darling. Sal is not surprised at the baldness of the story and that Tiff gets the detail fuzzy. Obviously she only hung about the end of the street like a stalker. Sad. But Tiffany has her ways and means and hardly cares whether Sal sees her game or not, for Sal is to blame by osmosis for most everything.

Saturday comes. At six the Toorak bedroom is a mess of fallen clothes. Our Karenina our Bovary stands willowy before the mirror, her make up masking what was hitherto a dream in peach. The black-haired one, the Siren, waits on her, and (not to outshine our tragic heroine) fusses with the chosen party dress of snake green. It's sexy poisonous like the Narnian Witch (but Tiff has no plans to play the callous bitch). Her mother, also dressed delightfully for dinner in green, checks in for a check up. The wish (as ever) is written on her face: *a few years hence my daughter will be me.*

- Darling, daddy and I will be with the Gallaghers, just a few blocks away if you need anything.
- I won't mum, but it's sweet of you
- You look lovely. We're both in green
- If someone's there and then they're gone, what does life mean?
- Darling? I don't understand your meaning
- You wouldn't. You're a lawyer
- Are you all right? (She looks at Sal, or whatever the girl's name is)
- She's nervous. Turning seventeen. And the 'boyfriend'...
(Tiff picks up the cue)
- That's right. I'm an adult now. I make my own decisions
- *That's* nice, darling.
Mother steps away, harbouring a nasty feeling. True, my daughter has had

bruises of late. I hope she's not planning to do something silly. She asks Sally to help her carry something. They step out.

- Is my daughter all right?

(What to say?) - She's sad, Mrs Haigh. I'm trying to help. All her friends are

- Of course. What can I do?

- Just let her be. She'll be jake

- The green doesn't suit her. Did you choose it?

- You're wearing it

(Who *is* this child?) - My husband requests it, that's all

- Can't have your cake and eat it

Why doesn't she take care with this woman? Answer: had it with the pretentious *crap*.

- Hmm. I'll call her on the mobile later.

In the taxi hardly another word was said, but Tiffany slowly bled. Let's see how sensitive my parents are now that I'm dead!

At Swaggers on Little Collins everything is Chi-Chi Frou-Frou as required and the gang make their various entrances (merely players) in their besty glitter and swank. Everyone videos and it's soooo awesome darrrling. Tomorrow's stars and social pillars (their various perfect skins glisten in pearly light) gather for group shots at the entrance. Let's freeze the Future, and all the world's a stage. There's Mona and Antonio, already the arty couple, jazzy-iconoclazzy; on the other hand there's 'Boner' Hodgson, the first fifteen dude with the big blond back who'd carry Tiff to hell and back; there's Jasper Cork the gawky joker, crudely amusing in the adolescent vein; and Polly Winters, ever keen to be Tiff's Best Friend. Oh no, and Cute Adelaide, yunga than the rest (gotta give a mark to hot and cute tryhards). Assorted 2050 Liberal worthies bring up the rear. They always know it all, knowing not a thing. Who needs to know shit anyway? Not fools at all, but tomorrow's people.

Everything's perfecto in a noisy sort of vein, and the other patrons smile. Theirs is the shriekiest rowdiest table, the funkiest hoedown you'll ever see. Tiff and Sal arrive 10 minutes late to applause (why is that Goth Sally

B always round her?) but when Tiff sits down the general blah tones down
a bit (she perspires a certain angst behind her makeup nowadays) and
glasses are raised, led naturellement by Polly Winters. Mercifully a load of
silver platters are brought and people re-descend to gawking and howling,
and the Centre of Attention in her snake green entertains her mixed bag
of soul mates according to their gaudy personae. No particular thing
ever gets said in this din, so miming the part is pretty much it in a sped-
up youthy world where tragedies and comedies fly past by the minute,
where eager students of life learn a dozen social lessons in an hour, where
protagonists shame themselves never to do it again. Sal grunts the odd
ironic quip to maintain the social mask and sucks on the red.

But Tiff is more and more looking sideways as if she has something she
needs. She clutches her silver handbag (diamond clasp) a little closer.
Polly notices of course, and after Hodge has had his hug and slurp and
Jasper's told his dirty quip and Mona's bagged the latest Art and Cute's
compared her tits to hers - Polly taps a glass and introduces Tiff who
mounts the stage at last.

- Guys, thenk you. Hands off Hodgey, you'll get a grip later (ha ha). Jasp,
that tie is outrageous, you are insane. Sal, thanks for helping me out.
(Mmm) And Polly, you can have this handbag when I'm 70. (Oooooh!)
Mona, I'm jealous: latin lover at 17? Go wild! Antonio, here's my address.
(Haa haaaa) And everybody, you're all cool as, and thanks. And if my
mum and dad were here, which they're not thank you God! (Huuurrgh!)
- no, I love you mum and dad; seriously I'd say to them:

I'm seventeen now. It's been a bit of a journey. Am I an adult? Hell no! (Yo
baby, rip it off!) I've had a few things to work out... get through lately...
(Respectful hush) and Sal: you know how hard it can be sometimes
(Deeper hush) or maybe you don't. That's for you to say. 'Cos like... I
had my heart broken and... (Deep freeze) I don't know why! (Sally slides
lower in her seat) I didn't think I'd say this but... Jean Paul. Have you
heard of him? No? (Glacial stares) He showed me... something that I
could be... something *real*... What am I saying? This is a party, my party.
I... just want you all to know that I care for you... and some of you know

that I… (she whispers) lost something. *The Baby.* (Eyes dart about the restaurant, faces twist, grip something hard) I lost the Baby! And I didn't *realise*… who I really was… It's very *strange!* (Polly stands up, touches her arm) No no Pol, it's okay! So guys, I've got something… to share with you now. If you can just wait a minute…

She grips her diamond bag, moves away from the table. Polly holds on. Tiffany eludes her.
- No no I'm fine. Talk amongst yourselves. I'll be back in *one* minute.

She moves swiftly to the ladies room. Major pause. Things have been overheard since table twelve went quiet. The clientele seem antsy. Heads confer, eyes wander, waiters loom. At table twelve no-one's talking at all. No-one can stand the suspense. Revelations? Shit that's enough! Jasper Cork has a shot: There's an Englishman, Irishman and Lebanese who wanna get to… Shut the fuck up, Jasp! murmurs Hodge, who seems prre-tty disturbed. No warries, haf a drink, says Antonio. She is fine! He starts to pour. - Guys, it's a party. Chill! Polly says: It's been *hard* for her. Look, just go and check will you, says Mona.

At that instant Sally Bang shovels her chair backward and hurls herself in the direction of the ladies room. Knives tinkle on stone as Sal slams into a waiter at the far end before disappearing through the door. Mona and Polly go after her and Hodge shuffles to his feet looking baleful. Inside Tiffany is standing facing the mirror over the sink. Red splatters are all over it. The slim green girl's arms vibrate. The shiny porcelain is streaked in rivulets of red. Taps are gushing. A Stanley knife is on the floor. Sal sees none of it but grabs at Tiff and spins her round. Tiffany like a mummy lets her. Sal shouts at her face. Tiff bumps forward, arms rigid in a semicircle, hands grasping at something bulky. Sal slides on a wet tile. Tiffany is beyond the door, back in the peopled room. Mona and Polly are in her path. They scream. She shovels past them, aiming for table twelve. All heads swivel. But Hodge moves to her. She is gurgling in a half cry. His big arms hold onto her. She bends like a willow and falls but he holds. Awkwardly he lays her body down. Her hair is fanned out on the stony floor. Vibrating, she is clasping something. Her mouth is fixed. Everyone is standing. The Maitre D comes running. Chaos.

The Road to Damascus

Mrs Bang has been in the habit of attending her Catholic church for oh so many years. Ever since, in fact, she came from Ireland all that long time ago. Just once a month or so, alone. Her husband never comes. It's miles anyway. She's not the spiritual type, more the comfort type. She prays for her family, who seem to her like distant people, not really melded but 'functioning along'. As if some little thing were absent, something wrong? No, Life is never wrong, Father Lone had said. You have to lie in it, since it is your marriage bed. This is what Father said.

One day, some weeks after the time her daughter ran off to the country with that older boy, Sally comes to her and asks:
- Mum, what d'you *do* at that church of yours?
- Come and see for yourself. (Why did she say that? It seems so sudden)
Well maybe I might, her daughter said.

Now Alicia Bang's never a courageous soul, but she has her ways. And one of these is Father Lone, from long ago in County Athlone. She always came for his sake. And he always knew. How many years, how many tears? …Now Sally has come with her. Father Lone greets them in his polished way. Your daughter? How nice to finally meet. Your mother speaks of you, oh she does. Coming up seventeen? - a wondrous age. (How he knows her, barely having seen her!) Please please come in, our service is to begin. The priest takes his station. Mother squeezes daughter's hand. Sal feels the gesture is too grand, puts it down to over-feeling.

Meanwhile in the lofty hall a half-hearted preacher makes a call, and it stains his sermon and his prayers. A call not to god but to *himself*, to an inner reservoir of wealth, of love and spirit and health! The girl's a beauty no mistake! Up close it's personal. There's an ache that wasn't there, at least never like this. How many years have I skirted the truth, how many years have I denied my youth? A single moment changes a life, as if all moments were preparation: ushering, shuffling, waiting, glancing to the wings. Finally a strange wedding begins. The *bride* is there, the waiting over, the field is clover. God is here, and will marry us all. No angelic choir no hellish fire no sermon no water not even an oath. Just peace, simplicity, thee and me. Mother Father Child: a *family*.

* * * *

Weeks later, Sally Bang heads to the mother's church alone. She wants words with the Priest of Athlone. Ne'er to confess, for the world's a mess, and we don't trust elders, priests even less. The last was a fat man preaching love, and he fell on her like a Beast from above. She never screamed at all, at all, but now her soul is very small. An ant in the world. And I don't need a *friend*. Maybe I'll believe, but beware of my end! Why shouldn't I destroy the things I love? I refuse to believe I care. Why give, why live? Is there anything bigger? Couldn't be. There's nothing ever there, for me.

Dressed to upset, she scowls by the altar. No genuflect, to hell with that. Fancy meeting a guy in a frock. What'm I thinking? I'm SALLY BANG, don't fuck with my mind. Do we go in that box? Nobody does it? I say we do. Gloomy dark: love it. This all confidential? (Not a fool question) Yeah, *mummy's* okay, at work today. You in a hurry? C'n I smoke my durry? Dude, me too cool for school. God can see you're no fool. Don't worry grandpa! I'll get serious.

Enter the BOX.
- How many miles from nowhere is this church
- Home is always where we are
- This is your home?
- I like to think it is. Tell me what's on your mind
- How's this for starters: I dump my yogi boyfriend, my girlfriend slits her wrists, a fat guy rapes me, my oriental sister disappears, my mum is having an affair with a freaking priest.
She can hear breathing from far off. Anybody in there?
- Do you know who I am, Sally?
- Don't wanna

- I'm going to tell you
- No frigging way. I do the talking
- Then talk to me
- I love scandal, publicity. Evil child. Better that way
- You're far from evil
- Yeah? Check this: 'Kindly Priest. Married to god. Confession box. Mystery woman. Married to a butcher. Secret child! Gone to the *wild*. Truth gets out. Loses his job. Gets fucking old'
- Our affair is platonic
- Wassat?
- No sex
- No-sex affair! Like a bald man with hair? Or a girl with a prick? Man you're sick
- Believe me or not, I don't really care
- So you like fiction?
- There's no contradiction
- My mother told me
- I'm sure she didn't
- And how would you know?
- Oh I think I know that
- Smug, ain't ya mate?
- I hope I'm not
- Religious types are the smuggest. They got god. I got the devil
- How does it feel?
- Fuckin' unreal. Don't have to be pure. Eat manure. Life's a sewer
- I see you're clever. Maybe a poet. Don't judge me, okay?
- Why wouldn't I judge? I'm holding a grudge
- No, you just want to be. But I see that you're brave
- Just havin' a rave! Okay, I won't
- Won't what?
- Judge. Someone told me that. Fat Guy
- Who's fat guy?
- Rapist who wants to be Therapist. Cute. Remind you of someone?
- I don't need you to like me. I need us to talk

- Sure thing boss. I like a man in a cage. Not free to feel me up. Not without God's permission
- What are your dreams?
- Gonna explode
- Oh I get it, your name
- Gonna get the fame
- The friends you mentioned. Tell about them
- Thereby hangs a tale. All guts and glory. Not all about me though
- Glad to hear it
- Yeah well, Jean Paul's the Yogi. But to Tiffany he's the bogey! And my sister is Won. But my sister is gone
- A spiritual sister?
- I guess
- Sounds like your very own Soap. Tell the plot, if it's not too much trouble
- Prick up your ears then. Like it juicy?
- Juicy as you like.

From about the time Sally Bang started hanging at his church, the priest began to crystallise the idea that his future didn't lie there. Sally as Catalyst may be stretching it, but no doubt she reminded him with force that life beyond the church was a far more complex (juicier) affair than he lately, or ever, cared to admit. He didn't tell her this: religious men have their pride. They can also abuse what they care about: witness Jean Paul and Orwell. Fundamentalism suits men best since they're emotionally stunted. Details of the affair with Sal's mother will never be told either. Gutless priest. And priests shouldn't lie. Sal is right, it probably wasn't so platonic. Just like water isn't so wet. Just like Tantra, the root you have when you're not having one. Ah, there's the thing with religion, the life you have when you're not having one. Turn it to Abstraction and whip yourself with it. All this truth-telling's hard on a priest, but he'll handle it, he likes a bit of whip. Sal finds him amusing in his adulty serious sort of way. She discovers he keeps a diary. A closet writer? She wants to see it but he draws a line. Am I in it? she says. Is the pope catholic? he replies. She sees this humour as a sign of life. But he knows humour well, as a part of himself. She has lots to discover about me, he thinks. If she wants. She's not sure she wants, considering her mother and all. In fact the new liaison has made mother fret, for Sal and the priest are in selfish cahoots till both see that Alicia's dignity is on a knife edge since she has her family to think of. The priest has mislaid his 'balanced view', created embarrassment for all. Sal is too interesting, being young and new. She inhabits a speeded-up universe, he a slow round of seasons and balances. She the dabbler in fashiony fads, creator of postures, player of cameos, holder and dropper of attitudes, maker and breaker of friends, juggler of worlds, mystery guest at the dance. A bacchanal. He, the apollonian Listener (and the old wannabe whose slow fragile pact with time is coming undone). He hears about her polyglot people, role models, losses, diseases she got. He comprehends this Jean Paul boy, though is critical of him to her face. She needs that. He even sees where Orwell is, but holds his nose to moral disgrace. She needs that too. And he feels for the silvery Tiffany, whose odyssey of love ended at her doorstep. And he is strangely stirred by Won, whose Asian intensity tilts at the heart of whether to die or live. Sal takes him Manga comix. Amusing, all these heroines in deadly scrapes. He talks in low tones of Hamlet's dilemma. She points out he's gay (Hamlet, I mean). He gets her point. He warns her not to disappear. She says she probably will. Gotta be the tragic child, no matter what.

- What have I got? All this posturing in backstreets, hanging in holes. I want them to *notice*. I want it all. And I'm definitely gonna write about you and my mum.

He hides his panic, says that's therapeutic! She means to the papers. He doesn't get it.

Guiltily he knows he needs something she can't give. *She* doesn't know she wants something life can never give: something elusive, already lost. Life kills! So at last there's a point when this draughty ghost box in a vault of a church in a faceless suburb, is suddenly nothing to her. Irrelevant, lifeless, depressing. And at once he feels the same. Their meetings are over… not one of them face to face.

Willed Spontaneity

One late winter's morning on a school day, Sal gets herself up early, prepares her limbs with care, places special bits of underwear in her school bag and heads out into the drum of the city. A long coat covers her uniform, she has on her fingery gloves. Avoiding the usual route she takes the tram south of the river. Anonymous carriage, steamed-up windows, crush of bodies, their vacant half sleep: all convince her somewhat she is doing the right thing. No matter where it brings you, do something! Let things be *different.* She alights at a seaside suburb, walks a way up narrow streets, arrives at the house. Mist of morning clings about her. By the gate she notes a gleaming Audi, lightly coated in frost. Cars always get me, she says to herself. Up the path to the side door. The key in its place. That's a miracle or she'd have to knock. In the dim corridor floorboards creak. Enter the front room. On the table a briefcase, smartish. A laptop, a scarf. *Women's heels…*

Oh shit! Oh I get it. Shouldna come. Shouldn't have. I'm a *schoolgirl.* Her eyes turn misty, and she breathes right out. Sits on the corner of the settee, scrunches up her knees. Morning shadows shroud her… Now a door clicks at the back. The bathroom. Footsteps in the corridor. Enter a woman. Sal sees her first: blondey bob, business skirt, blouse. Slips into her heels, clicks her case and turns. *Oh my god who are you? Oh, it's you! What are you - ?* The English Girl from the Retreat! Waddaya know? No sari now. *You're here to see Jean Paul?* Sal is mute. Undignified pause. The girl steps away. *Jean!* His voice comes back. Her skin tingles. Soon, both adults are there.

Hi guys, I'm the child. The Anglais stares at him, but he won't meet her eyes.
- Jean, you said to me she… okay, all right.
Old cadres and lovers say nothing. A cold wait.
- Jean, what do you say to me?
- I'll call you. I'm sorry
- Are you? (Pause) All right. So be it. Then I'll say goodbye.

She packs her remains, opens the door. Keys rattle in her hand. The lovers seem sorry. Down the path, the low click of heels. Car door, the engine, she's gone. Quiet in the house. I never knew her name, says Sal. He stands about, not looking yet.

- I came to see you one more time. It's early I know. Will you let me be here?
- Don't know.

But in the morning silence, Sally Bang starts to be at home again. Why shouldn't I? This is me and this is he. I'll be his proper wife. *And this is my life.*

Sally stands, drops her coat. Come with me, she says. He lets her lead, up the hall to the bathroom. She turns on the shower, unpeels his gown, drops her clothes one by one to the tiles. She and he stand in the mist. Sal pulls him close. They're naked in the stream. Sal feels the power of her beauty, she enters the dream that she dreamed. This is going to plan! Out of the shower, no towel. She runs to a cupboard, makes pools in the hall, hurries to serve him, his geisha. She leads to the bedroom. Quiet trance for them both. Her skin glistens. The bed is dishevelled. She searches his drawer, takes a purply pink sheet, makes the bed they will lie in. Now she slips on the garments she brought. She's a beauty. He gazes. She pulls him down. They're body-entwined. He understands to go slow, the goddess is guiding. Beauty takes over, she is supreme. Yet this is *his* dream. He loses control, and it hurts her! - but no, she pulls him in, far in. He tells her *no!* She cries *Yes! You do as I say.* Enfolds him crazily, clings to her man. And she knows when it happens. Let me have it! she says. Your hot hot river, let me have it. For this is mine, all mine, she says, she says.

Eternity reigns. Then years and hours. Then minutes… She opens her eyes; he is there. And his eyes are just melted pools! At last he slips out, away from her. This action brings her back to herself. He lies beside. There's a coolness, a lightness, a beauty to me! And just for a time… maybe I am free.

Sealing Envelopes

A week has passed. Sally calls up Boner Hodgson. He's nearby so they meet on Chapel Street. Yep, Bone was with Tiffany Haigh just yesterday. She's all stitched up. There'll be scars, biggies. She'll be right though, Boner's gonna make sure. Gonna be her future. Says Hodgey: I'm not the judging type but what made her do it? What kinda guy was he? Sal claims she doesn't know too much. Tiff made an error with that Jean Paul for sure. Experimented a bit ya know, bit off too much. Desperate for an affair, wanted to claim herself. Thought she wanted a child, thought she could be adult, thought she could be free. Went bonkers really. She'll never love like that again.

Sal finds her stomach in knots as she says all this. Does anything ever go away? Hodgey gets some of it, but sagely knows the key to life is Keep It Simple. Hodge is the no-shit guy with the big blonde back, who'll save the deep stuff for his girl from Toorak.

- All beyond me, mate. But I'll treat her right. Just you wait.

What's to become of Tiffany Haigh in her frozen future? Will she be a silvery exemplar of the upper echelon, firm in the knowledge she dodged a bullet at seventeen? Or will she be slowly unhinged by the burrowing seep of neurosis? What could I have risked, what could I have been? No, she'd be far too mature to be fooled by *that*, fooled that love was more than the fenced-in rituals performed by Tiffany Haigh the adjusted adult. And so she'll teach her children… or perhaps not. For who knows what contrariness lurks in her silvery soul? Who'll bet that some irrational groundless stupidity does not await our ashy blonde at some future time - when the sown seeds, utterly discarded in the fertile ground of her need to grow, ERUPT? And that will be a *spontaneous event*. And big blond Hodgey won't know what hit him. Bummer.

* * * *

One day Sally finds a scrap of brown paper in her schoolbag. In block

writing it says: *Manindingah Township. Pass Gunderoo. I am Geoffrey. They call me Arkulula. 'Cos of my eyes. You come.'*
Well well. The koori guy from the retreat, with those liquid eyes.

* * * *

And did we forget old Johnson Toast? Toast holds a candle for Sal, believe it if you want. Glowers at her from a distance at school, and in a rough ceremony one day he offers her one of his (old) gaming consoles. Sal should consider it a gesture, so when he presents (in monosyllables) she avoids to wrinkle her nose. Now she can massacre any number of boys! To him she'll always be updated Lara Croft, tomb raider. *She can murder me any time she likes.* Sally Bang made Johnno grow up a bit.

* * * *

Sal is sowing some bad seeds too. In a crevice of the Art Room she fashions a careful letter. Heads it up *Family Secrets.* Addresses it, businesslike, to the editor of *The Age.* Copies in all the email addresses she can muster. Concerned young citizen has a big thing to divulge. About ADULTS, about Clarity. Respect. Not about Judgement. Or Revenge.

Belonging

Weird how old people seem to get dimensional as you grow up. The psychotherapist Bilk at 45 going on 150 now looms as some kind of nutty sage, and Sal feels glad to be back on his grubby couch once more. (She heap older and wiser too) Once again she can be Queen of his Attention any way she likes. Bilk is incapable of acting the adult or ejecting her from his office anyway. (Sal on a whim rocked up one afternoon, skipping last period maths ugh. To hell with minutiae and abstraction, personal life is too much action) Not that his place looks like any kind of shrink's office. Bilk gives the impression he sleeps there. Lucky there's a toilet. Though Bilk seems to have no connection at all with the world outside his grimy window, people seem to do business with him since he appears to be no thinner than last time. He is *forever falling away* as the poet Rilke might put it. Sal on one of her nosey rummagings once found a toaster and a loaf of last century's bread (plus dead cockroach) in a cupboard designated 'academic research'. Now she assumes he's fairly legendary for not givin' a fock about bourgeois boundaries, man. Truth be told, the cleanliness bit or lack of it, claws at the borders of her female sensibility. But, with a studied abandon of her very own she nestles in the nutty abandon of his life.

Today she dumps on him a curly question (something about being an alien) and lets him ruminate in his teddy bear way before delivering the gospel according to Freud Jung Adler Reich Skinner et al, which allows her to feel lazily important. Not that Bilk is unaware of the requirement to flatter a teen voyeur, specially a little babe like her. The daddy's-girl routine or owner-and-pet routine (on her part) of old has yet to establish itself but the seeds are there. Letting B. rave in his self-absorbed Germanical fashion entertains the mysterious mystic self-child that Sal likes to mock up around intellectuals. Not being one herself, Sal pushing 17 nonetheless has a nose for irony slash absurdity. And pity.

- *Belonging,* vat is itt ektually? In za beginning it is only biology. You are nothing but biologic consciousness. You are subject to heat and kald, to hunger, to discomfort, to painful simplicity of helplessness. Later your family take over, and parental relationship is most important. You copy, you try to complain, you copy some more. And you suffer from your parents' unresolved relationship. Zis you eat up as well! You are victim of emotion and senses. Zen you go to school, meet peers and friends, zuffer the pain of discipline, of lessons in behaviour, moral code. And then there is peer pressure. This is always stupid, according with the mob. So many mistakes and fears and needs and doubts. And you are not capable to solve zese, since no-one has ability to teach you zis. But you taste bitter fruit of experience. And later in life, you *regurgitate.*

Zen you discover media, and it is always telling you to be perfect consumer! So you consume ideas and fashions at greater and greater speed, and you haf no thoughts of your own. And you haf no silence. And your culture is pushing you to conform. And your family history becomes your mythology, with all petty beliefs and assumptions and conditionings. And zo you are reflex being, automatic being. You see monkey, you are monkey. Zis is true, no? And so you seek the role models. And all of zese are only a part, an unsatisfactory part, a marriage of convenience. And you are *restless,* no? (Sal is quietly spellbound) At your age now you discover reason, power of analysis. You like to destroy systems, you like to argue, you are ironik and everything is *scheisse.* You say you do not belong. But still you want more than ever to belong! Becoss your will is strong and you want to make your new identity, to return to za source. Adolescence is paradox no? And it is zo painful. But pain gives you a sense of being alive somehow. Listen to me: you haf no identity except what you have been giffen, and you do not *know* zis! You *sink* you know, you sink you are original, but you are neffer zis. And so you try to act. To act faster, to act some more and some more. You want to taste everything, like the sous chef, no? And you are so sophisticated. You know everythink but you know nothing. We are educated dummies. Parrots of the surfaces of things. (Bilk now works himself into an emotional knot) But where is *ourself?* Does it exist at all? No. Or it neffer was. Maybe we shall come later to... to what? Some humility? Some love? To laughter? Shall we give up all things? To try to haf the silence in the mind! What shall we *do?* Hmm? What is *needed* now?

- Spontaneity.

Sal has no idea where this word came from. But it crystallises out of her mind like an eagle in a wide sky. Terrible, full-formed, inarguable. As soon as it is spoken, it is her truth.

So er - what could it mean? Could it mean... the 'spontaneity' of trying to get herself pregnant by Jean Paul for instance? No, I planned all that. But I was reckless and I didn't *care.* Yeah I did. Gah! Maybe Bilk 'll tell me.

The spontaneous never know that they are! Bilk knows she is a beautiful girl of substance. He always did. But at this moment he feels... with a strange deference of the aged to the young... as if they are messiahs, because they glitter with forgotten wisdom newly found: that she has something to do that he will *never* do. He feels his youth is gone, right there. That the baton has passed. (It hasn't) He goes quiet and looks at her, with his sniff and his rubbery lip and his hairy arms. She is aware that, like Little Jack Horner in her corner, she has completed his erudition with a coup de grace. And he sits humble at her feet, at the feet of the young. But she is not proud. And he has not the stifling adult ego to try to deny her. Instead, he bows to the beauty of it. *Spontaneity. Spontaneity.* He is a loving simple manchild under all that dry grudgingly-won intellect he never believed in. He hails the glittering child sage. And *she* loves him out of loving pity.

Repression

Spontaneity (the premeditated kind) seems to be working its work. Young Sal has rushed in with the insouciance of youth where angels fear to tread. That email she sent off with devil's wings into the cyber blue has had a result. By Murphy's Law word reached Dad that his Irish wife had an affair with a *priest.* Such nuances as 'platonic' or 'spiritual' fail to prompt our Melbourne butcher to finesse the issue with any reasoned analysis or discussion, these tools being foreign to his nature. Still, he knows when time has come to put the women in their place. Sal arrives home to find mother standing in the kitchen with a handkerchief over her mouth. There's a nasty bruise. Ron emerges from another room and accuses daughter and mother of being 'in it together'. Claims he's not sorry. Sal tells him he wouldn't know shit from clay which earns her a sudden slap too. At this she grabs at a knife out of the drawer, but Ron ironises that he's more experienced with those items than she'll ever be. Sal suddenly realises that she sides with the mother for the simple reason that she and she already have an understanding and that Dad is quite possibly a *stranger.* Neither of these women has reflected to any depth on the effect such news might have on a simple man, much less a man who 'as his pride and who's for years provided for 'is women without in the least whingeing about their wishy-washy womanish ways, and now they're in cahoots. Fact is, Sal hasn't talked to her mother much either, and in fact no-one really talks to anyone else in this family. In facty fact, this fam. is a bunch of scaredy lazy strangers who mole along in life without any real objective.

But this is no time for introspection. Time only for hurt. And for repression.

What's a real man to do when he's been lied to - or at least not told truth for a hell of a long time? For a man as uninvolved with the world as Ron Bang, it might be easier just to act as if yer wife's gone bananas, as this is what women are prone to do according to mate Georgio with whom he shares his customary 2 beers down the pub after work and whose trouble-and-strife once had a fling wiv a janitor after he let her go and work and stuff.

Couple of days after, there's a mumbled sorry all round, and when Mum tries to tell it like it is to Dad, he says: 'That's Your Business. But no wonder that girl o' yours is a tearaway'. That girl of *yours?* Shee-it! That's how it was all those years ago! It turns out Ron had a deal with his wife all along. 'If you don't mention the boyfriend ever again - then I'll marry yer'. The mother was desperate, she with the little baby - and he saved her hide. Great way to make an honest woman out of Alicia Mary Connaught. And a great way not to come to terms with a little human being called Sally Bang. Lazy as all fuck, eh? And thick too. But a good man all the same. That's why they all come in me shop everyday 'stead of goin' down to Woolies. 'Cos I'm honest. Tell it like it is. And I know the price of a lump of rump. Or hide.

* * * *

I suppose your ghost writer should quit being too hard on Ron Bang. But why should he care? I mean, your ghostie never ran from any ghosts. No skeletons banging about in *his* closet. Besides, a work of fiction is a work of friction. Deal with it, Ronnie boy.

And Alicia is really not sorry for all those years of going to the church and mutely confessing to the proprietor her deep attachment. She even hints this much to Sally, through a screen of tears in the kitchen. But mother's also sadly unschooled in the art of analysis. A life opportunity falls away and gets lost.

Sally, you should feel a stab of regret at your parents' failing. And you should vow never to fall in the same trap. Never repress! Show me your spontaneity now. You are romantically young! Life is too full, too strange, for repression ever to win.

But the wounds of experience have come thick and fast for our Sal. The romantical girl, having sown her strange seed with Yogi Jean Paul, has tasted the awful complexity of caring. Tasted the despair of her semi-friend Tiffany Haigh, tasted submission-as-death through the low karma of the fake guru Orwell, and is forced to heed phantoms from out of her family's past. But to stay reckless is still her guiding force. *She will not freeze the future.* Old Bilk reminded her: to fail to understand how you're conditioned is death. To run away from the desire to change it, is death. But Bilk also boosted her, told her she's all at once ageless and a growing gathering girl. Told her it doesn't matter what she is or what she'll become. The romance of the future is still alive! Still, the long year of living dangerously has dealt to Sal a jaundiced air. She needs to get out, away. Only one person in the world to fill the gap. *Her Oriental sister Won.* But how to find her?

Decadence

In the Uni café one spring day, Sal spots… rabble-rousing heroine Red Kar-en (!) K. seems to have tamed her exploding hair to a cutesy platinum blonde which at first glance fails to match her famed image as an espouser of any political cause that'll get her laid by the right people. She greets Sal with an affected tone as if someone offstage were scrutinising her performance. She is dressed expensively in faddy fashion items, seemingly chosen to impress someone not here. And when questioned re. old Animal Road, she scales the heights of scorn. Under no circumstance would she associate with any plebs from that zone. Kar-en does the talking as usual, Sal takes the passive role. Why not? She has only one question anyway, but it's a while before she can negotiate the wall of aggression that passes for conversation. *Still a commie then?* What are you talking about, Sally Bang? I was never a commie, not even a pinko! *No?* Wake up girl! Our duty under western late-capitalist consumer insanity is to exploit the limited resources left! No future! Every man and girl for herself. Idealism is absurdly hypocritical. This, with the urgent chutzpah reserved only for the indefensible by the vulgarly indiscriminate, and all intended to flit over Sally's head. But things have changed. Sal merely shrugs. Who's the new boy? Stinking rich? (Flash of inspiration) Wouldn't be *Marcus Factor* by any chance? K. summons her steely look. Why not? Marcus is a trend setter. - And you're Paris Hilton. Still got his Maserati? They look each other in the eye. It is at this point that they'll either hate each other for good... or develop a steely camaraderie based on sardonic irony. Fate hangs in the balance.

- Come to a party tonight.

A dare. Kar-en also evidently craves to know where Sal has travelled in a year: to underestimate might be a mistake. Besides, razor-tongued people need a butt or a foil. This is the only way girl-on-top Kar-en makes buddies: through put-down love. Which the buddy's supposed to get, and to love. Sal knows all this. Yawn.

- Yup. Okay. Where, and how do I dress?
- At Marcus's. Dress rich! 9 o'clock on. Not past your bedtime? 48 Fullilove Road, South Yarra.
- By the way, would you happen to remember a Korean girl named -

At which point, K. needs to greet a crucially important person across the room and hurry off.

Following several excuses to parents and dredging the depths of her wardrobe before settling on a retro red skirt number plus red top under see-through red lace, followed by fifty clammy minutes on a bus, Sal arrives in front of a platinum knocker attached to a heavy green door. Some elegant ditzy chick answers without a pause, champagne flute at the nub of her fingers. Claims she's *not the butler* darling and who the hell're you 'cause I'm little sister to Marcus Factor and *I don't know you*. Sal says charmed I'm sure and steps right past. What a wacko. Yet the place is a classical dream in marble: central atrium, sweeping stair to the right, hall leading inward to a big open lounge, terrazzo beyond. Gold light, swishy palms, swarms of princesses in heels and tinsel-tiny silver skirts, all class arse. Sal is way out of place. Good.

Kar-en spots her and affects to be acquainted. Come and meet Marcus if you like. Sal notes her outfit seems more strained than apposite. K. is not necessarily the Belle of this Ball. Into the lounge. Note the jazz quartet darling. Marcus is there. His blonde fine hair and all-over Gatsby sheen gets Sal tingling ever so slightly. He greets Sal with studied nonchalance, but doesn't pass her by either. K. seems to want to say things. And Marcus doesn't look at her.

- I'm launching a new clothing line tonight, Sally Bang. Informally of course. Selected people, you understand. I like the outfit! Yours? I'm reminded of 'Kate Middleton Slut'. Hey, come meet some people.

He takes her hand and leads her away, and K. doesn't follow. Sal looks back, sees her standing askew in her heels, a vacuum in the crowd. Sal suddenly sees: Kar-en doesn't know what the fuck to do with herself. That's very interesting. But Marcus is talking and folks are listening, especially females. Precious few appear to know each other, mind. On flows the babble and clink, and music and light gild the beautiful youth in an unreal halo…

Later, Sal finds herself in an upper bathroom of the boundless house. Factor and she have already soaked up three private lines of cocaine amidst the gilded flush-plush. His show was short and smart, and Marcus has the easy way of a rich boy who's learnt to use his resources. Now he slips the door wordlessly to and cleverly removes Sal's relevant underwear. She has no specific objection to spreadeagling herself atop this rich boy, though the tiles are hard and cold against her knees and remind her of another blood-violent bathroom in a restaurant in a city. The present bloodless affair endures as long as Marcus Factor wishes it to. Following it Sal retrieves her bits, wipes herself, looks vaguely in a gilded mirror at a person resembling someone she knew, and totters in her heels out of the salle-de-bang into the glitter and hum. Marcus is gone of course. Sal dawdles down the upper corridor, past an open door.

In a shadowed room she spies Kar-en. She is kneeling on a rug, head down, hair lolling over her face. She looks up in a jerk and Sal sees a smeared countenance: indistinct lips, runny eye-pencil. K. is mouthing something, clearly harbouring a substance she can't control. Sal feels she ought perhaps to go in. K. suddenly appears to recognise her since she intones something like *Fugg off Bang* before putting her grimy head to the rug and starting to weep. Sal pulls the door to like the undertaker at a funeral. She knows what *that* is all about. Marcus already in the bathroom offered *her* the-career-in-modelling-with-the-big-heap-of-money blaa blaa. Which she accepted like the coke and sex, without the ghost of a thought.

She now nears what seems to be a last door in the gold-velvet corridor. At this point a blonde boy lunges out of the door toward the back staircase. Master of the House Marcus Factor… scowls at her and hurries away. Sal rocks faintly on her heels. She wants to sneeze. The warm light sprinkles her eyes… Next, a figure in knee-length white appears in the doorway and slips past her shoulder. Sally stands still like the elf goddess. Long seconds flitter before she registers. She turns, starts to totter back down the hall. Quicker, she reaches the big stair. At the bottom that girl in white is disappearing across the atrium toward the front door. Sal starts to waken, clicks down the steps. But the Marcus sister is there at the foot. A drunken siren, she tries to grasp at Sally and lick at her face. Sal pushes the girl to the wall. She falls like a ragdoll, uttering nothing, her glass shatter-echoing on marble. Sally slips, and her hand closes on shards. There is blood. She staggers but aims for the great door. The heavy wood yields. Down stone-dark steps she totters. And Won the Korean is standing in the middle of the road, in the still of the night, gazing at her. *I thought it was you,* she says.

Sally unaware of blood streaming from her hand runs to Won clings her arms about her neck and pushes her cheek in the girl's face. There are tears. A minute, a year, goes by. At last they look at each other. Won's neck is stained with Sally's blood. A car growls out of a nearby driveway. They slip hurriedly to the pavement as Marcus Factor's Maserati roars by. Won clasps Sally's hand… and they step off into the night.

Contradictions

They're in a little graveyard. Sleep shrouds the city. Sal is wild awake, but Won speaks as if in a trance.

- Often I try to come to a graveyard. To feel the impermanence, to feel the empty nature of all our works. I do not care what I do, but maybe my - how do you say - abusers will start to care. They are weak humans, not so bad. I love them, pity them. Maybe I will help them. Sometimes they need the violence done to them so they will wake to themselves. And sometimes they need to dominate so they can be strong in their primitive way. Or else they need to cry and I am there to catch their tears. My father taught me. I will not forget. He was not all a good man but he loved me. I believe it. He was strong, so strong. And they put him away for all those years - and he died. I do not forget. But he said to me: *use* the victim in you to make you strong. The more you know the victim, stronger you can be. And I *will,* always. For death is nothing

- What is 'strong'?
- It is purity
- Is all that sex and abuse gonna make you pure?
- No. But it is what I must do. Only I can do. I am loyal to my father's spirit
- And what does 'loyalty' do for you?
- Makes me free
- Did you really know your dad though? I mean, was he around - apart from teaching you martial art stuff?
- You question me, Sally Bang. And you are right to. But I am tired. I am not so well
- I want you to live. Live with me. We don't need anyone!
- We are directed by ghosts. We cannot escape

- I will

- I deceived this Marcus Factor boy. I said I had disease, disease he could *catch*. He was so angry and crazy then! Maybe this will shake him, make him see his arrogance. I entertain many people for him, boy and girl. I must pity this pretty fool

- So that's what you and him were -

- He uses lives. He will not use mine

- He used me too. But I wanted him to

- You are female. Still lazy, passive

- Passive?

- You are not *serious*.

Sally looks at the immutable girl. Can I ever measure up? Is she superwoman? Or is there something - that has to give?

- I never asked how old you are

- One thousand years. Does it matter? But I am twenty-two

- You want me to be serious?

- Sally, you must

- My life's a serious fucking contradiction! I'm lazy and passive and cynical 'cause I don't believe in a thing but I wanna be strong. Too strong. Gotta be independent right? No victim! But Bilk (my psycho dude) says there's a bunch of things I belong to that I don't even know about (most of 'em shit I'd say). So I'm trapped. Contradiction. He says 'find identity', 'cept can somebody explain what that is? Maybe it's not even there. Tall Uncle Bill (my cool mate) reckons I'm totally focused on myself. Well I'm not anybody *else* am I? Don't need anybody, right? ('cept you, that is) Mind you, I put on identities all the time. How many masks can a chick put on! Contradiction. Most people are morons anyway. Why should I care about all the tossers trying to make the scene? Then you feel like FOMO FOMO if you don't grab all the experience. Contradic... you get it. Maybe *I'm* the tosser. Better than sitting home with a finger up my fanny.

...Then comes along this priest guy. Mum hints he could be my real dad. Bilk says I crave a father. So I got a daddy complex. Woo-hoo. I need multiple daddies! There was this guru guy. I let him play fuck-daddy. Weak arsehole couldn't control himself

- To worship a father-figure? No Sally, not for you (Won murmurs)
- Old Bilko 'd never hit on me. I encourage him but he won't! He's my pet actually. Ugly little *spunk* he is. I'll have him for a daddy. Doesn't judge… But who'd wanna grow up if that's what we're in for - turn into fossils with old fogey smells? Like why fucken bother? What if I live and die and nobody notices? Gotta *be* somebody, gotta be noticed. But then - urrr, I'd have to *work* at it like forever. No *time,* too many things to taste! Gotta kick arse. Like Kar-en used to do…

…So along comes some guy. You dunno why you're into him, you get totally sucked in and then you're *in love*… Awesomely complicated, JEAN PAUL and me. So I do stupid stuff (don't ask) 'cos I wannabe somebody for Him. And I'm thinking it's about commitment and I'm gonna settle down like forever and it'll be jake and lovely poos romantic. But I don't want *responsibility*. Kar-en said control everything or you're the loser! Now she's controlled by Factor and his car and his drugs and his bullshit money. Contradiction! Sucker Kar-en's a nobody. Don't feel sorry for 'er. Yeah I do. Won't happen to me

- I think it just did, Sally
- What? Jean Paul? But I don't want to control him or be controlled. Wanna risk, be *out* of control. Do stuff without needing to think. Just do it. Maybe I don't have the guts. *You* do. I know you do.

Won is gazing at her with her eyes closed. Enough contradiction perchance?

- Take Tiff my rich-as school bud. Everybody wants her, full stop. Slashes her wrists: that ironic or what? Barges in, gets tangled with *my* guy! (To be fair, I hadn't met him yet) And she says to me romantic is not about commitment or settling down, it's about *risk*. Fuck, she's braver than me! I'm jealous. Couldn't chop *my* wrists, wouldn't have the guts. Mind you, pretty stupid over a guy. Got people's attention though. …Me, I'm a vain cow. Love dolling up to be top girly working class underdog. What a wank! 'Cos I love my clothes, oh yes I doo. Supposed to be gritty proletarian but I'm not in any class! I'm not *anything* or *anybody*. And

I've no frigging family! Yeah I do. Sad crowd, have to care about 'em. Shit, CONTRADICTIONS! *There's something I want and I don't know what the hell it is.* Won?

Won opens one eye. She hasn't snorted three lines of coke.

- Let's get out of this. School hols is coming up. We'll do it. Have you got a car?
- I will not come, Sally
- You have to come. Besides, I can't drive
- I am not for you, Sally Bang
- You have to. Have to!
- You do not want me. I cannot give my heart to you
- I don't need…

Wired-up Sally stops, looks at the grave girl. It starts to dawn that Won can only give if she gives away everything. This is some kind of wondrous strange commitment. A real fanatic. What a burden.

- We'll go for a little while then. (Eager Sal is negotiating)
- If I go, you will never speak of me
- Huh?
- Never speak of me or my feelings or my body or my life. These are my conditions
- Then there'll be something between us
- Yes. And there will always be.

Sally is mystified. But the Korean withdraws. Her eyes are hollow. It's time to go to a place called home.

✳ ✳ ✳ ✳

Two weeks later. Sal has successfully manipulated the parents to let her do a 'study tour of spiritual slash aboriginal sites'. She'll be writing it all up for her final Religion Elective. Biggest thing since sliced bread. Yo, Sal. Dad has no influence with her anyway since the Big Family Secret got out. No more meat in their relationship now. Seems to be drinking more, four pints a night with Georgio. Mum's alone, worrying double. And there's no church to run to since the priest has fled. Where, only god (and Sally) know. But mum 'll explain this to her husband right? Nope. She might like to though, if ever she could. Sal has no appetite for communication with either of them. They'd never change anyhow. Jean Paul on the other hand has texted her multi-times. In his stand-offish way he now offers to *photograph her* Bill Henson-style. For the exhibition he's planning. Exhibition all about ME. Tempting. (She's seen Henson's stuff) But she resists - for now. Contrary girl! The guy even talks of 'revelations that are new to him concerning her'. She hesitates…

Screw it all. Not now.

Into the Wild

Sally Bang and the Korean set out westward on state highway ---- early on October third. The Korean drove a nineties Porsche she apparently borrowed from a 'friend'. The girl notified no next of kin as she appeared to have none. The Bang parents assumed their daughter, though not strictly a minor, was in the care of an adult. They'd given her money, though assumed the Korean had money. The assumption was they'd be gone up to fourteen days. No forwarding address given, except one, for a remote aboriginal settlement.

From the start it's plain that Won is fatigued by something more than the exigencies of pursuing her mysterious amoral city profession, but Sal's not allowed to speak of it. Not that she has more than a inkling of how Won conducts business in the social shadows. Won takes the opportunity on back roads to show Sal the wheel, and she does not hesitate; after all it is a Porsche. How did Won procure such a vehicle? Oh, a client offered it in lieu of payment. Though at ease with Won's inscrutable cool, Sal now feels she will need to negotiate the relationship with more rigour than before. But it's the unknown that attracts and thrills, so for now she basks in their reckless romance. After all, here is our adventure to the *spiritual heart.*

Open spring skies converge on the tip of the horizon-road, inviting the two to drive forever. One day, the glistening bowl of sea to their left, its endless breakers clawing the gleaming coast as if to beg the future, Won asks Sal to stop - which she does on a rise overlooking a silver curl of beach. Now Won with no words exits the car, starts down the dunes and onto the sand. Sal watches from the height as the lone figure, her lace-form tracing the strand, disrobes piece by piece and steps toward the surf. She stops not at all, and the greening white surge beckons her into its maw. Won's arms are spread as if in bridal supplication, her hair a flag to the wind.

Sally Bang is slow to comprehend the unfolding suicide - but when she does she flings her body downward through the dense consuming dune; lurching sliding throws herself across the yawning beach and into the spray-sea that's swallowing her sister-soul. The curling tops come crashing; a rip pulls her sidelong as she claws at the form of Won who makes no investment in her body or breath. Sally wrenches at her, catches the neck; the naked form slips away! Sal lunges again, this time an arm; her lung-breath is water and she's screaming WON come back come back don't do this I need you. But the girl has liquid eyes the text of glistening water, hands of foam she makes no moan and baleful feeds the deep... Now Sal has gripped her, pulls her throat, and several times they drown together 'fore Sally drags her onto sand then drops on top, her lungs a galloping chaos in the pouring wind - which tugs at their sodden forms lying under inhuman sea-foam.

Two human specks on a desert coast, the echoing wind, the creeping tide, suck clean.

* * * *

At length Sal takes her up and lays her in the dunes, collects her scraps of clothing from the strand. Later, wrapped in a blanket on a sheltered sponge of grass, Won apologises with all the finesse of the aristocrat, and thanks her friend for the deed of assistance. Sally tells her she is welcome, says nothing more. Absently, she picks a shard of driftwood, clutches it in her hand, and they drive on.

Unfulfilled

Later. They come upon what seems like a seaside suburb of caravans. Strange little roads with cute verges, kids with cricket bats, pot-bellied men in flimsy chairs and beers in hands; flotsam and washing and women with folded arms who gaze at them like watchers at a match. They sidle in on evening shadows. Won doesn't look at anything. They park and Sally in her arse-torn jeans chains rings and whatnot steps up to reception. We'd like a caravan. The manageress smiles a craggy smile; she's seen a few. Pay me when you leave, she says. Two alien girls crawl into a box on wheels. The Asiatic one lies down and drops asleep. And Sally lies beside her, cradling with her body-warmth.

Next morning early, there's a knock. Sal swings the door and sunlight blinds her eyes. A large blondish woman's standing there.
- Saw you come last evening. Your friend all right? She looked a bit… come over, have breakfast with us. Just there
- Er, okay. Give me a minute.
She rummages for clothes, serves water to Won, who's aware and listening.
- I feel better, she says. - Don't worry for me, Sally
- Uh, we're invited -
- I know. Go. I will come
- Will you?
- Whatever I do, I shall do. (She smiles) But I will come.

Sal steps over to the neighbour's site. Looks fairly chaotic with jetsam stacked about. Several adults in camp chairs blink in the light. Sal notices hairy knees stubbies thongs reddish faces. Two males: one stocky, the other wiry. A weighty woman in a slack t-shirt with loose grey-blonde hair.
- Hi, I'm Sal.
- Gidday Sal. Bit early ain't it? But my wife wanted to knock on yer door
- No. It was nice of her.
The guy extends a hand. - Me name's Tommy. This is Kurt. And Greta. And you met Linda. (Sal shakes awkwardly) Saw yer Sports. Like a Porsche meself. If I could afford one

- You can afford it Tommy. You just don't get round to it.

This from Kurt, who seems continentally factual.

- Don't get round to a lot of things, mate. Hey Lin! Ready yet? Starvin' out here! (To Sal) We're

'aving bacon sarnies with our booze this mornin'. *Her* idea. Never catch on

- Give her a chance, says Greta. (Her T-shirt says: *You'll love every piece of Victoria* over a jigsaw of the Great State).

- Whatever. She's cool

- I doubt that, says Kurt curtly.

- So is that wagon yours?

- No. My friend Won's

- Won. She Asian?

- Tommy! (Greta hisses)

- Here she is. Won, this is… sorry…

- I'm Kurt. Greta my wife, and Tommy. And here's our sweet Linda.

And Won the perfect, in tight slacks, delicate top and two-inch heels, shakes all the hands with a bow and a smile which leaves the company impressed. She's in control. Sal breathes out.

- Which country you from, Won? says stocky Tommy, eyes a bit wider.

- Actually Tommy, I am from Australia. (Smile) But my father was North Korean. You may be aware of the political situation. He was a victim of the regime. I am his only child. At ten I was sent by my aunt to your Lucky Country. After we fled to the South, you see. I am 22 years of age, and in hospitality industry. It is a pleasure to meet you all.

There's a pause in the morning light. Linda, dishes in hand, directs at Won and Sal a scrutinising gaze.

- Nice to 'ear English well spoken!

- Tommy, you're a clever fellow but you've no class (says messy Greta).

Linda serves bacon sandwiches and orange juice. Won offers help.

- No, it's my pleasure. Fresh young faces. Nice to meet

- Jeez, this stuff puts hairs on yer chest. Tryin' to kill me with yer health kick, Lin?

Kurt: - Ignore him please. So you are travelling? We, as you see, enjoy our spring holiday together in the cute Ossie way. We work and socialise together in our city suburb. So we are unable to be apart in our other suburb, by the sea.

Too much information, thinks Sal. Won smiles her delicate smile.

- Yeah, we love each other so much (Greta)

- Get me a beer will ya, Lin. Jesus

(Kurt) - Tommy is my partner in our boat firm. I am a designer from Kiel. He is a rich man but wishes to deny it. Why, you may ask. Because he knows money and booze but not the art of boats. Friend does not know one end from zu other.

- For a kraut you're remarkably polite. Money makes the world go round, mate.

(Linda brings a six-pack) - Don't drink them all at once, darling

- Nah, I'm house trained. Drink 'em one after the other. (A wink) So how's about a spin in your Porsche?

Won to Sal's consternation immediately assents. - *Soon!*

Tommy swallows a mouthful, tries not to turn red. Greta being female, sees all.

- Mmm yes. Our country's future is multicultural… And what do you do, Sal?

- School. Year eleven

- Oh! You look older. I recall year eleven. Wanted to be a model. Now look at me: haus frau

- Muzzer to my children! Und she has a business. Women underrate themselves, no?

- A bloated success. I'm what you'd call a winner who lost

(Sal) - How d'you mean?

- Kurt won't like this, but we're the classic smug Haves. Got-it-all, overweight bourgeoisie sitting on our real estate. Too damn lazy for a love affair! Be *quiet* Kurt, I'm talking to the young lady. And dear, with your figure and your charm and your looks, make sure you don't become what we are.

Sal returns Greta's bitter smile. But Linda gazes at Sal as if at a long-lost daughter who's going away. Husband Tommy feels the need to crack another tube. Which sprays over Won.

- Tom! She's our guest!

- She's all right. Sorry love (wink)

Won gazes at him and laughs a tinkly laugh.

Kurt: - And what is your purpose for travelling?

- *We're on a trip to the heart of the spirit.*

Sally doesn't know where this phrase came from. But as soon as it's said, it sounds as if it had always been. Nobody speaks. Sal smiles to herself. Yet Won seems agitated. She excuses herself and steps away.

Linda, finally: - That sounds romantic.

Greta looks hard at Sally. - And why not?

Since Kurt needs to question this young lady about her curious statement, Sal is dragged into a turgid chat. Linda clears dishes. Tommy though, looks about. Finally he mumbles: *Goin' for a slash.*

* * * *

Hours later, Sal returns from the beach. The wind is up. Linda had come after her. Seemed to want to talk about herself, her feelings (many unfulfilled it seems)… but Sal's mind is reliving the horror-scene of yesterday. The car is gone. Where *is* she?

- My friend. I have to look for her

- She took 'young Tom' for a spin

- Your bloke? You don't mind?

- Why should I mind? I've no control. Oh, I used to like his rough and ready ways. Until… you see, I came from Denmark to marry this man. Australia was a ticket to money and ease. You have it all but *what* do you have? This beach is lonely, my children are gone. I used to paint - I'm not so bad - I don't do it now. There's no reason. Our suburb, our big house… there is no culture here. As a child I loved the windy coast of Jutland. It was romantic. But now, nothing.

The car is there, in the beach car park. Won stands next to this Tommy creature, looking out to sea. Tommy notes the 'weird one' approaching.

- Come for dinner you guys. I'm doin' prawns.

And he and his wife step away. Sal knows it is better to say nothing to Won. But she says it anyway.

- You gonna fuck every tom dick and harry you come across?

The first time she ever spoke harshly to her sister. Won turns toward the sea. Sally pulls her. The wind whips the dunes into their eyes.

- Get away, Sally Bang
- No way. I pulled you out of the sea
- You should have left me
- What is *wrong* with you?
- It is the world that is wrong, Sally Bang
- I want an answer. Not some Asiatic crap!
- What do you think I am? We are nothing. *Leave* me
- Why do you want to kill yourself? (Won moves away. Sal shouts) Did your fucking father teach you?

Won turns dagger eyes to her. The wind flings strands across her cheek. She is like some Asiatic devil-ghost in white. Sal shudders. - I didn't mean that...

Won reaches down, scoops two fists of sand and holds them rigid before her face. In slow motion she opens the palms and sand writhes and swirls in a cloud about her. Then a sudden flick or bow of the head, and she is running. The other girl pursues.

Casual observers would have seen two dots, tottering down a far sea-combed beach. The one behind will catch the one in front - who pushes her away, and the follower will seem to lose heart then gather her strength for pursuit again. The one in white seems to slow, to stumble, even fall to her knees, then as the other reaches her, she'll dither forward again. Pursuer will hesitate, wrap her arms about herself, then on, once more! Thus it goes, far far down the strand... until two specks are lost in the sea haze.

That evening at Camp Desperation it's middle-age grunge not bourgeois as these people cultivate their favourite sodden games of love and hate. Sal is all for driving out, but contrary Won stays put. They haven't reconciled. Rich Tommy dumps a great bag of king prawns on the caravan bench (his contribution to the evening's culinary arts) and lunges for the fridge, where solace lies in cliffs of beer. Curt Kurt, his tipple of choice great flutes of white, sweats red in the neck. His glasses fog at the sight of his big grey whale of a wife. And Greta, parked with cigarette in hand, is holding forth.

- There's no romance. There's no romance! When's the last time my picky German husband took a risk? All picky perfect clean and nice. Gotta let it all hang out! (This to impress the young ones no doubt. The opposite effect)
- You're drunk already, woman. Where d'you put it all? Ah, why did I never marry Linda? Sit with me. Sit, baby.
Linda says: - I-have-to-barbecue-the-prawns. Who wants a prawn? *Anybody* want a prawn? So specially original! On the bar-be-cue. Like yesterday. We got dead prawns from yess-terday. They're in the bin!
- I'll cook 'em Linda, says Sal, keen to get out of the fetid van.
- Nah nah nah. Oim the cook tonight, you're the guest. And our little Asian too!

This from cultivated Tommy who puts his arm round Sal and smooches her on the shoulder. Sal puts him in his place and slides out, to howls from soggy Greta, and Linda too. Kurt is swearing.

Won is standing bent over the grass, her hands to her stomach, the blue silk of her dress creasing green in the barbecue light.
- What is it, Won? You're sick. Come here.
And Won is crying tears she can't control. They drop to the grass like little diamonds. And Sally's heart is keen to burst. She holds the girl to her. Won's eyes are hot on her neck.
- I'm sick. Oh, I'm so sick.
A bawdier argument erupts within. There's banging on the window. *You cook the fucken prawns!* Linda lurches down the step, spies the children standing there. She gulps, goes quiet.
- Are you two going to stay for tea? Please stay. Please? Oh, is she sick? Oh, let me help.
But Won is sinking to her knees and Sal can't hold her up.
- I have *disease*. Do you not know?
Sal kneels, holds the girl's head. Linda kneels too. Now Tommy, beetroot-red, appears. Kurt is shouting. You dare insult your wife? She's too good for

you my friend! *Well fucken take 'er then! I gotta better fish to fry!* Tommy sways there, his Tube in his hairy slab of fist. Greta squeezes through the door. - He already had his lil' fish today! That one there! That be right, Tommy boy?

- What do you mean, *disease?*

Sal whispers. Her hand slips on sweating silk. - What do you mean, Won? What do you mean disease! Linda: - Let her be. I'll take her to her bed. But Won now vomits in a sudden arc that catches Tommy's shoe. He grunts and jumps aside and his hand lands on the hot griller. He howls like a dog at the night. Won's face is disfigured over the lurid grass.

- *THE AIDS.* She chokes it out. And Linda sits aback. - The what? *The AIDS, you see?* repeats the girl. Her words seem disembodied in the drunk light. The women kneel there, force the shuffling-sweating others to slow and cease. Their breaths insult the silence.

- Yer what? says Tommy.

- She said nothing. (Linda, holding Won) Not to you, anyway

- What the fuck'd she say?

- *What the hell do you want, man?* This from Kurt, shamed by his uncouth partner.

- The fucken dame's got AIDS!

- Oh Yess! (says Greta) She's a whore! Couldn't you see it, stupid man! Now what'll you do?

- What does she mean? says Kurt.

- Kurt, wake the fuck up!

Greta lets her fat frame slide into a chair. And Tommy doesn't know where to put himself. But Linda has taken Won aside, lain her in her caravan and covered her with blankets. Won, sweating heat and cold will push them off, pull them on again. And Linda gives her water, bathes her head. Our Sally has shrunk to a child meanwhile, so Linda soothes her too. An hour goes by. Won is asleep. Linda leaves. She'll come back in the morning.

Somewhere in the night, a banging on the caravan door, some guttering voices raised, Tommy being pulled away. Sal wanders on the beach under the moon. Black surf rumbles in a tawdry dawn. She feels her heart's been torn away. Morning comes and Linda is there. Sal says: I'll put her in the car. We'll drive away, back to the city. They bundle Won in blankets into the seat, and Sally takes the wheel. She says thank you and goodbye. And Linda stands and watches till the car's a tiny speck rounding the headland road. Until it disappears from view.

The Undiscovered Country

Sal drives, not caring which direction. Her driving's rough and basic anyway. At times she goes reckless fast, at others she crawls as if to spare the insects. They abandon the main roads for the inland and the country turns lonely, scrubby, nondescript. She pays no heed to sign nor civilisation, such as it is. It's as if there's no-one else in the car, as Won has withdrawn into a semi-sleep or trance. At a lone gas station she takes on junk supplies, fills the tank, talks to no-one. It's as if she wants to lose the thread, drive to the moon. In the noon-day glare red dust cakes the car, seems to hang in curtains about the skeletal trees, rises like a shroud behind them on the metal road.

At a comfort stop she watches over Won who crouches in the dust without dignity. Her pale effluent makes a little stream in the dirt. She inhumanly spits. Sal is grimly lost. She told them AIDS - should anyone believe it? The red ants swarm about her feet. The car's a monster, metallic-heavy by the roadside. She wants to walk into the scrub, forget. She does it finally; cicadas rattle and hum in the secret places. Crowds in, this tempting empty loneliness. She's gone for a time she can't recall, as if the dreamtime. Stumbles back in panic, lost then found. Won is lying by the wheel. She stares ahead as if her girl had never gone away. Now Sally puts her face into the sun and looks at nothing. She lies down in the road. No vehicle comes. She sinks into a dream. The heat and dust are cradling her, and ants negotiate her disparate parts. She peers into the bowl of sky and finds some clouds to mesmerise her by. Let the war be over, give me peace. For corpse-like Sally lies like Tolstoy's hero, lost at Borodino. The clouds resolve themselves according to her mind, their shapes assembling life that's gone and done. Her future reconciled, her past a story, romance lost, no battle glory. All times are gone. Forget and leave this earthly. Let it be. Let me be.

…Sal discovers she's been dead asleep. She finds her body in the road. She rises, looks. The shadows of the trees have lengthened, the car sits heavy in yellow sun. There's grit in her nostrils, sand in her hair. And Won is not there. Sal hurries to the left, then right. But Won is in the forest by a white tree. She's studying a gumnut in her fingers. Look, she breathes, as Sal comes up. Here is the universe, and this is me. They stare together. The insects make their rustle all about. Won takes her hand. Together they listen. The weight of the vast continent holds them in its timeless afternoon. Now descends the embrace of eternity. Here is the still end of it all. This is all there ever was - is - or ever will be.

Back in the car, and Won is quiet. Sal is mystified at the girl's untouchability. And do you have the proper drugs? she asks. Of course I do is the hasty reply. But it is hard for you? Of course it is. But what am I to complain? And how could Sal any longer know what is fact and what is fiction?

They drive on through the yellow afternoon. At length, a settlement. By the road a pub, a store, a house or two, some cars and motor bikes. They stop. Sal turns to Won, a question on her face. Won says: - I'm better now. Don't worry Sally Bang. All in its time and place.

Won changes into jeans and jacket, boots. Sal does the same. Both apply make-up. They look at each other, the old female collusion. Couple of dykes? They step up to the door of the pub. Inside there are fans revolving in the roof and a heavy bar straddles the room around which are seated men and youths with their girls. All turn to look at the Asian and the Goth, whose studied denim shouts their aloofness and guilt. No-one says hello except the girl behind the bar. Sal orders beers; they take their bottles, sit to the side. An older man in a hat regards them from a booth. That weirdly futile air of country pubs pervades the room, as if life happens elsewhere, as if in the collective grief of a pantomime collusive strangers share their resentment in public places, let it fester to vent itself upon the new and different, the very thing they crave.

Like in a slow-motion play, two dudes step up and say g'day. Can we get you a drink? I'm Watto, this is Binge. Not our real names. We ain't from here, fuck no. Came through from Charlton, got the bikes outside. Wanna spin? We'll have a party at the pub tonight. You stayin' round here? Dunno, says Sal. Know a place? Maybe, says Binge. These tools round here don't know much I reckon. Need some stirrin'. You chicks from the city? C'n tell straight away... The allure of craggy boys in leather, stubbly beard, a ring or two, on motor bikes, should work the trick. Crotch of leather and ironic lip puts 'em a cut above the local boys, of whom there are plenty skulking about. Sal smells the sexual danger, but Won invites these males as fodder for her abnegation-quest. Easy Riders, not born yesterday, they understand the mating ritual (got their dignity after all); 'cause boys need signposts on a road, and drinks with chicks had better go somewhere. Sal is all for the Lesbian routine; strung out, it'll make the perfect sting and put these Aussie penises in their place. Won wants meat and gravy but. Fanatically tragic, she's wilfully blind. Any moral compass she has these days is not of the human plane. And Sal has felt too much and too deep of late, and needs to drop to a baser plane. So the drinking begins. At first she'll fool herself she's in control, that her city wiles will serve her, veteran of a dozen weird eclectic roles. But here in the bush a baser instinct lurks, and booze feeds it now like a croc in its lair. Out of depth is what we want! And why should I fear it, being a girl? But Won is older, ruthless; for her there is no 'out of depth'. Herein lies her abominable perfection, the fruit of her works in the underworld of revenge. A nature weirdly absolute: deep hate and joy and grief trained to feed on each other; deep nothingness too. Not suitable for any girl, you'll say. Well, you will witness where it leads.

Our outsider party makes an island in the room, and the local goons and girls wanna join up. Here's the class act! The boyz in baseball caps need to impress but their bloky jokes are in-bred, their courtesy a mess. Drink gets the upper hand, universal means of social ingress! The molls who hung off chosen guys affect an indie mien as if to collude with these city feministas, so the lads just rate 'em Hard To Get. And Won! oriental artiste of desire, she should be be demure and cute - not so! She prattles to the populace, exudes rice-paper light for all, never offends their girlboy loyalty webs but lightly super-siren sexy is wild-awake and super-free! Sally lets the punters think she's slave-girl to the Asian Exotic. Her punishment is to fret inside, to dread as her own the fall of goddess Won. Now look at the competitive want that grabs our gang of thirsty new chums, excludes hangers-on, binds and entwines as the drink reaches deep. Two chicks suddenly risk unseemly attitudes of jive, the bar-girl cranks the music up and piece by piece the thing gets wild. Local elders slip to the other bar, and the field is clear for bacchanalian rites. No social strictures, adulty reference, social nuance, class, religion, cops, creed or stamp can tame a local mob in season: wild colonial boys and tarts, easy riders, city chicks in denim - all blossom into glazed revelry, wild breathless secrets told, hard skins shed, hides revealed, hot feelings offered and returned. Heated bodies touch, women go pussy-loose and brazen boys with leering breath and yellow eyes, bottles clutched and rolling, suck the nectar from each other's lies. A clamour of voices incoherent swells above the throng, shout to rough gods in hoarse inhuman song. The bar is tossing drinks about like sweets, and cash is hurled like confetti. Listless lives in farms and fields and fetid factories squander and nullify in a night to remember!

Sally sees things have travelled far when she's under a table with someone pouring liquid in her mouth and some other trying to yank her jeans off. She staggers up, sloughs off cries of protest from her five-minute paramours, stumbles past heaving couples on the floor and out the door, where the clamorous night hugs at her like a sponge. This is surely the epitome of grunge, she foggily reflects. But wait, her eyes adjust, and she sees a leathered figure by a wall. He's panting 'gainst it; underneath a girl is tending to his call. It's Won of course. Stomach reeling, she wants to pull her friend away. An irony you'd think since Sal might do as much on any other day. But Won is fragile, not of this earth, diseased, and needs a friend's protection. - *Jesus, what!* Binge the Biker tells her get the hell away but Sal persists, grabs his leather wrist. She's surely pissed! And now he curses, pushes her off. Grips the face of Won, pulls her like a rag doll over to his bike, fishes for keys, starts her up and Won climbs on, a spider on his back. His middle finger's all Sal sees as the couple roars out into the night.

She stands awhile in the dark yard, stares at the spewed-out tyre marks, wonders if Won will come back. An elder man in a hat steps out from the other bar. He asks politely, is she all right? She tells him yes. *Are you staying here?* She says she has no place to go. He hesitates, says good night, turns back. *If you need, my house is down there, couple of miles. My name is Edward Joy.* No thank you, she says. No more joy tonight. ... Sal wanders up the dark road. Soft warmth and soundless stars bring her back to her skin. Each step I take is a moment of the future eaten, gone... like telegraph poles on a deserted road. And there's nothing I can ever do. It's good, because there is no right or wrong. No-one really knows what they are, where they're going. No-one can tell it. I'm on my own. This is the dark life... and I like it. Be kind to yourself. You ARE. Have no debt. Take no revenge. Not on Jean Paul. Not on anyone.

While she's gone the bike returns. And this time Watto parks the Asian on the back of his monster and heads out up the road. So Matty's confused when Binge informs her Won is not about. She waits uncertain in the dark. At last, a rumbling turns to a roar, and the biker and his floozy turn up. Won steps off. She looks dishevelled, tired, distracted, pained.

Sally Bang feels the car keys in her fist and as Watto pulls his helmet off she punches his face BANG as hard as can be - just like in the movies. Fuck, sudden revenge! The bike keels over, traps his leg. Won screams at her, tries to pull the bike off. Exhaust burns into his calf. Impolite! Sally bundles her toward the car but Binge bursts through the pub door like a mad bull and Watto's staggering to his feet. There's blood to be spilt. Binge seizes her throat and shoves her over the bonnet. *Fucken bitch I'll sort you out.* But Won stamps him in the leg! which makes him buckle quick. Now Watto yanks his sometime lover by the neck; she chokes and falls! and now he comes at Sal with murder on his mind. She's spreadeagled on the bonnet again, her keys fall, he has fistfuls of her hair. But he grunt-squeaks like a startled pig when she shovels fingers in his eyes. And Won grabs at the keys, dives in the car, clump it forward though Sal is still pinned. Won brakes, and off she slides. *Get in!* Sal claws at the door, they lurch ahead and Watto is knocked clean aside. Crazy Won fishtails down the road, ramming the motor reckless fast. Sally tells her slow down, slow... and at last she does.

The lights illuminate a figure on the road. He slides by, possum-ghostly. Sal tells her, *Stop!* Won lurches to a halt, the heavy engine guns. Sal steps back down the road. The figure comes. It's Ed. What happened? *Can we come to your house?* Oh! Sure you can. Lead on, he says.

* * * *

Won's strength is gone, her nerves sapped to powder. The eyes in her rice-paper face no longer comprehend. He offers her shower and bed. She drops to listless sleep. *They'll come for us, I know they will,* says Sal. He tells her no, they're out-of-towners, won't know this place. *My friend is sick and she doesn't care. I think she wanted to infect those men. It makes me sick to think of it. I have to guard her now. I have to save her soul.* Sal starts to sweat, then gasp. The night has torn her nerves. She throws up on his floor, retches again and again. The collected tension of the days has cornered her. He wraps her in a blanket like a refugee. She falls exhausted on his couch. He watches her awhile, cleans up then kills the lights.

…Sally's dreams rush madly at her eyes. Armies of men are raining blows at her, she's constantly about to die. She struggles to breathe and somehow crawls away. But her body is agonisingly heavy. There's no escape, they come from all quarters, again again. For hours the dreaded violent spectres come - at every turn, whichever way - and she must fight and scratch and beat and massacre, warrior-girl of a hundred sordid skirmishes. At last she begins to clear a space - forever watchful, ever alert, with deadly weapons she never had at the start… And she jerks awake, sweat pouring in her eyes and chest. *Oh god. Where's this? Oh. The real abominable world…*

* * * *

The problem with the young, Edward Joy likes to observe (he has time to observe) is the extremes of passion, the absolutes they live by. Or if they have no passion they live by listless dropping away, and drugs and dirty dreams ambush their tender minds. Everyone has their crutch I suppose - some little myth, be it love gone by, hope turned to fantasy, God put on a pedestal and cultivated fetish-like. Or a simple wish to return… and that would be me. To return to days when you thought things were different, to a Narnia of the spirit where we claimed to be free, full of hope. And what of you, Edward Joy, hidden in your rural retreat without a link to past (because severed by you), without a way to say goodbye to undigested things? Your choice to be a hermit wasn't thrust on you; you ran. You thought 'here and now' should be anywhere, but you made it exclusive, saying it must be *here*. And that it must be faced alone. Who has the guts, the stamina, to face alone? You know the ache, know the contradiction. You said a ruminative peace would serve you well, but has it? Hell no. And where is my darling wife, where is she now? Does anything ever resolve? Ed, in your house today are kids - from the other world, where you used to want to live. You made a dirty pact with thoughts you couldn't resolve, with that ever-restless mentality like the sea. You tolerated it with sophistic balances but you were never a monk. How easily the old ache returns! Two fugitives from a soap-opera land at your door - and you invited them! You're seventeen again. As Faulkner said, the past is never gone, it isn't even past. And you embarrass yourself. *Well, I don't care...*

The girl named Sally has finally come round. She talked in her sleep. I would that she'd talk to me. Yes, she seems to want to.

* * * *

- Then I punched this guy in the face. Why'd I do it? I'm better than that
- What are you hiding if you punch a boy?
- Wanted to *kill* him. Kill for Won's stupidity! But all he wanted was a root and a good time
- If you don't mind me saying, you blame him for your insecurity
- Go on
- You want to be strong. Want to be impenetrable. But it's no excuse for insecurity
- Guess not
- And why? Because we're afraid to love
- But I love! No, I don't, I'm a selfish arse
- Don't be hard. We all fear to admit we're nothing special. Let's face it,

men want what they want. Like all of us. And if they can't get it they fear and they lash out. The drink is testament to that

- Yeah, we were tanked. But maybe I hate Won. Maybe I think she's a fucking fool. No, I love her. She's me

- Does she love anyone?

- Nope. Or yeah, just a sad vision of her dad. He died in a camp or something. He's her god

- You say she has AIDS?

- She says she has. Could be a sympathy trip. Never know with her. She's so unbelievably fucking unreadable. I know, 'cos I wanted to be unreadable. Loved the risk, the power

- She's taking a risk with those guys then

- Blow jobs only, she reckons. Shitting men. Do we want 'em or don't we? Do I hate 'em or don't I?

- Both, I'd say. Life's always both. Never black or white

- Is it true?

- I know it is

- I'm glad then. Too big to handle. I knew there was something too big to ever handle. Love that desert. Love to disappear. Get lost for good

- Yes. And then you can come back. And do the things you have to do. You know we're always failing, failing and dying. But it doesn't matter

- So we don't have to be any fecking thing at all. Cool

- We're cradled somehow

- I feel cradled now

- There's nothing to do, nothing to be, except be here

- And here we are

- Wish I could do it though

- You've done it

- I haven't, Sally. But you might. We're always at the start. All these years. Nothing ever passed, nothing ever changes. Young ones like you put me back at the start

- Me? Woah

- You're a bit of a sage and you don't know it. Good luck, Sally Bang

- I actually feel sorry for those goons on bikes

- Guess they wanna break out. Life 'll teach them what they need

- How will I save Won?
- Looks like her grief is deep. I hope she survives. I do.

* * * *

In the late morning, Won appears at the front door. Sally and Ed are seated at the table drinking coffee. She's been to the car, changed to a white dress, made up her face. Her black hair cradles her skin in a soft moon form. The eyes seem calm again. But her make-up is a mask; she's a night-survivor in the morning.

- I'm going for a little drive. Thank you, Sally darling. Everything is all right. Thank you, Mr Joy.

She walks out to the car and steps inside, starts up. The other two follow. At that moment a rumble is heard on the track leading to the house. Two heavy bikes curve into view. Won glances in the mirror - then jerks out and off down the track. The boys have seen the car, they're giving chase. Their bikes roar past the gate. Sally shouts into the air. Edward bolts for the house. The girl is running down the road. Ed charges out with a rifle in his hand, throws it in a truck parked by the house, starts up and lurches backward to the road. Sal turns, her face is distorted. She claws the door, he barely stops as she clambers in. This is grim, both know where this could end. They clatter onto the main road, still dirt. Four hundred yards ahead a demonic dust shroud curls backward from a scene of chase. They reach a ridge, dip down into a gully filled with heavy trees. It's hard to see but livid tracks are slashing the road in front. And then - Ed pulls his truck to a shuddering halt. His eyes have seen. He stares. Sal cannot see. *What? What?* She falls out of the cab, runs into the glen. Two bikes like angry flies are jerking on the road. They turn and roar at her, she falls aside, they grind up the ridge and disappear. Dust chokes her eyes and mouth. Now Ed is running down to her. He reaches out but now she sees: a smoking thing at the end of a gash in the road. The car is lying askew beneath a great white tree, its backside in the air. She skelters forward. Stops. Shall I look? Ed takes her arm, wants to pull her back. But Sally

Bang must etch the future onto the slate of her memory. That is the way of the young.

In the sardined car the unrecognisable form of a girl in white. Glass and metal and blood are everywhere.

Her lovely girl has fled to the other country.
Her darling father greets her there.

Be Yourself

- What I wanted to say... to say to her... was she was loyal to her father but not *herself.* What I mean is, she could be light and simple, kind of transparent, free, peaceful. Should've been kind to herself. I mean nobody owns you. Have to be yourself. She was like owned by an idea that her dad needed to be revenged. It was just an idea. She had no debt but she thought she had one. All that respect and none for herself. All for some kind of purity. Fake! ...Couldn't believe she was so disciplined though. She was like a martial artist. Did she *use* everyone she met? I've got a feeling she was trying to *love* them. Ed?
- She used discipline to try to love
- But while they were treating her like shit she let them, because we all need to like 'go through it all'. That is fucking strong. I'll never be lazy again. But did she love *me*, need *me*?
- Don't cry. I'm sure she did
- I'll never know if I was special. I need to be special to her
- Maybe you were beyond her. In fact, I believe you are.

After all the police interviews, media splash, parental calls and injunctions, Sal decides to stay with Ed a few more days. She wants to visit the death place after the circus has gone away, and carve a message in the tree. *Be Yourself*, it will read. Bereavement, like love, is a discipline, and Ed helps her through, as if she were his own daughter. In a strange way (he said later to me) he saw this event as a gift. It stopped him fearing the passing of time and the futility of worrying about it. And Sally appreciated him a lot. There was a bond, which made him feel special again. Perhaps she felt he was a man with true grit. It was a moving time, such as only happens once. The spiritual heart. Never too late. They took walks in the lanes and the bush and at night he fed her and talked to her about any and all things that came to her mind. He saw her soften and deepen. He celebrated in her the insight and ageless perfection of the young. It didn't even annoy him any more, when he smilingly dreamed she were his paramour in another life.

$$* \quad * \quad * \quad *$$

The Manga comics don't turn her on so much anymore - we don't need to live the desperate trials of Asian heroines - but Johnson Toast's video games are quite addictive. The muscly loon even turns up at her place. Sal puts up with him as she knows he's basically in love with her. And who can resist that, since she knows he'll never have a hope? She murders 400 men in a single session anyway. You gotta admire that, Johnson my boy. Juice Nick turns up too, says 'cool' too much, and Sal observes he's conspicuously reading a Russian novel about a loser who stays in bed for ever. *Oblomov,* he says it's called. The guy's got a brain but is really too spotty. He remembers the pass he made at her once, and won't be such a fool again. He won't forget to be serious and solicitous and sophisticated when he grows up and gets married to a girl who reminds him of Sally Bang.

Lotta BS and Rude Boy keep a wide berth. They've read the papers, heard the Twitter: they know a fake legend when they see one. Jealous tongues as long as your arm. It'll cement their relationship till kingdom come no doubt.

One day on a whim Sally sends a little note off to some koori settlement in the dusty outback. To her surprise it comes back, with a scribble: - 'You come see me some time. Soon maybe. Geoffrey.' Just might do that, thinks Sal.

'Speaking of 'come see me': That priest turned up again at our house the other day. He's something *weird*. All sorry and stuff about not telling mum he dumped the church and fled to New Zealand or somewhere, to go live with a flock of sheep or something. Now he's back. And man, does he ask questions. Wants to know everything about me! Quite flattering reely: what happened here, what happened there, what happened everywhere. I told him, go read the papers. Like a possum in the headlights when I said *that*. Threw him some juicy bones, mind. And a few porkers. Reckons he's gonna write My Story. Let him *try*. Wonder if his story about being my dad is a porker too. If it isn't, he'll have to earn it. Bit of fiction bit of friction. Boys love it.'

Then there's the tiny matter of the pregnancy. Jean Paul had a feeling something went down that day The Bang turned up at his place like Mata Hari and shooed him into bed like Venus rising out of Port Phillip Bay. Never got it out of his mind. Why would ya? Now he wants to fossilise her form and worship it in photographs. Crikey, she's a goddess. And if I've got the nerve I'll get her to marry me one of these years. It's gonna be a hell-ride since I never bothered to get to know her properly (too obsessed with *me* and that arid spirit path I thought I was on). I'll crank up the *artist* instead, keep the designer stubble (I know she likes it) and maybe maybe fingers crossed in the meantime she won't leave me flat-footed in the dunes... Weeks later it's confirmed. Yup, a little Bang in the oven. This dawns on Sal after she's thrown up 3 times in the school toilets. 'And I didn't eat anything macrobiotic. Better check it out... waddaya know! (mental note: don't tell Tiffany) What'll mum think? Like mother like daughter? What-evs. And whose could it be now... gotta be Jean Paul! Cool, keep him on a leash for a year or ten. Doesn't pay to let boys dominate. *Be yourself.* Besides, muscly old Johnson Toast's getting pretty keen.'

Postscript to a Fiction: She and Me

It's time for our hovering ghostie to take a holiday. Last thoughts? Why oh why must our heroine always lust for experience, travel further and faster than anyone else? Because she WANTS IT, THE ULTIMATE, NOW. Why should a ghost writer scrabble to catch that story? Because he needs to get to the end of his own daydreams, trawl his own undigested experience quicker than his limited time will allow. Your dog-with-a-bone writer wants to drag back time, count the waves breaking on the beach of his life. This heroine will to do it for him! So when do we get to grow up: when we see our youth is gone? Me, I feel like I was never young. When I recall I was 'happy' it was never it. When life was all promises, none were yet fulfilled. Sally sees already that no promises are fulfilled: when they are, they're not promises any more. No appetite is sated: when it is it's not appetite. No life is ever done because when it's done it's *no life*. Our teen affects to act it all out in a big flurry. Why the hell not? All we know doesn't have to be conscious, especially at seventeen. Sally sees (with crystal wit) that nothing's really here, and she cares nothing for it. I reckon she's a sage! I thought *spontaneity* was absurd, a dream in the air. But it's what I want Sal to want: to be spontaneous, which is supposed to be freedom: action without goal, creation without purpose, love without asking. Our past has no existence unless it's present; and the future is never, the future is *Now*. The spontaneous inherit the Now and they're unaware of it. This is a mystery, and a reason for longing, since it can't ever be. You'll say I look back and see some foggy thing I hoped was real, then force it on unsuspecting Youth in the form of Bang. Like the tarot's Last Card, she walks by the cliff edge surrounded by snapping dogs, her head in the sky. You can see why my heroine Fool will never die. Because I adolesce. The old nutter can't say goodbye.

And the fickle world won't care how Sally Bang treated her wretched ghost writer. She doesn't rate me (though I like a bit of rough). The first time I really faced up to her was just before she departed childhood for good. I dumped that Church straight after, and turned into the (daughter-obsessed) wannabe you've been putting up with. At first (as you saw) she sneered at my presence; later she decided I might be of some servile use. Finally she warmed to the idea of me and my kinky role. Wouldn't want her to actually like me or anything; that'd ruin our partnership. I got to challenge her - and we took pleasure in annoying each other with our embarrassable privacies, pained contradictions, untouchable brilliances, pathetic plot twists: hence the whole she-bang you just read. Before the Butcher came and whisked away my Irish Milkmaid (not that it ever would've worked, and besides, our furtive churchy arrangement was better) we had a thing going, me and little Sally in her pram. Now you see why Sal liked to say her elders were dead. She needed a *real* parent. It won't surprise that our relationship is a jealous demarcation of rights, since her chaotic surge to 'adulthood' is a battle for identity at the expense of anyone close (eg, me). At the big cusp that is sixteen we're delirious to escape people's definitions and enter the streams of chance. I don't mention we're also desperate to be accepted - then give the middle finger to those who'd actually accept. Effing teens. But since Sal made it to adulthood (you did sweetie, don't argue) and since the Prima Donna agreed to be chronicled (too damn lazy to write), it's *my* business to reconstruct her. She is the voice of my sixteen year-old heart, who keeps alive my hope of wanting more than I could ever get. I look back and see something I'm unsure I ever had: suddenly this chick wants more than she can ever have, and she dreams a whole bunch of things! So this fiction is born, ficted by a ghost writer. Who's writing who then? Is the man father to the child or child father to the man? She and I end up victims of each other's imagination, and (since we feud) begin to need each other. Whatever crap she thinks about me becomes *her*... and what I think of *her* becomes fiction (sucked in, Sal)! All that pained beauty, idolatrous wanting, piteous courage, knowing naivety, arrogant affection is mini-me. Our heroine's my drug of choice (bad pun, dad). She yells: you're a literary paedophile! (An ex-priest? Come off it) but why shouldn't I fool myself at fifty? Who invented the pantheon of middle-aged nostalgics: Bilk and Bazzy and Orwell and Edward Joy and Tommy and Greta and Kurt and Linda? Even Jean-Paul? ...Still, I'd be toast if she *went away*. Or like a bottle on a sea she'll always return... otherwise the news I'll report of her death will be fiction! Long may she hold up a middle finger to those who care for her, long may she seek her noisy quietus in a lonely place. And if I were to fix her identity, I'd have to grow up and die. Fixed equals dead. So never grow up, never fix.

Yet will she grow up into me? Bullshit! (she'll retort) There's a place in me nobody'll ever reach, that's never been exploited, that's always young, that hasn't *happened* yet. You are what fiction made you, I reply. *Fuck you, ghost writer!* she says. So: either this work of fiction will end according to the logic I set out or its heroine'll will her own surprise. Sal's last iconoclastic act of 'willed spontaneity' was... the pregnancy thing. A child of Bang! Now she can discover how it feels to give birth to something murkier than her own ego. Mind you, though she's not really self-centred and though she wills herself to care, I always liked her *don't give a shit* destructive act. The way she darkly cared enough not to care about any freaking thing. There's freedom there, a future! Personally I want her to have something beyond building the legendary soap opera of herself, beyond childy attention-seeking, beyond what the pressuring knowing world will make her into. I want her to have that *mystery,* lodged vicariously in the heart of me, where I'm inspired to rebadge my own history, never fix but dare my limits, heal up, dream an impossible spontaneity - at least in my fetid imagination. It's all I have, imagination. But it's richer nowadays. 'Cause I've been round the block. With Sally Bang.

THE ELUSIVE

COMMITMENT

NICHOLAS FROST

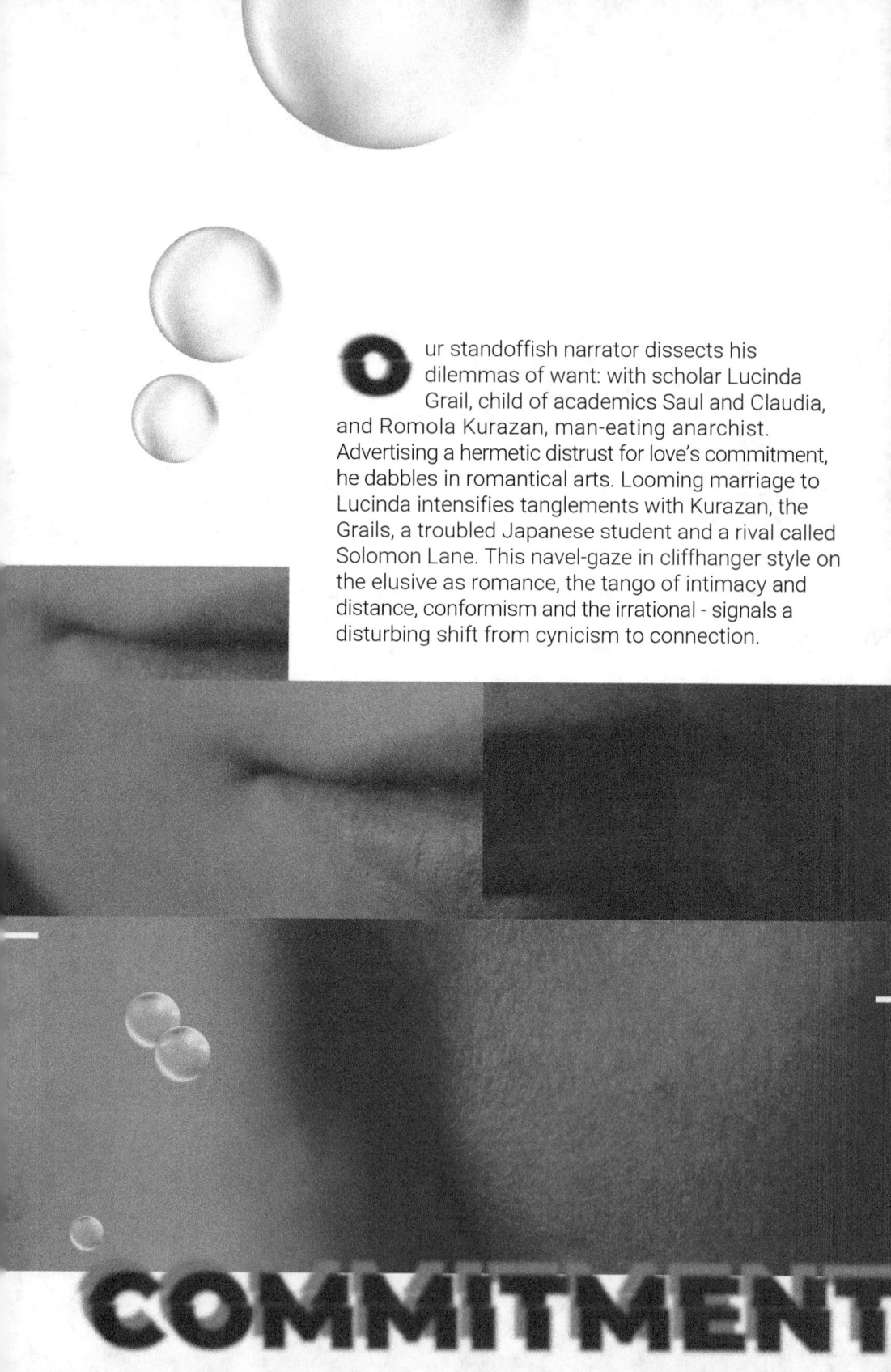

Our standoffish narrator dissects his dilemmas of want: with scholar Lucinda Grail, child of academics Saul and Claudia, and Romola Kurazan, man-eating anarchist. Advertising a hermetic distrust for love's commitment, he dabbles in romantical arts. Looming marriage to Lucinda intensifies tanglements with Kurazan, the Grails, a troubled Japanese student and a rival called Solomon Lane. This navel-gaze in cliffhanger style on the elusive as romance, the tango of intimacy and distance, conformism and the irrational - signals a disturbing shift from cynicism to connection.

COMMITMENT

Commitment

The Perils of Emotional Engagement My story is about a tangled psyche, and a web of people on whom I sprinkle its delicate contraries, who in turn inflict summary lessons on me. Romance and betrayal, intimacy, escape, the irrational: I hope these add up to an intrigue worth telling. You'll be asked to swallow overweening rants on the perils of emotional engagement and the limits of commitment and responsibility. It all amount to the progress of a pilgrim not a rake, to be sure. Your budding sage will encounter folks who interest themselves in the world so far as they can have sex with it, or who want to forensically study it, or who'd use it as a platform for their ego, or else weirdly sacrifice themselves on its altar of feeling. Me, I claim to want to fathom its essence for the sake of a persona I can bear to live with. You, reader, are bound to question my attitude to the politics of love and sex, but I'll ask you to hold judgement; there's always complexity, a reverse side to everything. I'm not begging to be liked, I'm looking for something else.

Above the Sea of Possibility Around the time that the fact of girls started to loom, I thought of living in a house of my own above the sea, wherein I'd inhabit society's fringe and dabble as 'master of hearts' to those who sought me out. In this vision there'd always be several candidates, who might share my house but never be encouraged to stay. Some would accept this with a tear or a guffaw and come and go. Others would appreciate the nuances of intimacy without commitment… though never commitment without intimacy, for this is cruelty, it seems to me. My fantasia flourishes by the sea, for it, though lonely, is the sea of possibility. I'll sit at a bay window in the cosy lee of a gale and watch how waves are whipped by invisible air, how they surge forever to the land and never alter it, not to the faintest degree. So I say, here's perfection! To be a hermit romancer, unalterable legend, closet sage. I'll never age and nothing need but poetry and sky. I'll celebrate loneness, and call it romance.

Contradictory Business My father, whom I never bother to know since he inhabits a similar arcane egoistic world, is an actor and sometime entrepreneur who dabbles by the name of David Darkness. No more pretentious name exists. Have you heard of him? And my mother whom he dumped when I was ten is also near-unknown to me, and I hear she lives in another city. These facts bother me not at all from the position I write to you in, except that they inevitably add to any sketch of aloofness I might reveal in these pages... So, following a humdrum higher degree in languages at a provincial university, and while doing the needed to secure myself in work demanding minimum effort appropriate to a lightweight personality, I took to casting about for useable friendships (read affairs) in the guise of barely being interested at all. Let me begin by mentioning two of these.

Following a certain public lecture by a certain big-headed intellectual whose daughter was present in the hall that afternoon, I by and by manoeuvred to share a coffee in a bar with said daughter, by professing in a beguilingly naïve but promissory way a deep interest in the subject it turned out she was completing her PHD in. As one thing leads to another we got to know each other better than I'd dared hope. Since I soon detected her inexperience in every sphere but the exigencies of Mind, I elected to 'put myself in thrall to her' to glean whatsoever I could of the delicacies of her chosen Art. She in turn responded to me with what I later discovered to be 'a quiet satisfaction'. I made up my mind there and then to pursue with her the 'holy grail of experience', wherever it might lead. Her name? *Lucinda Grail.*

At the very self-same time, due to sheer circumstance beyond my control, another woman by happenstance and serendipity crossed my path, and disliking what she saw doubled back to re-cross it twice more before I had the presence of mind to see what was occurring, and finally by hook or by crook - for she appeared out of nowhere and re-disappeared in a whirl and hubbub quite unlike the cool dependable wide-eyed Lucinda I mentioned - this second female contrived to turn up at my apartment in town, at hours quite unsuited to civilised repartee of the type I had become habituated to with the other, putting me in the angst of a dilemma as to where my attentions should lie, and then feeding this quagmire with quirky delight... a mercurial ingratiator called *Romola Kurazan.*

And, despite other contiguous experiments in the supermarkets of romance, it presently seemed as if the yin-yang force of the world were nudging, prodding me to engage in the curliest dilemma my hermetic psyche had yet dreamed up. I thought I'd tease you, nosy readers of the world, with my problematic privacies. Follow me then, as I dabble in the vacillatory business.

Lonely Lucinda   At such a stage in our liaison where we've begun to entertain thoughts of engaging in ways beyond coy abstraction, Lucinda has prepared a candle-lit dinner for two at her elders' home above the sea. In her apt, frugal way, my future nun of academe pursues a knack for cooking, which without guile she puts to my account. Where in the secluded footnotes of her heart does she yearn to partner the likes of me? What this neophyte knows of arcane rites of sensual dealing she's no doubt studied, since no social or family role has prepared her. Lucinda is poised for the role of 'untutored participant', along with a horror of clumsiness or failing to please. Tonight, 'prudent attention' constitutes her duty and contribution, for she knows I sense she's all at sea in the filigree of feeling and close-up dealing. She hopes and expects her man will 'pen the play, lead her in the pantomime of hearts, do the needed to achieve the assignation'. No doubt Lucinda has witnessed on sensual sites or at parties, close encounters of the corporeal kind: dabbling of hands, sensing of breath etceterah, from which she'll pluck jewels of apt experience to be turned into nuggets of metaphysic to be put in a book and savoured by those who'll applaud her archaeologic accomplishment in the field of sense-research. Cool bearded professors twice her age will schmooze with sensualist talk in her apartment, uttering close-lipped colloquies while her Great Work waters their idolatry. And she, slim-legged mind-aristocrat, all committed without commitment, receives the accolade, fingers it lightly and coyly constructs the literary odyssey of herself. I wouldn't marry you, Lucinda Grail, not if you begged me, you with your wondering eyes who puts me in the position of the missionary. Yet what would I commit, since we circle the whirlpool of commitment? You've set the candles with quivocal hands: how should I not notice? You've warmed the dishes with studied care: how could I not be pleased? Unstrategic in quietness, make-up lightly put, you assuage my taste for bossa nova. And what shall we speak of: one's late work? *Mais certainment*. But I'm distracted. Marital persistence with you... it tickles the vanity to think I'd be your comforter and saviour, but for how long? Till your scholary senses withdraw to the next lonely vale in quest of a lofty grail? You'd not seek it with me, though clearly I should be quietly flattered by association with the 'coming girl'. Daddy too will remind me of it, as he daily reminds you inside your lettered head. He doesn't think you suitable for husbands, self-seeding professor in his smug tower who never thought to endorse your luscious half-Italian mother as anything but a tidy exemplar of woman-as-thinker. Are we only daddy's girl then? Tradition's pedestal you certainly bow to. I picture you as a celebrated writer in a rarefied French film, where the exigencies of 'feeling art' for which everybody is to be bled, allow you (so continentally) to require a Special Fellow for bodily things you'd never stoop to understand. You flatter him to feel he's indispensable (maybe he is) but never grow up to acknowledge him (you lick the feet of an unforgiving muse) so that our partnership is as master and pet: you the vulnerable pet of course, with him so flattered to be your protector, all practical and steady - while you, lone savant, know and care for him but too too well... meaning never at all. Thus the minor artist in you calculates. But I've enough gumption to know I'll never play rescuer. I could rock up as your Heathcliff instead: rough aristocrat exiled from himself, despising connectedness, allowing you and me to bewitchingly fail, where we succour up a taste for sadness, interrupted wasted pleasure, bored martyrdom, tragic falling away. Great fodder for lonely learned meditations preserved in books! So, around and about we'll go.

But - Romola   Meanwhile, hard-nosed and youthy enough to survive our failure and label it experience, I'll be tilling crueller sexual pastures. Romola Kurazan! I wouldn't rely on Romy K. to endure my tragic pity for Lucinda, how I'm bound to her in some kind of long slow ruin. Shit-free Romola will demand: which of us does it for ya? I'll tell her: exploit both without the faintest loss of feeling for the other? As a man I can. Perhaps I'm an uncommon man? Alas, I suspect I am. Leggy loud Leo Romola barely bothers to put up with me, and any reason she would demeans her. Only nice girls are breathless to possess, and Romy's mystic mission is to slaughter the field. Knowing Lucinda and me (as she does) she'll guffaw as I sweat to serve two mistresses. That's the beauty of her, she never bothers to endure anything. She serves up a procession of tragedy-farce-grotesque but that headless energy of hers won't be flouted. She's like the murdering sea: love it to death but don't expect it to be other than what it is. Drown! - and don't quail in front of her either, or seek any vanity massages. Lose your mind in her Amazon of red hair. Survive if you dare. Win her grudgy respect.

But - one little thing. Romola has the hots for me; there's a thing about me she can't box up in her febrile nativist vision of the politics of sex. She stomps about and conquers, but only from me did she ever get the notion it's artistic to cry. I got a corner on her crying one time when she was flailing under some dreggy love affair - some manipulator who despised her headlong juiciness - and she 'got lost' for the first time in her strong-legged life. I who have experience at jilting tough girls (by calling them vulgar) saw her dilemma and exploited it. She let me save her from massive drowny death while I licked up her tiny tears. Romola's got the energy of a Minotaur but flails in the labyrinth of subtler minds (I flatter myself). I let her play the field but rein her in on invisible threads, while she deigns not to mess up our complicated rescue-thing. Rock up to my place Romy: you'll never get betrayed again. Or if I did I'd tell ya straight. She covets the role of betrayer too: to be exact, the exacter of advance revenge on me... But she's too hearty, too brash in her ways! Where's the cheat if nothing's hidden? My WYSIWYG girl can stray away, madly rut in her dens of sense, then turns her nose to loyal lurve which I serve up. All the other bastards are sport. Runs amok 'cross city and field but home and hearth is here! - a wink from me and a fake blush from her, and in our wide bed her splashy tides come to rest in our homey casual hot love affair. And I guess the wild world takes its toll. Never would she let slip any tantalous details, but ensconced in my bohemian loft she shuts out dirty life and nestles in cutesy reverence for 'our little here and now'. Naughty puss, no mistake. So no... we don't fool each other at all, at all.

Why are women never ideal? If they were I could ignore 'em. One's *conscience* with its sly little caveats, how did it get so jaundiced that even perfection mocks? Me, vain as fuck but made in the image of a God who suffers to lave the feet of callow dickheads: at least (kindly note) I see the irony therein. I perform duty as a young prick, that's all.

Entrée and Main Anyway tonight I'm charmed our willowy Lucinda can cook, since she barely studied it. Mummy's cookbook perhaps? Forget the cool genius your daddy broadcasts you as; I'm ready to mess with 'feral teen hiding under coyly virginal twenty-four'. Girls who don't know what they are? Hot. Also I'm betting she longs to be clear she isn't gay. Which makes me think of girlfriends. Keeps *their* names under wraps; not guileless there. This evening she's selected a knee-length blue dress which suits her, god knows how. Protected by the innocence? The legs are a mite slim, she's taller than average at five foot ten, spare in the disciplined way of a scholar. Could be sexy in a mortar board and gown. Light glasses when she reads betray her coy affair with books. Quite cool. Fullish lips, pools for eyes, breasts a touch prominent. Slave-girl shoes tonight, stylish in a childy sort of way. Best of all, that richy brown hair that tucks with comfort about her smooth neck and frames a guileless face… Yairs, this just-done PHD of yours is too too elevated for me, I confess. She knows I'm in jest but wants to 'explain'… 'mmm, post-structural poets fascinate, though we misconceive the term, which requires to be corrected, thus the world requires my services'. Does knowledge matter, I counter, other than being a stepping stone for ego and the world's accolades? She feels the critique (as a critic will) and turns her mouth from soft to ill. I fear her not; on my terms we'll discuss since I'm the ignorant party. She smells my arrogant side, and will ignore it since it matches hers. Hence we collude: our game is fought on other turf, not academic. This she sees and is all at sea. How can a girl of brilliance appear so fooled (take it from me)? Our options are three. One: she likes me more than she can say, and dares not think of the headlong rush were she to fall in love. Two: she has no imagination, thus secretly fears she's as stupid as the ox. Or three: the love phenomenon is too uncertain, too unrulily unkempt to fit with her studied vision, thus is absurd. Next scene. After the seafood cocktail I take hold of her wrists and kiss lightly the lips. She accepts my assay with a musy smile, and clears the dishes. I don't help. Something to chew on in her kitchen. And here's the point at which I feel The Pause. I slip to the door. She's over the bench, her back to me, richy brown hair about her neck. Here's the bit where I see our future: we have no children, we have our friends, she has her work, she cooks for me... The slender waif's afraid: beyond careful dishes she is lost. I admit my heart went to my mouth... I come from behind, put about my arms. She sighs. I kiss the tawny neck since it beckons. I'm practised at this. Yes, we're idiots in the world. One jewelled tear caresses the marble. I partake in her loneness. Is it not the function of knights gallant to rescue damsels in distress? Which bit would *you* respond to, steely intellect or lonesome heart? I feel the pull of the castle, of downy custom, imagining myself the son in law and forever (since daddy's approval counts for all) in receipt of her gratitude. Obloiging, that I am sirrr. To worship me distantly's her way of love, and I'll dig the hoary romance of it, the highland-snug romance of it, the quiet heroic of a husband's calling, austere duty to the eternal upper line to which she's tethered... There are selected tears. I'll never see this like this again. She can't fail now. Pity wins. Our romance is defined. Now Lucinda's exposed she'll always be there for me, meaning never. Ah, and pity's our pale aphrodisiac! Yet at this still point in her kitchen I think how a girl should *challenge*... To be told to fuck off, curvy arse in heels strutting away, running to stop her for crikey's sake, itchy physical tussle that morphs to huffy semi-sex - then being told you're still nothing, till next time, till she's back *on her terms*. ROMY KURAZAN's back... (though she's never there really, except in our psycho moments.) Yep, wankers like me need dilemma to feel purpose in this hollow world.

So so. Lucinda and me. We'll inhabit a maison overlooking the sea, not immodestly far from university, provided by daddy but later our own. I'll dabble in writing, teach a bit, half inhabit her social scene... and choof off to town where I keep a room in a ramshackle flat to remind me of student days, anarchy and all that. At first I'll 'teach her the arts of sense', and she'll attend physical class with enthusiasm, a touch fey and distracted but faithful to our private romancing. This will dovetail to her bigger romance - the academic, poetic, metaphysic - in a way that suits her 'sense of balance with a dash of wild sauce'. Once a week we'll dine with Daddy and Mummy and play family, content in the mouldy mould of Daddy. And she'll wink at me in their presence as if to say, we've our little secrets don't we baby! Little minx, your pussy'd better be wide enough.

...I steer Lucy to me. Her willow form bends. I whisper, let's have main course now. She leads me up her stair. It's inevitable, now she can win, time for commitment of every sin! The bedchamber looms. She's as if in a dream... 'Did this happen to mummy? He's fingering my dress and it slips away down... his hands grip my backside... we lay ourselves down... he's surveying my eyes, I feel all his weight... I don't breathe at all... his lips touch my face... his fingers are *in me* and I'm gripping his hair and we're rocking and rocking I love you I said, I said *oh fuck me fuck me till I am dead*! (did I really?) There's a point where the world is suspended in dread, then the rush, the *rush,* he's coming in me hard! And relief, relief - and then *there's no grief.* I'm a woman in love! He's quietening now so I hold him about, let my fingers imprint in his back. And we did it, it worked. All that fuss, all those years... Should I show him my tears? I can see he's quite pleased, with me here in my childhood bed. And really he helped me, saw all my doubts. So I'm safe... *And now I don't care. I'll dare, I don't care!'* The lady's keen, and love crazily happens twice. Then, surprise... we slip to a curious quietness, a half hour or so. And then, sudden hunger: back down those stairs, and we eat and we eat and we laugh! Seem terribly at ease, half married already. Lucy inhabits a different plane! And I like to see happy, certainly I do. Not the least bit mannered, spontaneously her uttermost best. Amazing how easy, an upper-class dream. And really I like her. This evening with you I'm slightly in love, Lucinda Grail.

Melancholic Winds   Next day we walk, on the headland and winter beach. Lucy's inspired and wants to report to her mother, but I insist our time is our own. Kudos to Claudia, but this stuff can't be shared. She sees my point (being nimble of mind) and lets me stow her phone in my coat. Wind tugs at our noses but we're incomparably snug in our love. On the shingly beach in the gloating tide we play games with the seaweed, reckless inside. *I'm a madwoman released from asylum,* she shouts. I weakly exclaim 'such beauty can't be trammelled or kept!' She appreciates my poetry so much that she wept... so I hold her as close as two bear-coats can hold, tell her *whatever whatever, with me you'll be free.* In turn she enwraps me, smile as wide as a beach, and I note her pearl-cut teeth each in each... framed like a dream by her broody brown hair, that in turn brushes lightly her blossom-pink cheek. And the wind sings our praise in indelicate ways, for two hearts so ecstatic this midwinter's day.

Fickle boys may dream up superior futures, but they'll base 'em on things that tickle them now. Such that love's eternal summer shall not fade, I'll settle for a pantomime of gestures. This wind is my compass, and rails where it wills. Impermanent, lost, it erases my soul! In the winter I stand, regarding the spume of the sea, affirming there's nowhere, nothing for me. To play this game or exit the world? (as the monks of far Iona did a thousand years ago...) At the razor's edge of dilemma is *romance* - it's what these choices have in common. If we combine them - live in this world but alone in grief - then romance is our succour, friend, relief. All a game, a trance, a buffet? I'll declare I'm 'eternal', beyond debt and regret. What about karma? It's illusion if we believe in nothing! There, I'm a sophist, like a Buddha of glass. I contain all the worlds. And I choose to reject 'em all.

Lucinda climbs the slope. Her shining face is held to me on a golden platter. Wind whips about her head and she waves to me like a ghost in the wind, and sun gleams on her slender frame, haloed against the sea below. Already this affair's gone too far to annul. These horses'll be ridden to their very deaths. May it be many years hence. Mustn't disappoint, nor tragedize, try to show respect. The thing is to entertain: the dreams fears and tears of the one who loves. Be present and absent at once? Melancholics crave the world as death, as fall; don't choose to be here, so let slow bone fingers reap their spoils! Yet at the base is shame: we daren't have our cake and eat it. Why think like this though? I'll have my cake and vomit it and gobble it up again! And in the roiling wind I'll laugh like a bacchanal, strike fear in the pretentious and proper. My pity drowns the world in pity's tears. I'm the boy god Siegfried, I'm licensed to arrogantly *kill.* To hell with domestic pantomime, tilts and journeys, bookmarks and jottings and critiques and dottings, dotings and gloatings, obsessions and blathers that feed the day-world, its pathetic book-ends, its duty and dribbling time, domestic crime, turds among teacups, banalities sublime. We two will succeed if we avoid to talk. My respect for Lucinda is as deep as it'll ever be, here on the cliff top framed by the sea, where we suffer no human nicety. In this sea wind we're not human; thus we might be more human. Not to be small, but to merge in this vast inhuman nature and its urgent whisperings of death, eternity.

Lucinda Learns Abandonment   Whoa, lighten up dude! says my Lucy, eager and lovely. Are you game? Here's a hollow, and no-one's about. She tugs me in; already she's unzipping. Shall I be ironic, block it for today? But cherie, you have to play! Besides, it's something new. Lucinda, brave as hell, strips naked in the tooling wind and laughs, like Botticelli's Venus in Seashell (minus veiling golden locks) so long as we ignore the goose bumps. *Now you!* she says, hands hovering about her pussy. My turn to strip. Wedding tackle: shrivelled like kelp. Can't we do it with clothing on? No! The point is we're naked in the storm! All right all right; she's in charge unlike last night. How far she came in the glaring daylight! One hoary greatcoat will make our bed, the other will be our shroud. Lucy's on top, her buttocks a-gleam, goose-bumped in the scrabbling wind and sun. She rides on a cloud of her own high making, whispers to the skies with enormous eyes, and the wind melodises her sexual lonesome song. But dangly limbs and rustling sex are not enough! I pull her roughly to me, she spreadeagles out and I journey far far in. Lucinda is shockingly lost. I taste her browny hair, whipped by the gale… we rock in love's eternity… and then she's come… and come again… and now she's gone… and gone again… as girls seem wont to do.

The reproachful wind ebbs and moans. I want to cover her thighs, soft bottom, back. She tells me no! 'I'm nature's nymph, all bliss and sorrow; we shall lie here, die tomorrow. And I love you today! With you I know I'll always be free…' Damn poetry! Or maybe she *will* transform to a conquering nymph of beauty and sex? Maybe if I let her, or imagine her so? Us dilettantes ruin integrity in our stunted souls. It's in my hands and I have to *fail*. Ugh, who'd wanna join a club I'm a member of? …So we're homeward bound. Lucinda's eyes shine like Venus, and she's certain I'm the sea-god despite my averted way of participating. Oh, she'll definitely live with that, in fact it'll never be an issue. Who'd want a guy who fawns and fondles when one is distractedly busy? The Boy is Perfect. I think even Daddy will approve. A trophy then. No! Ladies have to own their man. Let 'em. Applaud how she is when she's confident and smug. Sweet girl just had the best fuck of her life. Normal people won't see smug, just *happy*. Me, I'm not normal. I'm an aristocrat, see.

* * * *

I forfeited the phone back to its owner, now curled in her daddy's favoured chair overlooking the coast and conversing with mummy with enthusiasm. Should one flee back to town? No no darling, one's parents return tonight from their trip to Spain. A country one must visit! Andalucia, Grenada, Alhambra, the rest: classical glory, a civilised story. Lucy so wants me to greet 'em, wants them to share in our new novel thing. 'Can't we hide it? It's all been a whirl.' 'Oh baby, who'd understand? - but may'nt we give out a hint? It's like Christmas - and this me is impulsive, the persona you like!' She gazes with pity. 'True true, I do.' Now she beams, and her sensible beauty cocoons us right in. Cardiganed arms surround her peculiar boy. She offers lips and he samples. Time ticks. It's suddenly erotic in mummy's big lounge! Wee boy slips two digits in young mummy's cave. She frowningly guides them to home. He licks at her face, cleaves to her secret place. Her leg slips about him… oh slutty disgrace! *Please fuck me forever,* she breathes in his ear. His throat's gotten dry, romanticness tugs at his heart. Oh she's coming all over him, long, lithe and soft. His mascular straightness supports all her willowy love.

Could one get used to this? Quite possibly. 'So what time do they come, your people?' 'My people! You're delightful. At six. We must cook for them now!' Now Luce in the kitchen is supremely in bliss. It will never ever be better than this. Tag along like a beast to her siren song. Who knows, tomorrow I may end up her husband. Can any of it be wrong? Listen. To fail to plan is to be faithful to NOW. I'm here if my paramour wants me. Shallow reckless guiltless irresponsible empty: not fickle but ironic, in no way a fool. Eternity's a cloud of moments and I shall 'be here'. Shallow is all we are since this ghost world is nothing.

Enter the Saboteurs   I wander upstairs to check out my phone. Texts from *Romy Kurazan*. A thing has happened. She never says what. Can I claim I'm holed up at the Grail ranch? Huh, she knows it already and 'll turn up, knowing her. Bull in a china shop, I kind of love her. Righto, read 'em since we're tempted. *Yo there fuckbuddy, need a favour. My aqaintence* (spelling) - *a Japanese, needs your help. No friends no boyfriends, been here a year! Go see, talk, make her happy 0412 0412 0412. Do it for meee darling or else! PS: She's a bit weird. PPS: I'll be cheking your homewerk.* And another: *Get my message, you who need a penis enlargement?*

Reader, I shouldn't show you Romola's texts. They tend to show me as a dupe she twists round her finger. There's more to us than that, to be sure. I'm not inconfident, I let her tempt me test me roll right over me. And without boys like me Romy's pose as Boudicaa doesn't mean jack. I get it, unlike her other boys who sweat under its exigencies. Her irony sense needs an outing and I'm ironic and vain enough to applaud. Why doesn't she mix with other 'subtle' boys? Funny how the big wind of Romy's soul needs a fickle bendy reed like me to blow and blast - and finally to hang itself on like shreds on a wire. I'm her best audience. The Big Wind is nothing without things to blow away (I confess she blows me away) and being a Leo she needs applause. I don't compete, just see right through. She knows it so I give the *needle*. 'See babe, I've other girls you just can't fathom, like Lucinda Grail.' (She knows her, as it happens) *Grrr, then I'll add to your harem with a Japanese! And the Jap 'll do you in, then you'll see I am Queen.* Queen of my heart, baby? *Fuck off!* Nothing so romantic for arch-romantic Romy. Romy's lost in the world for all her chutzpah. Extreme extroverts never reflect on anything except to affirm their own existential posture. And witness the pity they feel for we more shaky mortals. But hey when *she* doubts, it's back to her boyo with the nihilist wit and ironising lip, 'cause she was all at sea for a minute or three. Why don't her other fuck boys appreciate her waif-like side? No worries, she knows I know she's the only thing that'll make *me* come in from the cold, forget the cool fish that I am. And she'll exploit that to the fag end. She and me, we get by. Our little hell ride.

* * * *

Back in the real fake world, Lucy is delivering the summons. Mummy and Daddy are here and I'm to come. Lucinda's flushed cheek and possum eyes greet me in the atrium. She pulls me with a little conspiratorial *hmmm* to the lounge where Daddy awaits. Daddy's grave gaze skewers me like a bug but I advance to shake his mitt anyway. Grave is the best I'll be getting for the time being. Vast intellectual Saul Grail, when he gruffly stoops to this level of earth 'tween empyrean thoughts, is stung to vanity by noticing his protégé is no longer all his own property. Especially when his Petal gazes at Alien Boy with a face somewhere between rapture and pleading, unconsciously clinging her hands in prayer to the parental gods of which He Is Chief. But then mummy comes in from inhabiting the scullery and saves little girl and new boy from ruthless husband, as she is wont to do being part Italian and a knower of lovers. She got the crucial text from Lucy anyway. Claudia Grail (nee Gonne) kisses both sides of one's face with an appealing moisture one cannot fail to note in such taut circumstance with Lucy looking on. To compare mother and daughter is instinctive to boy-lovers... as it is for mothers of girls with new boy-lovers, especially hot ones like Claudia Gonne (sorry, *Grail*. Gonne there for a moment). And daughter-lovers witness it all of a sudden, illumining their eyes to the enormity of the future. And father-husband of said luscious women, who hitherto maintained a dry counterpoint to their womanly juices, is dimly aware of a game-breaking shift that lurks from below in the form of me. At this moment then, it's as if we're required to join hands as a New Family, and it feels like putting on wet pyjamas. No-one fails to be embarrassed, but we all have our tricks. Youths and elders step up, like veteran actors at the first rehearsal of a new play while flailing to recall a familiar one. Lucinda our protagonist has a steeper road: she keens for lofty summits, being only twenty-four. Yet adoration lends her inspiration, and mother will obligingly serve the banquet as we speak our lines. For myself, I experience a sort of fearing joy at this novel experience, sliding into a whirlpool of family entanglement up to my neck. Spy and imposter in the rooms of the great: how accomplished am I at the dice game of appearing naïve? Pay attention now. Daddy and daughter are testing their arcane bonds.

- Did you really enjoy Spain, daddy?
- Indeed, though I fear the Moors have much to answer for, since their art exceeds our own
- Oh you mean since we're Christians, daddy
- I refuse to denigrate art as religion
- But for Muslims there's no difference, since art worships god
- I bow to my truth-goddess, who's a demon
- Spawned from your own seed, papa
- Don't talk of seed. It may spoil my digestion
- Don't they scare you though daddy, the Moors? They do me, being darkly un-Christian. Though, like the *Jews* they're hardly pagan either
- Our dark believers may have something to teach us. I propose a comparative paper on Muslim - Christian art. Would you write it for me? Daddy would enjoy it (he pouts)
- Too dry for me, papa. Care for some juice? (She winks, little show-off!)
- I see your attitude is somewhat loose. Could it be due to your new boy?
- Daddy! Don't embarrass.
She's laughing, but at this point I feel compelled to say that nothing could ever come between Lucy and her scholary career. Daddy ignores the obvious ploy.
- My daughter, if I could embarrass you we obviously wouldn't be sitting here with our young friend. I bow to youth's superior will.
(This guy is good! A mug of beer over his head would be amusing)
- My wife is Catholic you see, while I affect the pose of Atheist. My daughter is Confused. Hence it will be the topic of a book. You have a particular faith?
Me? I'm a killer of daddies, violator of daughters, stealer of wives, breaker of families, embezzler of hearts.
- Er, I suppose I have faith in my own judgement. Though my father claimed to be Catholic or Atheist or Buddhist as it suited him

- Hmm. And what do you judge my daughter to be?
- Daddy! Let him be
- No no, quite all right. You see Doctor Grail, your daughter is an entity I guess I wouldn't care to judge. But I can worship - she being superior in every way.
(This makes Lucy light up like a Christmas tree, then frown)
- I think what he *means,* daddy, is that I intend to be a scholar like you -
- But the fact she's a *woman* (I butt in) - will make her superior to any scholar.

At this point Claudia sees fit to wade in and deposit her bowls of nibblies or whatever. No doubt she absorbed the convo from the kitchen. I admire the classy rump under a soft beige dress… snugly evocative breast, rich russet shoulder-hair framing an elegant face…full lips, glitter-green eyes. Stop! with all this MILF talk. But, what clandestine roads does this woman travel with no husband in sight?

- You are a connoisseur of women then?
This from Claudia, who it seems, knows how to talk to a guy.
- Not really, I'm just too young! But I'd certainly like to study that subject. By the way, can I help you serve? (That bit sounded vaguely genuine)
- Come with me.

I'm thinking I'll come with her to heaven and back - and I yet might, since here's a girl who knows boys better than any of 'em ever know she knows. The fickle smile says: I know what the fuck *you* are and I'll deal with it without batting an eyelid. I ask her what's cooking. She says taste. I do, from the spoon she dangles too low. So I stoop and her cheek's a bit close. She wipes my lip with a digit, says 'Careful!' I tell her it's tasty, she says 'Should be, it's my daughter's.' 'Team effort?' 'No, Lucy likes it thicker.' (Fuck!) I giggle like a loon and she taps my nose with the self-same spoon. Suddenly I see she's a fun-loving girl. I note a pearl earring, tell her it's 'nice'. She says 'Two grand, keep fingers to yourself'. New tack. 'I see now why Lucy's a doll!' She tosses a wink beyond Mother's duty, tells me 'Handle with care.' So I finger her hair, say 'It's a tad like hers'. She pats my cheek (just the right level of sting), plants bottles in my hands, sends me packing.

A serious pro! So dinner goes off without further incident, thanks to Claudia's steadying hand. True, we all drink too much, as you'd expect since the rhythm of our play veers to the jerky and unnatural. But four clever folk can put on a show, and with the umbrella of irony full-opened over our heads, the sunny event succeeds. That is, no-one sees a need to reveal any more feelings than when they started.

The Moon's Madness   Late. Lucinda comes to me when the superiors have gone to bed.

- Thank you sweetness. I know they can be a handful. I'm proud of you, I really am
- Despite my cutty wit etcetera?
- I know you need to defend yourself. And good on you. I would
- Your mum's a sport though
- Sport? Interesting word
- Sorry. She knows how to… handle people
- But a little dominating, don't you think?
- Unlike dad?
- Actually, daddy under that gruff exterior is a kind man. You'll see
- I'll take your word for it
- Do, honey. I love you. But d'you mind if I go to sleep tonight?
- I'm gonna pout
- Tell you what. I'll suck you then I'll sleep. How's that?
- Deal. But don't make a habit of it. Could be contagious
- I won't, hot boy. So bring it here.

My Lucinda in her upper-middle-class fairyish way is a sensible sensitive girl. And I just know I'd be good for her, she for me. Yep, we can be a fairytale. And she sprung out of her reticence already! …I generously gesture to nimble night air over the headland field beyond the house, which crouches asleep. It's two am. Lit by a galleon moon, there's the vaguest path underfoot, sloping to cliffs where it ends abruptly, inviting unwary travellers to drop off and crash to sea-guzzled rocks. But such a heath upon a cliff suits me. I crave its solitude. The long-necked grasses bow under the moon's blade. Oh ghost moon, glitter on us all, we mourners in our seedless feeling. Aloneness tempts us, and love dashes our hopes. … Lucinda's downy moon-hair is there again under my fingers. How deftly she swallows the aching fruit of her night work. Looks up at me like Cat who got the Cream, her head framed 'gainst our night window with the black sea beyond. Lucinda lowers her luscious head and sleeps content with the oil-ed seed of her future husband still in her throat.

There's power in such intimacy… and abuse! Go back to bed, dude.

The Child of the Father   We must now report an incident that comes from that Other world, the Irrational, being as it is the fruit of Romola's machinations on the state of my sorry soul. Back in town days later I've called up Romy's Japanese (her name is Miki) and we rendezvous at a café. At first blush she's keen, affecting a chatty mild-extrovert tone that fills the space and averts embarrassment. Forthcoming in the manner of those who hide? The girl is apparently twenty-two, and clearly a princess with nervous energy to spare. I wonder what Romy put in her head about me. I'll not be privy to it (as part of Romy's torture method) but she obviously palmed the girl off.

- Actually, I have been here one year only. I like to meet people, yess. Thank you for coming today! You are handsome. Yess, people are kind but how you say, not so intimate. Maybe you are different?

Two black button eyes gaze out from under a fringe.
- So you study university, Miki?
- Yess, Master of Literature. Doctor Grail is my teacher (Whaaat? Romy!)
- Oh, I know that man (Don't say *that*. Idiot)
- You know Doctor Grail? Ah! He is great man. I am lucky! So strict and demanding, mmm. He challenges. This I need, to be tested! This is Only Way. Then I will learn
(Bit of the kamikaze about this chick) - I've only seen the Doctor around, I mean
- What is your father? (this is abrupt)

- How do you mean?
- What is he? Professor? Doctor? Scientist?
- Er, I guess he's an actor
- Actor? What kind of actor?
- Narcissist kind of actor
- I do not understand
- Me neither. Any reason you want to know?
- A father tells us what we are. In what class we are perhaps
- Oh. Well, mine would like to be upper, no doubt. Piss on the populace from a height in fact
(She gazes) - So you do not respect?
- Probably not
- So sad! Shall we come to my house for tea? I want to tell you things. About my family
- You don't like this place?
- I know this place. Please come.

Next stop, Miki's pad. The place looks expensive. Someone's paying.
- My father gives me all things. I am sorry for you that your father does not. Shall I show you? Look please, here are photos. I make tea for you. You are guest!

Miki bats her eyelids and bows her head in little jerky moves, as if someone is instructing her from the wings. Then she grins at me and stalks into the kitchen. I'm mystified. Is she fragile? I dutifully look at her album. There is nothing but posed shots. Three family members, some in traditional dress. All formal. The father stands erect in all of them, and the wife sits prim in kimonos of various ilks. The daughter, dressed in monotonous white with ornaments in her hair, resembles an oriental Dresden doll. Later frames exclude the woman, and Miki sits alone below the father's severe moustachioed countenance. None of this is at all interesting, except for a hauntingly impersonal wax-museum quality. Finally Miki brings tea. She serves elaborately. I feel like a statue undergoing worship.

- 'All very Japanese,' I find myself saying.

- Japanese are, how you say, stoic. We accept, never complain. But we feel. Ve-ry deep
- What d'you feel when a Tsunami rolls over you?
- We accept, but we feel. We feel.

There is someone she is talking to who is not present. Now she sits beside, taking both my hands. Slowly she bows her head; blinkingly considers a gravely important thing… now looks up, her black eyes like an Anime heroine.

- I like you. Trust you. You are so nice. Come to my room. We will lie in my bed. Come.

O-kayy, this is her routine then. She leads me to a room. It is unadorned but for a single picture on a low table at the bed end: a handsome young male Japanese in white suit and hat, haloed against the harbour of a city. Her bedspread is silver, a black dot in the centre.

- Allow me, please
- Miki, it's really okay. You don't need to -
But the Japanese girl has made up her mind. I am her accessory. What? Traditionally one would regard such a girl as a sex aid.
- I undress you. So.
Now a pantomime, geisha-style, of disrobing. Like a beetle at a wall she goes about the business. Clinical precision: first the man, then herself. Now she must lie within the sheet. Now he must lie too. Here we are. It's solemn and sad. Miki awaits. I turn to face her. She lowers her long lashes under the black fringe. What to do! Touch cheek? She closes her eyes, breathes. Lengthy pause. I'm feeling annoyed! I climb on top and pin her arms. After a tiny pause, as if to make a decision (everything is artificial) she flicks her black eyes open and glares.
- *What are you doing?*
- Going to have sex I guess
- I do not give permission!
- Cut it out, Miki (I still haven't twigged her game)
- We do my way or not at all

I stare.

- Sure. Your way.

Now she smiles like a wee girl. - Yesss, my way. I know what we must do. *Like you have made me.*

Ooh, I just *grocked* it. That young man in the photo - has to be her *father.* Ugh, what next? Miki decides.

- I trust you. Here for you. All of me. Do you want me?

Black locks splayed over white breasts are not to be resisted. Female readers, indulge me a moment. I can't say how, but it feels… abusive.

Miki proceeds - to a new phase of her illness.

- You see, look look! I touch all over my skin - and here - just here - as you taught me… in the *secret places.* Are you happy? Yes? Now take pillow and put on my face. Take it! Put it! (Umm…) I say you will do it!

So I have to perform. I do it and with a muffled shout she kicks out from underneath right in my own secret place! I lurch out of bed, shamble off, stunned. She's coming at me. Slams the bedroom door. The key in the lock: she turns it, snatches it out, clutches it to her breast.

- You see what you make me do! You see!

And she takes that key and shoves it under, into the secret place! Eyes are unholy wide. I tell you I'm getting pissed.

- Get it out. Get it out! Aaagh! Take it out of me!

She starts to *scream.* Who will hear us? This is the trick. I'm her *Rapist Father.* Here's a sudden fucking nightmare. If the police come how will it look? Got to cool this down. But agh my sodding crotch.

- All right! Little Miki, let me take it. My little Miki, let me take it away from you. Shall we lie down now? Shall we lie?

- Will you? Will you do it for me? I will let you. If you tell me. Tell me!

- Tell you what, Miki darling?

- Tell me I am the only one

- You are my only one, little Miki

(Now we lie down) - Say you are my daddy. My daddy!

- I am your daddy. Yes

- I hate you, hate you

- Yes, but you should let me, let me

- Yes, I will. I will. Come to me
- There now. There. Will *you* take it out?
- Do you ask me to?
- Yes… my little daughter
- So. This for you. (She puts the key between her lips) Now kiss my little pussy mouth.
I do. And I take that little key in my fingers. But we're not out yet.
- Shall you and me lie awhile, Miki?
- Will you lie with me always? Until tomorrow comes?

I lay her down, arrange her hair, pull up the covers. Wait. She's breathing soft and low. Seems asleep. Time to bail. Discover my clothes… softly unlock the door. Exit.

Take No Responsibility　　The very next day, black-eyed Miki calls me up! Seems altogether calm.
- Did I upset you last afternoon? I'm sorry, so sorry. Please forgive. May I see you today? (Pause) Oh, may I?
- I'm called out of town. For several weeks.
Following this lie, I fight to ignore the regret in her voice.

And then (swipe me with a spanner) Romola calls. How'd it *go* then? I hint that Romy shouldn't wanna know. Girls think they own ya though. She announces she's coming. Soon, she enters in belligerent mood (a mood I dislike).
- You know she has a mental illness, right Rom?
- How might I 've known that?
- Female intuition. Set me up for a fall?
- No way. Are you sorry for her?
- Almost castrated
- Then you'll see her again!
- No chance
- I say you will (She gives me the *look*)
- And Romy gets her way. Are you gonna stay?
- Gimme a reason
- A Japanese one?

- Clever boy. See, it matters to me that you Feel Stuff In Your Life. (She pins me to the sofa)
- How d'you know I don't?
- You'll feel *this*. If I squeeze more
- Careful sweet Romy. There's a limit
- Not with you.

Huh. And our fizzical encounter follows. Which allows us to discuss our *special dilemma*. I quite regularly chat with her while we're doing it. She enjoys it for some reason.

- H…oww! much sadism can a boy take? Brutal Romy likes to test (don't squeeze!) but if she's got a bee in her fanny why dump it on him? (Ow!) How long d'we ignore that Romy 'doesn't do intimate'? Kills her to think she's just a *game* to me. Galling to be taken for less than what she is. Intimate strangers… who never… let go! Just wants to play Angry Mum (not my nuts, woman). Okay, I'll see Jappy again but I won't let *you* in on a thing. Beg for yer supper since you need to prove what a bastard I am. A bastard you *want*. (Don't bite!) One of us'll end up killing the other. Or I just might be in love with a *gyppo's* daughter. (Izzat your new Brazilian?) My Romy's in love! Huh, wanna piss on that too? Ugh! *Bathroom is over there, bitch.*

Etcereraaaa. Ruffian Romy needs to prevail in our slimy-sweet masochism tango. Discussion on me must continue post The Act as well. She's gonna force me to care, gonna be my conscience. Sure, takes the onus off me. Attention flatters vanity. She's all bluster anyway. 'What you need dude, is not just to be abandoned, which is your way of getting attention. What you need is to be ignored and forgotten.' Dang, she's actually right. Romy is preternaturally stern. 'Think of aging, my irresponsible spoilt friend! Martyr, outcast, loser, tramp: none of 'em 'll be any use to you *then*.' 'But Romy, I'm required to be narcissistic and spoiled since life showers riches on me without cost in the form of you.' Krazy Kurazan says 'Watch Out'. 'Okay, but my doll Lucinda will feed me and serve me like you never will. Which of you will gimme my fill?' Yay. Me one, Romy nil.

The Green-eyed Monster I don't like to harp on the topic of abandonment, but time has come to prepare readers for a shocking little incident that occurred preceding my MARRIAGE to Lucinda. Yeah, the marriage you assumed I'd avoid. Truth is, I'm not a principled guy, on principle you'll recall. Now I'm not sure if I taught her or if she taught herself, but Lucinda was inspired by our sexual coming out to the extent that an unseemly unseen world suddenly revealed itself to her, whereby her round eyes got the bug to *experiment*. I refuse to monitor how I feel about this. Grimly glad that reality has struck? No luck. It isn't just 'men in general' Lucinda is ogling at (who'd no doubt resemble me) but a particular one! called *Solomon Lane* if memory serves... and it fucking does. Yep, a Jewish fellow. An outsider in the vein of me, I'll vainly suppose. Resemblances seems to glare between him and me, and therein lies my succour: that Lucy's in love with an idea, not some other fucker. Here's an irony: maybe jealousy will ensure commitment! I commit to not much (as you'll have grasped) but suddenly jealousy's got me by the balls. I'm blackmailed, stymied, caught in a knot, castrated, impaled: what the fuck has he got? Superior nose for chicks maybe? And the worst worry of it is: how well did she know him before she beckoned at me? I shall find out. And how did all this dribble out? We need to rewind.

Goodbye, Fairy Tales Right after our first parental party at the Grails I had every reason to think Lucinda was in love with me, or at least in love with the idea of me. All right, she was in love with the idea of love as maybe embodied by the idea of me. I told you, her ideas are 'academically romantical'. She would ask: is there a true emotion in this world that cannot be set down in a book? I beg the question since I tell my own story here (without committing to feeling). Her incisive mind roams lands of conjectural romance, and must include our tryst in her vision of life as literature, as fiction. At the same time she wants a fairy tale. Why not, bless her. As handsome prince I might appear, since for all her grown-up theses she is in the land of fairy faeces. And with a coming marriage, we need all the fairy tales we can get. Yes, I patronise her: she who wants to be feared as clever and wise, to distinguish verities from lies! But Lucinda's still unequipped, since she never sweated in the labyrinths of a sordid relationship, with me for example. She might grow up then!

Instead she's always been lauded as the fairy on the Christmas tree by her criminal Daddy, her supposed champion who in fact declines to take her seriously since he won't take Women seriously, including his Wife. By the way, he and I have sexism in common, and he's as patronising as I am. There'd be more parallels I suspect if I dared to look. Anyway, Grail wants her to be 'mature scholar in his own image' but still preserve his little girl. Maybe I should be keen to prise her away. Only way to do that is, don't be like him. But can I be bothered being different from him? Ha ha. And can I be bothered turning Lucy into a project? Do I want her to enter the labyrinth of a sordid relationship with me, and all that responsibility? We'd both have to grow up. Can't we just keep the fairy tale? But with my vanity (complacent repose) could I cope with that either? Cripes, I lose on all counts: (a) too sceptical (b) can't be bothered. Let me then transcend Jaded Adult and 'find the child in me'. How to become naïve again? 'Feel', 'connect', believe it's all real? Lucy wants to be both naïf and all-knowing adult. Maybe I shouldn't disturb since 'childish adult' suits me better. No! A gentleman must respectfully consider the needs of Lucinda. While she wants romance she needs the 'mature' version. But it can't exist, don't ya know! Plus, any grown-up girl would never cling to a naïve guy in the form of me. That means I'll never replace daddy. Sadly, Lucinda and me can never co-habit as children. We are led inexorably to do the adulty thing.

To Commit Uncommitted So Lucinda and me the very next day set our course, upon the shingly beach under the downy headland, along the narrowy path of the secrety way, through crevices only the rock crabs know… on our private coast at the cusp of sea and sky, where our troth will be plighted, encircling a miniscule lie. I told you it's possible to be happy in the hinterlands of *casual* love, where we keep to our privacies but meet to share rituals. Can human beings ever merge? We are alone: it's silly to believe we are 'as one'. Such an idea interferes with simple affection. Cosily-shared romance is not real. Romance must be tense, lone, unrequited! Both of us know it. So we're cosily matched, in our studied but cute little love.

- These last days have been magical (she says)
- Do you think our days will always be?
- How do you mean?
- No, I really hope they can be
- But you fear they can't
- In differing ways they will
- Do you believe in us?
- Certainly I do. Though I'm naturally scared
- I'd think it natural, if one cared for someone
- And I do, definitely I do, can I say?
- I believe you can, mister Formal
- Now you've embarrassed me
- Can't think why. Are you lost for words?
- I think I am
- Let me help. *I love you, my baby*. Now say it to me
- That'd be cheating. But I do. Yes, I love you, Lucy
- Is there something else?
- Will you *marry* me then?
- Yes, I will. …Yes I will
And a pause.
- And would *you* marry *me*?
- Yes I will. Yes, I will.
And a beautiful pause. And she sighs. And some tears. And I hold her. And I set her down amid the stones on the beach in the winter. And she holds my lips to hers for a longish time. Then we lie side by side and look up to the sky. Later we walk, and we've both relaxed. She can see I'm amazed at my courage, and laughs. Don't worry, I'll save ya, she says. We'll save each other, I reply.

There's a way in which nature fills all spaces, and we walk for miles. The gulls would have noted two human people, looking far ahead, measuring distance with a brittle and studied respect, helping each other cross crevice and rock. And the sun in their hair haloes the beauty of their novel affair: solemn, solicitous, private, aware… of the distance that marriage demands.

* * * *

Following this betrothal event, it's hard to believe that I barely saw Lucinda for three weeks (during which gap I first encountered the Japanese). Except that a family pow-wow was called that very night, and Saul and Claudia were delivered the news. Neither are fools to be sure to be sure - but grace personified, and Lucinda is childily nervous (as always around family matters) so they cheer and toast her decision, and I gratefully help them out. Claudia regales my cheek with selected tears, and Saul delivers a comradely pat on my arm. Promise of things to come no doubt. Later Claudia calls me outside to the headland, away from Father and his Beauty and their intensified tete-a-tete. The wind has dropped. The moon is there. She takes my arm.

- So now you'll be my son
- Claudia, I know it's sudden
- She's my darling girl. Will you treat her perfectly?
- Maybe I'll let you be the judge?
- This is not about me
- Why, Mother to be? We're going to be friends. I can talk to you
- You know you can. If you really need to
- Tell me what to do
- You're not scared?
- 'Course I am. Freaking out
- Come here. (She studies my hands, then pulls me close) Listen to me. It's hard at first, but in time you'll come together. I'll help you both
- Thank you Claudia.
And I kiss her just near her mouth. She regards me for two seconds, smooths my cheek. Takes a step away.
- Oh, look at the moon on the sea. It reminds me of home
- This country's your home, isn't it?
- It has never been, though I am loyal to it
- Perhaps renaissance art is your home, since it's your specialty

- It is, but I crave the *physical*. More than my daughter perhaps
- What kind of physical?
- The water, warm hills… lush valleys of Italy, stone uplands, vineyards, palazzos, the pots and the wine. Romantic fool, no doubt
- You cherish romance then
- Why not? Do you doubt it?
- I'm not sure I know
- You are too young to doubt.

She regards me with a summery smile. Gorgeous woman of forty-six who's seen so many things, and felt them all.

- True, I am.

And one I couldn't touch with a fifty-foot pole. Unless she touched me first.

- Shall we walk down onto the beach?
- No, young boy. You and I shall never go there.

And her no-no remark sends a shimmying spark right up my spine. But she walks away from me.

Back to the manse. I resolutely follow.

Faithful Friends   How do I tell Romola Kurazan that I her amigo am engaged to be wed? She'd think nothing of tossing little bombs at *me*. Miki the Jap for example. What'll she try to do next… though surely she gets it? Lucinda is her opposer, her 'shadow', all that. She's not intellectual, old Romy. But don't underestimate! She blows where she wills like sere winds of a desert. Oh, she'll claim I'm her compass in a void that she sniffs out from a hundred miles then must come a-hunting even when it presages her *doom*. But it's me who feels like prey, the assailable fool who got engaged. Imagine marrying Romola! She'd pay me attention in ten-minute dollops at random for the rest of my days. And she'd make me confess every itty-bitty thing to her and give zip in return. Finally she'd spit me out all over my bedroom floor. Reader, remind me never ever to confide in her. Remind me when my head's on a pike.

Lucinda's gone quiet, except for a few fervid phone tete-a-tetes where she comes across a bit breathless. Still, she takes care to talk of thoughts, to encourage, to 'be there'. Willing bride, duty and presence personified, 'has her plans but isn't revealing yet'. Tells them instead to Lilian Bourne and Tessa Branagh, two of her (and my) better friends, both married last year and free with advice.

Now three weeks have passed. Ms Tessa Branagh calls up one morning, informs me Romola Kurazan has 'sent her a text'. Branagh remarks: how curious it is! that Romola would ask about *Solomon Lane*. Do I know this Lane? A Jewish friend who was close to Tessa in fact! Well, who once was her *lover* (she admits) at the time before her own marriage. All 'amicable' now, but a curious thing. Might I care to slip over for a chat? In that silvery Tessa-tone we'll surely discuss nuptials as well, since she is to be maid of honour.

Soon I'm present with Tessa, at her impressive house in the leafy part of town. Husband's away, no-one's about, and we sit in her garden porch. She's donned subtle makeup, a classic scent, and I'm sipping her tea with a friand. She exhibits cool perfection in the upper-class way, with a knack for explaining without explaining. The sort of girl one could sit near all day, admire in her bath, get close to in the blueness of her pool. But her mood today suggests cause for discipline.

- Now darling, are you comfortable? Because a little thing, we need to discuss. First, is Romola Kurazan a friend of yours? If she is, I'm not sure she's *reliable*
- Will you show me her text?
- No, my sweet, but I will say this: people like Solomon Lane, whom we *think* are clever or gorgeous, I'm not sure we'd trust to marry
- You were lovers, you said. Why didn't you -
- He was present at my wedding. Surely you remember? Son of the Dean of Arts and a student of Doctor Grail. Soft-spoken, appropriately handsome?
- Ah, I begin to remember. (I don't) So what's his crime?
- I'm desperately sorry to tell you this, but feel I must for all our sakes. He and Lucinda are having an affair.
Pause! She regards me with her scrupulous stare.
(At last) - What's your evidence?

- Not your Romola girl, that's for sure. I tackled Lucy myself, and she confessed. I can see how it happens. And I hardly approve
- You've done it yourself
- Do you *want* my help?
- What kind of help?
- What d'you mean? You need to know
- Do I? What's *your* intention?

Oops, we're suddenly claws-drawn. Cool it down.

- All right Tess. I'm sorry, thank you for telling. You're right, it's quite strange
- Would you like my advice?
- Please. Go ahead
- Go to her now. She's waiting. And she'll tell you the truth and she'll ask for forgiveness
- Ah! Tessa the faithful friend
- I like to think I am.

And… now we stand up. But she hugs me. Pretty close.

- *Try* to understand her, darling. I know I do. She fucked up, all right? Easy to do. C'n happen just like that. Mmmm. (Now she breathes in my ear) And do stay away from *that girl* - won't you?

She kisses my lips. A hot little pause. Incipient heat below. Our breaths mingle. Then she leads me to her door… and gently pushes me out.

Nice work, Tessa Br'naaagh. Sorting out my basket-case wife-to-be through your girlies' network. Atoning for your sins! Reminding me of mine too, no less. You who'd lecture about Romy when you and me were eyelashes away from committing an evil sin. What a piece of work is Woman.

I'll bale up this Solomon Lane though. Should be a doddle to stalk a colossal hunk of spunk like that. Nevertheless, I shake within…

Anarchy Will Save Me   Whether a thing's done or not done changes nothing in heaven or earth! None can control the world for she is infinite in her subtlety. What fool will influence destiny? Even as we manoeuvre our clever positions, the forces of consequence invade us like clouds of flies around shit. Oh but it's good to know that no matter what we do, life is our teacher. Even if we live forever, or half live at least, we can be sure it all works out in the end. Ughhh! Will I change the course of things… alter the wetness of the sea, scatter the wind from these cliffs, defy this winter coast? Anarchy lends me courage, and today I baulk at nothing! *Oh crikey. Here we are already.*

Mon Semblable, Mon Frere Lucinda's Jew boy opens the door to his cottage. Turns out to be hardly a mile from her elders' house, so I introduce as 'friend of the Grails' which gets me through the door. Grand view of the sea, eh what? Now that I see him up close I remember him. Odd that I'd forget. He regards me solidly in his room ringed about by books. Cosily unkempt, but he's got the looks… air of containment, moves with ease, steady eye, measured tone. *Tessa Branagh sends you a greeting, Mister Lane.* Ah, Tessa. Is she well? *Not entirely, no.* Oh, sorry to hear… He appears to listen as if all the world were an inevitable consequence of himself. (If I mentioned his mother were dead I expect he'd nod sagely and thank me.) Why did I blank him then? Is he altogether too solidly mature? Now he waits for me to continue. - Er yeah, Tessa has some news. (Why dissemble with a guy like this?) She regrets to inform me that you are… having a fling thing with my fiancé Lucinda. (And it is almost a pleasure to tell him.) Yup, his eyes definitely widened. - Lucinda? I didn't know… that she was your fiancé I mean. (Whose might you think she was then?) I… never actually asked the fellow's name, you see.

Should have denied you even knew, you idiot. I would've. Speaker of qualified truths, Mister. Not a Yiddish moralist at any rate. So, Lucinda told him she was engaged, but not that it was me. Me, a man of consequence! Who dares to not have knowledge of me! What difference would it make to him though? Or maybe he does know and merely tortures me. So you're a Jew, I say. He blinks. *Why mention that?* Well, you'd have a couple of scruples would you not? At this point we seriously look each other in the eye. He asks me to sit, then says: *I'll make us tea.* Something absurd about this! He steps to his kitchen, solid with style. Appears vaguely troubled at least. So, Lucinda felt *guilty.* Spoke of a fiancé. That makes things better. Or worse! Can't decide. I find myself noting his sea view. Best I've seen on the coast. I almost bloody compliment him on it. But he's back and he says: Are you sure you should marry Lucinda? And his manner *excludes* me. Fucking egotist! (Truth is, I misconstrue his attempt at complicity as an insult. Too late) I find myself growling: *Do you want me to ruin you?* Right, that's stupid. He overlooks the absurdity. *I'm not so sure you could...* is his reply. This is going to take effort to maintain the rage, or at least the veneer of contempt. Would mild disapproval suffice? Thank god my vanity lends me weight. So I stand there, uppity and silent, and he drops his head. And he *apologises*. Fuck.

- Is it over then? I say.
- How can I say it is? he replies with delicate gravitas.

And we're complicit in our dilemma: neither of us wants to give up what we know we shouldn't be having. As vain and narcissistic as each other. We're both cunts! And we might have been friends.

Whether a thing's done or not done changes nothing in heaven or earth. What fool can control the world? No matter what we do, life will be our teacher...

Getting out of there, I stop in the lane and admire his damned view. But out of his presence (which was weirdly calming) I stoke up the rage again. Damn the cow! I put major effort into our love affair. Agreed to marry her for fuck's sake. Does she know what sacrifice that is for me! Who does she think she is dealing with? Dash it all, I don't just marry any tomasina dicklicker or harridan (oh, that's quite funny). Slow down here. All he's done is show me my hollowness, my fear of commitment, how I feel sorry for myself. But he excluded me, *they* excluded me, and that I cannot stand. I'm the one who excludes! Or maybe I should suck on it. Teach me a lesson. Good for me to lose once in a blue moon. *Blue mo-oon, you caught me standing alone...* Shut up! What about him? He's worse, for all his sexy measuredness and his manly dependable shit-fuck. He's getting a massive free kick! Better save him from himself then, make him lose. If he's as vain as I am, I'm doing him a favour.

My Guilty Child   Etcetera etcetera. Suddenly I find I'm at Saul and Claudia's. Ooh would they be home… would one talk to them… will *she* be there? Nnn, can't face this one. Turn about. And Christ, there's nowhere to go. What is it when we don't even know if we should feel sorry for ourselves? The lid's coming off my box. My melancholic fatalism is not working. My studied irony is not working. Superioric spiritualism not working! Romantic narcissistic farawayness - not working! I spot the beach path. Down, onto the shingly sea strand. Stand and gaze. Noisy waves don't give a damn. Cold wet splatters the rocks, brown seaweed slurps and eddies in the surge. Inhuman world, you really get to laugh don't you? *And, but - there she is.* Curled in her blue coat in a little hollow in a rock, her knees scrunched up, her bonny brown hair whipping about her, staring lost at the soupy sea. Regard her thus, a little wee while.

She turns, and sees me. The embryo releases. Stares out at me. Stands, totters forward like a child. I imagine her straddling the other's body. It stabs me. Her white sea-hands twitch by her sides. I reach out with mine. She accepts. The wind lends a moment's impersonality. We step like dancers to the strand, that crunches unstably underfoot. Eyes set far back in sea caverns of her white face, she looks out to me. I've no idea how to reach or rescue. I see how eternity annihilates our lives… What is past is lost, as this moment shall be. What to do? Accept the futile-forever, carve out our little cave of consequence. So I hold her… as close as I dare. Has she decided to hate me? If she has, you never could tell.

- *I'm so sorry,* she says in the whip-wind.
- I went to see Lane
- You saw him? But how?
- I wanted to know if he's better than me. He isn't, so I came.
That's it. If I can be superior to this life I can do anything. It's detachment I need.
Then she says: - I *will* marry you. I promised you. If you'll still have me, still marry a bitch like me. I'd never hurt you again
- Don't speak too soon. We have to stay real
- You're trying to help me, I know
- I will if it makes you real. Though I'm not a saint either

- Why, did you betray me too?
- No, I didn't. (I think I believe it) But you owe me. No, not fair, you don't owe me. I'll never betray you, not really. I can promise it.
We stand and collude in the spume. Puts her browny soft head on my neck.
- Shall we go home? she asks.
- Yeah.

Just as guilt seeks punishment, she clings to me. And I help her do it, all the way home. In the most delicate way I've ever done.

Betrayal for Own Good   By and by it occurs to me that the simplest answer to all this guff is (wait for it) pre-marriage nerves. Such insight momentarily plugs a yawning gap or two. And helps me deal with Romola. We've not yet remarked on her role in all this, on her clever liaison with Tessa etcetera. They fully loathe each other no doubt. Or on Romy's spirited concern for my future, to be my (wait for it) 'moral guardian'. Betray me, punish for my own good! But what does secret agent Romy K get out of it? She gets *me*, but needs to betray me to keep me. Uh, but she doesn't want me apparently? I'll flatter myself she does. Or could she just be as mad as a meat axe? How she wrestles with her own need to care! She's as lost as the wind that rolls over these moors. No-one will ever keep her or make her sane. That spirit gypsy blows where she wants, a girl we all covet but never will have. I'll have to leave it that way; I won't wrestle with the wind… though I keenly await its next outrage.

* * * *

Reality is yet to catch up with the Grail family. It seems that Saul invited Lane for drinkies more than once in these weeks, he being the fellow's PHD tutor. And Lane indeed was 'known', at the very least, to Lucinda before. Solomon being son to the Dean of Arts, it might be incumbent 'pon the great Grail to entertain a future academic colleague. Not to mention he considers the boy not wholly unwholesome (unlike me) where daughter is concerned, should he ever pluck the nerve to actually recommend her to someone other than himself. I wryly ruminate that since the engagement

Doctor Saul has morphed into Doctor No and is taking *steps*. What could the Grails know of the Lucy-Lane liaison? Not a lot I'm guessing, since they've invited the guy to their 'engagement celebration' two days hence. So this tender trap creates a panic for poor Lucy. We're forced to talk in her room.

- What'll we do?
- Nothing, Lucy. He will come, I'll come, you'll come, your friends and parents' friends will come... and we'll all toast each other
- I feel very bad you know. I don't deserve you
- I understand, but bear with me. Tell me one thing before we proceed. How many times?
My eyes broadcast what I want to know. We look at each other. Her eyes are round.
- Three. No... four
- Not forty?
- Don't torture me
- Okay, four. Lane is one up on *me*, then. Why does daddy suck up to him?
- Sol is his PHD –
- I know that. What's the real reason?
- I don't know
- Yes you do... And what about Claudia? Does she like him?
- Oh no, she doesn't -
She stops, having said too much.
- Too interesting. What does she *know*? About your little -
- Nothing! I tell you
- Not *much!*
I'm getting good at cruel. Lucy now weeps. At least, tears drop from her open eyes. She's not one to bury her face.
- How's this: Claudia sees more than you give her credit for
- Oh. And you're so up on Claudia?
(I refuse to bite) - I'm guessing. Could she be concerned about, say, 'pre-wedding cold feet'?
- My mother is not concerned about that! (Again, too much. For a clever girl she's less than tactical)

- Really? And by the way, are we gonna marry in a church? (Pause) Or do you prefer a *synagogue?*
Now Lucinda stands up. - What do you want from me?
- You tell me what the fuck you and your old man are up to, and I'll think about - just think about - joining your fucked-up family
- Oh! Mummy would be glad to hear you say that!

And we eyeball each other. She's not sorry and neither am I. So we leave it there. She cries nonetheless. And I don't like to see it. I leave.

The fact is, I spotted the 'religion problem' right back at the dinner party. Saul actually mentioned it. He's a closet Jew posturing as an atheist. He needs an ally, which is where Solomon comes in. Wife Claudia is a great big Catholic but so lapsed in Saul's eyes (he channels his own failure as a Jew) that he pisses on her from a height. And encourages daughter to do the same. Which she does. And Lucy's wicked conscience tells her she shouldn't. Which is the point where I rode in on my white horse. Now I'm ruminating on why mother and daughter have both been so cosy to me: I might be filling a conscience gap for both of them. But under it all I'm out of control, more irrational than suits my usual irony pose: another way of saying I don't know what the hell to do. Me who affects superior detachment as his bulwark, now must decide if he's to get involved. Me, who knows he doesn't have the guts to face the size of his problem. Commitment! Responsibility! Dirty filthy words. Wait though. The problem lies with others, not with me! Solution? Let me sort out others' issues. Thus get a convenient handle on my own. Easy when you're angry, when you're hard hard done by.

Claudia, Come Rain or Shine   I'm sitting in my car as rain curtains the headland… Ready to decamp, I spot an umbrella by the hedgerow and a figure hurrying toward the car. Those calves, those shoes… Claudia. She raps at the window, clambers in back. Dripping squalls crowd in with her. I spy elegant apparel. (In this weather!) My nether region registers heat. *Drive,* she says. After a miniscule pause, I do. Where to, m'lady? Claudia motions ahead. Soon the windows fog. She tells me suddenly, - *In here.* I recognise the place, an old gun emplacement high above the cliff. Not a soul in sight. Rain streaks the panes.

- Want to come in front?

- Are you going to marry my daughter or *not*?

(Ah. Careful now) - I believe… I may be

- Let us assume you will *not*. Do you know why Saul and I will not let you?

- Uh…

- Look at this. Look!

She thrusts a phone at me. I scan the text. Ah. Aha! '*Concerned third party… best interests of the family… Japonese girl… moral imperitive…*' Okay. Only Romy Kurazan can't spell.

- It's unsigned

- You know this person, no doubt?

- Obviously Lucinda does

- Don't you dare lie to me

- Steady on, Claudia. Could be anyone. Anyone jealous that is

- Who is this Japanese girl?

- Your guess is as good as mine (I'll fib if I want. I'm not taking this shit)

- I am not a fool. I check. She has been mentioned as a student in my husband's faculty

- There you are, then

- What are you hiding?

- What are *you* hiding?

Pause.

- My daughter barely speaks to me. Why?

- Ask her

- You think I haven't? And she tells me… you have no religion

- That's a joke! So you eavesdropped our conversation

- What conversation?

- Fuck off, Claudia! Ask your bloke about religion, why don't you?

- What are you talking about?

- Come *on*. I'm not stupid. The closet Old Jew who pisses on your Catholicism? The darling daughter who obeys her daddy then dumps her guilt on me? By going with a New J -

- How dare you? That is a family affair, long ago resolved
- Shit yeah.

And Claudia looks at me with round eyes, just like Lucinda. I feel sorry. Now she lunges from the car into the squall, minus umbrella. I bang the wheel. Shit! *That was way out of control.* And I nearly mentioned the Jew Solomon! Okay, what? Follow her. Grab the umbrella. It's howling out here. I make out her form by the gun-turret wall, in the lee. I totter over, try to stick the umbrella over her head. She shoves it away, it drops to a puddle. She shouts. Water flecks her face. Her make-up is running.
- I hate this country. Fucking weather, look at it! You want to marry my daughter? Well, you will marry a family! Our pretty little family. And you'll hate us all! Do you hear me? You! are like my *husband.* You see how you are like him? Men are all the same. Everything is hidden. My daughter *deserves* you. My darling daughter - who hates her mother…
- No way she hates you, Claudia. She's all held in, that's all
- And *you* will save her?
- Come on. Get back in the car.
I retrieve the umbrella. She grabs it and whacks me, really quite hard.
- Get away from me. Get out of my life!
And she lunges into a passageway. It's a tomb in there. I follow her in.
- *Your* life. *Your* life?
I grip at her arms, and at the concrete tunnel wall with rain and wind howling over us, Claudia Gonne bites at my mouth and I jerk her in and she has my crotch and I shove her blouse up and squash her breast and she's pinned, and she splays her legs, shovels my hand between them. No panties at all! It's too late. She loosens. Soaked. We hang there, languish over mud… She shoves me back! lurches to one side, wants to run. I catch her from behind, she doubles over… kneeling, cursing in mud. Come to sense, try to pick her up. Out of my grip, she lunges at the cliff. Rain surges horizontal. I drag her. She falls in sodden grass. I pin her. We lie heavy like corpses… time on end. I brush black drops from her cheeks. Sodden hair flecked with green. Wind-rain billows my coat, spatters my back. We stir. My pants go awol this time. Our stomachs slide, her green eyes close.

She's a rag. I push far far in. Her mouth is far open. I yank her up out of the grass. She cries out. I crush her. It's fucking beautiful.

At length she goes quiet. We nestle there… time in the wind… Finally I sit her up, escort her to the car. Er - we'll drive somewhere. Find a motel. Can't go home like this.

Later in the dark, beside her in an actual bed, it occurs to me she knows not a thing. About Solomon Lane and her daughter. Maybe she really likes me.

* * * *

Beyond losing her rag in a rain-doused affair, Claudia Grail is not a fool. She comes to me two days later, and we walk on the headland. The weather has cleared and the sea glitters a heavenly unguarded blue. Height gives perspective, she remarks. I am informed that while she 'won't guarantee' that she'll never want to (how to put it) fuck me senseless again, she is nevertheless glad to have 'expressed her truth'. And is ready to accept me as son-in-law. The reader may find this astounding but I don't, because Claudia Gonne is disciplined - and real. Frankly yes, she can do without the fireworks and we should be 'proper friends'. I cannot but agree. With a bit of forbearance we'll make it work! And may we not *choose* our friends in this world, no matter if they be mother to our wife or husband to our daughter? A secret is the spice to subtle romance. Take it where you find it eh? She and I collude and smile. I tell you, I never was one to plod along with just one girl. Today in the big blue it's easy to be faithful as long as the heart is in it. And this is where she takes me up: are you going to be faithful in heart to my daughter? Yes, just in a different way from you, and that will be *our* business. My good boy, smiles elegant worldly Claudia Gonne. And today, I believe it can only be true.

Master and Manipulator   I'm on the mending trail back to Lucinda, 'Sorry, but the Lane affair upset me,' I tell her. 'And yes, Claudia fears her Catholic faith has been vilified by you.' - *Do you mean she knows about Sol* - I doubt it, I interrupt. I feel I can say what I like for Claudia, since our covenant is sealed. And suddenly one re-appreciates the charms of a daughter... Lucy is *sexy*. Result of deeper penetration into family secrets! Flippantly I say: I'll marry you in any church and any dress so long as you *wear no underwear*. Lucy's roundy eyes widen up. This'll fix her guilt, let her channel all the sap and nectar she offered to Lane. And she offers me the pudding-proof at our private hollow on the heath just an hour before the party (wherein family and friends will toast our untrammelled love and fortune). At the coming moment, too clever by half I invite her to call me *daddy*, a game which after breathy stares and wild-eyed blushes she shoutingly assents to.

Despite all this mastery, meeting Lane in the presence of Saul and the party cronies is a stressy affair. How to cope with that smug superior bonhomie, that clubby intellectual shield Saul raises to the inevitable fact of my existence, which hides his involuntary scowl when I tend to come near? I affect a bonhomie all my own, not to mention solicitous smiles to Claudia, who accepts them with boundless irony. Meanwhile Solomon Lane regards Lucy and *sweats,* so I'm just as nice as pie to him. Lucinda must be shown how she marries a man of bigger heart than Lane can ever understand (not that I know his heart) - and to that solid-reasonable exterior I flaunt, as in the lion's den, my red-cheeked paramour flushed with the scent of the heath. At my hands she's suffered guilty pangs, and fears to return to those devil's lands. And Tessa Branagh and Lilian Bourne with glittery eyes keep a lid of shame on Lucinda as they bask in their own matrimonial chess with husbands they already betray. Ta v. much girls. Such is the foolery of social reckoning. Yet I know, my mastery is paper thin.

Not Contempt, Compassion   Hands up those who think me an arsehole right now? The truth is more mangled than that. Lucinda in the end is guileless, and here's the source of my attraction to her over all others. We all need to grow up no doubt, but I hesitate to admit if I ever did seek 'innocence' amid all this grown up frippery, I'd want her to share it with me. The only way she's actually guileful is in intellectual trysts with her father, a measure of their poisoned relationship as far as I can see. She'll not think it poisonous while he's her entrée to the world of academe, that safe option that circumvents life's nasty realisms. And he encourages *that* since he wouldn't want her to marry anyone but a clone of him, being the outsider and Closet Jew with his fetid inferiority complex masquerading as superiority complex. And the shame at his wife with her bumbling Catholicism (without the guilt) who's really too intelligent for him, distracts and complicates. So daddy and mummy are rivals for the soul of Lucinda. And guess which side I'm coming down on. Again I admit, I show a dearth of compassion for life's outsiders. Annoying, since I wish to be one myself. At least I'm freaking honest about it. Saul Grail is really an emotional illiterate, since he threw the switch to intellectual supremacy decades ago, a defence no doubt against the other grasping academics who inhabit the ideational rat-race he competes in. Where's the point, Saul, at which your self-absorbed posture gets set in stone, where you no longer have the stamina to question the cabined world you inhabit? The trick then is to fetishise it, make it seem more important, all the while masking your massive boredom and the inevitable emptiness, behind the legend of your reputation. Claudia Grail on the other hand, is content to keep her academic aspiration within the bounds of reality. In other words she never takes it seriously, not in the heart. She's far too keen to experiment in the currency of feeling. Where she and I stood in rain and wind on a lonely cliff above infinite sea and sky, what could the miniscule pickings of academic rumination matter to us? Hereby, a kindred spirit.

It is within the bounds of possibility that I should feel sorry for Saul and Solomon Lane and all those others who upset me, since we're all pathetic in our ways. First step is to admit it: that is, if we can recognise the ways in which we are pathetic. I have my blind spots no doubt, but if I didn't, what would be the point of living? The fun's in letting them stay blind for a while. No, I lie. It is painful. I know what: I'll publish a book about it… and I'm catching the Lucinda and Saul disease. See how it works? I *am* like them in my fear of facing the uncivil knobbly rawness of things. It is true that what we fear we become, what we hate we become. Pity me! Truth is, I can't stand people who ignore or write me off, framed up in their own self-referential smugness. It strikes me as not only cosmically absurd but dangerously autistic. Call me a self-centred feelingless little cynic if you like, but it is the pretence of this world that makes me so. I have to be bloody-minded: armed thus I may ignore you, write you off in my turn. To survive on the battlefield we have to kill everybody else. Is it not our duty? On the other hand, isn't it said that if people knew how to laugh then they'd know how to share? Well, we can start by laughing at each other. Then maybe you and I can one day *share* a laugh at the expense of someone else. Then that bright day may come when all god's creatures will join together in one great burst of cosmic laughter at themselves. Not. (Now *there's* something to laugh at.) So where is compassion in all of this? It's no use if I don't feel it but play at it instead. Hard to have compassion for those who have none for themselves, who instead ignore you as a means of ignoring their own nasty selves. Hard also to have compassion when you fear you will become like these minions you secretly despise. And hard when you can't admit you are not at all superior to anyone, since superiority is the basis of your posture, and detached non-commitment the basis of your *defence.* All in all, 'tis hard to have compassion when you are but flotsam in the great churning washing machine of life, and when you won't even admit it's true.

How then to get to Saul Grail? How to slide in the knife that punctures that puffed-up pompy pretence and that curmudgeonly sluggishness of feeling? Or to plant a bomb that wakes him up to his daughter-hugging selfishness - without actually destroying our chance to one day become something resembling friends?

Bad luck. The knife is taken from my hands. A terrorist enters from nowhere.

The Irrational Strikes Two weeks have passed, and Saul Grail is to deliver this year's Hacking Memorial Lecture at the university's Hacking Hall. His subject, following a recent tome, is: *The Role of the Irrational and Female in Art.* A majestic subject only a genius would undertake. In the meantime I suffer the inexorable return from her wanderings of the irrational Romy Kurazan at my flat in town. To grab the initiative I thank her formally for her toxic texts to Claudia Grail and the compassionate way she outed the unfortunate Asiatic. I entertain myself by explaining that it has had the desired effect of turning the whole family against me but that I will nevertheless prevail in the end. My bantering tone has her totally unconvinced, but she's not foolish enough to show me *that,* as I discern immediately, which she in turn notes with irony. We're so well matched (except for her physical superiority) that we really should get married. Then she can torture me for the rest of my days and I will no doubt benefit by it, far more than I ever would by 'that Lucinda' for instance. But Romy Kurazan would never stoop to such a course. Instead, my beloved informs me she'll be attending the Grail lecture, as she feels she has so much to learn concerning the *irrational female,* and that she is even considering joining one of his courses at the university this semester. I claim to note several pigs flying past the window, but at the last, recognise them as bloated gulls searching eagle-eyed for little scraps of detritus left by me. My admiration for Romola Kurazan is really as boundless as the sea. Although she's but a rabid spiteful street-fighting spoilt gypsy daughter of a disgraced foreign potentate (so she likes to tell) she has a spirit as big as a big dirty planet. And with her great scraggly hair like a comet gone bust and those great strong thighs that protrude from those absurd Boudicaa skirts of hers (even in the depth of winter) and her pink-purple knee-socks and all the other outrageous bits she splays about on her directionless march through the cosmos - I would go to hell and back for that girl. Thrice. But no-one will ever contain her. She's tragic. I know it and she knows I know it, and that is where we end: in the eternal absurdity of Now and this conversation, and all her plotty plots, and my open-mouthed wonder at them. Whatever next?

* * * *

The tribes of academe gather for the one o'clock start. Enlightened gales of voices ring out across the green quadrangle, and the rustle and twitter and babble and banter of privileged minds distils itself at the entry to Hacking Hall. There stands Lucinda in her pale-blue best, nervous at all the proceeding. Her cheek reflects the pink-white blush of a spring sky, that floats beyond these sturdy stones and spires. Her bag clasped in front of her, jew-eled but simple, will be void of items save those that might powder a nose, brighten a lip or dab a tear. No heaviness here, just a child's admiration for the dream of Idea. Thus we hope it might always be so. At this moment she turns to me: for undoubtedly, proud daughters need husbands. I smile her smile and greet her crowd, and shake the hands of her colleagues and friends.

And so we are seated. Claudia joins us. Several rows back is Solomon Lane. Then, through the door comes Romola Kurazan, and she parks herself at *his* side. Her great outfit is green and purple, matching her lips and hair. Several academical necks turn her way and gawk, as they indisputably do in whatever company she stands. But why oh why does she sit next to Solomon Lane? Romy and He wave to Lucinda and Me, but only Lucy smiles back.

And crikey, fancy that: there at the fringe, by the aisle, sits Miki the Japanese. She carries a little jewelled handbag, just like my Lucinda's.

Saul Grail disports with solid confidence, and in professorial spirit of independence fawns to none, not even the Dean, who now introduces our renaissance man. In the kingdom of the mind he'll cut it with man or woman or race or creed. Thus begins his rational discussion of the irrational.

- Since the dawn of civilisation, two great forces have contended for the mind of 'civilised man' (and with man we beg to include *woman*): the search for rationality, order, light, balance - contending with the presence of the irrational, chaotic, dark and wild. And art like no thing else, offers a window to this eternal struggle, which is of course, my friends, irreconcilable. For what is art but a restless struggle to *contain* the upwelling of the unconscious in a form palatable to so-called civilised tastes? Yet who has not experienced the terror of the new, when injudicious art conspires to reveal our civilisation to us in mirrors most dark? And do we not *yearn* - 'midst the safety (and the boredom) of organised thought - and when that strange wind shall rattle at our casement, invading the houses of the great and good, do we not clutch at our holy books, turn to remembered wives and husbands and say: oh lord of rational good, please save us? What machinery have we not invented to shield ourselves? My friends, our shield is learning, is thought, books, Art. And this may be our *undoing*. Let us consider the plight of Leda, and Zeus in the form of a swan…

But our professor gets no further. From the body of the room comes a foreign voice of undoing. Not imposing at first, but thinly determined. I know who it is without looking.

- Why did you say to me you were my father?
- I am sorry, I did not catch -
- Why did you speak the word 'father' to me?
- Oh Miki. Friends, welcome our student from Japan. Shall we hold our comments till the end, Miki?
- I only want to know why you call me daughter.
Doctor Saul stares. Lucinda looks at me. I shrug.
- Do you… do you… speak of the irrational in parent-child bonding? Of Leda and Swan perhaps? Do you have some example from Eastern art?
- This man has called me *baby*.
A bunch of heads now turn. Doctor Grail blinks several times. His mouth is half open.
- Dear Miki, are we quite well?
His tone is hollow! She jumps from her seat.
- I am well. I am well. Do *you* think I am well? Or am I *irrational* to you?
Miki starts down the aisle. Two hundred heads follow. I slide into my chair. Lucinda cranes to look. Miki steps to the stage. And she calls in her high-pitched voice:

- Misser Grail! You know my father! This young man of Osaka - he come to your country - he is master of art - this university *ridicule him*. Now he is master of all Japan! And he send me - and I study for him - and he *love me* - and I love my father! Why do you say to me *you* are my father! In our *fuck room* you say to me I am your father! You not allow. *You not allow.*

There's a thing in her hand. She stabs out at the doctor, a flurry of blows! We all gasp. He falls to the ground. Lucinda screams. Oh my ear! Some guys run at the stage. The Dean tries to wrestle but the girl's on top. Saul is prone like a barrel. They drag her off him, to the wings. Her feet scuff the stage: she's foaming, howling. People are seething and milling in their rows. I gaze to the floor. Irrational just struck! Lucinda totters up the aisle but Solomon Lane grips at her. I spot Kurazan making for the exit. Where is Claudia? On stage, staring at her man. Someone shouts to people to get out. A guy on a phone charges down the hall. I sit in the midst, lift not a finger. Minutes flick. Medics arrive, then police. I don't wanna know if the feller's alive. The cops shoo us out... The Hacking folks cluster outside. Claudia and Lucinda and Solomon are gone. I call Romy's phone but she's not answering. Lilian Bourne is there. 'Who the fuck is this girl? Never saw a thing like that. These Asians are *crazy*. Was she a student of his? Poor Prof! Did they have an affair? Someone said he was alive when they took him out. Have you heard from Lucinda? Have to text some *people*, darling!'

Get ready for the Twitter Feed: new-minted case study for the great Industry of Talk! - of two disparate people, irrationally tethered, neither of whom had any ground, for coping with the Irrational. Fact is we can't, darlings. It's irrational.

* * * *

That night back at the house with Lucy and Claudia and the burly Solomon, I learn that Saul Grail is still breathing and propped up in intensive care. The familial world can now begin to cerebrate on sordid facts. Only thing to hide from them all is that I know That Girl. Lucinda is claiming she wants to *kill* that girl. Can't bear to think of the cesspit of daddy's undercover doings with a student. Or the effect it'll have on *her* future. Who'll believe now that Evil Saul didn't drive Miki to it, that she's just a fruit loop? Our Lucy golden girl really wants to chunder! She rants at Mother and I have to step in, so she goes and cries on Solomon. Look how cool this cunt is in a crisis. Must be feeling sick himself, poor boy, though his Dean daddy seems mainly unscathed.

No doubt about it, Romola sniffed out the affair. Maybe set it up in the first place? And Romy won't answer her phone. Oh when she wants to disappear, she does. Now I'll need to squeeze from Solomon what he knows about Romy and *me*. Right now this bothers me more than punctured Saul. Romy, answer your fucking phone. If she truly is mad and wants to put in the Boot I guess she could ruin me. The way she smiled at Lucinda today. I'm getting very nervous, I want to just *go*. But I'm not leaving Lane with Lucinda. And Claudia is clinging to me, wants me to hold her. Shit, we're supposed to keep a distance. Go and mother yer daughter. But Sol the Creep is muscling in. Come hug *me*, Claudia.

Perversely I'm even concerned for little Miki. And it's obvious that Saul's going to find himself in the Polar Arctic. Especially when the Dean turns against him. Poor demented Miki. She has no-one in the world.

The girls drift to bed. At last Solomon leaves… but I can't examine him on anything. Of *course* Romy told him about dirty she and me! Bastard's got me over a barrel. I see now that Lane will always be around for ever and ever. Can't affect a moral stance with him. Biggest headache of the lot. I wander out and loiter by the cliff edge. Nice bit of moral high ground? Pity he ain't standing next to me.

* * * *

Six days later Saul Grail is slumped in his own bed in his own den. He's looking glum. At least, glumness clouds the brow of the great unreadable head when I steal in with Lucy to greet him in the morning. It appears Miki's thrusts of love-hate were superficial at worst. The work of an amateur, thank god. It's the thought that counts. One might say the whole affair was superficial. But wounds inflicted on soul and vanity? Saul ruminates alone. No doubt Grail just encountered the irrational in fervid female form and that can only be to the good. He may have to revise his book and lecture though. Loss of position will not be long in coming, and the brooding of the Outsider looms in his eyes. Though he evokes no sympathy, Saul is defenceless in a welcome sort of way.

Shit that befalls others is a blessing, and this suffering world revives by schadenfreude. If close up, we have an unsurpassed chance to analyse the misfortune. I wouldn't point this out to shaky Lucinda right now. Let it be grist to experience instead. Lucy, I can tell, has no idea what to say or do except to be belligerently glad he's okay. Shall I educate her in the requirement to forgive, explain that his crime was not monstrous but human? I need invest no energy in the Saul problem, yet feel that I might for the family's sake. The judicious outsider and son-in-law might exploit a chance for them all to learn and grow. Because Saul is myself, in a way, though I'd never feel at home in that skin of his. Vanity wouldn't allow: too fat, too bearded, too gruff, too glum, too internal, too *sexless*. Maybe that's why she stabbed him! He shouldn't be flattered (though he might since murder's a form of flattery) but I'd like to know, as we sit there regarding Father in his bed, if he actually made our little Miki *gasp*. Or is he a lump of meat that got in her way? I assume he's brooding on this too, since Miki is a dream he might cherish in his bloated whale-like way: is this the girl who nearly killed me for love?

Lucy says she's 'going to make a cuppa', and slithers off. There's a pause. I smile at him. Friend, it's now or never.
- I also suffered at Miki's hands. But don't tell a soul. And I know you won't.
His great head slowly rounds on me.
- What do you mean?
- You may imagine what I mean. But I see you played a better 'father' than me. Me too young.
And his eyes blink at me like a wounded seal, as if to say *God, I'm hurt.*
- You can trust me (I say) because I doubt that I'll judge you. Tell me though: was it a real affair?
He stares at the boy who impales him with honesty.
- I... believe... she wanted me. Yes, I believe it.
(Unutterably frank. This is sailing good) - And there were good times?
Jolly good question, though I say so myself.
- There were two.
This is clinically silly but sort of nice.

- I don't blame you. The Dean will though. And the Me Too brigade. But was Miki a lover to you?
- Yes. She allowed me to be... for a moment... free. Somehow
- I understand. So you never did it before - with a student? (He stares at me) Don't tell me... Anyway, put it down to 'research'.
And wonder of wonders, he gets the joke.
Enough for now! So I tell him:
- We'll talk again.
And Lucinda is back, with some crappily-brewed tea from a bag.

Paralysis Solomon Lane over the next weeks performs the role of solicitous judicious faithful family friend. You might say he knows which side his bagel is buttered (mind you, bagels aren't) or conversely he might be expected to desert the sinking ship since Saul Grail's future will undoubtedly be under review and with it his offspring's. Or perhaps Lane suddenly feels that *Claudia Gonne* 'needs succour'. I would back Claudia to have the taste to see through this feelingly unprincipled hunk of dependable slime, and even if she *were* tempted to abandon herself to impulse (as she did with me) she is sensible to take the longer view. Which involves me, I'll assume. But I note with a hot flush that Claudia likes to tempt the devil, who is ne'er a Catholic. What then, I shudder to contemplate, is the difference between Lane and me? In the cosmic scheme none at all, except that he might be superior in a way I can't fathom... in mind or heart, or (worse) in his trousers. Perhaps this world is not a level playing field and ministers no justice. What horrific awakening has fate in store for me then? The trouble with Lane is he's a brilliant player of sincerity such that the line between actor and role is as thin as say, the sarcastic smile on the lip of a jealous looker-on, one who knows all too well how the role is played. Mon semblable, mon frere I must therefore tolerate. Nay, more than tolerate, must entertain - as if the honoured guest at the unholy feast of my own conscience. So what might break the circuit of my impotent paralysis with Solomon Lane? You guessed it already: my fearsome Boudicaa, Romola Kurazan.

Now, they say Boudicaa sought to save her faithful masses from the hated Romans but in the process had them slaughtered. Do we think it mere courage that led her on, or hatred of oppression? Maybe it was love of death itself. Maybe Romola rides that tiger. She hates something, but I don't know what it is. I suspect it's a class war without ever being spoken that way. Or the eternal saboteur. She certainly doesn't know. The irresistible Glamazon: as fatal as all hell *because* she doesn't know. And like a Beast she'll swallow Solomon Lane and spit him out, and spit him out again. How I hope she does, even though I couldn't take it myself!

This is all embarrassing farce, this stupid rivalry with Lane, where I stamp my foot and rail against my paltry human predicament. Is Solly Lane better than me? It takes commitment even to *talk* of it. To stoop this low takes commitment! We aristocrats of the mind would relegate it all to a lower-world grotesque. And there's no confiding in Lucinda, because she will make herself immune from her own sin by writing it as a Study, and publishing it, and winning her paralysed happiness that way.

Desperately Seeking Daddy Bravery is a thing I never factored into a picture of my own father, beyond bloody-mindedness and snobbery and desire to give the middle finger to the privileged world. My dad's is the inverted snobbery of one who never got what he thought he deserved. But if you choose a profession (theatre) that needs society in order to eat, and then feed and suck on society's perceived hypocrisy and blindness without a whiff of mea culpa, then you'll win no plaudits or friends. Still, for dad who's disdainful and aloof while stooping to cleanse the world of its triteness, to be friendless is a badge of honour. And possibly brave. Dare his son investigate this? No, I need to keep him at bay. I know nothing of my father's loves and losses, but I'll claim I don't care since he treats humankind in the manner of a disease. Could he be mentally ill? To classify him as such, the younger snob might manage to care, but how to cure his lack of care for me? I'd have to channel a better man, a compassionate, an understanding one. Or I could act a better part than him - which should be the supreme irony for one who knows 'all the world's a stage and all the men and women merely players' and stupid despicable ones at that. My act would skewer *me*, the fool who took the whole play seriously. Daddy would laugh out loud! Nope, I can't teach my dad compassion, but I can wrap aloofness about me. He'll resist my nuptual ritual as well, but I have to seek him out. Let him be chief guest at my Marriage of Compassion and Irony.

Uses of Art In the weeks preceding our putative wedding Lucinda insists, in a perfectly modern way, that I co-habit with her in the great house. To be her protector against the monstrous Solomon? Or so she can no longer be alone with Father? Or does she want to believe that domestic normalness can be studied? Meanwhile she informs me she is working on a Book. I acquiesce in all things, powerless no doubt in the face of female ill-logic. Meanwhile, my father's refusal to so much as acknowledge my wedding invite (delivered after an internet search) has caused some teeth-grinding. One frosty morning I spy an ad in the local paper. *'The Final Lecture by an Under-esteemed Academic on the Uses of Art'* - a curious title. Almost idly I slide it across the table to Lucinda. She, enmeshed in her morning crossword, murmurs approval as she always does. I suddenly find myself saying: *I'll go to that.* She manifests an ironic eyebrow. - *I saw the same ad days ago. Don't be tempted, darling. We can't expect to find the real goods in provincial university towns.* Back to her cryptic puzzle. For reasons only too glaring I want to defy the inexorable writ. Lucy is all poised tension nowadays. *I will go,* I intone to the silence. She fails to look up, no doubt searching instead for a clue that will explain her marriage to her.

At seven I shuffle into the car for the short drive to town, wondering if my late attitude is nothing but defiance of boredom or boredom at my usual inner defiance. As I exit the garage, Lucinda, wrapped about in her favoured blue coat, materialises at the house door and waves me to stop. She climbs in. I look at her. *Drive,* she says. Tonight she'll play the role of Mephisto: if there's to be regret she will share it with me. Lucy is like that: defiantly loyal, no doubt abetting her forensic struggle for truth in the entrails of our relationship. Perhaps she really needs. I fear she does. There's a frosty complicity no words can break into as we motor through the lanes and hedgerows and killed winter fields.

The following is the gist of what occurred in the University Theatre that night. I did not understand as we went in why this man hired a theatre for a lecture, but soon I did. A group of forty or so is seated and the lights go down. My phone is set to 'record'. We are addressed by a tall man of about fifty, who stands beside a low lectern.

- Because I want to speak tonight on the uses of art, on the limits of the rational and our fascination with the irrational, on our ability to risk, to leave behind our zones of comfort - I must ask: why have you come to this event? I have a list of your names and may buttonhole any one of you! We are in a theatre, in a temple of Art. Or did you come for a lecture? Then you will get one, on the uses of art. This is, as advertised, my last. And in a sense my first. As a professor at your university, I am retiring. It seems to me there is little to know except this: you came because you want to be entertained. You scarcely want to *change,* for who would want to tear at their own skin? We come for affirmation of whatever we claim matters to us. Why does Hollywood insist on positive endings? Because the audience demands it: life tied in neat bundles, where the religious habit in us seeks meaning, affirmation, balance and clarity in a world of frustrating complexity. And we want to forget. So should I offer titivation, a ritual of voyeurism? Is our theatre really a brothel? We could repair to a pole-dancing club and watch the girls perform fake sex in front of our noses, or enter their private rooms for a closer, more expensive look. Better still, we could participate with our bodies. Let me take this texter and mark a line at our feet. Oh, I mussed up the floor. Do not cross this line for any reason. This line separates Art from the World. In this theatre there's no crossing it because then our 'Theatre' is dead - and instead becomes *reality.* We will be forced to acknowledge what we are, and what we are doing; and we do not want that, because then we would be *dancing.* Who is able to dance? Ladies and gentlemen I challenge you - within the boundaries of a Theatre. Now, you will say that you're here on a cold night and may have paid money (but none tonight). You made effort and you want reward. Bourgeois living is all about reward. We come to be healed, not to be angered but soothed. Not to be patronised but served up 'truth'. We of the human university! Art should present us with curious symbols in juxtaposition, so that we pause to ponder their relations and contradictions. We are civilised, we can't bear to be in the dark, facing the irrational. We are happy instead to be *titivated* as we walk like smug proprietors in the thousand-roomed brothel of the intellect! But I tease you, and for this I apologise.

Now. What if I were to (for example) take some items of clothing off? Would you find it entertaining? Would you think me a lesser professor? I assure you I do not have a pleasant body, unlike a pole dancer's. I see you are amused. Where is the point where you are not amused? You are entitled to walk out - but why would you? The performance is finite. Why not see it through - not enough faith or spiritual resource? I don't blame you, I blame myself. It is usually me who has not the guts. Why am I here? Because I am retiring. What is there for me now but anonymity, to be shovelled to the back shelves of a dusty library - in the great two-dollar warehouse called society? I am a poseur: yet we are all selfish, we all crave comfort. Narcissists wrapped in winter coats, we want the world to cherish us, to understand *our* pain and sorrow, our delicacy and our subtlety and our need and our accomplishment - the fact that we *exist* but have not the faintest clue how we will cope with our *end,* with our suspicion that this grand parade of fractal pointlessness we call society and meaning is but a ghost dance of ephemera in a void of airless longing. We never want to meet, we want to *be entertained*… Well hello people! Here I am. Here comes the jacket - and the shirt - ah, these buttons are tight… and the shoes: one - two! And the trousers - whoops! That's it, chuck 'em away. No madam, don't stand up. You don't know what's waiting for you outside that door! Death perhaps, or deeper ugliness! Now ta-daaa: the underwear. Last bastion of dignity, last throw of the dice for a fucking fool. There we go, all gone.

And what an anti-climax. Feel the silence, feel the embarrassment. I feel it, do you? *So we meet.* In embarrassment we meet. Don't go sir, I need you now. I'm not mad. Are you titivated? Is there a policeman in the house? Pity, we could make a proper show. Now allow me to step over here (not to annoy you madam). Allow me for example to urinate on this lectern. Like a dog would do. I saved up the water. Ahhhh… here it comes… that's better. No sir, do not cross that line! Do not call on your phone, sir. Because the truth is here! Let me piss my life against this lectern! Let us all share the deed. *For I am you. I am you all. And you are Me. We are together.* Aaaah… Wait. Wait! I will fetch a mop and clean it all up. Stay where you are… all fresh and clean!

At this point most people have stood up. I keep my seat. Lucy says get up! I appear to refuse. We hear a clatter from behind and then the performer - for that is what he is - returns (in his socks) with a mop and bucket. He is ruefully smiling. He mops the floor and lectern with care. Some people can't help watching, others are half out. It's all wretchedly pathetic - and as brave as can be. He finishes, removes the bucket, returns. He retrieves his clothes. Puts them on piece by piece. It is agonising and ridiculous. At last he's finished. A handful of people remain. Lucinda is by the door. The man steps forward, bows formally. 'Thank you for attending my lecture on the Uses of Art. I bid you *adieu* and a safe journey'. And he stands there with a smile, until we all have left the place. I am the very last.

Out in the cold. Lucinda is standing in the lane. She stares at me in her blue coat. There are several audience members standing about. They seem to be arguing. One is jabbering angrily into a phone. We find the car, say nothing whatsoever at all, and drive home through the killed winter fields.

I did not tell her then, and have not told her since, for she has never met him, that the esteemed performer - was my father.

Old Man and Blue Girl   Beside Lucinda in our frosty bower bed, I start to dream. I'm a tramp shambling on a winter road. I meet a little girl, naked under a blue coat. She wraps it about, wants to step beyond. I reach out. *I won't face you, you are grotesque,* she says. You must, I say. The hedgerows wall us in. Do you want to be little forever? *I wish it to be nice forever. Are you my father? I must forget!* she replies. Where do you go this late? *To play in my mind garden.* Well you can't! And I sound quite firm. Where does the road lead? I enquire of the blue girl. *I will study to find out.* And she seems to cry. There are so many things left to wonder at, I say, feeling as if I am croaking. And she seems to grow in age, as if a married woman. *Don't ask me to stay a child.* Her hair rustles in the night wind. You wanted romance, wanted me! I cry. But she turns away, walks faster. *I'm not naïve, old man,* she says. I shamble to catch her, but she seems lost in the lanes. I'm cold and abandoned.

…One's father said that in the theatre of the mind, happy endings are what we seek. But such endings murder romance. I don't care: romance is too hard. What we *shall* dream on… is our spring wedding. Yeah, dream of that. Solution to all our cares.

Care   In these last weeks before the end of winter and the coming of a faux spring, I seem to think more on Miki the Japanese. What did they do with her? If I sought her out I might report to Saul, and I guess he might be grateful. Though I'll say nothing to Lucinda. Or to Romy Kurazan… My enquiries lead me to the security unit at The Fall Institute. I find the girl, seated in an upright chair by a long window. Black eyes languish under a dark fringe. Knees are together, hands clasped in lap, face averted to one side. It's breakfast. I slipped out early and I'm bleary-eyed. The female doctor says the girl is on suicide watch, and lets me know that apart from legal aid I'm only her second visitor, besides a demanding red-haired girl who brought her food. Would I know that girl? I say no, but ask instead: Has Miki heard from family in Japan? Yes. There is a letter it seems, the content of which the doctor cannot reveal. From the father? I ask. Has he disowned her? The doctor peers at me. What do you know of all this? Enough, I tell her.

- Hello Miki. It's me.
She raises her face. Oh, I didn't think to bring her anything. Suddenly I wonder why I'm here. In her pool eyes, black incomprehension turns slowly to comprehension… then segues to pain pursued by resignation. Nothing is said by the lips. We sit there awhile. I take her hand.

- Professor Saul wants to tell you he's sorry, and he hopes you're all right. And he will give you money, even a place to stay. And he won't press charges in any way. Everything's going to be fine. We'll even get you back to Japan. I'll write to your father. Your father will help you…

I don't know where this stuff is coming from. There is another silence. It strikes me she is more real than anything, perched on her chair beside the steel morning window. It seems she is not eating. And then I see. *She is not going to make it. Not going to make it.* For an hour we sit, and I seem to enter her trance, which is profound. But not actually more than I could ever know. When I finally get up to go I squeeze her hands, and she holds on to me for an instant. I wait. There is a little flicker under the fringe, a kind of nod. And that's it. I am not able to staunch bloody tears as I walk out of the door. It strikes me no-one is really a villain in this world… we are all weak and mostly lost, behind the facade of coping and arrogance. Better remember.

Back at the residence, I find Saul seated by his bay window looking out at a flecked greywinter sea. There are no books about him. I tell him where I've been and what I promised on his behalf. He listens, peers at me. Thank you for going there, is what he says. I know *he* never will. He returns to his own trance. I make him a cup of tea. Properly brewed.

Chaos   Friday evening three days later. It's to be drinks before family dinner. The latter is to be cooked by Claudia since Lucinda is immersed in research on her wondrous First Book. *Women Outside: The Pathology of Heroine and Victim.* Post-PHD Lucinda is determined to produce. I opt to endure (by day and by night) the steely hints, knitted brows, dismissals - as do the rest of the family, heroic victims all. The book is her refuge. Why should I worry? Write your fucking book but be sure to include a reference to a dying Japanese girl. Now Claudia has rushed in from somewhere unnamed, and she looks mightily flushed. I join her in the kitchen, pour out a big vodka and try to smile. She actually swigs it down, eyeing me with a look suspiciously close to contempt. I'm in no mood to be her insect. Is it time to enlighten her about her daughter and Solomon Lane? I murmur: *how can I help?* And she says *get out of the room maybe.* Okay, take a punt, let intuition do its dirty job.

- How does fucking a Jewish boy prove to your husband that you're superior?

Claudia doesn't even pause before gripping a steel pan and delivering it at my head. Naturally I dodge and it scones into the bench with a frightful clatter. She was already drunk apparently. Snatches keys and storms out. I'm smugly upset. The doorbell rings. No-one answers. Rings again. I'll go then. *Right bloody Claudia.* But swaying in the doorway, half in shadow, mushroomy hair, leathery jacket, skanky skirt, stick-heels… is Romola.
- Good god
- I went to yer flat but ya weren't there so I came 'ere.
Uh? Behind the slap of lipstick she grins like she schlepped a bottle of pills and washed 'em down with a flagon of vodka. Entirely possible. I note the car, parked any old how.
- What are you doing?
- I'm here to see you all, darling. Missed yous
- Fuck, no way. I text you fifty times and you never answer. Go home.
Her legs buckle. I'm forced to hold her up. She smothers her mouth on mine.
- Lovely boy, show me the way.

I plonk her in a chair in the posh lounge. Her legs are splayed out, comical and dangerous at once. In marches Lucinda, looking brisk. Obviously just gave birth to a paragraph.
- Oh! she says. Romola! And looks at *me* for some reason. Romy manages to throw up over the coffee table. To my mind this act suffices to cement the divergence in their two personalities. Romy starts to giggle as soon as she's emptied out. I note it's fortunate the parents are not present. Lucinda affects a surprising calm and fetches water. I volunteer to clean up. What a bore, Vanity Fair's winter edition is beyond repair. Romy hogs the sofa.

- C'm here Lucy, 'cos I want you and me t' ave a lil' chatty-wat. D'you know darling how long I suffered with *that guy*? Better specimen than that Sollymoan fellow bu' thas' not saying much. Men, can't stand 'em, can't stand sex without 'em. Not that I know about *your* sex life darlink. You reelly gonna marry this boy? 'Cause if you dump his *arse* darling, I'll take him off yer hands. Ha haaaa! And I don't recall bein' invited to your celebratey dwinkies. But I's prob'ly off my face in some *ditch* somewhere. Boo hoo I'm always the loser.

Wedged under Romy's arm, Lucy looks to me. I shrug.

- Mmm but who's gorgeous. Ever think o' going lezzy, baby girl? I'll teach ya.

Romy kisses Lucy's lips and flutters her eyes at me.

- If I did, sweetheart, it would certainly be you (Lucinda is surprisingly in control)

(Romy pouts) - Or d'you like *Asian* girls, darlink?

I step in.

- Come on, Romy, let's get you home.

But Lucy's face darkens.

- What does she mean?

- I meeeean, sweetie - d'you like *Aziatic* girls? But no! 'cos you're *daddy's* lil' girl. Daddy *protects* little Asie girls but daddy not so frigh'fully goo' in bed, dar-link!

I offer a helping hand.

- No toush me! Ge' filfy han' off!

This in an Asian accent. And she *punches* me. Narrows her eyes at me. Romy you're a creep. Lucy is on her feet and not happy. Saul walks in at that moment.

- Aaah! Ooh! Big ba' man! Daughter no goo' enough? Got to fuck Asia girl? Lucky she no cu' off balls!

Saul stands and stares. His face goes hard.

- Ba' bad fiancé boy like Asia girl too! Asia girl too!

Paroxysms of giggles. Now or never. Hoist Romy up and shove her at the door. This time she lets me. Sorry Saul, I manage to mumble. Lucinda glares at me. Haul Romy to the front door, out and into her car.

- *No wan' to smack me?* she says.

I glimpse Saul and Lucinda silhouetted like Nosferatu and Victim behind curtains. In the car Romy groans. The keys are where she left them. I start up, back the hell out, crunch a tail light on a wall.

- Fucking saboteur!

- Now now cutie. Truth'll always out. Try to *help* you, baby boy. Ugh… stop. Stop!

I do. Romy staggers out, crouches and waters the lawn. I shield her, like a waiter. She drags me onto her then rolls on top. Seem to be in the wet patch. Want to shove but she holds me vice-like, starts a knees-splayed pelvic motion. I hiss at her. A figure steps onto the drive. I discern Lucy's willowy form, crunching near. I give up, lie there. Romy farts, giggles, slumps, starts to grunt. Lucinda peers anxiously out of the dark. Romola settles into a snore.

Failure is Good   I need not relate how long it took Lucinda and me to get the embarrassing corpse upstairs, into a shower and into a bed. Lucinda set her face with steely dignity and performed her task. For myself, I swayed horridly between steely un-attachment, desire to kick Romy to kingdom come and desire to spit in Lucy's face. This last was the worst. When Lucinda's wide-eyed worry morphs to frigid slit-eyed anger, I will not take it. It's against the rules. Not allowed. In the end I had a headache to die for. I will not commit to disgust, or to anger or sorrow or decisive feeling in any form. Human life is a sorry, at times amusing, always farcical game. And I fail to see why Lucy won't share this view. Most women don't. They need order, take things seriously, responsible as fuck. Despise the messy anarchy of the absurd and unexpected. Me, I long for it, where it concerns *other* people that is. Once years ago I got home to find dad's girlfriend had taken all her ornaments and precious items and paintings and dumped them in a huge pile in the centre of the living room. And was sitting there eyeing them with grim satisfaction. This was the only time I ever remember feeling happy to know her. I think I offered her a box of matches.

You will see that the only emotion that matters this night is guilt, and in its shadow all others fornicate. A bed is a hard hard place when its inhabitants want to kill each other. In the morning, Romola is gone without a word. And I am left feeling responsible for her, which I am determined never to be. And Lucy knows I *am*, and I stare back at her with the word *Solomon* on my lips, and she beats at the tangled thicket of my unknown history with *Asian girls*, and all in all the day begins like we're about to get slaughtered in the shallows of Omaha beach. Romy has cut at the heart of my studied refusal to participate in reality. And it was she who put me in the way of Miki, and I marvel at her creative bomb-throwing brilliance, no matter how off her face she appears to be. Because Romola is always, and never, out of control.

Lucinda drags her spirit together at breakfast and adopts a tragic poise and sublimity I can only marvel at. Then she's gone, for a tragic walk on the cliffs in the grey wind. Saul comes in, sees my winded look and tells me to forget the whole thing. *Bloody women. What hope have we got?* he says. I am quite amazed. And oh! Where's Claudia? *Hanged herself with a bit of luck*, he replies. I grin heartily and so does he. Never thought I'd see the day. Gallows humour from Saul! Failure becomes him. I love it when the great are fallen. It relieves me, I don't feel so lonely anymore. Because you see, I suspect with tongueless horror that life is a serious deadly affair, where we all will dwindle and fail. All those outsiders and victims who hopeless stare at their demise out of rounded rabbit eyes in the traps and dens and hovels and streets and palaces, in the flotsam of war and human foolery and pompous grandeur and wanting, ten thousand centuries of sufferings and trepidations, a billion stories buried in the instants and tides of time, the blunderings, grievings, longings, stupid mistakes… And me? I claim to avoid all that. Maybe I can solve the human problem, stay untouched! But nothing is beyond cost. My unholy vanity leaves me breathless at times. I tilt at these tides of suffocating *care*, and scoff in the face of *effort*, fool myself I won't and don't suffer, cling to the notion of transcending it all. And I fear most of all… that I'm not special. And that I may be a fool.

I head out to the moor. Lucinda is not far away. In the grey morning wind, roamy seas are below her. I sit beside, take her hand.

- I went to see Miki the Asian girl. She's going to fall, probably die. Let's not worry any more. It's all too big to worry about. Saul wanted to go but I went instead. Miki was a real thing for him… And Romola is a part of me. Have to admit it, a too bloody big part. I'm in love with the idea of her. But I can tell *you*. Because your big round eyes will always haunt me, Lucy Lucinda.

She sits facing outward and never looks. Did she hear, in this wind? Quietly I step away, surprised at myself.

Healing   I think I said to you that a comely dream in the form of a spring wedding may do the trick, annul all this gothic Heathcliff morbidry, solve the world's jealous tangled sufferings, and let me idly detach once again.

For I do have schmoozing skills, and occasionally patience.

Claudia Gonne has been suffering. One day I pass the Solomon Lane cottage, half expecting to find her white Maserati there. On a gritty impulse I stop, knock on his door. He's in. Lane affects to study me as he would a lump of Roman pottery. I ask if he has seen Claudia. If he were half a man he'd deny knowing what I was talking about, but he's a whole one. I believe she has gone to her church, he says. Why do you ask? *Because I want to get my family back,* I say without the faintest trace of irony. And leave him at the step fingering something, looking faintly gormless.

She has two churches, one in town and a favourite in a village in nearby hills. My intuition is working today. Here's her come-hither motor. I step through a leaf-littered garden and enter the little white nave. The suggestion of faraway Florence welters in from coloured windows. And there she is, kneeling in her modish cream raincoat, head covered in a blacklace shawl. Whoah. Claudia Gonne, you're amazing. Who was I to claim you had no guilt? Wrong. All women do, even Romola Kurazan... In a church I usually feel like the joker, the guy who might end up praying one day by accident. And if people I know in less solemn ways (like Claudia) bow their heads to The Presence I am amazed and troubled, since sexuality and god don't mix. So I wait in awe... then step forward, sit near. She looks up, eyes widen at the sight of me... then drift ahead again. Soon she sits up, by me on the seat. We exist in the stillness. There could be a healing.
- Lane told me you were here
- I guessed
- Come back. We need you. I sure do
- You're the only one

- Saul's absorbed a thing or two. I've talked to him (slight exaggeration!)
- And Lucy?
- She's getting a new baby. (She stares) In the form of a book. But daddy's in her bad books
- The Japanese girl?
- Miki. I went to see her. I know her. But you guessed that. She's in danger of death. You could pray for her.
Pause.
- And how's Solly going? Or coming? On a scale of one to ten
She looks into my eyes. - *Quattro*.
And her gorgeous soft-skinned Italian face creases into a smile, and into a girlish grin, then a blush and then a pout, as if to say: I hate you. Now attend to my red lips, here in my little church. Do it now.
Which I do.
Later, we walk in the green park. Plenty of time. I take her fingers in mine. We're both lightly smiling. Strangely, the real emotion I feel is… respect. For something I can barely define. For her, no doubt… but for the moment, for the day, for the light, for the softness, the trees, the flowered lawn, the breeze.
- I'll marry Lucy here then
- Yes, she says.

* * * *

At home I find Lucinda at the kitchen bench beheading a pile of vegetables. Steam is rising from a pot and Saul is at the table with a mug of beer in his mitt. I step across and kiss her neck, a thing I usually wouldn't do in front of him. She chuckles slightly. He seems stolidly tranquil. Clicks open a bottle of ale for me. I sit and suck on it, cavalier with one foot on a chair. Long Lucy in her shirt-sleeves looks round at us, nods and resumes her frenetic chop. I've stepped into the middle of a reconciliation. Japanese veg perhaps? Suddenly I notice he has a skull cap on. At home. First time I ever saw it. I raise an eyebrow; he grunts. Enter Claudia in gorgeous cream coat. Summary pause… and she takes his chin, delivers him a face suck that makes one's fingers itch. Tinny sod doesn't even know he's married to her. Lucy looks back, a bit wild in the eye. Claudia gives her two lippy wet ones on the mouth. Go lezzo for that - but I'm no girl, I'm Pseudo Son in Law. Claudia drops her coat, has a sniff at the pot, grabs a loaf and plates, takes over the business. Even when she notes the cap on his head she barely hesitates.

- Put sage in, darling. And thyme and a bit of coriander. Sharpens and sweetens it.

Whatever the hell you say, Claudia Grail. Mum.

Lunch seems to be a successful affair. At table in the steamed-up kitchen Lucy jabbers about this book of hers, and her highbrow elders take to grilling her ferociously. She looks flushed and glances help! at me. My raised brow says you're writing the bloody thing not me. And she half-smiles 'cause she knows what I mean without our saying. We're communicating.

Later seems the right juncture for a light chat in the library. I mention Claudia's church, how I like the feel of it. Lucy reads my mind again (and doesn't ask how I got there). *Well, let's get married in it,* she says. You have yourself a deal, I say. *But Romola can't come, I'm sorry.* Then you'll have to put an electric fence round the place! No laugh.

- While we're at it Luce, what do you make of her?
- From an academical point of view? (She knows I'm fishing) I assume she's a very nice girl
- Whaat?
- You know her better than I ever will
- Maybe I don't
- Is she alcoholic? A drug addict?
- Er… no, because she chooses it. But would you say she's selfish? Or insensitive, vindictive, disgraceful? Pathetic, vulgar, jealous?

She ponders. - No. Not at all. None of those… She's lonely.

I'm thunderstruck. I never got it. At that moment my Lucy rating goes up ten notches.

- And that is why, my darling, she cannot come to our wedding day. Because she will steal you away. From me

- You are a genius. Lonely... I never saw it
- You're not a woman. And no doubt I shall put it in my *book*.

She smiles lightly, turns to go. Then as if on a whim:

- Tell me, this Miki girl. What happened to her? Where is she?

I tell her where.

- And what do you make of *her?*
- Hmm. She's in love with her father but wants to kill him as well. Had a *commitment*. And guilt seeks punishment. Now she's committed to a ward. Which she will never walk out of. Wretched and lonely. Put her in yer book.

Lucy stares at me. She got all that.

- Thank you. I have a feeling I might.

And she goes, in that courtly studied contained way she has, back to her booky refuge. And Lucinda will conduct that study. She'll meet Miki, and ponder on her, and reach Conclusions. With Endnotes. All done with compassion, studied compassion. And then she'll own it. Life by proxy!

My old ache comes back. I want a woman who's *dangerous*. But then all women are dangerous. To my ego that is. Lucinda informs me women are lonely. I guess that's why they have to own you.

The Uneasy Marriage of Commitment and Irony   Should I try to drag my own birth mother to my matrimonial hoe-down? This exercises my ironic sense for days. As for my father and his ghastly girlfriend Patti Lorr, I daren't consult Lucinda on that. What do I want by all this? The keys to doors long since rotted away? The girlfriend (the one who once smashed up all her stuff in our house) answers my phone call. The studied disorientation of the bohemian (why my father has presumably put up with her for so long) tells her to put no stock in me, but I get the sense she's tickled nonetheless. She'll play it hard though.

- Yairss, your old man isn't here, but I can tell you he won't be interested
- Not even for free grog? (Hide the grimness under banter)
- Well in that case I s'pose I could ask him. What day's it on... a Tuesday you say?

- It's a Saturday
- Is the previous woman coming?
- My mother? Err…
- Who's the unlucky girl then?
- Lucinda Grail. Her dad's a professor
- Oh. Marrying *upwards*. All right, I'll bring it to his attention. Send the invite
- You can come too, Patti. Say I don't need his money. Tell him he can give a speech if he likes. And tell him I saw his lecture
- You went? God, I didn't. Sounded bloody awful
- It was brave, believe it or not
- Him, brave? Ah well, pigs 'll fly. Don't expect us. Bye-bye.
CLICK.

* * * *

My mother is an even harder proposition for me. Word has it she re-married. That would mean a bloody brood. Too hard. God, I sound like Patti. All right, it was a lie that I said mum is unknown to me, but still, I stay out of her way. Lives in town, hubby's a doctor, she's a nurse. Caring profession, busy. She'd be embarrassed anyway. Why don't I call? Told you I'm a mystery. Question: would she approve of Lucy? I go to Lucy on this one, and she glares daggers at me. Of course you are going to bring your mother! Oops. Lucinda raises her eye to heaven like men are the lowest thing in the evolutionary chain. And we are, right now.

Lucinda and Claudia and Tessa Branagh and Lilian Bourne organise stuff in a brisk way I could never emulate, and frankly I leave them to it. Never interfere with the workings of a fete, I say. Although I drop in on Tessa once in a blue moon and share a bath with her. Mustn't neglect one's friends. Besides, I need to get The Information about my own wedding. Which she doesn't give me. Actually my current lightness of tone masks serious nerves, as if a grizzly bear were coming at me over the horizon. And I find myself using more time trying to get Romy to turn up at my apartment. Oh, she's sweet as pie since I told her she's been wedding-banned. Ominously so. To be frank, she's not exactly jumping on me:

claims to be 'tired' or 'busy', even 'disappointed'. Something's going down. I won't tell you what it is. It's shit anyway.

There's something decadent and flattering and lazy-cool about turning up to someone else's glittering event in which one is supposed to play a leading role. Perhaps I'm just an excuse. With these girls you'd think they were planning their own Super-Hens Party. Is this the price of being a poseur - to get ignored? Although Lucy is determinedly democratic with me you can tell it's a put-on. Her precious book and nuptuals don't co-habit the same hemisphere, so lately she's developed a short fuse with me. And as the welding sorry wedding day approaches, I appear to appear more curmudgeonly and introverted, except for momentary outbursts of bonhomie which have others looking at me as if to ask whether I should alter my drug of choice. My main concern is whether I will get the usual irruption of cold sores and whether my hair will look boofy and whether I'll look like a stuffed-shirted alien in the relevant clobber. Before inevitable change we mostly cling with the fury of the damned to our old ways. Lucinda is busying herself with The Book with increasing fury, spitting out fierce paragraphs (I've seen 'em littering her desk) and challenging her father to read 'em in a way that suggests a level of parent-child rivalry even I've not grocked before. Meanwhile Saul writes the expense cheques and darkly waits for his bloodless execution at the hands of the academical world, who it appears cannot tolerate research beyond the bounds of word and lecture and conjecture, especially not into the frailties of human feeling and the pathologies of female flesh and madness. In life, if you want to avoid experiencing something you can do it inside the academical industry, with its hierarchies and layers of mutual congratulation and febrile denunciations worthy of any Bolshevik party congress. I should have been an academic! It's the Great Escape. Even pesky research can be got round if you pass it off as 'serious duty and contribution to a needy society' while being provided with a permanent meal ticket inside its immutable establishment. My father doubtless was jealous of all this, hence his frightful lecture. Go dad! You can see how superbly narcissistic it all is - much more than I am. Lucinda will boldly go where her father has gone before, and will catch and surpass him on the road and beat him into a submission that crowns her as the glittering child who martyrly paid for her father's excesses with her career and happiness. In other words she's almightily pissed off with him. Go to another bloody university, I tell her. Or d'you fear you're not good enough? Meanwhile why not pity poor me, lowly translator and purveyor of the French language, most of whose clients are tourists, whose last book was *Drinker's Guide to Marseilles* preceded by *Paris for Americans* or some such bollocks. Missy should try stooping to my level.

But she will avoid the pained issue of The Outsider too... by studying it. Lucy has slipped away on several occasions in the early morning and I know where she's gone. Gone to observe the Japanese. This might turn out to be her real book subject since *The Woman Outside* is what she may fancy herself to be... if she had the necessary experience, the necessary guts to avoid marrying me, to shove Lane's head in a bin, drive a creative schism with her father and rush off round the world for five years and eat and pray and love until her blessed academical head falls off in the Congo jungle after popping out her fifth child to a great black chief's son with a bone through his nose.

And now the perennially delicate issue of religion in this house is negotiated by its protagonists with a spidery distance I can only wonder at. No doubt their academical prowess allows them to do it. My previous criticisms now smack of the intruder who disturbed their subtle debate. The holy wafer-and-wine mass, we have been told from the start, will be included in the service. Claudia must have it, but Lucy doesn't want to talk about it. I have no particular objection to slurping red plonk and chomping tim-tams in a church, but Saul will need convincing, since he sinks into the gloom of his armchair whenever it's mentioned. I'm sick of the tension. Time for us to have a boy-chat. And no mucking about.

- Claudia wants the full mass. Is she going to get it?
- If we're in a church I assume she will. Do you object?
- No Saul, but I assume you do
- I do not

- You do, like hell. But listen, we'll chuck in a Jewy reading (and a Muslim too if you like) and we'll all live happily ever after
- No
- Yes you will. Go and write one or choose one - or I will!
- What do you know of Judaism?
- As much as you know about women. But you never wrote books about it. Why not?
- Not my field
- Get Solomon to write 'em then. (He looks at me) Still want him for your son-in-law?
- Not at all
- Good. Listen, let the girls do their thing. A mass in a church won't change a single damn thing in heaven or earth. Take it from me
- I was not aware you had a view on religion
- Not having studied it, my view might be worth listening to. You are wise not to make it a life study. Art is safer. Would one claim that religion is rational? Try telling Claudia her faith is 'merely' irrational - especially when she's far more interested in feeling things than thinking them. But what would she *know* of Catholicism, since she's useless at it in your eyes? (Just a joke, mate) The irrational is more fun, don't you think Saul? Except when you get stabbed. How's the wounds, by the way?

He seems to be swallowing my brusque irony.

- Coming along. I expect to develop stigmata next
- Your daughter's taken a frenetic interest in Miki. I estimate she's visited four times. The girl didn't say much when I went, nothing in fact. We'll have to hope Lucy cracks her.

He drops his head to his chest.

- Cheer up, Saul. Lucy's kind of fiercely faithful to you under it all. I'll never change her, except to get her to take an interest in the bed department. And actually that might be a way in (since I'm anti-academical) to get her to do something *irrational*. Which she already did, mind you. She already did.

(I did not expect to go this far! But there's power in it.)

- What do you mean?
- Lucy's been a naughty girl. With *Solomon Lane*.

I eyeball him. And funny, this is the moment I realise I might actually in a perfect world be able to experience a thing resembling commitment... to Lucinda Grail. The truth will set us free. Blundered in where angels fear to tread, and learnt a thing or two from Romy Kurazan at last. And Saul's reaction will define our relationship.

- Choose your reaction carefully, Saul

- Okay. You win

- No, I don't *win*. Because I'm the one doing the marrying. And you can bet it doesn't come easy. You and me need to get along. And since I realise you had the presence of mind to (a) marry a peach like Claudia, and (b) have a mad affair with a mad student (I didn't get past second base and you did. Hats off, mate) your cachet has gone up in my book. Let's get irrational. Break the frigging rules. I'm not quite as dopey as you took me for, am I Saul?

- I did not take you -

- Yes you did. I was the Insect. Until life shoved its blade in your heart. We need to value things (I don't know where this is coming from) not for what they're supposed to be, but for the simple fucking reason that they exist. They exist. They ARE. Do you think I care how anything ends up? I'll do my best I suppose, if I'm not too damn lazy, but in the end there's no morality in this world. There's nothing to do except DO - and to hell with the result. And if you don't like the result? To hell with you too.

I had no idea it would get this far. I look at him. And then he nods.
- Yes. You are right.
It occurs to me Saul Grail has thought about all this before. He's older, after all. And I guess that's what they pay him for. But he doesn't display it to me, to his credit at this moment.
- Indeed you are right. Congratulations
- Okay okay. I'm the young fool and vain as you like. But guess what, Saul? I couldn't give a rat's arse right now. Reckon I should marry your chick or not?
- Umm... why don't you toss a coin? Try the Yi-Ching. Or tea leaves perhaps. But not in a bag...
Now we're in a better space.

- Cool. See you on the day then. And lighten up. And make the speech *you* want to make. From the heart. And get pissed. See you later.

He raises a hand, and almost smiles.

Be Loyal to Me Post the Saul chat, my sudden awareness that not caring about much lets me care about all of it in a passive sort of way, is a nice present to myself. Neutrality to this world may be the go. I always thought I should resist, or at least treat this life with sarcastic disrespect, but there's no need. I was simply anti-bullshit, that's all. I'm really no intellectual, and I take ages to feel things properly, but by the same token I need to back myself. If you, reader, accept my frankness and frank lies you'll get an insight into an amoral lazy player of the field who really seeks to be no menace to anyone. Don't be offended if your own moral codes of affection and loyalty get their arse kicked. Maybe you like it. Life is the teacher, and it will get round to doing the teaching in unusual ways. Getting married is the most artificial palaver you could ever imagine: two big planets colliding and buckling over the bitsiest things, bound to the absurd ritual of declaring love and loyalty - where *to be alive* is nothing but love and loyalty. I mean, if you're not loyal to being alive what the fuck else is there? Can't escape your own skin, and neither can your partner! Oh, we'll be talking about God next. Frankly I have no objection to God. I am the Real and so is he, right? Even inside a freaking church... Dear reader, you can tell I'm getting antsy, hence the foregoing screeds of febrile self-reflection, complaint and lashing out. The dreaded day has come.

A Guest At My Wedding Darkish dawn clouds seem to have passed away eastward, the wind has dropped, and blessed sun has come. Spring is definitely here. At one o'clock I find myself standing at the entrance to the nave, talking in low tones with Tessa Branagh, who locked up the gig of best man-girl since I've no particular male friends. Tessa is a good lurk anyway, and alleviates the portentous nature of the occasion by telling me how her husband Troy, not a year ago, managed to get his pubic hair jammed in his fly not ten minutes before he was due to step in and marry her. I remind her lightly she's told me this before, and she reminds me equally lightly that she knows it. I tickle her gloved palm and admire her champagne silk outfit and hat, which is a mite too sexy. People are gathering, their various elegant dresses and suits framed against the speckled lawn and big chestnuts under a delicate blue heaven. The tableau seems fine enough, but I wonder if I am a part of it. Tessa, not a fool, adjusts my face and outfit more than once. Anyone'd think I was marrying you, I remark. Could do worse, she retorts. Actually the suit is almost luxuriant: silver with black silk shirt and silver tie. She assures me for the third time I don't resemble an assassin. Truth is, I've already espied Romy Kurazan under a chestnut, holding on to Solomon Lane. What is one to do?

Now a Jaguar rustles on the drive. Out steps Claudia, then Saul with some effort (he's still strapped up) in black with kippah, and finally Lucinda, holding a little posy, in simple body-fitting ankle-length satin, off-white, and a long blue wrap about the shoulders. Cherry-brown hair worn down as usual, with a light silver band. The effect is… calming. Claudia meanwhile rocks up in brilliant green knee-length silk, plus a disc with half-veil and blossom filigree above hair worn up and pendant emerald earrings. Like nobody else.

Not too formal, I said to them. We meet and kiss at the door, a tableau. Lilian Bourne films it all. The guests file into the church, and we the family greet them and smile. Following on, we enter the nave as one. Thoroughly modern. Our priest, a manifestly good-looking fellow garbed in purple and white, greets us at the front. Claudia has chosen with professional care. Ahem. Father acknowledges Saul in his Judaic attire; we're all equals here. First the Mass. I perform my duty with light detachment as if participating in an interesting game. Claudia seems to exude emotional charge; her acts are impulsively bold. Lucinda is serious and contained, dare one say scholarly. Even Saul in his stolid stillness seems to accept the ritual with courtesy. There is a moment of comfort when the priest places hands on one's head and blesses the marriage, and when he looks into one's eye with solemnity and urges one to love, honour and cherish, one can readily see what he means.

Nearby Ranelagh House, the venue, gives out onto lawns and chestnuts too, and I am glad, since in gentle nature I may hold onto a semblance of myself. Wide terraced steps herald a big room with French doors opened to the spring, framed by white, pink and turquoise blossom. Seating nooks are democratically arranged for seventy in white and gold. With several statues and a fountain, the effect is comely, quietly Italianate. I am impressed.

I take care to ask the Maître D. to set a place at Solomon's table for Romy. She peers from across the room and I signal to her. She blows a kiss. Beyond the somewhat solemn service, faces seem to lighten, and so arrives the bubbling of chat. Waiters flit about and ply people with sparkling flutes, and the patter and clink grows denser. I step over to Solomon for some reason, and as we shake hands I note he is sweating, exudes an ill-at-ease redness under the beard. Strange. Maybe his balls hurt. Romy sails out of nowhere (on cue) and theatrically clutches his arm, then ensconcing me inside her white shawl bites my ear and whispers *Congrabulations, darls. Thanks for my invite.* Beyond this I have no clue what to do with myself. Lucinda takes hold, leads me about. Handshakes, chat, kisses to a plethora of uni people. She's animated now, seems determined to enjoy. Sorry about you-know-who, I say. *Forget it, darling!* Lucinda is a dream from which light oozes. I seem to enter a passive state of awe, which happens to me when confronted by class. I never can fathom how such a human gaggle can be so richly healthy, how effortlessly the web of invisible class flaunts its attainments in a cosmos all its own.

And, there is my mother. She came to the service and sat at the back. I slip over and greet her. We stand, semi-formal, side by side in the throng. She tells me she felt it best to come alone. We appear really rather similar in places like this. To my eyes, she seems... contained. We chat as if she's the nice lady next door and I the boy who comes to mow her lawn. This seems a safe arrangement as we warm bit by bit to facts of each other's lives, quietly looking to discern the filigree of their separateness. Claudia has other plans. She comes at us with determined zest and sweeps mother away to the top table to be seated within her encompassing. And suddenly there's Patti Lorr, and beside her... the Man. So. The fellow decided to turn up. What to do? I see I am alone in this. Who would understand, since I never spoke to anyone about him? Patti is dressed in an unbelievable theatrical hat under which she glances about like a frightened pigeon. Then realising it, the expression defaults to vindictive pique. She nudges him and vulgarly points at me. He turns, in some unutterable posture, all six feet four, and espies me from said height. I am forced to walk across. Gutless Patti grips him.

- Welcome, Patti.
She attempts irony. - Charmed, I'm sure
- Hello dad. Thank you for coming.
He achieves irony. - Oh I wouldn't miss a wedding in which my offspring is to marry the daughter of a Professeur. Ha ha!
- Jolly good
- Am I to be introduced? *Saul* Grail, is it not?
- Yes, and his daughter's name's Lucinda
- Is that *him?* Look, well done, chap.
And he claps me on the arm and heads for poor Saul, Patti in tow. He'll ask him for a job no doubt.
At that moment, a vibration in my pocket. My mobile. Should I? I step aside.

'Mr___ , this is Doctor Barr from The Fall Institute. Would you be so kind as to call or come to our premises at the earliest opportunity. We also seek to contact Ms Lucinda Grail. We regret to inform you that Ms. Miki Okono, the Japanese girl, passed away last evening. With best wishes, Alicia Barr.'

I stand there staring at the screen. My eyes cease to focus. Lucinda is eyeing me from the far side. She beckons. I point to the men's room. Inside... take the end cubicle, lock the door and sit... close eyes... breathe in, out. The muster of humanity seems to fade. Gradually there comes from afar, a low bumping sound in its place. I recognise it as my own heart. I attend to it now, and it leads to a closed place.

Fear. Never without it. Everything that's born will die. Not a creature stalks this earth without fear. The little gull who squawks and eyeballs me on the beach will be carrion. Did I say goodbye? Even the big eagle in the sky will totter to its last crevice, shroud itself in its wings and close its eyes. What is there to do in this world? Acts let us forget, but as soon as we cease to act, fear returns. After the time of forgetting, fear will exact its price. At the going down of the sun and in the grey dawn… Why are we born if there's nothing to be done? Even when we know there is nothing to be part of or commit to, even if dying is but a shifting forever into rarefied worlds, we fear returning here as helpless children, to relive all this ignorant absurdity. Never gone, that nameless *loss:* of my body, of my mind, of my mother, of my father, of my friend, of my wife, of my life. … Poor little Japanese girl.

There is a knock. *Are you there, my friend? It's me, Solomon. Lucy is wondering where you are. We want to start, you see.* I step out. He is embarrassed. Touch his arm, apologise, walk out to the crowd. Lucinda is there. Are you all right? *Fine, no problem. Dizzy for a moment. All fine now.* She looks at me with round eyes, then she leads me to our table. Everyone applauds us. Sitting there she clasps my hand under the cloth. Saul stands. There is silence. He sniffs, surveys the room.

- My friends, in this life we must face the truth, whomsoever or wheresoever we are. We must be ourselves. Let us seek help, where and from whom we need it. Let us look forward, for nothing is lost. Let us have courage and acknowledge our fear. I myself have never acknowledged in public the reality that I am a Jew. Although most people will actually know it, I have never *allowed* it. Today I wear the kippah. My own wife Claudia I married in a church twenty-five years ago. I hoped then that my fear in this life would be taken away. Perhaps she felt the same in regard to me. To some extent we can help each other, and to some extent we cannot, for we live with our history. Let me raise this simple glass. This is the cup of Miriam, sister of Moses, who led her people out of the kingdom of Egypt thousands of years ago. This was the Passover. Throughout history Jews have been victims of the irrational in man, and you will think of the Holocaust. But I am here today because I believe that the simple things - love and marriage and family and hope - will prevail. And whosoever my daughter marries, I wish it to be known that she embarks on a great *feeling* adventure, into the heart of herself and the heart of another. And perhaps I myself have not done that, have failed to do that. And perhaps

I can begin anew, with my daughter and my wife and my son-in-law. Ladies and gentlemen, let us toast the bride and her groom. They will stand together and they will stand apart, but today they commit. Today they take responsibility little by little through each other, for each other, and for themselves. Please raise your glass. Let it stand for the grail we all seek. For truth, understanding, feeling, love - and commitment.

Saul sits. He is sweating. I didn't think he would or could deliver all that. Just goes to show. There is studied applause; the crowd appreciates an orator it seems. I catch his eye and nod to him. Lucy is shedding tears. And so is Claudia.

Now my own father stands up. What could he possibly say? But I forget he is an actor.

- My friends, I am David____ , father of the groom. Some of you may know me as David Darkness. But today I come not to speak of darkness but of light. For we are suffused in the pearly light of this happy gathering. Ms Claudia Grail, whom I have but lately come to know: thank you for this lucent celebration. And for your own remarkable beauty. It is truly a light to our weary eyes. As is the light that shines from your beautiful daughter, whom my son has the honour and privilege of coupling with today. And Professor Grail, we thank you for your superbly honest and courageous words. I myself well know what it is to place my heart 'pon my sleeve and face the slings and arrows of outrageous criticism, in exposing the truth of our failings, of our vanities, our fears and our ignorances. For this is the role of the artist. But let me not dwell on myself - although I note the opportunities afforded by a captive audience! To my son I say, although we seem to have but tarried here a moment together in this life, I feel that I know you and have influenced you, that you have made the right choice, that you marry into a family of great merit. And for this alone I congratulate you. Ladies and gentlemen: the Grail Family.

This is greeted with a bluster of applause, and father seems satisfied with himself as he cheek-kisses all the good-looking women within reach. He even tips his glass to me. My poor mother sits quite still.

Lucinda has opted not to speak. Her expression tells me she has finally recognised my father - as the man in the *Theatre*.

But now Claudia stands and invites the world to eat and drink and dance. No-one asks me to speak, which is just as well since I probably would claim Saul has said it all. What can a man say at his own wedding? We stand in the midst of nothingness and claim that it means something. Best to shut up and drink.

But no public moment would be complete without Romy Kurazan. She totters to her feet. Looks tragic, dangerous and lovable all at once. And says:

- I just want to say... that there's nothing deeper in this world than two people together in *love*. And no-one should ever be allowed to get in the way of *that*. You see, I don't know my dad or my mum, not really, and - oh sorry! my name's Romy - and I'm really not a bit drunk - well a bit tipsy - but where's the crime in that? Uhm where was I? Ah, Lucinda and Jean Luc: you are so perfect. My *friends*. May I speak on behalf of your friends? From Solomon and me? 'Cause if it all falls apart, you just give old Romy a call and she'll come running and fix it up. Fix it all up. Yeah.

And Solomon pulls her into her seat. She smooches him loudly. Scattered applause, smug sidelong looks.

A wedding's a great excuse for mindless carousing since it celebrates LIFE. Claudia has arranged a sumptuous buffet and swing band, and now eager punters spill out over the premises and onto the lawn. A lot of babbling and squawking and stuffing of faces is going on. Lucinda is hovering about like a moth, glancing at me. Finally she pulls me aside.

- I didn't know that man in the theatre was your *father*! My god
- Sorry darling. I really didn't know how to tell you.
She looks a bit demented. I squeeze her hand.
- Have you had a single thing to eat?
- And your poor mother. I really have to look after her. She is *not* happy
- She'll be all right. She's tough

- And what's got into *you*? You look like you've seen a ghost
- It's fine. All fine
- And *please* keep Romy under wraps, will you darling?
- I'll get Solomon to do that
- Will you? I've got to mingle. Eat something won't you? I love you darling
- You too.

And she slips into her crowd. I watch as jolly Solly Lane pats her baby backside and she mocks up a shock and slaps his cheek, and 'little boy' pouts claiming hurt, and several rowdies laugh. And eagle-eyed Tessa slides over, shoves a tart in my mouth and squeezes my nose till it stings. *Keep away from that Romy*, she breathes in my ear. The band revs it up. I note the Italian trumpeter, sassy Claudia's boy no contest. Look how she's beaming at him right now. In this rent-a-throng people spout their mouthings each to each since conversation's off limits. A welter of food is getting guzzled, half an ocean of booze. I manage to drift about and play the innocent abroad amid the hooting crowd. They seem to gape in surprise when I enter their kooky conclaves then compensate with hasty slurps on my cheek or muddled shakes of my foreign mitt. Old Saul manages to look conspiratorial, claps a drink in my hand and whispers *well done son* in my ear. I hug his shoulder and feel like a fool for doing it. His speech was all right though. How to avoid father (and floozie Patti), who triumphantly regales a sizeable clan 'pon the terrace with the tallest of tall tales? I find myself wishing he was a nice guy since he's far too entertaining. And Romy K. stands in the midst in her four-inch heels, toes pointed in and face askew, with her leathery bodice and her nutty knees, tart half in her mouth, peering at the populace through saucer-eyes like the five-year-old at her own birthday. I dare not approach, though if I would, I'd never leave her in a thousand years.

And at length there's a ceremony where a cake is cut amid a flurry of flashing snaps, and apparently people think I'm a jolly good fellow since they sing it out loud, more for their paramours I suspect than for me. I find I'm the centre of a thousand poses, and people are getting friendly friendly. Now it's darkening out, and terrace lights come on. There's a girl I know… I think she's called Lucinda, holding onto Tessa's big man, and a fuzzy yid called Solomon who's cavorting with shady Lilian… And poor dear Romy, swaying swaying wivout no partner at all. Dazed, distracted, she did some crime 'cause something oozes from her skin in the hubris sublime. And the Uni types and the gung-ho rowdies, and the fluttery elder dowdies with their in-laws and out-laws, all the shiny reckless people, myriad colours on their ripe-tripe faces, rolled liquor in their eyes, are dancing in a bacchanalian confab of lust and throwaway lies. For gapey happiness never dies, it's what we're living living for, on our boozy oozy dance floor, on and on through the arcadian night. I just got married. To what? Life is embarrassing.

So at last the white corpse of Miki slips my mind, since somehow along my way a dozen glasses have emptied down my throat. Out in the bowery garden there's the faintest sniff of wind, and glimmering light spatters the grasses, silhouetting a perimeter of heavy trees and a couple of lone stars in the black bowl of sky. I walk abroad. Below the rustle of a massive tree I spot Lucinda, her cherry hair… and a solid back - that'll be Solomon - unseen by all but me the husband. And she seems to be pushing him back, but he's coming at her again. There's a pantomime. Finally she lets him close, and he makes the most, 'cause his hand's between her legs and her dress is lifting lifting and he fiddles about his fly… and I think she wants to *die*. But my precious wife is disciplined! She pushes him into the dark, and her guilty hands feel over the dress, to straighten her creases, to hide her mess.

Should one interrupt? I'll turn away. Observe luscious Tessa instead, with her big man Troy. There's an altercation it seems. Marriage not going to plan? I step across and Tessa turns, and behind me she spies my Lucy. Darling, come talk to me! she cries. And Lucy tipples across, out from under her tree, where the other guy lurks embarrassed, seeking a way to flee. But the Moment has arrived. To make our scene complete there's criminal Romy standing on the step, and pointing pointing at Lucinda's dress. *Jean Luc!* she cries. (Yeah, that's my name) I can see in her eyes she dreams of murder, some wild surmise of a potentate's daughter, uncivilised. - Jean Luc, look to your wife! Look at her, why don't you? So everyone looks, and Lucy startled wants to cover her body from prying eyes but Romola runs at her, flings her aside, cries: *What do you want with my lover?* And she drags Solomon Lane into the light, and she clutches at his hair and shouts: *Is this man your husband? I saw them, I saw them at it in the shadows! See, see! Oh oh have pity on me!* And she makes her pantomime, such bad acting to be sure but quite enough to make me love her, the crazy crazy whore. I don't want to hurt Lucinda because I feel just how she feels, but here's an excuse to knuckle Solomon Lane. The time has come. I step right over and whack him as hard as I can, right in the face! And Lucy starts her screaming, and we men flail our arms in guttery disgrace. Now Tessa and Troy try to pull me off but the Jew and I are scrabbling in the dirt, locked in our fool's embrace. He's quite sodding tough this Solomon, and he gets in a couple that bloody my visage before Tessa's man, strapping fellow, pulls us apart. Solly's bleeding. Tessa shouts at us both. And Lucy is sitting leg-splayed on the grass and she cries and she pouts. *You louts!* And I feel rather sorry, and nearly apologise. Where's the devil Romola? Nowhere to be seen. Good riddance says Tessa. Now Claudia comes running, alerted by some people, and demands with green-wild eyes to know what just occurred. Solomon shuffles his feet and says: a misunderstanding, nothing. And she sees her baby daughter splayed out on the lawn, and clasps her arms about her, glaring up at us all. Alcohol lends its patina to our scene, and we're haloed like criminals in the gaudy shadows. We stand ashamed, and I feel oddly lonely. Now Solomon wants to help Lucy up but his face is bleeding and Troy plants him to the side. Lucy stands, and she curses at her mother, warns her to stop her fussing! And Lucy looks at me, and her round guileless eyes crumble and melt away. And I tell her don't you worry, it'll all be okay. You're not well, she says, we must get you a doctor. Absurd remark. And oh, she sees my mobile lying in the grass, and she picks the thing up, and I shout no! and she says what? and wants to make it go. In the shadow-light we stand about, watch the dishevelled bride fiddle with a phone. Now she squints at it. What's this? she says, and I wonder what she means. Tessa takes over and reads out aloud. - It's some message from a hospital. About a Japanese girl - who seems to have died...

We gawp as Lucinda totters away into a darkling field. I wave the others to let her be. No, Claudia: it's my job now, to have and to hold from this day forward.

So. Lucy and me. We enter a bower at the end of the lawn.
- I'm sorry
- Why didn't you tell me about Miki?
- How could I, on your wedding day?
- But you found out alone, and told no-one. My baby, why did you not tell? I'm your wife and you have to tell me
- I thought you wouldn't cope, but I see you really can. It's me who doesn't cope, and I'm a stupid man.
Pause. She stands and sweats, and stickily so do I.
- I fucked up with Solly. I'm a stupid fucking stupid bitch and I deserve to die. I was so pissed I didn't know what he was doing.
What *he* was doing? And she's balling her eyes out in the dark. I let her do it for a minute or two, then wrap her with my arms. We both feel stupid empty lost. We both are fools. And we'd better get used to it.
- Don't apologise, I don't deserve it. But crikey, my male ego can't take it. If you care about him go ahead and do it. If you don't, give it up. He's a jackass don't ya know
- Will you give up your Romy?
- I never had her. She's completely untouchable
- We can be adults about this
- What does adult mean? I'd rather die first
- Die with *me*, then
- Okay. Can you wait fifty years?

And she pulls me down. We lie askew all over the grass, stare at the sky. The dark rolls over us. Neither of us cares. 'Cause it's our fucking wedding.

Picking Over The Corpse   It's been my intention to tell this morality tale from the eyes of one who refuses to believe in morality. Post-wedding, you will point out that a married man needs to grow up, accept new rules of behaviour. You'll note the multiple ways I've labelled myself shallow, dilettantish, embarrassed at life, irresponsible, amoral. But how can I explain the absurdity of morality? I refuse to dwell on good-bad, right-wrong, where we judge with our famous discrimination and bung on our moral stamps. Meanwhile all we've done is create great tangled messes called intellectual tradition or religion. What happened to real feeling? And what's so sacred about my marriage and the (lurid) circumstances of its coming about, that 'love' should now be placed as if in a sealed jar and worshipped? Although Rules might apply in relationships, you can't expect me to take them with any degree of seriousness - even while I play along, admitting their annoying presence. Irony is my refuge, even in love. Don't we know the springs of happiness are contaminated by the politics of love? Happiness lies in the simple, spontaneous, thoughtless. And spontaneous acts and feelings are the bloodied victims of morality. Yet I, who fretfully dissect the roots of relationship happiness, have turned into the judging intellectual! Lo, by writing a book I become my Dreaded Shadow. Why write such guff anyway? I know I'm a mirror gazer who doesn't offer much (there's too much disappointment) but my real wish all along, reader, has been to show myself as *vulnerable,* as really feeling behind all the contradictions! Scary don't ya know? In other words I am *special,* and deserving of your love. Forget I'm a narcissistic praise junkie. You are too I bet. Just appreciate that I'm not fossilised by stupid rules, not a hypocrite in a right-wrong straitjacket.

Meanwhile, having sought to surrender to feelings in all their horrific modalities, one finds one is fairly useless at them, and that one's intellectual wife does rather better! Let's segue from marriage to morgue. On day two after the wedding, which you will be pleased to know sputtered out in a detritic miasma at two in the morning after the last fool-reveller had left and after tearful Claudia had been assured by all that her efforts had brought peace to heaven and earth, Lucinda and I made our pilgrimage to the hospital place where Miki's soul had breathed its last fanatic whisper. Directed to the morgue, we were asked to identify a white body.

And Lucinda plunges into the pantomime of death with a fervour that deludes her. Miki has become mythic since she didn't know the girl: victim, heroine, daughter, grand metonym of unholy experience she might yet strive for. Or maybe Lucy wants to somehow exit herself? Now that she has a corner on the feeling business I bow out, and in the way of 'young turk with whole life ahead' (my new pose on becoming a husband) try to affect the sort of solemnity I would reserve for say, an unfortunate cousin who has 'popped over the border'. The truth is I *was* sad for Miki - but Lucy hogs sad and tragic. Women steal one's feelings away.

Should we laud the outrageous Miki? You'd think we would: bravery, courage of convictions, no compromise, heroic, all that. But my response is pragmatic, even defensive. Sure, the girl was true to her fruitcake dream, but where's the romance in throwing your life away? As a woman Miki was over the top, and I have to admit my ego is threatened by women like that. Suicides are beyond me since they *ignore* me. One might counter, we have to be alive to be brave... and cowardly and stupid and wrong and egotistical and ridiculous and in love and all the rest of it. I myself need a stage where tragedy and comedy and farce can play out, with living women as antagonists. My soap opera must live for its own benefit: I'm the vain actor after all. And why do yourself in if there's no-one watching? I can't see why Miki wouldn't want to be an attention seeker. We're all self-centred. Life is for self-centred living, and the unhappy, restless and wanting will inherit the earth. Her death thing destroys romance because it is *certain.* And it's uncertainty that keeps us alive. And in love. She had to punish her dad after he'd pushed her to hysteria. He was just a punisher who refused to be the guy she could fuck and marry and have babies by. She was too fanatic, and in dying too pragmatic. Love is ironic don't ya know? And she'd do it all again no doubt. Bad luck. Oh well, at least she broke the rules, and she felt something, and was true to herself. Hats off, etcetera. What now? Nothing. Sayonara.

At a café afterwards, Lucy recounts that she visited four times, but only once did Miki speak a few precious words - and that these words related to a need to die in order to be purified. And that she forgave her lover, her father. (Forgave? Should have stabbed him as well) Lucy wrote the words in her book and they're sacred now. And she will write to this man in Japan and it will be solemn and putrifying - sorry purifying. Death is sacred, right? I tell you it isn't. But I'd not say it to Lucy. The dead can never be confined to the little hole of another person's fancy. And I the melancholic who visions all as romance, I myself seem to have been dying beside the eternal wind and sea for so long that death is but a condition of living. I've prepared for it with the rising of the sun and its going down, so am detached at the prospect of a corpse in a morgue, albeit a lovely one.

Except that I will use death as a cause to scorn all experience, all moments, all relationships, all life. And scorn is my great excuse not to participate - in this ghost-dance, absurd corpse-dance of the never-never, this always-might-be, this never-was. Participation is embarrassing, I can't bear it, I lose control. I cease to be. Participation has always signalled death to me: controller, watcher, non-combatant, ironist that I am. But I also know scorn is but desire inverted. And I desire. They tell me, these whispering ghosts of desire, that therein lie spontaneity, gaiety, thoughtlessness, tom-fool insouciance. No place here for death or any reverence for it! Instead, happiness, innocence, simplicity, love, participation! I'm trying to tell you how I would like to live but never have, never could, maybe never will. Oh fuck writing about it. If you get my drift, you get it.

South Of Solitary   I did not realise that the depressing corpse of Miki signalled the incorporealness of me and Lucy. Should I have forced myself to talk to her about too-big thoughts and feelings? Would our post-wedding blues have been a chance for caring and sharing, for unpicking my morose fragility and her mood for exit? I didn't get a chance to find out. Days later, with the assurance of the truly serious, Lucy tells me she has accepted a tutorship in a university in our largest city. Many miles away, for a year. And yes she's going. And that it would seem to her at this juncture that a bit of distance (a bit of death) may be appropriate for both. She will of course visit and no doubt keep in regular touch. Besides, she has a book to write. Fait accompli! I nod sagely. Did she plan it all? I am quietly flabbergasted, but what do I do? How could I not concur after all I've said? You dear reader are my refuge: who else to talk to? I'm cornered. Lucinda dictates terms and I must according to all principle let her go. What happened? No no, I merely acknowledge the presence of regret. And regret is bad. Lucinda is gone.

So Romola wins. But she is gone too, naturally. To central Asia I hear, perhaps to make determined love to her roots on a great empty steppe.

She sends me a postcard of herself sitting astride a yak, which looks a trifle disconcerted, as yaks might with strong-legged weird foreign girls parked on top of them. One day too I stop in at Tessa's place. But she, beyond our usual conspiring of touch and lippy kiss, 'says without saying' that our game has been ever-so-slightly compromised, and that she has *some* duty to her husband Troy (whom I quite like, to be fair) and that in all gallantry I might see that our window of intimacy has narrowed just a tiny notch, sweetie. Only for the time being, you understand. And this will amaze you, but I am smitten with the curse of tears, beyond the garden wall on her deserted avenue of leaves, that I never saw coming.

In Claudia's case, the topic of Lucinda's departure is barely raised. Except that one time she and I walk out on the moor above the cliffs and the sea, and I'm forced to seek her advice. In truth I want to rekindle our own subtle cohabitation in the fields of sense. But Claudia has seemed distracted since the end of *that* wedding, as if exhausted by the prospect of moving on in time, as if required at last to face her accustomed husband, to fight no more the battle over their daughter, and really to say adieu to the girl in herself. Am I relevant to her now? This is my real question. Instead she talks luridly of her husband's prospects, then relates to me some turgid story about how Solomon Lane had come to her and sought her motherly advice on 'whether to remain or whether to seek a position in a certain university in our largest city'. This I don't want to hear at all. Yet Claudia, being not a fool, takes me down to the beach below, a place she never overtly would go, and we say goodbye to liaison and hello to formal friendship with a quiet event amid sweet tears upon the stones of the beach at the entrance to a mossy cave I once dreamed of she and me in. Then she resolutely wraps herself about and walks away. And I sit and stare at a buffeting thoughtless inhuman sea.

One time, I go to town and without warning call on my mother at a hospital. She greets me with candour but seems occupied. She speaks of her busy job with the needy and dying. Our meeting is weightless and brief.

Such a man as me who claims to 'have no pride' shouldn't bother himself if he sheds another great skinful of it. To commit to befriending a lesser self than you thought you were - despite the defiant shout that you are as infinite in faculties as the eternal sky and deserve no less - takes courage that I've not yet discovered. On the beach the seagulls seem remotely concerned. Or not, as they please. I make a point of feeding them. And by some strange chance I discover a stray cat (a white one) on the moor, which I take back to Saul and Claudia's and offer to their care. Later, I snatch the furry one away in a midnight ride to my town apartment. And I implore her to live with me there, which she deigns to do after I fed her the best salmon and caviar. For five days running.

Little of consequence passes between me and Lucy since there is little prospect of D and M while her head is absorbed in The Book. *Women Outside* Etcetera. Live the dream, Lucinda Grail. I realise I'm actually jealous of her since she is committed to something. It doesn't matter what or how inconsequential, but *being there* with something, nurturing it, is a simple expression of forgetting. And forgetting is eternity writ small. But eternity beguiled by loneliness, places its head in the noose of time, shuffles its shoulders in the cage of the months and weeks, paces moody in the glass prison of the hours. I can't forget. Can she?

The Arrival Of Shakti   Months later at the start of winter, I receive a handwritten letter from Lucinda. This is the crucial part of what it says:
...On this day I sit on the floor in my chilly big room by the park (which you have never seen) poring on my rigorous work. The snow has fallen for days, and a skein of white shrouds the alien-familiar outside (as you know, I am a stranger in this quiet suburb) leaving all objects, dead or undead, in a limbo of blank whiteness. I work as usual alone, within my mind books. But today I seem to stare blankly outward at all the white. As if to mock my dogged journey, some romantical distraction of non-intellect tugs at my shivering shoulders. Then a passage of poetry: *For when this quiet swan in restless flying, shall find her own eternal life...* I tell you there came a white force like some ghost in spring, descending from above and into me and down my spine and into my body and across the floor with what seemed a sigh or a cushioning. A clear light enveloped me, and I felt myself opening out, as if the confines of the body couldn't

hold, as if the confines of the room no longer held, as if the confines of my thoughts had never held. Then there was a timeless peace - of secureness but aliveness - and a sparkling opening of my two eyes. And it was *as if this had always been.* The wonder! Like a resolution where all made sense in some thrilling perfect dance of clarity and spontaneity. I think some older self has died. I feel younger!

And you see, Jean Luc, I have been in this state for several days. And I have really not eaten. And I know I should but I don't care. In fact I care about nothing in the world except being as I am. I am so excited. Things are so beautifully uncertain, yet they are secure. Strange paradox. I hope I can always be like this…

I thank you for your texts, but you will see now why I wanted to write in longhand. Well, I have decided, reluctantly but firmly, to come back early, and for good. And I expect that you will be there. In fact I know you will. I shall be at mummy and daddy's by Saturday week. You might like to call me.

* * * *

There's no aphrodisiac like loneliness, and today I'm like the cat who got the cream. My detached little white puss (apparently someone named it Lucinda) eyeballs me from her windowsill atop the heater, since I had the temerity to disturb her seasonal repose with a bit of thumping and jigging about the room. Don't disturb! Back in your box, she warns. Don't worry, I say. Normal ironic transmission, from a lofty romantical distance (not a bit arrogant or take-for-granted) will be resumed forthwith. More or less.

Commitment Is Impossible   In the presence of the irrational, in the presence of death, in the presence of sex and love and women and men and relationships, in the presence of the wind and the sea, in the presence of change and emotion and delusion - how can there be, on this earth, any such thing as commitment? Yet people want certainty: certainty of ideas, of tradition, of religion, of morality, of habit, of rules. We have to fix something, but the moment we do, it kills us little by little.

Perhaps we may commit to the uncertain, to change, to nothingness, to the sea of possibility, to the ocean of being, to centreless bliss? Would these not lend us majesty? Only then may we surrender to the irony and embarrassment of the trivial, of our daily mortality: the little, the empty, the shambolic, the absurd, the Sisyphean, the ignominious… which again all demand the bliss of forgetting. Ah - but if we forget, we're *gone*.

Normal Transmission Resumed   There are things in life I sagely know are beyond my ken. Mind you, if I write about 'em, how would they be? My ego is sticking forks in, but I really will have to let Lucinda become special to me, on a pedestal once and for all, otherwise all our previous angst will be wasted. Because reader, you surely didn't think I don't want to reform, not be other than the curmudgeon I present to you? If you cut me, do I not bleed? Do you know how it hurts to play cuttingly ironic devil's advocate? And without my smug-clever raft of evasions, how could we 've had a story anyway? But you can't expect me to change all at once. I'm invested in my lack of investment. Give me another century. And should my epistle contain 'character-development', 'journey and happy ending' (as my dad debunked in his wacky lecture)? Any ending at all? I tell you life's never that. We serendipitously take on this and that along the way and meanwhile our familiar parts ossify or drown in buckets of self-justification. What parts? Attention-seeker who craves validation! Righteous critic of the human bullshit game! Scoffer at tradition and intellect. Sexist who parodies sexism, narcissist in his bubble, self-sorry manipulating egotist whose self-put-down is pre-emptive defence, booster of outsiders 'cause he himself is ignored, ironic actor hypnotised in his own play, fool taunting at others' foolery, dupe who can't decide whether he's ironical or romantical…
Blaaa. All these. No change.

So, what pearls shall we glean from significant others? My look-at-me old man won't give up his snobby posture, his delicate outsider-insider pivots, but he has his moments of outrageous bravery! My no-nonsense mother I should honour I guess: a professional carer. And luscious Claudia, goddess of feeling (though a narcissist like me) will never take seriously my brand of distant posturing. For Saul, the old monument, getting stabbed was the best thing since it woke him up to honest feeling, humility even. Even Solomon I can feel for: so desperate to be the schmick inside guy. And Miki. What to say? Mad and beautiful suicide who's *gone*. And Romola. So lonely wild she'll always feast on human flesh, and never be touched or touchable. Love that girl.

Which attitude then? Engaged or ironic or slimily elusive or morally firm? To be present or not. To feel or not to feel. To be adult or child. Close or distant. Commitment or knife-edge romance! All of them are just my clever armoury to dodge *discomfort*. No-one, least of all lazybones me, likes discomfort. Reason enough to enter the fragile mists of commitment with sweet Lucinda? I guess we could bask like kids together, novices in the currency of feeling, cravers of each other's intimacy, always sorry for each other. Me, I find it hard to respect. Breeds contempt. Easily put off. Good at pity though. I'll just wither on back to the lonely wind and the sea, and she will clutch at her books. God alone will know what we want. Till I miss her. And she me. Until I recognise I can't be without her. Then romance 'll be back... etceteraaa!

* * * *

Today is Sunday, one day in eternity. She's back, for good apparently. I've decided to place myself in awe of her. I bow to that luminous letter where she abandoned intellect, bowed to spirit, tapped great wells of feeling. She's a goddess, got it sussed. I'm not in her league. Not today. Though if she won't jump in the sack with me quick, I'll divorce her arse. So for the next formal hour or two I spruik self-abnegation and flatter myself that a dose of humility will not be lost on my scholar. Does she concur? Pleeeease? She does. We progress to the bed thing. It's all gooooood. We're not divorcing.

And I shall experiment with Lucinda, shall worship her in the distance of romance. Love, honour, obedience, respect and... oh, all of it at one juncture or another. We'll negotiate sweet limits in our house above the sea, with Saul and Claudia down the road, and in our separative togetherness we'll live half-committed and quasi-happy. Commitment to the asylum of marriage? Who can really afford to get used to someone? It'll morph to pity, and there's no respect in that. So on the basis of never veering close enough for boredom, pity or dislike, we aim for 'the balance of the unpredictable'. Who the bejesus can say we'll succeed? You *can't*. The point is it's unpredictable. Thanks Romola.

But one day, according to some whispering ghost, there arises what they say is an ideal state, beyond self-centred embarrassed fickle bored pitiful unpredictable… *Appreciation.* For one person. For their sweet limits. *Appreciation.* For you, micro-symbol of the great eternal. You, tossed by nasty winds just like me. Kindred soul, quiet and small. Both relieved! Goodbye tangled soap operas. Peace. Calm. Simplicity. Comfort at last… You reckon! I'm twenty-six for Jesus' sake. That old cardigan 'appreciation' can wait till I'm a hundred and sixty.

Just Do the Opposite   I mugged up a story for your entertainment about the ins and outs of commitment. To be brutal, I did it because I needed to address how intimate feeling is crushed under the mask of (my) egoism. I wanted to address a loner's nagging wish to find a place, and not least to satisfy my anarchic intellect's guilty want of *order*. I'm told we all must face our shadows, welcome and accommodate the opposite in ourselves. Maybe I actually want to learn to value myself through another (Lucinda), beyond all the self-posturing and self-talk. So how to be, if you really seek a relationship but want to not kill it? I've perfected the distant aloof outsider whose solution is to put the other on a pedestal and worship with faux humility. I've contemplated the serious-supportive-committed-responsible adult (for five minutes) and I've accepted the possibility of innocent spontaneous childlike intimacy (in some other lifetime). We float in a myriad universe. We are untouchably complex beings. Amid chaos we struggle for order, and having order we long for the chaos of possibility. In our souls anarchy and responsibility, aloneness and connectedness fight it out. My orderly analysis in this story has to admit its nemesis: we may have to succumb to dumb anarchy, and this may be a relief. So try this: Be lazy not studious, irresponsible not earnest, thoughtless not thoughtful, tom-fool insouciant not ceremonial, amoral not moral. Ignore significance, eschew self-analysis, abhor predictability. Play it as a game, not as serious war. Whatever you do, don't *commit.*

Meanwhile the ironic wind and sea outside our bedroom window roll on regardless and forever.

…I hear in the twitterverse, that a louche louty redhead named Romy Kurazan has just departed far Samarkand. Tossed out of that land as well no doubt. She is, as we speak, crossing the great sea. The Sea of Possibility. Apparently heading my way.

THE ELUSIVE

IN SEARCH OF FRANCESCA MARS

NICHOLAS FROST

IN SEARCH

OF

FRANCESCA MARS

Francesca Mars carries the world about her, dispensing waters to the downtrodden, scandal to the press, charm and stress to family and satellites. Self-immolating media star with a child's secret, she tilts at strange awakening, toying with all who need to put her on a pedestal or drag her down. Musician Nicky Bright and journalist Lena Duvorchek orbit Mars in an erotic triangle, fending off stepdaddy Peter, socialite mother Carolyn, great doctor Cotillard, Mister Bouseri the Eritrean and Ayaan his daughter. Bright claims to win, in a close-skinned contest of ambition and use, the politics of giving and wanting, glamour and ugliness, the artifices of art, the problem of value.

In Search of Francesca Mars

Lena Duvorchek shovels through the street door at a pace only a hack can generate on the scent of a story she thinks is going to make her. Dumps her bits, plants her leggy frame, commandeers the remote. Your writer tipples in with his miserable Indian takeaway. Life as we share it in this house careens around Lena's moods. Today's is the equivalent of a bloodhound at a hunt, and jackbooted Lena is ready to rip a rare bit to bits. Attempts to eyeball her, retreat to the kitchen, out loud protest that the tackies are getting cold: all a failure.

- Who cares about food? says lofty Lena.
- Me, though 'tis scant reward for my musical exertions
- Don't pout
- Not
- Your concert was a freak-out, okay?
- Yay
- And I've got shit on my mind. Come *on*!

She snarls at the TV. Life trumps slender art. I'm the idiot who tickles a piano.

- Is there news or what? This crap country! Aha. This is the girl I was telling you about, and that's her old man. Stepdaddy. Rich as fuck
- You mean the guy who looks like -
- Sting. Shhh. I need to hear this.

'...Police sources say Francesca Mars, daughter of prominent businessman Peter Mars, has been bailed following arrest near the scene of yesterday's fire which destroyed an outbuilding at the Wellcome Laboratories near Bath. It will deal a further blow to the reputation of Mars, whose company has been embroiled in controversy over alleged payments to locals in Somalia following deaths during a trial rollout of the anti-Ebola drug Demzyn...'

- Stop rustling the bag. She's talking...

Her Goddess Mars looks all at home in front of a camera. Swarms of pre-raphaelite curls are what we feed on first. Late twenties, romanish nose... it appears she's beautiful. Firm carriage, glittery vibe, strings of sculpted sentences tripping from the lips. Speech of a practised activist... ironic, challengy, enjoying her ego.

'- My father already told you there's no connection between my presence in Bath on Sunday and the fires at Wellcome - which I don't welcome by the way. Is it possible two great events can take place independent of each other? Whilst my person may be a source of continual gossip, we must assume that each and every attack on Big Pharma in this country is not necessarily orchestrated by the likes of Francesca Mars nor tied to the business dealings of her daddy...'

- Is she something or what? I did the personal interview
- One usually interviews personally. (She ignores) Personally when?
- Told you, a month ago. Before all this shit hit the fan. I offered to do big articles
- And she turns you down so you offer to write a big book
- So?
- Gonna offer your big head on a platter?
- Fuck off. Everyone's writing about her. Had to go one better
- Does everyone try to get in her pants?
- Possibly. I intend to beat the queue
- Looks like it'll be a long one
- Guessing you'd like to be on it? (Lena thinks she has me sussed)
- And you're certain she's gay
- Why do you assume all Serb girls are stupid?
- Only met one
- Listen upper-crust music man: I judge character better than you
- That's why you love me, and *I* don't love me. As we discussed
- If I get her you'll be more lonely 'cause I'll bring her here
- She's a goddess. She'll never come 'ere
- And *I* am not? I who you love unthinkingly?
- You're a glamazon. And your dinner's cold
- Microwave it then
- Yes master who's never my mistress

I head for the kitchen.

- So you liked my concert?
- Sure. I love ugly music

- What - a whiff of Stockhausen, bite of Birtwhistle, smidge of Xenakis and the world has a hernia
- World is full of shit and so are you my boy. We all prefer Mozart. ...Shall I call her now, tonight?
- Uh? But d'you think the punters got it?
- Got what, poser?
- The program! Pay attention
- Usual BBC *rubbish*
- Hate you.

Lena smiles at last. She's quicker-witted, crueller than I. And more fanatic.

- I must call. Establish special relationship. Be attentive, show concern
- She'll roll right over you by the look of it.

Lena's turn to pout now.

- I am not all sex and hunger. I am also professional
- You're a Serb. You bombed Sarajevo.

Oops. Lena glares witheringly at immature me.

- So my Lena has her personal number. I'm amazed
- You should be, Bright. I'm amazing.

She's grabbed her bag and bits and slammed the door to the midnight street. My Serb bombshell is fine when you're in the up mood, but seek a bit of nuance, bit of empathy for sensitive labour in the Feeling Arts, and the pragmatist bares her teeth. Now my curry's inedible; with her about I don't care what it tastes like. This fact suddenly looms as a harbinger of unease. If I could be number one for Lena I'd celebrate. No win with this female freight train though. Are they all built like her in Bozznia? I even fool myself she might ditch the lesbian pose for me. (boy shit) But is this Francesca really a girl's girl? Lena's fooling herself. Note to self: your habit of wanting to muscle in on other people's realities is an 'only child' thing, and probably the reason you insist on posing in front of crowds. For attention-seekers no amount of affirmation is enough. And I find I don't get the adulation I might presume to expect, since after my gigs people tend to say significant things like 'I note the way you mix Corea with Liszt, but did it make Liszt sound better?' Or 'I wonder how Shostakovich would react to having half his prelude played inside the piano?' I assume my faux-boyish manner invites them to twist my arm conspiratorially thus. But I can't hack it, I loathe criticism. I'm always right. Don't people see the effort? *You* do it arseholes. (Ye who paid good money) Okay, back off. I always get negative when it's late. Something to do with cracks in my aura.

Dump the curry for toast then. Ugh. I've an impulse to go find Lena. She knows I worship her in my nonsympatico way, and she'll fail to be surprised if I turn up at the *Split* bar where she'll undoubtedly be at this hour knocking off pricy cocktails to remind herself she's a real force in British journalism despite being born in the Balkans. She'll be on a stool fiddling with her phone and 'll already have racked up five calls to this Francesca Mars and will have put her foot in it since the more she pushes the more they all shut the door on her... And she'll be accusing the poor sod at the end of the bar who accidentally looked her way of sexual harassment while she's engaged in crucial business of national impotence, sorry importance. And the make-up 'll start to run and the long legs will get in a tangle as her skank-skirt slips about her bum 'cos she chooses to *not* be in control of her life anymore and let 'er hair down which is therapeutic for high-strung ambitious tarts... then all the guys 'll cop it (me too) 'cos she's out and proud and won't be fucken exploited by anyone. I'll slip into the *Split*, find her in a bluey corner and steer her out to the street, and she'll curse me louder than the rest but I'll smile like the martyr with a heart who bears the heavy load of Lena. I affect this pose because though she'd never let me anywhere near her heart, she kind of likes me slash loves me, whatever. But she also pities me and I pity her. So we get on like a house on fire. I choose this simile because our relationship is conducted as if our house were perpetually on fire. I'm always wanting her to be nicer to me, or at least appreciate my prowess as artist. This is a mistake. Here we are then, tottering down shadowy streets with misty rain in lamplight. Alcoholised Lena is occupied by deepy things.
- You know she keeps extensive diaries?
- Who?
- She. The One. Francesca Mars.

The thing about Lena is she can't hide her enthusiasms in the English way, and hence can't hide her failures.

- I guess you'd like to see 'em
- I *will* see them
- She hide 'em in her pants?
- Little shit. Just wait
- No really, I wish you luck. (I don't say she needs it) Invite her to our house. I will cook for us all. Stroganoff. And I'll talk intelligently about Big Pharma and Animal Rights.

Lena looks at me and smiles a little smile that I know is good.

- And then Nicky Bright 'll vanish. After he's played some tinkly preludes to get you pair in the mood. For *lurve*.

The Problem of Use

After Lena splashed into a bed (mine, I note with dismay) I feel a need to wrap my coat about and walk the veiny lanes of Chelsea. It's my habit to contemplate the minutiae of concerts when they're over. The world breathes again, seems solid and simple, reminding me my flight into art was a strange exercise in the fantastical and forbiddingly neurotic. Most concert musicians pop anti-nerve medication but not me. Why do art? I always ask and I never know. It's a problem of use: is it *useful*? Is there value? Or is there value in anything? If not in art then I suppose in nothing. When it's finished it's forgotten - and to be forgotten is a curse in this pastime paradise where we all grope for sense titivation, meaningful mind fodder, self-validation. Odd as well that I'll expend endless effort to get a perfumed result (phrase, nuance, structure) for a validating moment that (a) fills a faceless longing, (b) feeds my absurdly arcane taste for cosmic order. If I don't re-create the microscopic essence and make it sparkle like nothing else so I can strut about like some man in the moment ignoring all memory and time, I will be forced to face the airless void of all my acts. I'll be a nothing. I play for amnesia, to be present, to 'live'. And yet, though people might want what I give, I fear they don't need *me*... the pampered artist (in my own dream anyway). And I think of all the lowly ugly forgotten people: what do they ever do? I graze elysian fields and pay not a tithe in return, or I perform 'a duty of sadness' as if

Weltschmertz were my duty. Middle-class guilt! What a fake. Oscar Wilde would piss on it. Lived round here; that blue plaque says so. Jowly old T. S Eliot as well. Quiet stone, white plaster, boughs hanging over walls… wrap myself up, sufficient for a moment. But when the gossamer logic of that musical fragment falls into place, when all ears and eyes are trained on my gesture-conjecture-consequence, I'm indispensable then, bloody near happy. There's *suchness* in it, holding the now in my palm for all those hearers, as if at the birth of meaning, the coming of a child. 'Tis I who resolve the world's hiatus! Between the act and the consequence falls no shadow (mister Eliot). That comes *after*. Art can only translate the suffering of the outside, and since I feel guilt at suffering and wish it to stop and don't know how, I binge on art's empyrean fantasms. Patrons come for soothing and healing and we get a nice dream. But it embarrasses me; I feel the cost, I forget the ugliness. I run to obtuse risky places since music must be a mountain not a valley, life a hurdle not a cradle, art a burden not a gift. Self-flagellation is my duty while I cash in on sadness and joy. The world's flounderings and blunderings parade and resolve in miniature, reduced to gesture in an artist's hand. This escapist begs to suffer! So I toss in clangs of ugliness, dare my audience to get it. I won't feed their love affair with comfort: we all must suffer! Beethoven would assert it. Und Wagner. And mad Berlioz.

Dude, forget this arty web of emotional conjecture, focus on concrete pavements. But who even hears these steps: the darkness and silence? Imagine a *pure land* where no-one thinks or dreams or plays or walks, where life exists without the aid of will or eye or you or me, where music plays itself, or not, as it pleases, where the wind dances alone and where silence harkens only to itself. Perfection! *Escape.* Meanwhile I claim I can't do anything but play, that art is my penance in the absence of any other. Absurd are the subtleties of mentality and feeling! But art still steals, its exertions steal from me. How convenient: a paradox I don't care to settle. Walk on. In the comfort of the dark.

Aid Star

Lena struts into her own room next morning, yanks me out of her bed. I wrinkle an ironic eyebrow. With all speed she whips up the big wind of herself, and as flotsam in her wake I retreat to the bathroom from whence I am similarly ejected. Woman has the greater cause and need, and Lena is a woman of consequence. Her breathless readers await.

- What's the rush for a Saturday?
- You don't know?
- Apparently Nyet
- The press launch! Francesca Mars and her father are launching a partnership for Eritrea with an African businessman. The Savoy. I'm going
- There'll be high-class booze then?
- Your point is?
- While I know in my heart you're no alcoholic -
- And I know you're not my effing father, last time I looked
- C'n I come?
- No way
- I'm an asset. Legend in my own lunchtime. I'll schmooze for ya
- Mmm. Might be some arty wankers there. Stick to art, no politics. Get it?

Any grown-up wouldn't put up with this, you'd say. But Lena needs to play Grand Expert in her Field, and knows I affect to regard politics as mostly absurd tittle-tattle. Truth is (I claim) she's more interested in sex, gossip and corruption - no political heavyweight - and really she should take my advice and treat it all with irony since irony would give her a niche in the op-ed columns of her nauseously earnest weekly. Her writing's too heavily un-English, too east-European, though I forget those guys spent a century doing War and Commyism. She in turn points out I'm naïve (true true) and that she already mastered Balkan irony wherein all politics *is* sex, gossip and corruption. Since the Brits are famous for ghastly phone-hacking tabloids she claims she fits right in. *I* need to get my feet in the muck, she never fails to remind. That's why she never fails to undermine my so-called art. I guess she and me compete, but on completely different playing fields. Who knows, one of these days they'll coalesce and the contest get explicit. Today, maybe? At the Savoy door, I'm not sure how I'm dressed or who I am, but I hold to luscious Lena's coat-tails as she surges through the English plush toward the ballroom at the back. We're late. She eyes me as if I'm a smell, but it does me credit to be near: people gawp and I get benefit. I remind her I did in fact wash this morning and that some folks actually regard me as a human being. Thus goes our banter, and we bustle into the room.

I don't fail to recognise Francesca Mars, who stands upon a dais. The pre-raphaelite lush of curls is poised with nonchalance behind the head and she's holding forth to what appear to be a press gaggle and a coterie of well-dressed beautiful people.

- Your question Marty, says you're either ignorant of the situation on the ground or you prefer gossip to reality. While I'm partial to either, since we're here for the people of Eritrea I assume we focus on reality.
Lena wrinkles her nose at me. Stay put, it says. She heads for the front.
- Oh! says Francesca Mars. - This is Lena Duvorchek, people. Come up, Lena.
Lena looks pretty staggering. All the jocks roll their eyes. Marty protests:
- But Francesca, there are more brigands and warlords than even you can shake a stick at. Shouldn't you put focus over the border in Ethiopia?
- We go where the need is, Marty. Mr Bouseri will no doubt agree.
She glances at an elegant East-African-looking gentleman in a silver suit. Another journo sticks his hand up.
- Yeah, 'Michael at the Mirror'?
- Ha ha Francesca. How'd you two negotiate this deal? It's a mother of a package even for you. And what are you doing *ce soir*?
Titters and groans at our gallant friend, who looks smug enough.
- Washing my hair, Michael. Need to shake some men out. Look, Mr Bouseri is one of his country's philanthropists as well as a financier. My father and I are proud -
- But who actually clinched it - you or Peter Mars? And how'd he get the Foreign Office on board? It was *you*, right Francesca?
- Michael, take a look in the mirror (I'm sure you do by the hour) before you toss off-the-wall questions and rattle our guests. (Several 'oohs' from the press corps) No no, I'll answer. This deal's about painstaking negotiation, and without my dad's influence there'd be no question of -

- Corinne Davies, Financial Times. We know he's loaded but can he do it without your sex-appeal? - Andrew Card, Science Monitor. Is Demzyn actually safe? - Who paid off who in Somalia? (The pack's getting warmed up) - What exactly were you doing near Wellcome's laboratories on Thursday night? - Did you give the board the middle finger? - D'you have shares in that company? - Can you confirm a rumour you're engaged? - Is it in fact Doctor *Luc Cotillard?* ...Etceteraaah, generalised hubble-babble.

Francesca Mars shrugs and looks sideways at the man I assume to be Peter Mars. Dark Mr Bouseri smiles, and I notice there's a deep-skinned girl standing near him who'd likely be his daughter: tall in heels, hair set high over big earrings; a statuesque bored-looking Ebony goddess. Now Lena pokes her hand up.
- Can everyone be quiet please! I've a proper question!
The press gang ogles, mildly amused.
- Ms Francesca. Do you know how many landmines are in this area of Eritrea? And what effect these weapons can have? My father fought a war in Bosnia decades ago. That I am not proud of. And children of that country still die of landmines. Who remembers them now? Is it the right time to make a fuss about Ebola virus in Eritrea? Or is Ebola more *fashionable?*
Silence. Okay question. The pack smells a thing.

- Ms Duvorchek. Lena. (A glittery grin) You speak of fashion, and fashion is where money is, no doubt. I advise the moneyed class since I believe in the art of the possible. Though I can't contain the winds of fashion, and while I bow to the will of its arbiters (I note the esteemed press in front of me) I will pursue my course without fear or favour. I *will* stand up to the movers and shakers of this society and will use my influence such as it is. Ask Damien Hirst if fashion had no influence on turning 'artist' into 'billionaire'. Ask Obama if fashion had no influence on his becoming president. Mr Bouseri, you see the bourgeois games we're forced to play in my country. I hope you'll forgive. But money and influence make the world go round, and they alone decide which particular flavour of suffering we give our attention to this month. Come and stand where I stand, Lena, do as I do. Make your own decision!

- Do you imply I have no respect? D'you know how much respect I get for being a Serb in your famous country for example? Look at me, I can hit on any man or any *girl*. But do I want? No, I want respect for integrity as journalist, I don't waste time asking if you have a boyfriend or fiancé. I don't ask if you and the elegant Bouseri are 'close friends' or if you'll 'take me to dinner'. People here are pampered, spoilt. They should get a real life. I respect you if you tell them this. If you do not, I do not.

This exchange (if I got the gist) has a curious effect. We're all gawking like it's last set advantage server at Wimbledon. Francesca regards the lanky she-warrior with fear-free eyes.

- Yeah Lena, and you're right to say it. Perhaps you're too beautiful for your own good! Thank you for reminding us all of the *truth*. Now, shall we all have a drink and toast ourselves - the *lucky* people?

Booyah! Now it seems to me the subtle muso (and to everyone else in the room) that the subtext in this convo obliterates the text. Francesca knows how to orchestrate. How cutely she broke it up with flattery and the invite to drink. We masses follow and her cachet advances. Now we'll chatter and babble about exactly that. I cop myself fantasising what she's like up really close. Ooh, you don't get close, nobody does. Stepdaddy knows it. Look at 'im, smooth as you like, parking a public kiss. And are we assuming she's gay? Is she assuming people 'll soon be assuming she's gay? Next week, more questions! In this mingly throng I'm sweatily aware I've joined a pack that ogles the celebrity of Francesca Mars. What's she then? Saint-fatale? Gifted pollie peddling soft causes (pity / guilt) to get herself front and centre? Alluring, you can bet on it, guv. And knows no doubt how much this stunted community needs its stars. Rock star, movie star, porn star, Poof! Poor star, Aid star! Next I find myself standing next to that ebony goddess. How to strike up with this divine slip of elegaunce? She leans on her hip, flute in hand, nods to these whiteys with a demi-smile.

- So Mr Bouseri is your… father?
Voice from planet Mars is mine.

- Oh yes. (Offers a jewelled hand) Ayaan Bouseri. Pleased to meet. You are press?
- Actually I'm a musician. My friend is Lena
(She wrinkles her nose) - The girl who makes her question into a speech? So lively
- You're in business?
- Oh no. I am a student (student *what* - goddess?)
- Eritrea is your home?
- Yes. My father knows so many in the government. He wants to build our country
- D'you like UK?
- Oh I love UK. Bond Street, Knightsbridge, Kings Road. Beautiful. I am at home
- Francesca has a couple of things to say about fashion and money, right?
- Mmm… Francesca Mars gets what she wants from whosoever she wants. Okay… the girl just divulged a thing to a stranger. Avoid the bait though. Handy not to be a journalist!
- I don't know her at all. Why's she seen as glamorous, d'you think?
- Fame is aphrodisiac. 'Success' is 'the right people at your court'. My father must deal with such people. I tell you, women in my country do not like it
- Muslim, you mean?
- I mean dignified
- But you like the UK… women don't stay quiet here, right?
- Perhaps they should learn
- You wouldn't get much aid then, apparently?
Her jade eyes look through me. - It is not sympathy our people need
- But you're personally rich.
She frowns, ready to slip away. - Rich is not such a blessing.
This delivered as a lesson.
- I wouldn't know.
She moves. An absurd line exits my mouth.
- How would it be if *you* were to collect money for your country?
- Perhaps you'd like me to sell my sex as well?

Far out! I follow her with my eyes… and note how she touches (with her tippy fingers) a noble-looking guy in the crush. Not selling sex we hope. Should one've seen it? Next I'm elbowing Michael at the Mirror. He's stuffing a thing in his mouth.

- Grub's good. An' the plonk
- She spat out your question good and proper
- All sport to her. And to us too I s'pose. Still, gotta dig the dirt
- She's too ironic to be fake, you're saying?
- Nah, she's my kinda girl. That is, I'm guessing she is. Saw you n' that leggy babe walk in. Your squeeze?
- Nope. But she might be Francesca's.

(Where'd that come from?) - Don't say? Can you confirm?

(What's it to me?) - Your guess is as good as mine.

He curls his lip. Suddenly I'm a news bloodhound. I point to Ayaan's confidante.

- What's with that dude?
- Him? Luc Cotillard. Doctor, Medecins Sans Frontieres. One of the A-team. Could be more than; rumours rumours. If you're in with Fran I guess you're in - and all us proles are jealous. I'm off to chat up the black Venus. Cheers for the girlfriend tip.

No prob dude. Who'd wanna be in the A-team anyway? Fact is, jocks like him make me feel small. I'm a snob, despise this sort of shit. Lena needs to be in the *in* - or wants to manipulate it so she can despise it. She'd kill me if I explained that to her, mind. Maybe all journos loathe the mover-shakers: wanna set the world to rights but rely on them to do it? (Journos are like critics at my gigs: happy to be praised by 'em but as soon as they exhibit a view contrary to one's expert vision, it's 'You do it arseholes!') We *doers* are the real in-crowd. Actually, who could possibly be so un-ironic as to wanna set the world to rights? Suffering is endemic to this mortal coil: fix one thing, ten hydra heads pop up. Oh dear, I'm not equipped to deal with the serious world. Naïve I fear to be, idealistic I'm suspicious of, realistic I despise. Only equipped to 'finger it obliquely through art'. No woke idealist, or hippie or new-ager either, more a satirist-cynic (with a heart, otherwise I couldn't do art). This political bunfight, these ins and outs and low blows and subtle sallies, Politics of Giving Caring Aiding - they leave me cold. Possibly I'm lazy. I let this shit parade titivate like a soap or a good scandal where I loftily enjoy with dramatic irony the protagonistic twists. Why this dissociated riff? Mainly 'cause I'm overwhelmed by the fact most people on this planet live lives not remotely connected to higher things (in other words not remotely connected to me). Horrid, depressing. Not about not having material goods or entertainment etcetera, but how they just can't *have* 'the rare perfume of Art's subtle gift'. But then I wouldn't know if my world is superior since I'm a cossetted guy who learns about people and their shit from trash TV - and judge 'em. If you can't begin to fix things you can despise them, and if you can't be intimate you can look down upon. Oddly though, I feel that if I were forced to do a thing to *save* someone I'd probably do it. Am I saying I'd rather put food in the mouth of a bug-eyed dusty kid in Africa than play Chopin nocturnes? D'you know, I think I would.

Goddess Mars

In the crush the comet Francesca hovers. Sure makes a deal of mingling with the hoi polloi. Persuader, mmm, looks the Pro... carries no food or drink... light, energistic, calculating. Has to be ironic! One couldn't possibly converse with her. Quick, adopt 'disconsolate piano-player' persona, that'll save ya. She turns my way, like the Prime Minister would.
- Hello. You came with Lena - but you're not a journalist.
I take the proffered hand. Feel like I've reached a kind of centre. She holds for an instant. Special as the rest... but no-one's looking.
- I'm glad to meet you (a pleasure to say it!)
- Nice hand. You're a musician?
- Oh! I'm a pianist
- It's okay, Lena told me. Trick of mine to put you off guard. And your *name* is -
- I'm Nicky Bright

- Yess... I'm sure you are. (Impish smile; oh jesus) If there's a thing in this world that can make me lose my mind, it's music
- Oh?
- My real father Leo Gorda was a violinist. Have you heard of him? He died when I was fourteen
- I'm sorry. (Feel like I've been given a present) So... you lose your mind
- Not in anger, only in love. Daddy was a genius to me, but he's gone.
Either she's a magus who tosses spells, palm-reading virtuoso, or I'm number one boy in the room. Whatever, there's a cocoon.
- Do you play concerts?
- Yes, and I teach and compose. Like to 'fiddle' with the classics (ironic smile)
- D'you fiddle with violins?
That is sexy! - Oh *yeah*. Everything. I mix new media with classic repertoire (ugh, formal).
Francesca glances down, manages to seem vulnerably girl-like. I'm conscious of her hair. Red-gold curvy river, with estuary. Reassuring.
- *Play for me sometime.*
This is delivered in a whisper, but I get it. Vulnerable flirts with self-important, self-important with vulnerable. Could she be trusting me? Then Mars re-asserts.
- Okay. Great to meet. Enjoy.
One flash of the eyes in mine, and she's moved on.

Lena is looking at me from the far side. Seems agitated. I join her.
- Wanna split?
- Er - do you?
- What did she *say* to you?
- She said 'hello'. (Lena eyes me up) Actually, asked me to play for her. Did you chat?
- Everyone heard our 'chat'. (Uh-oh) No doubt you'll play for her.
I keep my mouth shut when Lena's in a mood. So we slip out and away, into the teeming Strand.

The Slaughterhouse

A week later, Lena lets it drop that Francesca Mars is making a speech at the Royal Society for the Protection and Care of Animals. Such a speech would never interest me, I tell myself, but I was alert since Lena mentioned it... though I doubt she wants me to go. Still, friends are bloody friends. The numbers are swelled this evening not by society worthies or hardened campaigners who'll boycott the event out of jealousy at a jumped-up media star, but by a nouveau crowd of young fans and the associated media scrum. Lena got her hands on the transcript. See below.

'- My friends, will I shock you if I say that a person who thinks that a dumb creature is born for his or her personal convenience and satisfied enjoyment, will be doomed to the repetition of a karmic cycle as *victim,* just as she was a perpetrator? This charitable society may dissociate from reincarnationism, but even the bible says the sins of the fathers are visited on the generations of sons and daughters. This institution is really a church, a holy place where we fight for the protection of the defenceless and the promotion of compassion. There may come a time in everyone's evolution where they will feel the call to be vegetarian, after which they will remain so as long as they are on earth, for howsoever many lives. In the slaughterhouses of the world, the beasts (loved by their guardians, we're told) are solemnly shipped to feed a great machine that spews forth its happiness on the human world in the form of food for tables. Our human survival machine processes animal life and wrings it out in blood, and we drink it and savour the flavour, convinced it'll make us healthy, make our children strong. Is it the place of the lesser animal to lay down and die for the intelligent and the good? And we won't neglect to feed their flesh to our beloved pets. By some miracle, out of this rouge threshing machine, comes enlightened thought and refined feeling, comes poetry, comes music, philosophy, democracy, law, religion and love. And materialists still say consciousness is just some creeping cosmic accident of the survival of the fittest!

Survival of the fattest, more like. Yet how do we at some point understand that non-violence lifts us, that kindness serves our purpose? Even gangsters are selective in who they slaughter, since 'to be happy' is their ultimate wish. But who can live in happiness where all about us is suffering? We must forget, ignore, or else trust that the dead are released to a greater realm where suffering is no more, ignore that this world is a railway station where souls come and go like automatons repeating an everlasting ritual. Moreover, this world is a killing field, slow or quick. If you believe consciousness is just an accident of experience then you will stay ignorant, will take a life, eat a life. Awareness is eternal, and if you know it not, you'll always kill or condone killing, since your survival is everything.

And it's just a step from animals to women. In Sri Lanka in 2009, as in China in 1937, as in Congo and Rwanda and Cambodia and a thousand other stricken places of the world, women are taken as meat to satisfy appetite: stripped, raped, shot, thrown on trucks, buried. Trophies! And the demented young soldier men who do it are moved to laugh. Women are cattle. Procreate, you women! There's plenty more of you. Create *me* - then die. But however and wherever, there'll be a haunting. Perpetrators will be victims since they deposited evil in their psyche. There'll be a filtering, as with water through stone, and as the years progress they'll be haunted by guilt and diagnosed with post-traumatic stress, which will fester and thrive and be visited on their families. Thus the blood of our country contaminates for generations. Through organised war we've contaminated the conscience of sons and daughters. Where is the victory? We drink our own blood. Perhaps what we need is farms that farm people. These will naturally be of a lesser race, except that human meat is just too stringy. Pigs and cows and sheep and chickens are better... Ladies and gentlemen, if we can kill an animal we can kill a human being. And we do. Our habit is embedded in the group mind; it is unthinkingly condoned. We must not forget this fact, we must face it. Then and only then can you choose: whether you will fight with anger, whether you will helplessly mourn, whether you will pass by and forget - or whether you will face your own shit. I leave it with you.

I have seen suffering and I have put myself there. I have looked and have forced myself to look. I have been to the slaughterhouses slow or sudden, to the fields of pain. I've gone there to cry (except that I did not cry much). It was my decision. I continue to do it. I don't ask you to do it. Tonight I have said hardly a thing that's new; it's ancient philosophy. But it turns out my passion, read my anger, is ever new. I try to heal myself since I can't heal people. What shall I do now? I don't know. Continue, I suppose. Yes, I will go back to Africa. And I thank you all for your support.'

This speech is hearty media fodder, not because they'll get it but because it'll discombobulate them all. Passion-ridden, shocky, calculating, philosophic too! Vegetarianism, Capitalism, Darwin, War, Grief, Women, Guilt and God, a hint of MLK. All conflated into an anti-establishment melange by an anti-darling of the establishment. Tricksy tightrope! Chutzpah and sexy too. That last bit (not in the transcript) about Africa? Nice vulnerable touch, cry for help.

I hang near the door (as I do in crowds) keen not to meet or greet. Lena pushes to the front, being determined to land some kind of fish. She'll not gut or cook it tonight though. I wander out, and Francesca Mars actually catches my eye. I raise a hand in salute. Very lightly, I assure you.

The Risks of Honesty

Lena charges into my practice room while I'm wrestling with bloody Schumann. That guy used to build torture instruments for his own hands.

- Her press secretary called. She's coming here for dinner. Tonight
- Uh?
- I asked after the speech. Said she'd consider
- Why doesn't she call or text?
- Guess she's busy
- Sounds like a set up. Suppose I'm cooking?
- You offered, darling
- Stroganoff it is then
- Are you crazy? She has to be vegan at least
- It's called irony? Right, roast vegan it is. D'you wannabe starter or main?

Withering looks from my beloved. She will blunder off in search of red red wine. I no doubt will drag my body to the shops and halfway there will notice I'm scurrying like a beetle… The Francesca of Mars arrives at eightish, didn't tell us a time so we had to guess. At the opening of the door Francesca smiles a little coy smile. The Audi is there under the street lamp. Her secretary man stands behind.

- That's fine, Adam.
She is dressed for I'm not sure what.
- Hello Nicky.

A fuck-me glam Francesca steps into our house. Her scent invites; she lets herself be kissed. The hair is beaded against her cheeks with the red-streaked rest defying you to take fists of it and shove it in your mouth. The skirt is rip-it-off short, firm-delicate legs drag the raddled eye down to cutesy strap heels. A spangle-green jacket opens at the throat, offering cleavage. A woman in girl's clothing. There's a petit purse under her dangly fingers and a hippyish fur coat (it works) which I'm not sure whether to butler-like take.

- And Lena is here too?
Her inflection suggests she and I are the last Adam and Eve on-planet.
- But of course. Come to the kitchen.
Yet she stands in my hall. Me too.
- I like your house. I'd certainly live here. Tell me - (she steps a bit near) are you and Lena…
- Flatmates
- But you're close. I know it
- I think you know a lot of things
- I believe I do.

She dabs a finger to my lips then walks on down the hall. In the lounge she stands, clasps her silvery wallet, rehearses shyability. An actor! Francesca Mars up close is all your dreams come true. Just don't touch. Besides, her sexuality's in doubt. And here is Lena, behind her in the doorway. L's had several drinks. Looks achingly at me. Our guest feigns surprise, takes her shoulder and kisses the lips, slowly, with a coquettish peck to finish.

- Darling. Thanks for inviting me. Am I late?

Tall Lena has decked herself in Madonna white: long boots, tight knee pants, lace-up blouse opening to lushy breast. As I said, why Lena Duvorchek wants to be a girl's girl is beyond me. Mars flutters her eyelashes in my direction. I step in, hold them both by hand in a clumsy troika and say:

- Let me water and feed you, and maybe later I'll play for you
- Oh, I hope you will!
And Mars kisses my cheek and sparkles her sage eyes.

We're in *deep*. The answer is to drink since it's dawned on Lena she's bit off more than she can chew and I can barely toss a salad in the kitchen 'cause my throat is dry, dry. Even goddess guest has bared herself by entering this house of the lowly. If we'd known each other we'd laugh but we don't so we can't. The kitchen's the place, and Francesca parks herself at table as I contrive to whip up something poco Italiano, de-corking wines and beheading beers and getting her to tipple. She who can hold a crowd of two thousand now deftly adapted to two, lets it be gleaned that intimacy is her forte. Francesca cascades her jewelly wit amid the breadsticks and celery and Lena stands and sits, drops her bits, laughs too loud, crowds my culinary stage, but I let her 'cause I love and pity her and the irony of this peeps out to Francesca which she and I scoop up with a wink. We all parade our generous parts, and nobody begins to think why she's come or how she must be sexually exploited… will our pricey guest put her head in the noose tonight? Anyway, que sera and Francesca has a wee drug in her jewelly bag which she slips on the table and ooh no Lena and me aren't just extras in her decadent little play 'cause she knows how drugs affect the vibe of wine and fun! so assures us there's nowhere she'd rather be since she knew straight away we were 'her people' the day we came because she has a nose for things like that, and speaking of noses should we tempt her little chemical with a 500 euro bill? We say yeah, and who'd refuse?

since Francesca royalises our kitchen and to be near her wipes all other considerations. And look how she mucks it all up 'cos she sees us watching and how she *really* isn't practised at this 'cause she's just a naughty wee girl who dodged the finger-wagging world but here we are together in your house, your lovely house - and Lena blurts 'if it were Christmas it'd be a lovely one' and she's all *emotional* so Francesca pinches her cheek and laughs to me, and we laugh since Lena lets her East-Europeanness get the better of her - and Lena darling! feelings *matter* nowadays where revealing yourself invites all manner of trolls. Francesca loves your honesty! (she wins a kiss for this, and yeah I do too). So we have a cuddle, us three, and we're all super-elated to be. The chemical ups the glee and we spill and guzzle and taste the pot and it's easy when I touch Francesca's hair to keep it out of the sauce and she takes my finger and sticks it in her mouth to 'taste the chef not just his cooking' with a look that makes me evacuate my brain, and when Lena clasps her from behind and puts her nose in the goddess' hair and she avows she's so at ease with her *new best friends*... I fall to wondering about the thousands she knows: how Lena and me could be her chosen, and could I play piano to please her eyes? No, I'm a simple girl, she tells us, even humble! An artist like you will see that, Nick! (there's no limit to her simple genius) and Lena, consternated with feeling from the blood of wine, grows solemn so we hold her bosom-close, parental Francesca and me, and to Francesca this stranger intimacy is a doddle as well. Fuck, why can't life to be always *this*, this desperate beautiful party where all's held in a promise! No future! And my cooking's no ritual either, more a clown show to the girls' powdery pantomime. Let me fail to rule myself, avoid the crunch of commitment, set up the mating ritual for beautiful women. But no, our guest aspires to more. And when we sit and (suddenly famished) eat and giggle and swap our sparkly wit for sexual quip and deflecting gossip on cool people we all claim to know, there bit-by-bit emerge some things, as euphoria crests to philosophy, that hint at weight or circumstance. Our Lena, prone to weighty toasts when drunk, who's making us fall about with stories of her randy uncles in the Bosnian war (how archly Francesca gives me the look) now peers into the past and lists all her English *boyfriends* from the early days of her ransacking of this country. All absurd and hilarious since she found she needed *girls* in ways that trophy boys could never supply… and Francesca concurs with gravitas while coyly confessing she has no funny stories of her own (which makes me lust for stories in my mind), so then she tells us offhand tales of boys who tickled her with propositions she never could meet. And Lena and me (I know her look) peer into the submerged gender-fluid iceberg of Francesca's life and wonder how it would be to be the intimate holy centre of her honesty.

Because - we're bound to wonder how a girl who masters all roles and gestures could ever be honest. Or we long to say, how could she fail to be honest, being a master? And why should such a woman reveal herself to us? I see why the whole world wants a piece of her. Because the goddess gives all of her intimacy but somehow not herself. She can dispense it all but deflects whatever comes back. Lena and I both want to claw out her secret, lick up the secret sex under the gorgeous clothes. But Francesca may be all comely and not sexual at all. Untouchable? Yeah, far too big to be anyone's little Francesca… but somehow desperate because desperately *real*. And it's as if I want to *find her before she's gone*. Or I'd want *someone* to find her, to swallow up all her love before she's gone. How long can perfection last? I want to know that she who seems to know it all, who laughs and cries with equal gravity, who spans the public and private, who summons destiny but is free as a child, who's touched by suffering but seems ungouged by horror - I want to know that she *needs*. Oh but what? I want that she'd need to confess, lay it bare on a sacrifice stone and bloodily surrender it there. Her need will make her human and make me human and lift up all of us! I want her to be great, to be *beyond*; but no, I want her to be little too, so I might feel better in my littleness. I wannabe a witness: not just to her genius, but to the revealing, the great falling out of her secret. And I want to believe the famous girl is there for me.

But being great, Francesca knows all that.

There is a point in the evening where Lena and Francesca could exit to bed still *fraiche* enough to tipple the superficial juice of each other in bedroom dark. Or they could stay (for me), and we could share a higher art: political-serious, musical-aesthetic, or just the confessional patient art of making friends. The choice is our guest's and naturally she says *Let's talk, listen, confess: the deeper road*. Whatever Lena feels about this she won't show; never so stoned or horny that she can't be strategic. She lines up cocktails of frothy pink and gelatinous green.

- I was a waiter once in a Beograd pole-dancing club. Hotter than the girls on poles I tell you. Used to pour shit like this into mouths of men and they'd throw money, which I'd *eat* or stash in secret places (she shoves a finger down her pants) like *this*, like -

- Oh god, I never would pole dance, butts in Francesca.

(Yep, Lena can be scary. Better rescue) - I could never stand up and harangue a crowd like you

- Oh, but *I* couldn't hypnotise them with my hands and my musical instrument

(I persist) - And you bewitch. I've seen it. I wonder how you do it

- Simple. People want it all, and what they want they get.

This topic seems reserved for she and me. But Francesca includes.

- And darling Lena makes her probing questions! You shook 'em up last week

- They were shook up by my tits and arse

- We're all manipulators. You go to Nick's concerts, Lena?

- Yeah

- And?

- Offers them a delight then stabs them when they come to collect.

Francesca gazes at me, mock-serious.

- Can it be true?

- Evil me

- Not so evil. (She smiles) I do the same in speeches. About slaughterhouses

- Guess I've a duty to entertain but also to educate. Shouldn't patronise, but why give 'em all they want? They come to me, right? *You* will know what I'm talking about

(I realise I've avoided using her name the entire evening)

- Yet if you give people all they want, they will destroy you.

This is where Lena and me eye each other up.

- How do you mean?

- We're all greedy yet still we complain. And the media feeds on it. We secretly think every 'third-world' person who turns up on our shores with their hand out is a threat to our precious life
- This society angers you?
- Oh, I wonder if we live in an obese society where everyone is a pampered bigot, or whether we're all just human, equally deserving compassion. I know what the answer is, but it rankles all the same
(Lena) - But you suggested it would destroy you *personally* if you give people what they want
- I meant if I gave everything, I'd give my life to it.
This is evidently not what she meant. Is she planning a reveal?
(Me) - You're doing a fine job. But expectations on performers are extreme, though we put our own heads in the noose. Attention-junkies, we want it all but it costs
- I am privileged. I can give my life away
(Lena) - Don't ever give your life away
(Me) - How does your family feel? Do they support you as you wish?
- I told you my father died when I was fourteen. And that Mother married Peter Mars six months after
- Actually, you didn't tell us
Lena butts in. - I don't know any of this
- And why *should* you?

And her tone has an edge. For the first time. Lena looks to me, I shrug at her. Don't delve in! But she does.
- How did you feel about this second marriage?
- Oh, I don't feel. It's all dealt with in the *diaries*.
Francesca turns to me.
- Did you know that if my father had got sick today they might have saved him?
- What was the cause of death?
- He stood on a tropical fish in the Bahamas. The same thing almost killed the writer Saul Bellow. We were on holiday. Picture an idyllic scene. I am in my summer dress prancing on the beach, calling to my father to come and look at the starfish I found. He is standing in water with a snorkel on

his head. I am running, lifting my skirts. I feel my hair flying in the wind and the sun in my eyes. I'm fourteen you see, I don't know anything much at all. And I laugh and make circles on the sand with my toes like a dancer. Then I see some people by the shallows. My mother, and our porter. Daddy is lying on the sand. No-one is coming, no doctor is coming. But the hotel manager, he goes to telephone, and I wait, holding my daddy's head. And daddy's not moving, just sweating and grinding his teeth. They move him into the shade till the doctor comes, and we take him to an infirmary. Two days later his heart gave out… There's an antidote now.

Silence, for the first time at our party. Is the great one's burden too simple for words?

- Hey, let's play you a song
- Yes, please.

So she follows me to my practice room, and sits on the hard chair by my grand piano. I give her a Schubert *Impromptu*. She holds herself with heels and knees together, hands clasped in her lap and peering forward as if in a church. Two corkscrew braids cascade down her cheeks. The rest fans out like a horde of richness. I don't know how she listens or comprehends this music, but she is solemn and still… a noble sight. I long to play well, especially for the girl of fourteen. Not sentimental, but clear. At the finish Lena is there, leaning on the door frame.

- Schubert. No more, no less
- But Nicky too.

Francesca slips onto the stool with me. Brushes the keys absently. Puts her arms about me. There's stillness, a spell. She steps over to Lena, takes her hand, leads her out. I listen for their bedroom door to click exclusively shut.

The Safety of Distance

At breakfast there's no sign of the lovers. Guess they had a 'late one'. Clear the kitchen? I want our mess to linger. I creep to their door and there's music. And why not? Francesca loves music. Or loves to cover the evidence. I feel a biting need to return to bed and take myself in hand. Next thought is, I'll be needing to practise piano this morning. It'll seem competitive. Chew some bread then, amid the party ruins, till a door clicks. There's a toilet flush and footsteps. Which girl? Our guest emerges, fully dressed. She sits.

- Thought you'd like some company
- I'd say you slept well
- Wasn't all sleep, my darling.

She puts her hands on my knees, and lets me see how risky-intimate she's being. Francesca reads the universe about her, knows she's indispensable wherever she is. Only a patrician lover would presume to read my mind without patronising.
- Don't be sad
- No.
I've known her five minutes and she's ruling my life.
- I am not simple, Nick. I do whatever I wish. Lena is beautiful.
And she stares at my eyes, quite stern. And then she stands, kisses my forehead.
- What'll we eat?
- Lemme do it
- No, I make breakfast for us. As the guest I'm your servant!

So I watch her flicker about the kitchen, deft-handed, eagle-eyed. And when Lena appears in the doorway wearing nothing much and sees the tableau, she grocks she'd better get dressed in her own house. Soon we're all three seated. Francesca Mars is all objectives in the morning. Elbows on table, toast in fingers, rills of smothery hair, all hard gossipy *business*.

- Told you in the night Lena darling, there's no chance my diaries 'll be published till I'm upwards of forty. And a book will embarrass me. You and me can do interviews. Ebola scandal in Somalia's off the list, too complicated. Besides, I don't wanna think about it though it's media-juicy. How the fuck, one may ask, could our medico officials mishandle the tabloids so badly? Fleet Street was on it like flies round shit. Oh sorry we're eating. It's what I need to control! They're telling us we exploited the natives. Hypocrites. Peter my stepdaddy could be a fool to throw his wealth at stuff like that, though it's me who says it. Knows jack-nothing about Africa though he says he does. Sick of me running off there I think. Mummy too. Well it's Eritrea next, and no fool officials are gonna fuck this up. You can't know how I slaved to get the foreign office on board. And you met Bouseri. Had to lift my skirt there, I can tell you. Mmm-hmm. (She crunches her toast) You met his daughter, Nick? Ayaaaaan. One spoilt little missy. No muck under *her* fingernails. Actually, *Luc* thinks she's a mythic African princess. *Precieuse cherie!* says Luc. Gotta protect the species: hanging round her might someday land us more dough. Though I don't notice *her* lifting a finger for blacks. And wouldn't want to upset her daddy by asking *him*. That'd be my job

- *Who's Luc?*
Lena and I say this at the same time, embarrassingly. Francesca trippingly giggles.

- Oh, didn't one mention Luc? He's my *collaborateur.* No party without Luc. (We're both staring) He's a *doctor,* darlings. Medecins Sans Frontieres. Met years ago. Love him to death. He's the guy who gets people vaccinated, pays bribes, sets up the supply chains, you name it. He's a beautiful beautiful guy.

This is one of those moments where lowly people get swamped in the wake of Francesca Mars. All through the speech I could see Lena wondering what was left to say. I found myself watching the flittery hands and toast and so-agile lips more than I was listening. Her self-cadences seemed judged for people far beyond our little kitchen, as if we peered into some churning world that she juggles like string beads. Too far from the charm girl we communed with last night, the girl we're falling over to be close to. (No right to expect, but feel we might) And the magus sees, then softens as if to say: darlings, I reserve the right to be complex! - distant and close, impersonal and personal, famous and humble and angry and gossipy, to *act* it all and laugh at my own act, to love you and mysterious others, have my secrets and worlds you don't reach. But have no fear, because here I am with *you*. Don't blame, it's me. Am I not obvious?

The whole human race fears being left out - by the famous rich influential and godly. It's why we have a tabloid press, the people's cudgel for assuaging lowliness and envy. We forget that our gods and goddesses are also little, throwing up their shields against fear and emptiness. The bitchy leader of the schoolyard gang was never so alone. And Francesca Mars, bravest of the brave and never so alone, insouciantly crunches her toast in our morning kitchen. You Francesca, are your own cunning enemy: your talk of Luc is too sudden, too nonchalant, nearly a challenge, a mask to the complexity of pain, ushering in a *coolness* at the table that none of us are ready to eat. And your eyes seemed to dull and dip a trifle, and we felt your world tightening. Or we're led to guess you must be tired... At last you enumerate a schedule for the day ahead, hints that help you depart. We take the cue and assume impersonal airs. By midday you're gone.

The Great Story of Ourselves

After the rush of beauty, one feels like a strange evil wind has blown through.
- Why the fuck did she drop the clanger about that Luc fellow?
Lena wants to push away her new mixed feelings, to grab back the hard-nosed persona she normally parades about. Me, I peck at her.
- Did you guys get on last night?
- In bed you mean?
- Did you talk a lot, or...
- I'm not going to describe to you how expertly she - whatever
- You were quiet at breakfast
- Couldn't get a word in
- Plenty to suck on there as well!
- What?
- Tension with stepdaddy... diaries waved in your face and whisked away... hints at a new war with the tabloids... in the pants of black businessmen with sexy daughters... the 'wondrous mysterious Luc'... thereby not failing to put it out to one hungry journalist that she's a 'weekend lesbian'.

Lena stares. Several dark shades cross her visage.

- But she obviously *rates* you, Lena!

- Get fucked

- Would if I could.

There's truly more to Mars than Lena and I can possibly talk about, so we'll avoid each other awhile - before collusive need drags us back together. I know too well: Francesca can easily be totally honest and ultra-manipulative all at once. I'm a musician after all. Lena should get it too, being a journalist. How would *she* as journalist address a fickle public about a thing she really cared about? She'd have to construct it, twist it, dramatise it, hollywoodize it, she'd need an agenda, a super-objective beyond mere honesty. Have to manipulate hearts and minds. End justifies means, can't be naïve where truth is concerned. Wanna get consumers of news to swallow your medicine, educate the dumb mass about the realities of evil? Better put your hard hat on, grit your teeth, put subtlety aside. But could Lena do that? She's a passiony emotional girl but the chip on the shoulder's still there. Wants to love and be loved but she's a slow-motion train wreck in love, and fools herself she can sidestep it. That's why I'm tender to her under my blanket of irony. We should really sleep together. But she wouldn't, she'd despise me.

And now we're competing. Our troika deftly ridden by Francesca Mars has unstablised us. And it hits me with creeping disappointment that Francesca *is* a Destroyer. Does she hold a flag for a cause or is she the cause? Finger that points to the moon or the moon? It should be obvious by now, the chief subject for Francesca Mars is Francesca Mars. Beyond the great aid donor philanthropist people's warrior and scandalist - is the painstakingly executed bloodsucking soap opera of Francesca. One is definitely in a bad mood this morning! Why be surprised though? Aren't we all like that? We're all our own subject, our own fetish. For a single sun-and-love-drenched moment last night I wished that here was a genius magician, beyond self-pity and selfishness because she somehow admitted to it, ironized it, tossed it away from her. A sweetly guilty but insouciantly smiling goddess girl who drowning in beauty walks an empyrean field, grace-handed pre-raphaelite nymph dispensing nectar under sacred boughs (cue the classic painting above my piano). How much the gulled fool does that make me in all my sophistry: how I wanna be dazzled bewitched bewildered? To be naïvely, painfully in love with something deeper and more beautiful than *me*. I believe Mars once greedily saw the possibility of her genius and beauty, but since fourteen sees it as a ghost and a dream now forced to express as haunted self-pity. Witness the story last night of her dying dad. Told with practised craft! And the young dutiful waif at my piano, lolling in Schubert. All totally real. It'll kill me if it isn't. Yet I know, and Lena knows and Francesca knows, what play-actors we are, what calculating watchers, narcissists, bullshit artists. How we *sell* to each other, embellish, propagandise, self-aggrandise - all in the service of our ego, the great story of ourselves. And Lena Duvorchek, when she weighs up love versus self, will be forced to lay bare the entrails of Francesca Mars for all the world to see. Oh yeah. Love will be spilt.

Through our front door one week later dropped a white embossed letter. Lena read it, thrust it at me. 'Carolyn and Peter Mars invite Lena Duvorchek and Nicky Bright to celebrate the engagement of their daughter Francesca to one *Doctor Luc Cotillard* at their town residence in Richmond on - '(three weeks hence). There was a PS: Would Mr Bright consent to offer a short musical performance for the occasion? Also a little note in Francesca's handwriting. The script was surprisingly unkempt, almost childish. '*Hello my friends. I loved our little party recently. It would be wonderful if you could both come. Dying to see you. F.*'

We stood in the dim hall.
- Is this what you English call a 'dark horse'?
- Why should you feel manipulated? It's a free country
- Political manoeuvre
- Lena! She has a life outside us and our egos. She's a national figure. (Boy, her curmudgy pugnacious face is annoying) You think Mars is going to marry *you*?
- Why not? Gay marriage is fashionable
- You're an idiot. She's not even gay. Bi, at the outside
- She fucks with heart and soul. I was there

- Apparently she does everything with heart and soul. But I can't work this out
- You'd kill for her. I can see it
- How can you see that?
- Are you crazy? I've seen one hundred boys look at me the way you look at her.

I was embarrassed, but she came close, and our faces almost touched.
- Are we agreed then?
- What?
- We expose this stupid farce. This 'engagement'
- Are you nuts! (Pause) …Waddaya saying?
- I will make up some stories. I have information. You can hear a lot when someone famous is coming all over your face.

I think I appeared stunned.
- And I will make it worth for you.

At that point she pressed me into the wall, slid a hand to my crotch, put her tongue nearly in my mouth. Well, you know what I said about Duvorchek and me… but I had to slip away. Too tough.
- Love you Lena. But we're going to have to think this through. You don't know who you're dealing with. In Francesca I mean.
- Huh. *I* will end up saving her. From herself.

And she walked on down the hall. I'm not sure I'd want to be saved by Lena Duvorchek.

To Be Good Enough

It's the Saturday of Francesca's engagement party and we're getting dressed up. What to wear and who to be? There's a spirit lurking in the back of my eyes (it catches me in the mirror) that whispers: are you not a person of *matter,* to be noted and lauded for your endeavours, to whom the world owes praise since by you it is inspired? I see an only child hanging upside down in a tree and calling out 'Look at me, dad! Look at me, mum! or prancing about at some party of inconsequential grownups with underpants on my head and a wriggly smile on my dial that says: All you people! Don't you see it matters to be *alive!* Now I think the same naïve spirit (which made me pursue art) is what filled Francesca

Mars and her golden-girl childhood with unabated love-praise, with a promise of world-shaping mastery, and which seemed to encounter its death at fourteen. I think she has never shaken away that spirit: she still bubbles and bursts with it despite the inky cynic poison poured into her pool of love at the passing of her father. Big people like her suffer big underground deaths, and she'll push it hard and far under because the death-spirit can't be allowed to block the march of her lioness light, her mountain reach for happiness. Perhaps she is vulnerable, lonely - and this is why she cultivates the great estate of the people about her, since in her little kitchen garden her vegetables have all gone to flower. But why, why marry now?

Lena and I have parked the car, and we walk the half mile through the Richmond green keen to arrive at the coupling of Francesca with our wits and selves firmly about us. And what of all the private souls who gather at the behest of the gifted one on such a celebration day, who might glance too often in the mirror, dab at a blemish and wonder, is my face good enough? Caught between self-sentiment and public duty, they think: what have we to contribute to the glitter-glamour of human competing that mocks us as celebration, we little springs who feed a great river? We need to laud the golden girl because we love her promise and spirit and little kindnesses to us. But doesn't greatness suck the life of the people, heroism the blood of its admirers, darkly whispering: in some other life you might aspire to something half like this! We'll scurry back to our hovels, to our private melodramas behind walls that hide unknown others who face their own. This, our limpet community of disparate souls. Yet still we wonder if beauty might save us from the lethe of ordinariness, the creeping lethe of years fading away. This country of England breathes its royalty in private, yet when royalty calls we jump to participate. So at the threshold, gripping cherished handbags, adjusting careful hair, brushing miniscule fluff from cuffs, fretting that our nails are clean... we step to our duty, half glad, half afraid.

Francesca is here at the steps, and not a guest shall pass her threshold without a kiss, squeeze of hand, personal quip. Today she's all studied honour and happiness. Reputation is heroism in the little things, and

Mars is all heroine. No recourse here for little folk who'd let their envy drain to self-pity or curmudgeonly want of revenge. How superficial is success! we say, snake-suspicious at this cap-tipping thank you ma'am queue for the lordly hand. But our Francesca knows all that. I'm super ordinary, not classist at all; how could you fail to believe in me? she smiles. Meanwhile Nicky Bright loiters in line on the yellow brick path by capacious lawns... In what actual way am I good enough? Because I see the price of her commitment and risk, the toughness behind, the tears she shed for influence. Bright won't be any fall-guy bit player to the nuance of an empress, he who sneers at all hallowed importantness, sticks up a middle finger to temples of culture! Not for him a glossy coat on a cadaver, mustifying all civilisation's yesterdays. Better to grab at the *now*, seize unuttered vulgar sad strange elusive beautiful life! With *music*. Offend as many stony egos as possible, force them into the mystery of the uncivilised. But it costs, and one slip from the icy path... I guess I know the price of bravery. Maybe that's why I'd go to hell and back for Francesca Mars.

And how does Duvorchek arm herself today? Francesca hastens down the step to specially greet her, stands with us a sweet moment, gestures to spreading oaks and highstone walls, shares the aura (and irony) of her resplendent residence. We're no damned Tory voters though you'd expect it! says her smile. She loves to be intimate, needs to be *with us,* and holds Lena's waist so cosily that I know Lena's heart is at war (I offered to be her date if she'd let me), so that not even Francesca Mars can take charge of Duvorchek's proud-volatile dignity.

All Francesca's People

Within the family seat is Carolyn Mars, birth mother to Francesca. In knee-length red satin she's all silver hair and slimness, though under the studied glamour-calm the pleasured eyes are tense. And Peter Mars in semi-casual black with designer stubble, reminds everyone of Sting the musician. Seems to me he's particularly keen on himself. Their beauteous res. is not ridiculously large: eclectic designer touches, rattan-chaired library, bay windows overseeing speckled lawn and trees, dining room set for buffet, teak table overlaid with delicacies, darkwood walls adorned in cubist masters, sideboards with Burmese figurines. The reception room in deft greens browns whites (with grand piano) exudes a modernist colonial air as if of Kenya. Peter and Carolyn cherish a romance with the exotic, and Francesca Mars in the midst is the jewel in their crown. Assembled today are Francesca's eclectic world-party people. All exude specialness in their ways: doctors, aid workers, government people, a lawyer or three, Africans in reds and blues, smooth South Asians, French and Spanish speakers, expensive-looking hippies, a rock musician or two, trusted members of the press. And not to mention, friends. Luc Cotillard the doctor, his own centre of gravity, moves about introducing each to each. He shakes my hand and Lena's and lingers a moment, all charmy French neutrality. A guy one might be happy to admire, especially if he saved your arse in a desert somewhere. Lena beats me to the inevitable analysis of his and Francesca's sex chemistry and concludes there's *none.* You're absurd! I whisper, relishing her assassinative tone. Lena's jumpy, goes off to roam. I sidle to the piano, brush the keys as is my habit. A guy whose face I've seen on TV catches my eye.

- Hey there. Eric Leavis.
We shake. - The guitarist, right?
- Yeah yeah. Special invite from Francesca. We go back a ways. Sentimental girl I guess
- Think so?
- Wants me to 'play for her'
- Me too apparently. A classic morsel
- Go for it. I'm making *noise.* Protest, you might say
(We eye each other) - Yeah?
- Would've married this chick myself, mate. And I'm not the marrying type, believe me. She was into me, bet on it
- Rumour is she's gay
- Are you fucking kidding? (He looks about) Sorry. You think all this shit is for real?
- I dunno. Tell me
- Had the affair like you wouldn't believe. All on. Then she runs off to

frigging Africa. Never see her again till she texts one day, wants to come to my concert. Nice as pie but cool as you like. What's a guy gunna do?
- Well, you're here
- Too effing gorgeous
- Stick to your principles, mate
- You try it. I'm heading for the bar
- Thanks for sharing, Eric. Catch you later.

Now *there's* a cute perspective on the goddess of Mars. But is the feller reliable? Are all these people casualties too? Course not, though plenty of 'em would want to know who the casualties are. Share the goss with Lena? Maybe get in her good books, help her on the trail of a scoop. The bloodying of Francesca Mars! - thereby asking Lena to betray her unique heart affair. Might even be nice to me. Ugh, when did I turn into a punter myself, inglorious scrambler for the Precious Touch… Screw it, I'm neutral! (as neutral as Spain after the Franco war). I assert Francesca's all out of my league - though this thought brings on a sickly feeling. What's my alternative: blessed music? *This* is the shipwreck she leaves in her wake: you cry to be good enough then abase yourself for love. I'll not be psychically manhandled! I do the pushing, I'm the artist. Don't panic. Ugh, why do I ruminate like a miseryguts whenever I'm surrounded by beautiful people? I know: impress the bastards with my piano technique. And behind their international smiles they won't even notice. But Mother Teresa-Francesca, *she will see,* will tend to my hurt like to a hundred others, like to the thousand poor of Africa. What's the fucking catch with her? Maybe there's a hundred little private catches like friend Eric. No smoke without fire… no sir, gotta be a nasty fishy *catch*. Now I get it. Lena is going to expose her right in the middle of this fake engagement party! Loony journalist thinks she can get Francesca to love her, need her, or worse, depend on her, exposing *the little-girl need, the private hell, the personal bloodied cross.* Gah, where is she? Stop this ego-drama! (why you play piano so turgidly like the critics say). Francesca Mars didn't get where she is today by falling under the feet of go-getters and hangers-on and heart-thieves and hurt lovers. So how? Uh… and the word *ruthless* emerges… from its lair, like a stink. Don't think it… or just say I *did.* What quality of darkness engineers ruthless? Here's the good dirt on our genie: ruthless is sexy, is power, is fuck-me fatal! No better scoop in journalism this week, exposed by the People's Press that marcheth on, scaling sierras of shit and slime. Slink and shrivel away Francesca Mars, lick your wounds, all vanity crushed! And who'll be there for you, faithful and true? Not the Lenas, doers of dirty deeds, but the *Nicky Brights and Erics* - true romantics who with music will nullify the world's savage laughter, take Francesca to their breast and protect her forever. Fuck, you're an idiot.

I spot lanky Lena at the bar slugging a green-looking cocktail with Eric the muso, and he's goggling at her the way men do. Bet he's the eternal fall guy. Unlike me. Meanwhile, since it all looks and feels like some frivolous high-ass cocktail party, Carolyn Mars brings us to order, and calling her husband and daughter to her side, addresses us all.

- Dear friends, it is a singular honour to have you here to celebrate a special moment in the life of my daughter. It is also a time for me to say a few serious words. I am no master of the spotlight, unlike my Francesca. My husband Peter and she are indeed a team, close, and strong. He offered her her chance to help the needy people of our world, and from *his* financial success her success has come. We should remember also my first husband Leo, Francesca's father, who left us fourteen years ago, and whose memory we cherish still. The precious things of life are fleeting: we must cherish. Luc, over time you've become like a son to us, and your decision to marry my daughter in the midst of your great work with the African people - is a courageous one. You have been a great confidant to me. I trust you and I welcome you. Will you join us?

The doctor comes and she embraces him with fervent kisses to each cheek. She kisses her husband on the mouth, squeezes the hands of her daughter. It is a studied performance for a discerning audience, with full marks for family subtext. Now Francesca steps up.

- I won't give a speech today. Mummy has said it all so well. How I think of my daddy today, how he would've played for us. How lucky I am to be with you all. How lucky I am to be Luc's chosen girl. And how important it is to continue our work. Peter - *daddy* - thank you for your continued belief in me. You've given so much. I won't let you down. And mummy, I love you. And I love your dress!

This is an amazingly sunken speech for Francesca. She pulls Luc in and embraces him tight. Luc waves at all of us. She pats him from behind.

- Oh… it is only for me to say my friends: merci. *Je t'aime*, Francesca. I did not hope to become your husband… you are so so wonderful. I am the luckiest man… I hope I can be… everything for you. *Cherie*. What can I say? Thank you. And I love you all.

Eager applause. At this instant there's the splatter of breaking glass. And yea - it's Lena. She steps from the bar, and she looks somewhat lovely in the alcoholic sense, and yeah, she's going to say something. Ugh. I grab at my musician's default attitude: 'If the sky falls in, it doesn't matter'. It's never worked yet.

- On be'alf of your friends and the Press of this great country of ours - and France too - and Africa - why not? - and *non gender specifics* for that matter - and everybody who ever got what they wanted - or *didn't* - I wanna say we love you Francesca, and whatever you do don't forget the people who made you what you are. You give us so much. It's true. But we feel things. We do. And love is bigger than… than even being married. Everybody loves you. Some of us too much…

At this point she grabs hold of Francesca and kisses at her, or licks her rather. Francesca cool as you like says: 'This is Lena Duvorchek, everyone. *My dear friend.*' And Lena sways, and Francesca grips her waist as if for a photo, and announces: 'Why don't we all sample the wonderful buffet? Then perhaps some other dear friends will play music for us…'

You know what? (I tell myself) The whole effing universe dovetails to the beat of Francesca Mars. She did not *bat an eyelid*. And she wouldn't even if Lena had told the crowd she was screwing her stepfather - or some similar *nonsense*. No no no, she sidesteps the speeches, ditto mother, nearly genuflects to stepdaddy and seems to cling to the Doc as if to the wreck of the Medusa, and *he* can't think why. But when the Lena threat came sidewise at her she seemed to *relax*. What the hell? I'm wondering if she's perfected the role of scandalmonger beyond all others. So what music to play on this faux nuptial occasion? *Girl with the Flaxen Hair?* Well it's French. Berlioz' *Danse Macabre?* Stop it. During the buffet Francesca pulls me aside.

- Congratulations Francesca. Are you excited?
- Oh yes I am, darling. Now look after Lena, won't you? She's a brave girl and very clever too. I'll give her the interviews she wants but she mustn't speak up in public. Will you tell her? And I'll come and see you both very soon. Expect me at night!

She is so charmingly conspiratorial that I visualise munching on her ear. Or at least burying my face in her cleavage. Instead, her hand gets a kiss.
- Will do. And don't you worry. But make it soon!
She touches my face. - *Darling.* And a little pause…
- Ooh look! The *Bouseris* have finally arrived. Better late than never.
She winks and slips away. I see her scoop up Luc, and together they greet the Eritrean and his cherishable daughter. Francesca is all raucous public laughter. All of a sudden.

Lena slides up and I hold onto her.
- Whoah! Stay, dodgy girl
- Look at *that.* 'Luc and Ayaan'. Don't they make a pretty picture? His African Princess. Think o' those thighs and that hot black pussy
- Steady on! She's quite chaste from what I gather
- Couldn't say that for her daddy though, according to Francesca. Hmm? And I've been cosying up to Peter Mars. Guess what? Gave me his phone number
- Shut the ff-ront door
- He will when I get hold of him. Gotta go and interview these blacks. A journo's work is never done. Play something nice today, will you?
- Oh I will. And *be* nice
- Oh, I will.

Soon I play for the assembly. Two Debussy *Images*... and for the duration Francesca stands alone at the piano and stares. Everyone shuts up for her sake, so I can actually do something. The Fazioli responds to every touch... startling bass fullness, dazzling top. Somewhere in Debussy's cascades and mists there's a corner of seriousness... and I watch her face as she looks at the piano, and we two enter a private garden, perhaps in Spain, and it is the seventeenth century, and she stands by a fountain in her white dress as clouds funnel upward in the blue behind her, and sun glitters on flagstones at her feet. And she seems to be waiting for her carriage, to take her to a ship to sail far away, never to return.

Dirty Money

A week later, evening. Stepping through my front door I'm diverted to the lounge by impressive moans of a Serbian ilk. Lena is looking persuasively sorry for herself, spreadeagled on couch attended by a decadent quota of beer bottles. I sit beside and enquire dutifully as to the matter. The gravitas: arms about my neck, significant breathy whispers in face, all make one feel privileged. For sure she's all broke and the paper is laying off and she'll be for the chop and she needs a story that'll run and run and 'll have to move house blaaa and it's all a *disaster* darlink. Frankly I'm never sure how Lena stays solvent with what she puts away in booze and all the guff she buys as if forever trying to prove she's well off 'cause she lives in Chelsea and wouldn't live anywhere else. And of course I offer the loan and of course she says never as long as she walks the earth. We collapse in a sofa heap, and my coat's pinned under her curvy backside and Lena wants to do the weepy bit some more then fall asleep. Etcetera.

Then comes a voice. - *Anyone there?*
It's Francesca Mars.
- Oh! You two are together. Front door was open. But I'll go
- No, come in! Help me sit Lena up. She's had a few.
Francesca stands there, eyes us up. I haul Lena off. Come along dear, greet the Lady.
- Nnnnn
- Wha's wrong with 'er?

- How d'you mean? She's drunk
- Oh. Yeah.
And her stoned-out eyes suggest this should not be so. She's in black, hair's something wild, lips brightly purpled. Not comely.
- Come to the kitchen
- 'f you say so.
I take her hand, and she lets herself be sat in a chair. Looks pretty damn loose.
- Where've you been?
- Oh I don't know, do I?
- Are you all right?
- Are *you*? Interrupted a little love-fest, din' I
(Tread with care) - No no, Lena has money problems and I'm her comforter
- Never heard from 'er once this week. Gotta talk
- Talk to me
- Girl thing, Nicky
- Bed thing, you mean
- Ugh, how crude are *men*?
- I wouldn't know, Francesca. Let me make a cuppa
- *Patronising* now. I'll go. ...ugh, this is really coming on.
She stares, mouth askew. What to do?
- Look, sorry! Welcome, nice to see you. How's Luc, and Carolyn? We loved the party. You were beautiful.
She stares, then grimaces like she wants the toilet.
- That fucker wan's to stop my money
- Who? Luc?
The face crinkles. - That fucker Mars wan's to kill my program. Thinks he can do what he *likes*. Know what he told me? Shouldn't marry Luc! Sez he'd never trust that black Bouseri either. Why not, wass he to *you*? I ask him. He shouts at me: 'You seen his *daughter*. Slut!' Was that alluding to *me*? Know what, know the irony? She ain't! I don' like her, little snob, but she's fucking pure Snow White! And my Luc acts like she isn't there, but she *is*. And Peter says *she looks at Luc and Luc looks at her...* and I can't stand it! My Luc's a gentle man, he's *my* man even though y'all think I'm a fucken dyke - and I am! Don't care what I am! But I tell you I'll have Mars's

money. And I'll shove it up my fanny! Funny. Nnnn! (She snatches at her hair) That Mars, wish I never set eyes on *him.* He's a racist! My gutless mother worships the fucken ground he walks. More fool 'er! I'm goin' back to Africa. Gonna help the pee-ple. And fucking cunt Peter Mars is gonna pay fer it all!

And she slithers. I jump to grab her head before it hits the stove. Cradle it awhile. Now Lena's there, filling the doorway. Her curlicued lip says: fix that shit, fella! I tell you girl, I will.
- Help me get her up.
Lena doesn't, so I stroke the victim's head. Presently she opens her opal eyes. At last we stand. Her head's buried in my shoulder. Lena's gone.
- Sorry Nicky. What'd I do? This is one evil drug. Ugh, makes me crazy... Need the loo.
I lead the way. She stumbles in, shoves the door shut. Lena is on her bed inspecting the ceiling.
- Fun listening to her barf up?
Presently Francesca stumples down the corridor. - *Sorry Nick.*
She rolls onto Lena's bed, brings a leg over, wants to lick her face... Shut the door on that.

Next morning Francesca hogs the bathroom for an hour then presents herself in our kitchen. Wet hair severely pulled back, she looks about with cat's eyes. I wait on her. Toast and tea. She chews. Lena comes in, pouts at the lady, sits. Francesca starts up.

- Naturally Mars is an opportunist, doesn't know the value of his fortune. How'd he get it? Cosmetics, developed and tested on animals. Claims there's nooo testing. Fuck no. Till some activists smashed up his labs. Ooh he's upset. So he muscles in on dengue research programs, and like the messiah bankrolls the biggest one in East Africa. But the price is too high for the blacks. Suddenly says 'we need the dough for research'. Big Pharma buys him out. Hey presto, money in the bank. Would have retired then and there 'cept little steppydaughter has her big idea to get him to spend it. On like, the *poor.* She's the best thing he's got but he's a *hero* with his hip little earring and his Bono-babble while she's his dutiful little nymph with her big hair and her shit-hot body made for camera, baby. Better than her mother by a mile. Stepdaddy *loves* little steppygirl all right. Trouble is she's got a *mind*. Fuckin' crystal mind. 'Cept when she takes the meth… Am I boring you people?

- Keep it coming, says Lena.

Elbows on table, Francesca goes on chewing her end of toast.

- Need to cool it, Lena. Anyways, you can relax when I'm out of yer hair. I need to lean on that black Bouseri, make him *pay up*. Hypocrite protects his daughter's little cherry. Dude's not fussy with the likes of me though. Still, no fuck no money. Favourite bit's watching me piss in his bath like an African

- Francesca! Give it up. That's it!

I've clearly had it. I'm on my feet. She wrinkles her nose at me.

Lena laughs. - Too too refayned. Go play yer instrument, Nicky

- Come on, Francesca. Let me take you where you want to go. Here's your coat. Let's go.

Out on the street her car has a ticket or three. She drapes arms over her male coathanger, breathes in his face, totters into the Audi, lurches off into traffic.

Back inside, Lena is seated in the kitchen in her legs-apart pose, fingering a knife.

- Know what she said in the dark? After I got her to scrub her mouth, not go to the toilet in my flowerpot and not put her whatsit in my face at four am? 'Mummy's jealous of me and Peter! Mummy's so *jealous* of me and Pete, baby! Over and over till I told her to shut it. Now what d'you think that means? Think it's time to write a *story*

- What happened to research? It's her stupid drug talking, that's all.

- Don't be naïve, baby boy.

Surely the drug thing was one time Francesca Mars was out of control? Don't be naïve, baby boy.

Burning Need

Nicky Bright didn't mention in all that flurry that he was getting ready to do a concert - for 'emerging artists' in 'one of the better halls'. He's fool enough to arm-wrestle with Schumann and his killing *Symphonic Variations*. Ain't so much Schumann but the lesser genius that's the problem. Being under oath from the producers to avoid 'avant-gardish adornments' he's substituting Ravel's *Sonatine* with Piazzolla and Satie titbits for dessert. They just don't get I play for *me,* he mutters... The day has come. Lately-rehearsed Sonatine requires perfect form which I ain't got. Excuse: the Yamaha is mud. All through the allegro I'm stuck in 'fuck this' mode. Then comes a doleful silence before the andante... and suddenly *she is there*. Francesca Mars slips into my hall, tipples up the aisle, sits at the edge. I've permission to play! Statuesque opening chords settle in the piano. There's meditation. By the close of the andante I'm on a new course in my *life*. Love is an abstract thing. The power rises now, of a sudden. Headlong rush in the presto... fingers at last whip up a fever to lick the keyboard beast. Applause. I'm unmoved. I look for her. On her face is sternness, a touch of reverence, maybe longing. I sit again at the keys. Piazzolla, then Satie. Hypnotic dreams beyond the shimmer-glitter of Ravel. My fingers touch for her. The sad coy music whispers to her.

A string trio follows. I step to the foyer determined to flee. But I linger... and my reward is there. She slips through the gilt doors: formal white shirt, satin black jacket, braided lushy gold spilling out, skirt undressing her knees. Crosses the marble atrium. Indelible Francesca. Spies me, with formal gaze of serious intent. Takes my hand, touches it to her lips, murmurs *thank you*. We slip together into the city. In the summer-cool night we halt by a brasserie window. Enter a booth, and by gold mirrors watch the doubled crowd, drowse without talk amid a thrum of low voices.

- Are you pleased? she says sometime later.
- Definitely in love with you
- Yes, she says. And holds my gaze. Yellow gold shimmers in the leather room.
- How did you know about -

- I find out things. Though you might have told me
- Didn't dare. Since last time
- Forgive me, will you? I can be horrid when the mood's on me
- You're a hundred things. All of them real
- Someday I will show you the little girl.

It's like she's just promised nirvana.

- Take it as a compliment, she says.
- Thank god I've an instrument to play or my feelings will choke me
- I've no instrument. I can only listen and feel
- I love the way you *believe* in music. Lifted me up today
- I believe in *you*. (She pauses) …Will you come with me tonight?
- To where?
- Outside the city. You'll be an accomplice. To my plan. We'll play a game in the woods.

She smiles a twinkly smile. My throat is starting to burn.

- Okay. Okay.

Francesca drives us out of the city. Gloomy yellow roads curl by in a speed dream. She's an urgent driver, pushes the Audi. Bach cello suites (Yo Yo Ma) fill the car with austere caressing. My eyes keep flittering to those knees under silk. That doom sense, that out-of-depth: always there with her. By midnight we find ourselves in narrow lanes. Still she seems to know the way. Now she offers a sidelong smile that says, *do you dare?* The music is cut, she slows as if to a prowl, looks about and about, turns abruptly into a gateway, cuts the engine. Come on, she says. Night air perforates our cocoon. Her crinkly locks shimmer under a moon. Francesca Mars pulls a bag from the boot and undresses. She lets me stare. In her new garb - black tracksuit and trainers - she hitches her hair, pulls some canisters out, hands one to me.

- We've a little way to walk. Through a stream to cover tracks. Are you attached to those shoes, because I'm throwing everything away. Don't look at me like that. You're seeing a side nobody sees, not even Luc. Joke, Nicky. D'you want to hold me?

She curls herself into me, brushes my mouth with her lips, licks my chin, steps away.
- Now you *have* to follow. (But I'm staring) Well?
- Not recovered from the body and lips, sorry.
She takes my hand. - This way. Do as I say at all times.

She straddles the gate with bag and canister. We tramp in silence through a wide field. The moonlight spills. It doesn't occur to me to ask a question. We skirt a little wood. I stare at the silverblack curves of her body. We reach a stream, she crosses quickly, disappears. I'm suddenly scrambling. My feet are wet. I bump into her. She steadies me and listens.

- See that fence? We go through with bolt cutters. Head for the building with low windows. (I can't see it) Break in, cut the animal cages, let 'em out, burn the whole fucking thing. You with me?

- I... do you... I guess I -
- We'll track back to the car another way. Keep close to me. Come here.

She holds my backside, slides a hand in my crotch, massages the place, breathes in my face then steps back. Her eyes are round. Jesus. But she yanks at my hand. I'm forced to run. There's a fence. The cutters. She's done this before! We crawl through. To the building. No lights, mesh on the windows. Hope it's not alarmed she says. She cuts, it's taking forever. Wanna go home. She suddenly smashes a pane. The trees glower at us. She gropes for a latch, clambers in, nearly topples. I'm holding her backside. *Not now, lover boy.* She's in. Silence... then the door. She flashes a torch. There are eyes in cages.

- Not a lot here. Enough to make a point though. Hello little beasties! Cut these locks.

We kneel. I can't hold the cutter. *He plays Rachmaninov, can't use a bolt-cutter.* She starts to giggle. I try to touch, she fobs me off. She cuts the bolts on six cages, opens the main door. Little animals scuttle in the dark. She's lopping petrol about the room. I copy. Outside! she hisses. My heart's banging. She pulls things from her bag: tapers and a lighter.

- When I say, you throw this through the door. Me, the window. Run for the fence, turn right not left, understand?

The tapers glower under her face, her heavy hair flickers. I don't know this girl. - You're a dirty crim now my friend! My hand's shaking. Wait… and go! We throw and flame erupts in our eyes. Back off, scramble through the fence. Flames tongue over the windowsills, sparks flitter out at the sky. Now a whoosh and a roar. She laughs out loud. Don't know what I'm meant to feel.
- Now do it to me. Here. And make it quick
- What?
The girl shovels down her pants. Her thighs glister in the light. She grabs at my pants, takes command of my crotch, wraps a leg about me. We crash backwards. Fuck! Francesca, we have to leave! She clutches at my head… forces me inside her. Rough. She gulps air. Her teeth are on my chin. She gasps. I'm licking at her face. We're clinging, I'm deep. She slows, whispers at my ear. Sounds like… Peter. Peter. Then the madness shoots up. We come at once, and oh it hurts. I clutch like a child, fingers in her backside. Her breath floods my mouth, we rock there for seconds, more seconds… more. Suddenly she shoves away, stands up, grapples with her pants. *Get up now,* she says. Flickering ghosts glare in the trees. I shovel myself up, woozy, almost tip; she grabs my hand, we run into the wood. Clouds obscure the moon. Where's the car? She hesitates, seems lost, but there's the Audi, ghost car by a grinning gate… Inside and away. At first she crawls, no lights. What goblins inhabit these lanes? We slip through a sleeping black village. Sudden pair of headlights looms behind. She mercilessly floors the car! It slews about but she rights it. Fuck, Francesca! Our lights flood on and we're gone, two fugitives in the night.

She looks at me. Her round-eyed naughty girl look.
- So how was I?
- I want dessert
And she laughs. And we laugh. We laugh and laugh.

Later I wake in nothing dark. Francesca is scrunched like a child in her seat. It's chilly, quiet. I finger the runnels of her hair, her eyes flicker a little. Comrade. I step out of the car. The moon's there. We're parked beside a field, high up. There's a wood on a ridge, and its edges saw the sky. With shut eyes I sway under the black vault. My city world is gone, lonely gone… Francesca crawls out of the car, clings to me. I know! she murmurs. Goes to the boot, pulls out a blanket, spreads it on the grass of the field. Now she strips away all her clothes. Her silver skin glistens. I stare at the bliss place. She kneels.

- Come hither lover. Do as I do! She straddles me, wraps the blanket about, cocoons us in. Sleep-honey voice says:
- Never escape me now, Nicky
- Don't care
- We'll go to daddy's house in the morning. I'll show you… our house. And she sleeps. Leaden deep.

Master and Manipulator

At her husband's death fourteen years ago Carolyn Mars (then Carolyn Gorda) kept on the country cottage for Francesca's sake, or so she told herself. She'd never felt at home there, and at Leo's passing sealed it up and couldn't bring herself to return for years. Leo had filled it with his dreaming music and his fire, his boyish self-absorbed quest for the 'juice of life', of which she never approved but felt guilty before his spirit. Nowadays she comes, not with Peter Mars but at times with Francesca, who is no longer the girl who sat at daddy's feet at evening, walked with him in the woods, meticulously set his place at table and let only he with his musician's hands stroke and master the tangled garden of her hair. With Peter Mars Carolyn married all the money she wanted, which Leo never gave her, and took care to worship Peter despite his self-regarding coolness. She also took care to ignore the way Francesca cleaved to him, and the way her daughter interested herself in spending his fortune. Carolyn knows her brittleness is ne'er a match for her daughter's warmth, and in secret even blamed her weaker self for marrying in haste like Hamlet's mother. She is afraid of Francesca, if the truth be known. And why shouldn't she fear that her husband and daughter will exclude her? Even though her daughter is marrying that nice doctor? Carolyn should welcome *that*. As if she could influence any decision of her notorious offspring. But all the media barbs against her family of late make it her duty to protect... because her Leo at least understood her, knew her for what she was, and warned her always to seek one quality if she couldn't achieve the rest. *Integrity, honesty,* he said. Still hidden under the societal façade, yet waiting like grief or anger unexpressed for the day it might fly into the open and spread its heavy truth, Leo's old warning now makes her ponder where her filial and motherly duties lie.

Francesca Mars calls out musically to her mother on the sunlit drive in the morning.
- Mummy! We got lost coming last night. Had to sleep in the car! I went to Nicky's concert!

The daughter will make no effort to explain why she's in the countryside with a man who is not her fiancé, and Carolyn will not ask. The boy is received with courtesy, and watches as a mother's eyes ponder the fact of him. Come see the property! says Francesca, but Carolyn intervenes. - I received a message from *Luc* this morning. He texts me most days as you know darling, and there are problems in Africa. Would you call at the earliest chance? - Of course mummy; you don't have to say it, though I suspect he's in total charge as always! And she pulls at her young man's arm. Come and see where daddy practised! '...This was my room... this wood is where we'd walk and tell jokes... this rotunda is where he'd stand and sing and conduct the trees. He was such a *funny* man...' Francesca Mars and Nicky Bright stand quietly in the wood, and she is prompted to shed a little tear. 'And now darling, I shall take a bath, my little ritual, while you talk to mummy. Think of me as I languorously lie!' Soon, as required, the boy is seated with Carolyn in her stone-floored parlour. With ritual nonchalance, they ply the conversational art.

- Yes, Francesca slipped into my concert. A nice surprise. Insisted I visit with her here. I take it she'd had a drink or two! Does she always do things on impulse?
- She is impulsive, yes
- Couldn't refuse. Though I consider it a holiday. The house of the great Leo Gorda

- You consider him great?

- Why not?

- Since I was married to him I can't judge. A prophet in his own land, etcetera

- I get it. Tell me, Luc is managing a new campaign? I assume your husband values him

- Indeed, and my daughter too

- Their engagement was a perfect outcome then?

(She looks at me) - Perfect

- And a wonderful party. Thank you

- And thank you for playing. Francesca adores music

- After her father, I assume

- It surprises me she is a politician, rather

- You see her as one?

- Apparently one must be so in order to help the unfortunate. Have you met Mr Bouseri?

- Briefly

- And his daughter?

- Yes. In fact we had a conversation. *Ayaan,* I think it is

- Indeed, Nicky. And how did she strike you?

(Mmm, she suspects about Ayaan and Luc) - To be honest, I think she likes to spend money. And they say getting Mister Bouseri was quite a coup

- Francesca has her techniques. Don't ask me what they are

- So it *was* her, as the press tell us?

- If they say it is, no doubt it is

- You're not involved in any aid programs?

- What do *you* think?

- I don't think. (She gives me a glittery look) Steady on, Carolyn. I'm just here for breakfast

- You and I both know that's a fib. (Pause) But never mind. What do you think of Doctor Luc?

- Well... I'm glad there are people like him around! I couldn't do what he does. So... that's it.

She stares, then studies the sky through a window.

- Does he *need* her, I wonder?

She's a player, this girl.

- Perhaps he wants a princess.

Her eyes glitter again. I'll toss another one.

- I don't think he'd marry for money. For pity rather. Pity's a form of love, but it's not sexy. (I smile here) All in all, a beautiful friendship.

Her eyes moisten suddenly and she seems to gulp. What's behind those eyes?

- Why should Luc pity my daughter?

- Take a close-up look

- She's a user. You know that

- I guess we all are

- Not good enough, Mister Bright. I love my daughter but she is an abuser. A powerfully charming one, as you will have learned.

(We stare) - Let's leave this, shall we Carolyn?

- Be warned. And I think that's her now. We'll enjoy breakfast… Darling! How was your bath?

- Hot and deep. (Francesca gives me the *look*. My lower parts start to ache) Now mummy, have you been entertaining Nicky, since he's my *friend*?

- Of course, darling. Why would I not?

The reality is, brittle Carolyn took me into her confidence behind Francesca's back. Interesting fact. But the Mars family dynamic has more to reveal.

- Oh mummy! I *know* we turned up out of the blue. I wanted to hear Nicky play before I go back to *Africa*. (Non-sequitur?)

- You don't have to go, darling

- But me and Luc are a team

- Your stepfather complained to me the mission's not properly planned

- Peter said that? Rubbish. He never said it to me

- I report what I hear

- Mummy! Where do you get these ideas? We've done meticulous planning for months!

- Luc talks to me about his feelings. And believe it or not so does your stepfather

- Fee-lings. That is *all* it is. How many projects have I turned around with my energy alone? You're out of touch, mum. (Haughty now) Africa's just an idea to you. May I remind you that people are dying, *children* are dying
- Not at breakfast in my own house. No
- This is daddy's house.
I butt in.
- Allow me to take a walk in the garden.
At that moment the mobile on the table rings. Francesca clutches at it.
- Francesca Mars… *Lena!* Yeah, in the countryside with our friend Nick. What? You want to see me? Not socially? Mr Bouseri? I *know* Peter said it. It was me who told you. *Publish?* Why would you want to - I told you I would give you what you want! Are you fucking *listening* to me? This is my family!
She slams the phone on the table. Carolyn looks at me and I at her. Francesca appears to be seriously shocked. Stares down at us like Empress Wu. Then slumps to a chair and pouts.
- Why can't I have what I want! Why can't I trust *anyone?*

Is it possible that Lena Duvorchek has knocked her from her perch? Was that call out of the blue? Couldn't possibly be. So where's Lena? Francesca bursts through the French doors into the garden. I make excuses and follow. Into the wood now. She's standing in the trees, fists clenched. I take her about the waist. She pushes me off.
- Your bitch wants to publish my quotes! How my stepfather fell out with Bouseri. How the Eritrea thing is 'under threat'. She has no idea what Peter will do to control! It's a *front*. It's because he doesn't want me to marry Luc!
- Why not?
- Oh, wouldn't *you* like to know!
I feel a churn of fear.
- Don't tell if you don't want
- But you'd love to know! Just like your bitch 'd love to know! The whole world loves to know!
(My bitch?) - Why doesn't Peter want you to marry?
- Because he wants control, you fucking idiot! Because I'm so famous!

And he has *such* a reputation as a philanthropist, he can't crawl out of it! Ha ha! And my stupid mother is desperate for him to pull out. If only she knew! She doesn't give a shit about my needs

(Why turn on Carolyn?) - I don't get it. Peter Mars can only benefit from your success. And Luc's. Unless you spent all his money

- How could I spend all his money? He could hardly bear to part with a few pennies for the children of Eritrea. I got the government in, and Bouseri too. It was me. Me!

- It doesn't add up. *Why is he down on Luc?*

- Fuck off, little piano player. Fuck off back to your baby music and your baby Lena.

Yeah? This is some fucking pantomime. I try to lay hands on her but she pushes away, runs into the trees. Now I hear a voice calling from the direction of the house. It's not Carolyn. Oh my god it's Lena. She knew we were here. She followed us. The headlights on the road last night. The call. Crazy cow! We've gotta dodge *her.* Stop! What kind of pawn am I in this? Gutless wonder grovelling to Francesca. Can't you admit she's puppeteering all this? How can she be so resourceful? I can't match wits with women like this. But I want the truth. From the puppeteer goddess' mouth. *Ugh, I want her version of the truth.* She knows I want to be complicit, to stick my head in her noose. Don't leave me out, I wanna be in the in-crowd! ...She's there by a little pond in the middle of the wood, kneeling in the leaves, back turned against me.

- Don't attack, Francesca. Whatever you've done for me or with me or to me, I stand by it. I don't ridicule it. (No response) I don't piss on it from a height like you do. And do you think I give a damn whether you lie to me? (Good, anger. Better than grovelling, or complicity or fatalness) You can wrap me round your little finger for the sake of your famous plans, for your reputation, for your oh-so-complex psychological journey, but I tell you this: in the end it doesn't affect me because I've got a thing no-one can take away from me. Let the sky fall on my head, *I don't give a damn.* You should understand that. Actually I know you do. But don't you ever dare call me a little piano player! Who the fuck d'you think you are? Trouble is,

I know what you are. You're some kind of genius and you're too beautiful by half - and I know I could...

Stop. About to say some emotive sludge I'll regret. Suddenly the notion's ridiculous. Man up, dickhead.

- Ah, screw it
- You don't know what it's like for me, Nicky. I... walk a tightrope. I walk a razor's edge...
- I know. The legend of yourself. You may have noticed I'm also a performer. I know about self-promotion
- Peter Mars has a hold on me. He hypnotises me
- And you're too weak to deal with it? Next you'll be telling me you need to be the 'vulnerable female', the 'helpless victim'. Put it on your resume, ha ha
- Nick!

Oh my god, she's crying. But a voice calls through the trees. Lena. Francesca must have heard. She fails to wipe her eyes. Is this the climax, the big reveal? Why lead *me* to the woods? Why the grand pantomime for a piano player? One can see why she got herself connected to Lena: she knew a rapacious journalist when she saw one, but me? Logic says she wants a friend. A simple lover, an ally maybe. Don't fool yourself! Even if she wanted any of us for love or 'friendship', aren't love and friendship just dumb arrangements in a world where nothing matters, where everyone perishes, mostly in agony, in a fog of injustice or disease or starvation? What's the point of friendship when you've seen the bug-eyed face of a starving child? But has she really seen the horror... or does she fear she *doesn't care* even if she has? The cynic battles it out with the lonely girl - kneeling right here in the leaves. And this lonely girl is her great embarrassment. Especially if it turns out she needs more than other people need! Oh what a beautiful tragedy, the unfolding tragedy of Francesca Mars, an ego that dwarfs the suffering of the lowly and starving and diseased and destitute. 'Screw all of them! (she seems to cry) Why does everybody assume I don't suffer? Do not the givers suffer? We who sacrifice our cocoon of gladness and innocence and security for the sake of some unknown blacks on the dark side of the globe! What about me, you bug-eyed victims in the Horn of Africa? I lost my father. Is that not enough!' ...I am speaking for you, Francesca. You ought to say it to me. I want to hear it from your mouth.

But Lena's there. She steps out of the trees like she chose her moment. Looks like she hasn't slept.
- *You* took your time. Where's your camera? Your recorder? I won't talk to *you*.
Francesca stalks away in the apparent direction of the house. I get hold of Lena. She shrugs me off.
- Don't you interfere! Francesca, wait, I want to help
- Keep away. Keep away!
Francesca seems to encourage the opposite. The conversation clearly has to happen in front of Carolyn Mars. There she is on the lawn as we emerge from the wood. There's another man standing in the driveway. I've never seen him before. He has a camera in his hands. Francesca starts.

- Mummy. Do you know that *she* has a private hotline to your husband? Do you know that *she* likes to make up stories about our family, how there's scandal in our family? Come on Lena Duvorchek, tell us what you know! Tell us how you think I'm a pawn of Peter Mars. How he hates my future husband Luc. How he wants to end our mission to Africa. And how my mother fears him and me so badly! (Sudden pause) But who is that man? I don't know that man. You journalists. Your little club!

Carolyn is staring, wild-eyed. But I have guessed. Francesca has set up Lena, forced her to follow her here, then tipped off *another* journalist to turn up and film the revelations.

- There is no scandal in my family, whispers Carolyn Mars.
- Oh no, mummy. That is what I told *her* - in her bed in the middle of the night - but she won't believe. Lena Duvorchek had to seduce your husband as well. Had to screw him in order to get him to say whatever she wants
- What are you talking about?
- Read all about it, *tomorrow.*

Francesca Mars retreats to the house of her father and slams the door. We stand and watch like figurines. Moments later she emerges, slides into her car. Its brake lights glower at us. She roars off down the drive scattering metal. We are flotsam in her wake. That was my lift, is my next thought. The phantom journalist has debunked as well. Lena and Carolyn stare at each other. Lena has nothing to say. Struck dumb for once in her long-legged life.

- *You may all leave now,* says Carolyn Mars.

* * * *

A local taxi gets Lena and me to the station. Grim ride to the city. Our little train rolls through vacant fields. Lena is silent and her made-up eyes are stale. I start to feel sorry for her.

- She cornered you there sweetheart. But don't worry, she cornered me.
- You? Don't worry, lover boy. She has no reason to manipulate you
- Why?
- Because you're not important enough.

Ugh! The train clatters over a cutting bridge. Yeah, Lena is right. Lena is very important with her Serb gravitas. But maybe I am too! After all, Francesca dragged me in front of her mother as if to rival her French doctor. Nope, I'm a walk on. But to be unimportant is to my advantage - if I wanted advantage that is. And yes I do. My Francesca might just care for me effortlessly, beyond a need to justify. But am I to be one of a mob? I am an exclusive, a snob. I'll not compete! But Mars has made me grovel, made me cling to the notion that her sage and sparkling gaze was the one unpremeditated thing left in her world. Last gasp of a fuckwit. This is why I'm a music man. And nothing but a fill-in for her lost father, a troubadour who momentarily salved a mood in her desert tent on the long march of her drear campaign with destiny.

But maybe Lena really cares about her too, wants to write her true story. I realise I don't know my Serb half well enough to judge. We all have someone we care for more than they care for us. Would Lena seek nobly to divert the world's attention to some luminous facts of suffering? Expose the suffering of the great ones in order to expose her own? Nah, too ambitious by half. Only the great can lead us to truth by their own trails and pathways. And we can but follow in the hope that they will acknowledge our effort, acknowledge our suffering. Francesca Mars, I suspect, worships the dream of her father, and wants to begin again from the deep age of fourteen. The attention-seeking little girl once perceived the fabulous fact of her own being, and wanted to scatter its riches for all the public world to know. But who could ignore its evil, its loss? So she aspires to be tragic, vainglorious, the arch-heroic public sacrifice who showed us our flaws by exposing her own. Move over Jesus Christ. In the media slush of public crucifixion and fleshly scrutiny and mass applause and public tears - brilliant Francesca Mars will lead us pied piper-like to the heart of her private tragedy, wherein we might see our own. And we shall thank her. Then one step more… By her brilliance will she show us the dark irony, the colossal *burden* - of owning that brilliance. Game, set, match. A narcissist fanatic, ladies and gentlemen!

You'll see I've fetishised the habit of speculating on her, and it's draining me. Romantic dreams are a waste. The Serb is more pragmatic. She sees an opportunity and takes it, knowing that her prey is a warrior and wouldn't hate her if confronted. All's fair in love and war, and Lena's aggression is a form of love. Yet I believe she feels the cost; in fact I know she does. The question is, will she admit to it? Lena has her steely dignity and her losses. Will she blame the famous for those? All the world's a stage and all the men and women merely users. Will Lena aspire to dignity, or to the mere tearing down of great Francesca in order to 'expose the lies of us all'? In that case what may any of us believe in? We badly need something. I'd say we'll be scouring tomorrow's media, and believing whatever we read therein.

Loyalty Test

Francesca Mars (you'll have seen by now) has perfected the strategy of promoting a scandal then rubbing people's noses in it, of flirting with enemies before cutting them dead. But again, is this her test of our loyalty, her cruel-to-be-kind exposure of our weaknesses? I am inclined to believe it, but beware! This might be her biggest irony: to make us believe she is a standard-bearer, a genius, when she is nothing but a little wee girl all the while.

Sheer infatuation born of vanity has made me deny that the public career of Francesca Mars is but a soap opera studded with set pieces. The mystery appearance at my concert, enlisting me to torch a shed (she must have thought me as gullible as hell), the poignant tour of daddy's house, dangling me in front of mummy as a rival to Luc… even the drug-addled invasion of our flat! and her 'breakdown' at the evil phone call from the ravenous journo who is scandalously revealed as her lesbian lover and who screwed her stepfather to get a story! All planned, staged. Whodunnit theatre! Sport perhaps? Foolish world, do not presume to fathom the perverse resourcefulness of Francesca Mars.

Me, I've retreated to merciful music, weaving up a score for an upcoming theatre production (a tragedy). How sweetly normal is that? Francesca looms, big-haired spectre in my study. Here's her chair… and I wish she were here, formally listening, appreciating simple time together, being human-sized for once. Fat chance. Several news articles have appeared in recent days regarding the scurrilous Mars family and the perfidies of the media scrum, notably one Lena Duvorchek. Lena's been AWOL for several nights, trawling bars no doubt, scum lying low. I don't judge; we're all insects crawling the earth, where the tyre tracks of doom forever lurk beyond the next furrow. Actually I compose better in a fatal mood. Gloom suits my Little Art.

Escaping duty one evening I find myself trawling (for Lena) up the King's Road. And passing the doorway of a bar… what do I see? In the shadowed interior: a dark girl and a man at a table. He leans toward her, her legs seem to invite. Several steps past the door I grock it. Doctor Luc Cotillard and Ayaan Bouseri, his *paramour*. Ta daaa. Isn't he supposed to be holed up in darkest Africa? That'd be none of one's business. On the other hand, should I pop in and greet? Through the door then, and sidle up. They glance up but evidently don't recognise. Nicky Bright. At your service.

- Ah! says the doctor, too late to be natural.
- Back from Eritrea then? And have we seen Francesca? How's Mister Bouseri? D'you live round here, Ayaan?

The brown saucer eyes look from me to Luc… and he being French invites me to sit, menage a trois-like. I note the long ebony thighs protruding from skirt, glistening curls framing the neck, fakey bored pout. Save us Allah from ourselves. Yet Lucky Luc's in charge.

- Ayaan, you remember Nicky and his playing at our engagement party? Francesca was certainly enchanted. In fact yes, I am back for an important meeting. Unexpected. Our Eritrea scheme has hit a bump. (His French lilt makes it all seem accomplished fact) I am fortunate to run into Ayaan. As you see, we have a drink before I undertake the business
- Oh *yeah*. Peter Mars is under pressure! About payoffs following those deaths in Somalia. Media's like a dog with a bone. I assume your dad's considering his options, Ayaan. (They're staring) Francesca is super-stressed; is she actually *going* to Eritrea?

Good at lobbing grenades! And Luc is going to cover it all up by confiding in me.
- Tell me, he says. Do you see her a lot? It is hard to know her mind. I've been worried for her.
(Why listen to bullshit unless you're going to spin some yourself?)
- She's seriously *pissed*, Luc. About some story that Peter Mars is going to jack in your whole Ebola program. Some say he's got it in for you. No idea why. And that Bouseri is getting jittery. Hope you're not killing yourself out there for nothing, mate. Though I wouldn't know. You're a Pro, take my hat off, etcetera.
Ayaan is getting nervous, needs them to depart. He kisses her hand. No fool! She glares at him, barely mouths goodbye.
- She all right?
We watch as she strides past the street window with her chin stuck out.

- I believe Ayaan is worried by the situation. She seeks private advice. Her father demands!

- Don't tell me: wants to stay in UK and keep her flashy life but has to 'give back to her country'. Rich-poor muslim-secular daddy complex!

(He doesn't flinch) - Actually you are right. Ayaan is a good girl but too proud. So we get on well. (A smile) One day perhaps she will join our work. I encourage.

We look at each other. He's smooth enough to know I can blow him apart. And pragmatic enough not to fret about it in front of me.

- Look here Luc. Francesca is really shitted about -

- Actually, Nicky... (convincing sigh) I have been concerned. Francesca is to be my *wife*

- She asked *you*, right?

- I'm sorry?

- She asked you to marry her. Sure, she admires you but I daresay she pulls the credit back here in UK for all your hard yakka

- What is 'yakka'?

- Your work, Luc. Work that save lives. I can't think of a single reason why that work should be interrupted. She does all the blabbing, you do the life-saving. But marriage, that gets in the way. Am I right? (He's glaring at me now) I mean you're a giver, but you have limits, right?

Doc Luc won't be rattled, yet.

- Let me buy you a drink

- Okay. Red wine.

And he slips to the bar. A cool operator, I kinda like him. But smoky Ayaan has reappeared. She hisses at him, points at me. He holds her arms at her sides, motions her to go. He brings the plonk.

- *Salut*

- I imagine Eritreans get sensitive about being patronised by us whites

- She is a rich child and naturally wants it all. But she must do her father's bidding since he pays for her education, her apartment and everything else

- One could go gaga over a chick like that

- Gaga?

- Lose one's famed French reason.

His eyes seem to harden.

- Actually I see disturbing things in my work. We come from 'successful' societies: there are no wars, no famines, droughts, earthquakes, crop disasters. We can be fed when we're hungry, aided when sick, helped when we can't help ourselves. With technology we create success. All we have to do is eat and procreate and consume and eat and consume some more. And you know it is sometimes meaningless. I have not been a victim of war but I feel the quiet horror, the absurdity, of peace. And at times I am disgusted

- I imagine you are. You want a trophy

(He leans in) - Look here, Nicky. I wonder if you can keep this quiet. The reason I have returned in such clandestine way is this: I must convince Bouseri not to pull out. Without him we are finished. And I must avoid the press.

Confidential, considering I've been plugging him about his dusky fuck versus his wife-to-be.

- May I hazard some guesses? One: Mars won't swallow Francesca's rebellion from *him* - ie, that she got engaged. So he undermines *your* program. Two: Bouseri doesn't like the way you're in love with his daughter. And you're desperate to keep her.

Luc stares at the table.

- What the fuck could you really know?

(Good, he's pissed off) - I know you're angry with her because she's a proud fucking African and her daddy won't do your white man's bidding

- You think so? Because I have been feeding and clothing and sheltering and injecting with medicines these people for years and years? I do it because I am a doctor, because I care, because if I did not...

- The fuckers'd die in a desert of flies and dust? Don't tell me

- Absolument! And the Bouseris of this world turn from me as if they did not need. As if their pride could put food in the mouths of their people! And it is the privileged, the tribal leaders who line their own pockets, who preach their pious Islam, who say they want self-determination not handouts, and that their culture is under threat from the white Colonialist who is historically to blame. And they come to Paris and London and Rome in their silky suits and send their children to be educated by colonialists, and they hold their fat noses to the air!

Luc breathes heavily through his nose. I feel a bit sorry.
- I agree with all that, Luc. But is she real, this Ayaan? You put her on a pedestal. I know because I do it with Francesca. And if your Francesca is a fake you should've seen it. Do you love her?
- Of course
- You know she champions your causes for selfish reasons
- She has her good reasons
- They're too complicated for you! Lemme save you from marriage to Francesca
- What are you to her? Do you imagine you can contain her?
- Not in a million years. But duty made you agree to marry. You're being dishonest. And ruining it for somebody else
- And you are that somebody
- Fuck *no*. Do you think I can't see how like a spider she wraps me in her charmy thread? Do you think she'd make such an elaborate effort with me unless she wanted a devotee, a witness to her incomparable secrets? Francesca dares, Francesca wins. Self-publicist in love with herself *and* who hates herself. Who longs to give and destroy at once! But someone must *be* there when she does it. She calculates it could be me. All too tough for you, eh Luc?
- Ugh, I don't know what to do when Ayaan tells me she hates Francesca's guts. It kills me.
I can't help the good doctor there. I stand.
- I won't spill the beans, mate. Thanks for being candid. And good luck
- All right. Good luck to you also, Nicky.

Night Dream

In my bed, past midnight. In the street window is a grand piano silhouette. The door slips open. There is a creaking and a soft rustling, and blue skin glints in the massy shadows. A form lifts my cover, slips in. Bundles of braid tickle my cheek. It's her. She curls about me. And whispers.

- I'm to be gone, Nicky. The dusty desert. Somewhere people need my help. I resent them for their suffering but I need them. I can face my own selfishness.

Her head is on my shoulder. I feel her balmy breath about my cheek. If it's a dream, let it be.

- Sorry I cursed you and cursed Lena. Do you see I miss my daddy? Do you know I always do? Can I be fourteen with you? (the honey voice) I know I'm alone but I don't want to trick you. I unleash things I don't want to control. Can you be in love with a mad girl? …You do love me?
- Are you nuts?
- To seek bestiality in beastly places: my solace. I am a voyeur of beastly things. Can hurt myself that way. I like to. I'm ugly, weak. I can hold on to you. Can use you and you'll let me. But Nicky, I'd die if you hated me
- No chance
- I'm spoiled, I destroy people. I fear ugliness but I want it too. Fear weakness but want it. Oh, will I ever achieve anything?
The sweet monotone.
- Don't have to. You just have to be
- I was never soft with you. In the raging fire I raped you. If I'd been the man I would have raped you
- Lucky me
- Let me be the beast. Let me atone for being a beast.
Low breathing, rustle of hair. Curl of naked leg, tickle of faraway toes.
- Will people let me heal?
- I'll help ya, baby girl
- Should I marry him?
- No. He's in love with someone
- I know who. I don't blame. I'd want her too
- He needs his African dream. Dodge all the futility of his work
- Can I still be his goddess?
- You're my goddess
- And you give me music. When I listen I remember… I walked in a forest, holding hands with my daddy. There was nothing under my skirt, only the wind. My daddy went away, and where the tall trees gaze to open

lands I heard the pipes of Pan. Now the new god Mars is there in the wood. I am his Venus. I can't resist. I pull away his cloth, he is massive, it's easy to give in. He's not daddy, he wears an earring. He flings me in the grass! I wrestle him and hold on. I want him to kill me. I want the hot death feeling, I always want it. When I wake he is gone. The wind rustles the boughs in the wood. My back hugs the turning earth. Clouds drift in a blue dream. I'm a girl spread out in the wind. It plays on my legs, I am filleted. That was our first time. Will you keep it secret? Nicky?

The girl-voice urges me.

- Yes. But why tell me?
- Tell no-one. No-one. *For then I am bound to you.* Are you bound to me?
- Yes Francesca. Bound to you
- You're my hope. Now I can burn. I go to my work. A hollow star, I burn out. Super Nova
- Come back to us
- I will. If you say I should.

Tears and serious kisses. Then she pushes me away, climbs out of the dream bed.

- How did you get in?
- Lena gave me a key long ago. Tell her I came.

There is a rustle in the room, and her soft breathing. The door opens, closes. She is gone.

* * * *

Deep at night I'm awake in my study. Lena enters through the street door, creeps down the passage, blinks in the doorway.

- Hello Nicky. You never came looking
- Sorry. Were you at the *Split?*
- Oh, I am drunk
- Hold me then.

We slip to the sofa.

- I drank all my money. Finally
- I'll help you
- You are best guy. Kiss my lips

- Francesca came. She missed seeing you. Says she is sorry. She's gone to Africa
- You know she is the slave lover of Peter Mars. And Nicky, that is how she gets his money
- I know no such thing. You imagine it
- I am so jealous
- Nothing to be jealous of, beauty. She loves you. We're a happy family. Wait and see.

She lets herself be cradled, then opens her eyes.
- I will go to the airport!
- You will not. Go to sleep.

And we let ourselves sleep.

The Forbidden Zone

Lena has been getting Africa messages from Francesca, which she passes on. Couldn't the girl write to me as well?

'...Finally I met Luc and we took the Toyotas into desert on the Eritrea-Ethiopia border. This is a landscape to settle our debt with life. No meaning or solace, savage, beautiful, rock and sand knuckled under steel sky. I said to Luc I feel like fly shit on the car's window, or scattered dust illumined by the sun. He liked that. Ragged birds wheel and watch, and their cold eyes know what we are better than we know ourselves. The heat is sapping. Luc is used to it but I am a little female and he had to rescue me since I threw up twice. I will get strong. I refuse to cut off my hair. I want to go to a forbidden zone miles from here because there are families who need our help. Luc says no, it is mined. But I feel lucky, I will go there... I think the sun has touched me! I thought of a phrase and it's been rattling in my head: *The reality is... it's all unreal.* What should I make of it: beauty in a paradox. I will always come to Africa. If you have nothing you can be yourself, if you give it all away you can live. Yes, I am a pampered westerner and it is not my money, but I am determined to make a difference. Whatever a difference is. You see how the desert swallows our notions and dreams. And yet we walk on, as nothing. At least we walk. Love you. Love to Nicky. F.M.'

I myself have walked into a thicket of stress with my *Antigone* soundscape. The coming production's rigid glooms make me long to tell the director: don't torture us! The deserty sets and blue shadows make me feverish, and in my mind I'm riding with Francesca in Eritrea. Strange dislocation settles on me and my musical offerings seem outlandish. The director tells me as much. I claim it fits his tone but he's not happy. Art is cruelty at the best of times, and at worst is merely irrelevant. I'm powerless, trapped in this box, required to comment on life in some parallel universe of art. I crave the real: no irony, no displacement, the actual sunlit Real. Not jealous of Francesca and Luc, for romance is a pang beyond jealousy. Why should I not have the romance of scattering beneficence to dwellers of the sands? Is it not simple love? I'm sad, not there in the wild with her and Lucky Luc. I think I shall just record a musical abstraction, leave this den of art, let the director choose the bits he wants... let vultures tear at the rest.

Late one night during final rehearsals, Creon is exacting his price of Antigone in her cave tomb, and the messenger is bringing news of her death. Suddenly my mobile yelps from the shadows. The director curses. But - Lena... she blurts in stabs of bloodied English... that *Francesca Mars has walked into her minefield and met with her Fate.* They've found the body, and brought her out... but Luc *can't save her* she's bleeding somewhere in a fly-blown hospital there'd be a plane coming to take her home but it won't land because rebels are all around. This is the news she has. Will I come? And she's crying and there's nothing on media yet but there will be, there will be. I lurch out to the night street, stumble-run for any taxi back to Chelsea... But the street arteries are clogged, the city's heart is clogged, its limbs white under shoplight cut off everywhere... I take the last mile by foot, shirt-sweat clings like cold glue, raw breath in my ears. At home I find her. TV's blaring so I kill it. She has a phone in her ear, is shouting, repeating to someone down the line. I hold her but she's not connecting to anything. I make her call up Peter Mars. Says he negotiated a helicopter - 'but the fuckers won't use it. British commissioner on the ground says they took her by road to Addis but I won't have her dealt with there, no way. We'll fly her here to London but it's touch and go 'cause they found her late. What the fuck was she doing? Where was Luc and his team? It's a fucking scandal, heads 'll roll for this. Do those blacks know who they're dealing with? You can't trust Bouseri to put his money where his mouth is; where was the security unit he promised! They're laisser fucking faire that's what they are. This is it, this is the end, she's staying in England for good, if she isn't in goddam bits when she gets here. I have to go. Luc will update. Come to the airport if you want.'

That was Sunday. By Tuesday morning following a torture Monday of scrapulous rumour they put her on a private jet to London. Luc fought with Peter Mars they said. Shouldn't be moved from Addis Ababa. Mars pulled rank and got her out. By late Tuesday afternoon she's at Heathrow and whisked to hospital. No value being at the airport but Lena's there. And a press gaggle is at the hospital so that's insult added to injury. By Tuesday ten at night we're in the ward. Carolyn and Peter Mars are there. Luc greets us, looks scattered. We tell him thank you, again and again.

- Another hour, she would have bled to death. She was lying in the dust. Luckily I am a doctor. She left the party and walked in a restricted area. I told her never to do such a thing. The foot is barely there. I think the rucksack in her hand shielded the impact. They told us in Addis they could save the foot but I could not say. Mars made the decision to bring her here so there is a delay. It may be crucial. Money talks. I suppose we should be glad he got his plane there. I am philosophical. The wound is bad. They are going to operate tonight. I am inconfident. It is simple. She will be an amputee.

We are allowed in for five minutes. Francesca is a ghost in a bed. Awake though.
- 'Lo people. …Din' think I see ya so soon. …Luc bin marvellous. Withou' him, I be gone.

Her eyes flicker. I dip my hand in a frazzle of hair, hold her forehead. Lena clutches at her wrist. Carolyn is sat there, gazing at a window. Mars in the corridor is mouthing off at two doctors who're failing to be patient. Throwing weight about; can't say I blame him. I lean in.

- You're gonna be a hundred per cent. Do you hear?
- Yess, Nicky. Than' you.
She closes her eyes. Wiped out.

Inhuman

They took her left foot off in the night. A professional procedure, to which the response is trauma. Francesca Mars is incomplete, and the bumptious press splash it, feeding voyeurs' ten-second attention-pang. I hate them. Lena and Luc and Peter try to slam the door on the media beast. Got fucking photos at the clinic didn't ya? *Too blurry innit. Doin' our job. Need more, want more. You guys own 'er do ya?* Next night I follow Lena to the Split bar and we drink. The theatre director barks at me down the phone. I tell him I made a recording: pick the eyes out of it. He loses his bottle and I tell him to shove it, I'm not playing live. Bright career move son. Days pass… laze about my room. Can't erase that crack-lipped visage on the pillow… time and again her big eyes will open out of sleep, wonder at something enormous, fall back to the void. Outside, a rump of wind shoves the city trees. What changes, even when the sky falls in? What's beauty where it only used to be? If we lost the body what'd be left: knowingness… transparent love? If I lost a foot I couldn't reach the piano pedal. Vacancy: best drug now, and when her body slips away there'll be whiteness, here in no nameable place or time… and exhaustion will slip to quietude. With no context she'll exist like that, float outside responsibility of a life, above the blue earth, gazing on old spheres that now seem so idiotic. The little bits of the world we cared for, the sallies and wrestlings we did: where are they now? But when the spidery world encroaches, as it will, her troubles 'll clamour in. The drug of unattachment will wear off. Francesca the Powerful will careen out of reach. Can't play any more the fields of possibility and push, irony and youth, posturing, childishness. Now the future yawns, and over the horizon like the slow trundling threat of a great herd of beasts, when the tremors of her End rustle the nerves at her fingertips, she'll know the wild nameless Hope she used to have is gone. Shut in the blunt awful present. And her grinding work will begin: to keep the spirit inside the flesh. She'll need a husband. It's going to be me.

Next time we enter her room she's sitting up. At the bed end, a single bump under the cover. She stares at the place. Shock has cocooned her. White smock, estuary of hair. Lady of Shalott in her boat, drifting in a river. But her smile is a merciful beachhead. Not quite human but wanting. There's lunging heat in my heart. We sit on either side and she says: 'An old man came and talked to me. He lost his wife. He told me to shine again since I was an angel, and I told him I would, but now *I'm not at all sure*'. I see a rim of tears ripple, patter on the snows of her face. She swallows and the eyes stay open. She will not stand atop the mountain so soon, but will water valleys below. Nothing in me (I tell her) can repeal the legend of Francesca Mars. Lena puts a massive bunch of yellow flowers. Can't ignore *them*, Francesca says. I stacked a phone with classic works. Choose your mood, I say. Slash wrists, melancholic, heroic, peace, clear thought, classic temple, surging seas, holiness - all for you. And here are books, says Lena. We'll come each day, I say. Do you have crosswords? Francesca Mars looks at me and I witness desert skies in her planet eyes. Don't *do* crosswords, she says. Then I know that to contain her in a place, will take all our will and will fester and be wasted. I pray it won't age her, drain her, make her hard. Forget *that* one then, I laugh. But she and Lena don't laugh. They're holding hands, as girls do better than boys. I feel like a stranger. We're all strangers to Francesca Mars - unless invited into her ruined house.

Ten days pass and we're gathered in the hospital garden. The city intrudes; she'll need a quieter place. Bailed-up eyes, cracked lip, cutty talk, non-sequiturs: the big torture's coming. And Lena has something to say. I told her to hold her vulgar wants, but she wouldn't listen. We must engage her mind, said Lena. Help her return.

- I thought you'd like it if I wrote new articles to keep your presence out there, help your cause. Also to counter the gossip
- The *African* never turned up. Luc wouldn't bring her. Where's a Doctor when ya need him? Dunno what to do with a cripple girl? All duty no love
- He's here every day, Francesca. He worships you
- Worships the Black. Guess what? Going home early. On the *mend.* Minus one or two *bits*

- What can we do for you, darling?
- All right, I pity you. You can peek in my deadly diaries! Only bits I feed ya, mind… Sorry Lena, don't mean to make you sound like a *dog*.
I daren't speak. And spite won't help. We're going to see ugly before we see beautiful, she's set her mind on it. Now she cries.
- Does he love me really? Luc?
- For god's sake darling, he's in shock as well. Don't you know?

And the girls hug each other. But Lena's got her dark look on… You're so premature! Wait, for god's sake. No-one's even begun to ask why she walked off into a minefield in a desert. Maybe Lena's cooking up a theory on that. The doctors don't want Francesca to go home but she kicks up a fuss. A private nurse will tend her. The so-called convalescence begins.

Selfless Giving

Lena Duvorchek's new tract soon appears on several media sites. Here's some of it, written in her archaic lefty style:

'How much do we give and how much exploit? Today, we reveal exclusive moments from the diaries of Francesca Mars. Maimed by a landmine in Eritrea, failed by people who should have guaranteed her safety, it should be argued that Francesca Mars paid the ultimate price for giving. Like a soldier in war her life is shattered. She is the victim of people she tried to help and those she strove to represent. Need is a relative thing. We say even the selfish, the rich and the ignorant have needs. Too often the needs of the middle classes outweigh those of the world's beggars. And giving is as vulnerable to fashion as anything else. How happy we are to let others do our giving for us. Authorities in third world countries do little to aid their people, but are sure to shake the anti-colonial stick at those who'd come to their aid. Instead, doctors under protection of international agencies allow an amateur onto the front line, and the consequence is another beautiful casualty. An African businessman from the horn of Africa uses a white girl just as he exploits his own people. Our own partner government puts no safeguards in place for the girl ambassador who did the work they are happy to applaud. Where was the security when Mars almost died in Eritrea? Who will take responsibility? Not businessman Peter Mars. It makes business sense to use his daughter-in-law's talent and charisma to enhance his reputation with at least two governments. And to use his considerable charm and closeness to her to exploit. Businessmen do this. Fathers do it. Fiancés do it. And our amoral media does it, insatiable beast that in celebrating Francesca Mars pushed her to a position she could not fulfil. And, as with Diana Spencer, cried crocodile tears when the upstart fell on her sword. Let her fail, she who demanded so much! But many prominent editors today, the Sunday News included, will rue their too-close association with Francesca Mars! Sad story now, worth a few column inches, photo or two. This media should ask: Did Bouseri the Eritrean impose sex on Francesca Mars in exchange for fund grants? Did Peter Mars suspect it but do nothing? Why is Luc Cotillard, faithful fiancé of Francesca Mars, seen constantly with Bouseri's daughter? We all must face our own need, and the paucity of our generosity. Only then can we really help. The selfless hold the moral reins of this life, while the rest of the pack do their tiny bit, guilty they aren't better people. Or glad of it! Why? The fall of the beautiful happens but rarely, so let's record the manner of their demise for the 'betterment of ourselves'. Indulge your schadenfreude, but beware! One day you and I might aspire to taste that beauty. And then we will realise what sacrifice it takes. Some say Francesca Mars lost her sanity, or loved too much, or inflated herself, drove herself to ruin. But who would willingly lose a limb, risk a life of high promise for the sake of a little notoriety, five minutes of fame? Only a mad person would do it. Or a lost soul. Therefore, Francesca Mars is a victim. But she is *our* victim. Ours.'

The net effect of this is wall-to-wall nuisance. Putting out flags for Francesca lets Lena serves herself. I can just about hear her. *No-one calls me a dog.* And the accusations (no doubt she has more) are just damning enough to feed the required shit storm while keeping her out of court. But Lena never anticipates the consequences of exploiting that chip on her shoulder. Chips blind you like that. Consequence one: today an editor has seen fit to reveal that the writer Duvorchek 'more than likely' had a failed lesbian affair with said subject. Lena may not care a damn but others will. (Lena hinted to me that Francesca's little bag of conquests included a couple of prominent editors.) Another claims Duvorchek had a 'liaison' with Peter Mars. Would she be bi-sexual in that case? Consequence two: Carolyn Mars rings me. Francesca expects me to 'visit'. (No problem, but why call me: can't cope with a stink in the house?) Three: Lena is absolute persona non grata at the Mars residence. Four: our cellphones are blitzed with media calls. Lena is rapidly becoming the story while Francesca languishes in her agony. Hence the last consequence: I don't wanna be anywhere near Lena right now. This is inconvenient since we live in the same house. I'm channelling my own fright over Francesca but I don't care. I order Lena to give the diaries back. She claims she was fed innocuous crap. I break into her room to look for papers, she tries to stop me, I wrest them from her grip and we have such a slanging match there seems no chance of comeback. Result! Sum total of world suffering just expanded.

Under this cloud I travel to Richmond two days after. Francesca left garbly messages on my cell in a voice I failed to associate with her, seeking items of an illegal nature. No doubt she has friends in low places. Carolyn Mars greets me at the door, shows me the stair but will come no further. From the upper corridor I hear a strange wailing. Behind a door a voice, presumably the nurse, is repeating a message. *All this won't help. Have to help yourself.* The wail is punctured by pitched sobs, then silence. I enter. Peter Mars is slovened in a chair. Francesca is deposited on a big bed in foetal folds. The nurse holds her strapped leg. She sees me, and drops it.
- Is this him? she says.
Francesca jerks her head up.
- *That's* my friend. He's allowed. No-one *else*.

Mars hauls himself out of his chair. Sleepless eyes, piratey little earring, designer stubble gone to seed: all exude meaninglessness.
- Do yer worst, 'friend'. And tell that bitch of yours I'm coming.
(Would he mean Lena?) He's out the door. Nurse is primed for accusation. Fran did a job on her.
- I really don't have to put up with it but the father insists. Do something for her, will you?
- Fuck off now, tart

- Easy darling, nurse is trying to help
- I dressed the wound. Painkillers don't agree with her. She won't take medication. Keep the leg dry
- Don't thank 'er. She's my enema! In the pay of mummy.

The nurse is gone. In the silence the stump announces itself. I finger the hand of the girl on the bed. The eyes are out of focus. A lunatic smile, as if she did a bad thing and the only way to atone is to do a lot worse. Her hair's a viper nest, the gown smells, she's sweating. It'll be the drugs? A crying sight. What do vain boys feel when their idols are desecrated? We're fairweather helpers, disgusted, embarrassed by loss. Francesca's world has shrunk to a bed in a sickroom in her stepdaddy's house. Where's my arty refuge now eh. Maybe she offers a new art: nihilist. I'm not cut out for despair: I finesse it as musical nuance! - serve it up for the delectation of connoisseurs (who want mercy, who listen to forget) so long as it *doesn't soil my life*. Now all this shit. Nothing to finesse here. The girl's sticky. Raspy cough too. Seems she amassed a flu into the bargain. Should we touch, do flu solidarity? She solves the dilemma by plastering my hand to her lips. Now she drags me in, takes charge of my mouth. Oh babe I'll let you. Time for me to slip to the (wherever) bathroom... Take me! she says, and drapes girly arms about one's neck. Now I have to carry her. Back can scarcely take it. Halfway she pisses and it runs down my wrist. *Francesca!* - Sorry! And she actually giggles. I put her on toilet, find a cloth. Next I trip over the leg and she howls in fright, slides off, bangs her head on a tile. *Fuck* this shit. I try to raise her but slither and bang my knee. Now *I* can't get up. Sit her here, can't fall any further. Accusing silence in the big house. Now prop her against a wall, try to lift - what the fuck? Oh yeah, she soiled herself. Shit everywhere. Coup de grace, Francesca. Don't gag, drag the gown off, chuck it in a corner. Gush tap, flush one's delicate hands. She's naked by a wall. Creepy. I'm like her *guardian* now? Pull the shower over, hose her like an animal. She flinches. Now she lolls, mouth ajar, head on the side, and starts to blub. Stump is reddening. Shove her to the bath, haul her in. My back. My sodding knee. Me me me. Keep the leg over rim. Come *on*, Francesca! Let the water run. Let her lie.

Look, you're talking to yourself. Exit, straighten the sick bed whatever.

Gaze at grey sky in window. Never did this kinda thing in my life. Too lonely weird. How do folks in hospitals cope? Jesus wept. So do I. All silent. Better check that bath. *Fuck, she slid under!* You moron. Drag the head up, make her breathe. All right. Watch over, watch over.

Suppose we cleaned her with soap? Ask the corpse. Nope. Do armpits, stomach, neck, hands. Contours slither under my hand. I hesitate - then run my hands over her breasts, crotch, backside. All flesh, all Francesca. My pleasure. The once-sturdy angel stirs a little. Towel her clean. The pit eyes open slowly. We hobble to the bed. I slip in, cradle her. She seems to appreciate. Silence in the manse below. Slow time. No-one comes. My vigil then.

There's a numbness about this house. Perfection shattered, none of the idiots cope. This girl can't stomach littleness, is histrionic, wants all *and* nothing. I'll tidy up her life. No dying female on my watch, thank you Jesus. Phone shoved under a pile of underwear. Lone Francesca shoe, no doubt flung at the window. Dead time slouches by. Three o'clock. The grey-wide empty day. My accustomed life seems sucked away. I'll move into the house. Carolyn can't object.

Later I wake in the dark. Here she is, beside me. The door opens a crack. Carolyn is there.
- You'd better go. Thank you for your efforts
- Have to deal with this, Carolyn. No crawling off
- What d'you mean?
- Don't you dare let her fade away
- You don't understand
- And get a better nurse. Live in, if necessary
- Peter will decide
- I don't give a fuck what he decides. I'll be here tomorrow. Her resurrection starts now. Get it?
Standing there, she starts to shake. Tears come. I take hold of her. We cling in the silence and the room, in empty time. I realise we're both exhausted. Take her hand; down the stairs.

* * * *

Lena wants those diaries back. I refuse and she gets doubly moralistic, says they were 'trusted' to her.

- Go see Francesca if you want to help her, Lena

- I did. Keep up

(A lie) - Go again

- This a caring competition?

- Could be your little loyalty test

- I care for what she stands for

- And what would that be?

- Her effort, her crusade, her truth

- Convenient. She's out of her mind, did you notice?

- She is never out of her mind

- Fuck it Lena. It's not all about you

- Or you

- I'll stand by her. Till the…

- What? The end?

- Whatever

- Never saw a war, did ya? Never saw bodies

- What, the girl who counts ruins in Bosnia? Dial up the moral superiority! Stop *using*, Lena. Makes ya ugly

- No stupid boy ever called me ugly

- Don't! You know I love you. Whether you notice is something else. (Pause) I'm stressed, not used to playing nurse. She's trying to do herself in

- *That* is why people need to see how she is fucked over by this society

- *You* said she was in control

- She is a *victim*. Does she control Peter Mars? Bouseri? Luc? Her dead father?

- She control you?

- I love this girl. You know nothing

- Yeah. Boys know nothin'.

We stare at each other, rivals for the soul of Francesca. It'll drive us apart, but should it?

- The thing is to save her
- You do your job, I'll do mine. Give me the diaries, Nicky
- Actually I burnt them. Don't worry, there'll be plenty more to plunder.

Lena comes at me and snatches at my hair like I'm a ragamuffin. This callous act makes me shove her sideways and she lands against the rim of a table which makes her gasp and fall to her knees. I stomp off, turn back, stoop to help her and she swipes me in the face. It really stings. *Fucking boys!* she says. Force myself to walk out... feel stupid all the way to Richmond, where my car drives me. Tough girls don't inspire sympathy. I'm sorry all the same. At the house I find Francesca trussed in bed, the surly nurse having done her work. Hair's been tamed but there's a sullen fog, as if she just presided over a perfect shit storm.

- Close the door. Come sit. You can do something for me
- Say hello to me, darling
- What? Yes. Now Nicky, the Pethidine is utter crap and I want smack. You can get it. Here's an address. I made the call.
She produces a dirty scrap of paper.
- This is miles away.
- You wanna be my friend or not?
- I'm more than your friend, Francesca
- Issat what you think?
This remark causes me to gaze at her.
- Now we're feeling sad and sorry? All right, you can kiss me.
I do. Her lips are dry.
- You'll do it for me won't you?
- Who else is gonna?
She regards me like a frighty rabbit, then curls her lip.
- You think I don't know a hundred people who would?
- Where are they? Where's Luc?
- I can call them!
She grabs for her phone but it falls to the floor. Tries to reach it and her foot is dragged. She gasps.
- Get it... get my fucking phone!

- Francesca, let's wait on this.

She eyes me, plainly deciding which tack to take. Decides on cruelty.

- All right Nicky, I'll be in your *debt*.

She pulls my hand to her crotch, starts to manoeuvre my fingers in. Her gaze is unsubtle. Not a lot to do with me. *Come on Nicky.* She pulls me close; her breath's not fresh. I stroke the hair… and quietly withdraw. Next she stares into space as if forgetting the whole episode. Shortly:

- Mmm… but Nick I promise I won't abuse, I'll only smoke it. (Brightly) You can have it too! And then we'll do things… we'll watch old movies or you can wheel me round the estate… we'll play songs on the piano downstairs… and we can go on a road trip, or… or…

She proceeds to cry. Next comes a heap of phlegm which she coughs in my hand. I laugh, wipe it on my leg.

- Don't do that, it'll stain!

She's solicitous now, looking with big eyes.

- I'll ask the doc for morphine, get you the real stuff later. Okay?

- 'Kay Nicky. You're my special boy. …Luc didn't come, his phone won't answer. (Pause) I'm a complete bitch

- You're not. Pethidine's bad for you

- Think so? Peter didn't come. I wanna sleep in his bed

- No you don't

- Oh I do, he's my baby! One time we slept the whole night. He's the best lover but I'm ugly now. Mummy'll be *glad.* Not jealous are you?

Grrr. Should I take any of this mouthing seriously?

- I am actually

- Noooo Nick! You'll get to fuck me too, promise! Hmm? Come here.

I've nothing to say to this. Feel profoundly shit of a sudden. Peter Mars? Bloody norah, that's worse than wiping up crap.

- What are you thinking? Have I offended you?

I'm above this sort of thing! Got both feet and all my fucking fingers and a great big gig in a chamber festival that's gonna be unmissable and I'm gonna fucking nail it. Gotta practise, gotta call my pushy agent and negotiate a big fat fee. In fact I'd better be *gone.*

- Are you going away from me now?

I realise I've stood up. Pre-raphaelite babe is frowning.

- Yeah, stuff to do (I hear myself say it)

- You just got here. I'm lonely. We'll watch TV, play a game. Stay and eat with me? We can sleep together if you like! Mummy won't notice. (I'm inspecting the floor) Baby?

- I'll see if I can't make it tomorrow. Till then, ciao.

Finger her cheek, exit quick. Duck to the car, lurch into a morass of traffic. You poor little bastard! Too hard, sad story, save arse, dodge future pain. (Not what I said to Lena eh) Some humans live on a different plane. Me, I'm a survivor. Hey Nick, slash yer wrists then she'll care! Who can understand *women*? Or maybe she cares already. Fucking goddess, everyone licking out of her hand, not so fucking clever now. Oww! *Don't ever say it.* She lost her foot, nearly lost her life. Grow up asshole!

Turn the car. Roady mayhem. Suck on it dudes, never saw a u-turn? Call.

- Er, d'you want the drugs tonight?

- Oh! Are you pissed at me, Nicky?

- Sorry, stressed. I'll come back

- Oh yeah… okay… come later.

It seems there's someone in the room. Mars? She's whispering now.

- Will you get my supply? Did I give the address? I'm so grateful. Thank you Nick. Thank you.

Solicitous as fuck! Now I have to do it. Little poor ego in a tender trap. Okay, drive to where the fuck: NE 25. Ninety minutes later, a cul-de-sac in semi stucco land. At the door a hip-looking fellow (could be a muso) gives me the once-over, says: Special delivery for Francesca Mars? There ya go son, don't snort it all at once. I assume she'll pay later. With interest. Tell me, how's the Empress?

- Stood on a landmine, lost her foot. Why d'you ask?

- Ha! Good one. Ciao, man. Drive safe.

That guy doesn't read the papers. Back in the car I dip my finger in. This'll do things to yer skull. Leave it leave it. To the highway and giddy up fair steed, for I am her gallant knight and foul Richmond awaits.

The Gods of War

On the orbital at ninety miles an hour I get dialled by Lena. Cracky voice claims wrong number, wanted *Francesca*. What's her game? Surely not feeling guilty. Call back.

- Lena, I'm sorry. Why are you ringing Francesca? It's late

- She tried to ring just now. I've got to confront *that man*. I won't be fucked over!

- What? Lena? Lena!

The Serb wants my help but won't say so. Put your foot down. If a cop sees me! Another call: Jesus Lena! - no, just a crackle on the line. *Nicky?* Francesca's voice. Then nothing. At Richmond all house lights are on. I stop at a distance, creep up the drive. Why you creepin' boy? Shit, a police car. Uh the drugs. Return creep to car, shove powder bag in hedge. Skulk in the house shadows. Through the window I see two officers talking with Peter and Carolyn Mars. No sign of Lena. The fuzz step out and up the drive. Right at that moment Lena's car pulls in. An officer signals. Conversation. The police go. Peter Mars is there. Tall Lena steps out and faces him. Mars shovels her against the car, her knee jerks up, he doubles over, she's headed through the door. Better get in there smart! Mars sees me. *Oi!* Nothing to do but protect bloody Lena from herself. She's in the room. And Carolyn confronts.

- Get out of my *house*.

Lena has walked into her minefield.

- Fuzz were here. Why?

- Because you called them, *bitch*. This from Peter, who comes at her through the door.

- Don't touch her!

And Lena is amazed to see *me*. - Come out, Lena. Come on

- Fucking saboteur!

I'm barring his way. There's an idiotic struggle. - Whoa! Slow down

- Stop it all of you! shouts Carolyn.

(Lena) - Why do you accept the lies, Carolyn Mars? All for money? To protect your daughter? Stupid woman, coward!

Carolyn Mars swings wildly at Lena's head. The blow is lucky: knocks her sideways, she tips over a low table, spreadeagles. I stoop down to her but she crawls off, heels cock-eyed, vinyl skirt and bumcrack prominent.

- Ha ha! I fucked her husband. I used him! All men are stupid, Carolyn Mars. But women are *worse*. (She's half on her feet) Why would *your daughter* go for such a bastard? Why's she worship *cock* so much?
(Mars) - *Shut up fucking whore!*
And I'm trying to hold him off but he's Raging Bull. I shove at him and we crash in a chair. He punches my head and I go down. Carolyn's voice screams. *Bastard! Bastard!* Never saw what happened next, but ten seconds later I crawl to my knees and Mars is spread on the floor with Carolyn on top and Lena on top of that. He's immobile. Carolyn seems to be writhing on him and sobbing, clutching at the carpet. Lena has the pair of them in a strange embrace, thighs all fannied out. I'm keen to lie down… keen to throw up.

Suddenly in the doorway… is Francesca Mars. Leaning on the jamb, in her slip. *Shall I call the officers?* She's freaking grinning. *Did mummy murder him?* in a voice that drips like honey off a spoon. Now she hops across, clumps down by the body pile, lays an arm theatrically over Lena's back. Carolyn is quiet. The scene is bizarro. There's a rustle on the drive. Cops are back. Who the hell called 'em? *Francesca,* duh-brain. The blue boys hasten in, eyes widen at the gothic people pile. They gawp at me. *Nicky Bright at your service?* One cop reaches down to Francesca; she shrugs him off. Lena slides out from under. Francesca clutches at her mother… gothic tantrum coming… wait for it… Cop pulls at her shoulder. *Agh! My wound! My foot!* Startled cop lets go. Lena steps between.

- It's okay officer, she's crippled. There was a fight. This man fell and hit his head, his wife couldn't stop it. Kindly call an ambulance. I will take Francesca to bed. She's in shock.

Francesca obliges to appear waif-like, clings to her saviour Lena. The cops examine Mars. Everyone is ordered to remain in the house. I prop Carolyn up, take her to her room, lay her on the bed. Suddenly we're alone.
- He tripped and hit his head. You understand, Carolyn?

She looks up. For a moment she's Francesca.

- Yes, that's it, Nicky

- You're not to blame

- Okay, yes.

I lean down, put my cheek to hers. She pulls me down, right on top. Ages of denial perspire from her eyes. I let her mouth couple up with mine. In time, it ends. No commentary needed. I don't even care who sees us. Poor uppity-class girl, your lackey is here: Carolyn slash Francesca of Mars.

Usage and Love

Time jump. Lena and Francesca have cleared right out. What would make Francesca cling to her old paramour when Lena just engineered violent revenge? As usual my boy-naivety leaves me flat-footed. Lena's crusade for truth is a crusade to validate herself. Usage is stronger than love. Under that sexual exterior is a child craving to be loved and despising anyone who offers it. Into the labyrinth of ugliness she goes, hoping to unmask beauty. There she recognises a kindred soul, and Fran recognises her... but Mars is the wilier one, better attuned to the wounded cause of herself. And she'll play little victim and Lena will play great saviour, and their corrupter's bond will carry them to a cliff edge, and like tragics clinging limb on limb they'll sail outward toward destruction. And at the last: each will find a way to evade the other and claim their hollow survival, alone.

Peter Mars' concussion (that's all it is) keeps him banged up for some days. Strangely, he calls me. I see a chance to apologise for my disgraceful journo friend, though the tough guy 'brushes off the flies'. He affects to ask where Francesca might be, since she 'disappeared'. And makes sure to ask after Carolyn, who 'exited too'. When I suggest she's run to her private Gorda-house in the country he claims he never thought of that. What's going on? I take up the cue and call Carolyn's phone. She divulges to me that the police at the house that night had in fact been tipped off about a certain Audi (numberplate xxx) recently spotted in the vicinity of an *arson attack* (that is fucking low, Lena). She of course explained to those nice officers that her daughter the owner had been safely with mummy at her country house at the time. Now I'm smelling collusion, a familial covering of tracks. Interesting how quick Carolyn's cathartic intimacy with me reverts to accustomed icy veneer. I don't doubt Carolyn and Peter Mars will endure any amount of marital stress in the face of media or police onslaughts. Catharsis is surely skin deep. She'll be co-opting Lena as her ally next. Maybe she already has. The deeper question surfaces: against whom is the collusion? And to my eyes the answer is… *their daughter*. With me as scapegoat. Shit, you're naive.

But even a naif can *spin*. Sure, Peter Mars will want to discredit Francesca. 'Yeah… (says Mars) it might be construed that she abused my funds to bribe that black Bouseri. It might also be circulated that she 'got too close to the black' and is 'not a girl to be trusted'. Then Bouseri will call off our joint deals. Good riddance eh. The only catch might be that the black will demand damages and there'll be a court scandal. But no, we can fob off these Africans, especially if Bouseri might be proved to have sexually compromised one's vulnerable daughter (we'll say thanks to Lena what's-her-faggot-name for this exclusive information, gleaned during one of our hot midnight clutches). And the bonus: I can get this Frenchy Doctor off daughter's back, then she'll hurry back to number one Daddy - if she knows what's good for her. No more gallivanting off to Africa with her stupid aid circus. Besides, who's interested in a one-legged girl? Stepdaddy'll look out for her. Wife can't object, even though the cat's out of the bag on our dirty family sex secret. She won't divorce me for years yet, she'll let me make lots more dough first. Hang on. Might still be able to parade dismembered daughter about and get sympathy vote for other projects. Milk this third-world aid bullshit, pose as philanthropist. Francie'll come to the party, since we covered up her crappy little Arson Crime…'

Bright, you could be a crime writer. Though I'd never blame Peter Mars for being in love with her. Should one do his bidding and run to find her? Nope, she's an all-grown-up girl. Lena will know where she is of course, since Lena has taken clothes from her room. I'll assume they're together, true lovers ripping each other apart. Or maybe Francie ran off to the good Doctor Luc? Fuck yeah. I've had enough. Bitter taste in mouth! I've a big fat concert to prepare.

Faithful music: the time has come to make love and offer allegiance to you. I have bravely decided to append a new-composed piano part to *Threnody for the Victims of Hiroshima*. Not a tad pretentious, and Penderecki would be pleased. Hundred and fifty thousand incinerated victims will be pleased as well. The power of art to salve! Sum total of suffering in the world will never diminish; neither will the sum total of art. Cute bedfellows. Day by day I claw at my creative cliff face, and the piece takes its bedevilled lumpen shape. Would it all seem so pretentious if *she* were here to listen? Its massed hollowness of suffering makes it aimless; thus am I aimless. Can I not exploit that feeling and make a success? No, for here is the last trick of art: real emotion is no guarantor of success, and is in fact its obstacle. Art is artifice; real sadness is mere spectacle and pretence, and even supreme ugliness is forced. Art is a border world in which we hover and wallow, neither true nor false, a razor's edge promising chasm falls. Art sucks your energy away, leaves nothing real as reward. But I'll press on like a pilgrim because I do it for Francesca… *'She walks with me perfect and intact, through the ruins of Hiroshima. And we hold hands and gaze at the dead and our love transcends the horror. Our romance is illumined by airbrushed backdrops. We are exquisitely young. She is all promise in her soft cardigan, her silken braids caress her noble forehead. She walks my lanes of the dead and sprinkles beneficence like water to parched mouths, and to mine…'* In such night dreams she is whole again. And since dreams are wish fulfilments I know she is far from it. So I want to find her. Perhaps she will come to my concert, will listen with serious intent, and the soft spark of our togetherness will rekindle. We may even hope to heal the seeping mortal wound of her father Leo. For are not the waters of her life seeping away because of him? Does he not haunt her, asleep and waking? Or has she made a fetish to hide her cruelty, to paper over the truth of her selfishness, her arid expectancy, her arrogant nobleness? Does Francesca Mars not suffer from the subtlest canker of all: meaninglessness? And is her sublime smile just a mask for her sublime *inconsequence?* Are there really no heaven-borne ones, merely people, made of flesh that smells? My goddess could be but a sham! But if not *she*, then whom?

Why should anyone else be allowed to keep her! It's me who understands her need. Or maybe that's why she avoids me. But I don't care if I'm the grandised fool-artist: when I think of Francesca Mars *I am not that at all.* Doesn't anyone see why? *Because she inspires me.* Whichever way, good bad or ugly or better worser richer or poorer, in sickness and health, till death us do part - she inspires me. I will be her artist of love. What'd be fittinger than that? Only music distracts her from her Great Serious Business, vaults her into dreams... and I'll be her enchanter, I'll give her respiration...

Prize idiot. One week to concert. I'm feverish. Call up Doctor Luc. Does he have access to The Cure? Hasn't seen Her, just a message where she said she 'craved a holiday in solitude'. Solitude with Lena? Luc wonders out loud if she 'has enough bandages'. Poor feller, he's in love with Ayaan. And today there's a call from *Lena.* I creep around to asking her if she'll come home. She avoids to say yes. I mention my concert date. And, (my tone is the mask of innocence) has one seen Francesca? In fact I have, is the deft reply. Often? We skirt about till I say: *Bring her back, Lena.* To which she is forced to reply: I will not, not to you. And then I know for sure what's going down between them.

Two days pass. Though I never watch TV but am desperate for distraction, so the synchronous cosmos orders me to flick it on. And there is Mr Bouseri! and he's railing against our country with steam coming from his ears and tells us he is breaking his contract with the British Government and with businessman Peter Mars who 'behaved so very hypocritically because this Mars sent me a certain letter the content of which I could not possibly reveal to the BBC but only in court, and oh it claims that Mister Mars' daughter has been *compromised* by myself, furthermore that I 'bribed her for favours' and this assertion I totally categorically deny since I am a Very Fine Muslim. But it is *Mister Mars* who used his own half-daughter to achieve business contracts oh yes, and now Allah has decided to punish him because she is gravely injured and has run away from the family circle to a place only Allah knows, and this of course could not happen to my own daughter who is so loyal to me and to her country, and I utterly reject filthy accusation that she is seen in company of a French Doctor who incidentally as you know is engaged to the half-daughter of the infidel Peter Mars. Thus I will make no further statement. Until possibly tomorrow. Or I will meet you in court. Although I do not trust British court. Goodbye.'

And garrulous Mister Bouseri, his nation's pride, is replaced by a gushing reporter who informs us the Mars scandal just gets worser and worser since police want Ms Francesca Mars to answer questions about a certain Arson Attack. Where is the mysterious Francesca? Gone to ground! Last seen in the West Country led by a foreign woman known as Lena Duvorchek, not to mention 'Duvorchek had been mentioned in connection with Peter Mars' etc etc blaaaaaa. I switch off.

Three days to concert and I've got ants in pants: the Chopin *Ballade* I am matching with *Threnody* is proving knottier than I dared believe. Goddam masochist, too late. I imagine Frederick coughing up blood as he writes. Fucking norah. Only safe ground is the Bartok *Variations* which isn't saying much. I took 'em for granted and now their depths yawn at me like black holes. But hang in there! / use the fever use the stress / when it's fixed it's dead / let the concert be a discovery experience... and other assorted new-age horseshit. Should I take a drug? Better not. I hate art so much. In the vortex I call Doctor Luc. Why? Because he's calm and a fatalist totally unlike me, and because he's seen such evil as makes him real. 'Cause I've no male friends. Shit, I have no friends period. Nobody actually loves me. I chase skirt, never needed friends. Always had the wonder of my own arsehole to explore. But has he heard from her? *Yes, today.* Where? *No comment.* Come on, Luc! *Not now, Nicky.* Has the media been at you? *Yes.* Can we meet for a drink? I had a talk to Peter Mars (a lie). We meet at a bar off the Kings Road.

- Have you been back to Africa?
- Certainly not
- How is Ayaan?
- She is scared. Her father is sending her home
- Listen Luc. Marry her. Francesca will understand
- Ayaan will not. She is a Good Muslim
- She loves the west and its money! Call Bouseri's bluff. Are you man

or mouse, Frenchie? (He peers at me) And have you helped Francesca's recovery? Answer: no, because you don't really want a cripple girl. I do though. You're a major giver Luc, but the buck stops here. Submit.

He drops his head. He is sad. I hold his shoulder.
- You're a great man, better than me: but get out of the way. (Pause) And now tell me where she is.
- Ah, she is deeply unwell. I don't want to think about it Nick. She was raving, psychotic. Loves me, hates me, wants me, hates again. The girl Lena, she is bad. And no doctoring skills. Demanding and impatient. She asks me for money! I say yes but it can't go on. Also Francesca is in pain. She will use drugs, I know her. There will be infection. Ah, I am depressed
- Tell me where they are, damn it
- In a cottage in Snowdonia. The village is Beddgelert
- Come with me
- No no, I will face Bouseri as you say. I will do it
- All right, you do that.

At home I google *Wales, Beddgel* or whatever he said. Fuck it, I need to practise. My agent Brand rings next.
- We're expecting a full house, six hundred. Are you on track? Key critics will be there, has to be effing perfect, Nick. Need to rehearse visuals for your *Threnody*. Soundcheck's tomorrow from six. Be there.
Love the reassuring tone. Middle of the night the phone rings. I almost miss it. And it's *Francesca*. The voice is distorted, line is bad.
- Nicky? Nicky? Where are you? Why are you never here? I am in Wales, in the North mountains. I have to hurry, she will not let me call. The village is Bedd-gel… something. Do you have money? Don't tell anyone. I need drugs to kill the pain. Can you go to my supplier?
- I will come after three days. I have a big concert. Wait for me, wait there
- Come now! I can't last. Bedd-gel. She is taking me some place else. I will never call you again. Never, do you hear?
- Francesca, stop it. I said I will come. Wait three days
- Not a chance in hell. This is your chance. Do it. Goodbye.

Click. I'm standing there in the room half-naked… SNAP! I fling the phone. It crumps against the wall. *Fuck off out of my life!* Why can't I do anything that makes me happy! My hand slams the table. Pain shoots out of wrist - oh christ I've *broken* it. Leap away, shove it in armpit, bung it under water! Bathroom... bandage. Every shitting thing in the world clatters from the cupboard. Wrap it just wrap it... Half a throbbing hour... and I know it's screwed. In the still night - comes a *turning*. There'll be no concert, no concert no crowd no music nothing. Is gone. Is finished. What'll Brand say? Can't even drive. Oh but you will; you're gonna *drive*. Why's this happening, why are *you* the victim? Four am. Call Luc. No phone, stupid arse. Out in the cutty night, blunder to a phone box. 'Luc, she called me. Have to go there. Wrist is broken. Can you come? Yes now, sorry.' He actually comes. A sprain, he says, and wraps it super tight. Change this in two days. And don't drive. - I'm going. Probably kill her but I'm goin'. Would you call this number: my agent? Explain this: an accident. Thanks, friend! I embrace him, too emotional. Call me, he says. Shoves a hundred quid in my pocket and some livid-looking pills. Shakes his head, goes. Five am. Sudden thought: go to Richmond, retrieve that powder stash from the hedge? Gather odd bits: torch, money, phone. Crawl to car.

The Mars villa crouches at the black drive's end. I fumble about and the blessed package is *there*. Deed done. Head north. Out of London on the yellow-slick motorway. Bison trucks thundering by, headed for Birmingham. Dawn on the bypass to that city: jagged buildings like upended keyboards strut ugly in groggy light. (For you who celebrate ugly art but gag at the real!) Out on the Shrewsbury road I feel greyly sick with fatigue. Eggs and coffee in that fair town... and on to Snowdonia. The land rises and falls, starts to seep in my urban eyes, wants to sere away the thudding familiar - which fights back. Black and ivory keyboards invade, mirrored in the road's white lines... wanna get me homesick for the safety of it all, for 'my little life where music's my little wife'... Hooroo ladies! Thought I'd pop up and visit you in the crags and fens of Wild Wales. Urgent package for Francesca Mars, sunken fair maid. Now kill yourself with it. Glad to be o' service. Forgive your onetime lover seeming abrupt, but he feels absurd, lost. Pull over by a farm gate, slip into a doze... half an hour. Fumble up the GPS. *Colwyn Bay... Harlech... Bedd-gel-ert*. Shit, it exists. Step out to the world. Touch some stones, mossy fenceposts, green fronds wrap-soaking my feet. I'm quite far up in the hills; the day is revealing its blueness. Here are walls and valleys. Road snakes through a glen and up a ridge, shrugs at the sky beyond. Sunlight tickles my face and for a moment I forget my wrist and the damp and dread and grind and visage of an embarrassed alien... and segue to hope and dream... to openness and peaks and blue and the far sea... I'm walking with my sole friends, who're a happy trio linked no more to heated worlds of city and past and jealousy and debt; we're human again and always young and sharing a life in our house above a valley and walking in the autumn noon in hills and roads, gazing along the coast's frilling line and to the ripple sea... snug in scarves and boots, all limbs intact. And we link hands and vow: never to go back to hot Africa and dust and money and ambition and sweat and machination and art - at least not while we're young. For we're whole, we are whole and young.

GPS says, you're at the village! There's a steep snaky street and a view of a lake. Tea shop, post office. I enquire. Perhaps the hotel, a mile further down? And suddenly there is Lena, across the road, exiting a pharmacy with a package. She hasn't seen me. Stops in the road and thumbs her mobile... And this is the moment where I turn into a *spy*. To face Lena is suddenly a crime. Dressed for cool in boots and ski jacket and sunnies, her Serbian red bob tucks about her face. She hogs the miniature villagescape like an invader of men's bedrooms, abhorred by secretly watching wives. Lena scans the sky, discovers nothing, struts to a car in front of mine, roars away. Follow then! Jittery rush along stonewalled lanes beside the river, a mile or so, sudden jerk to a driveway that curls up to a cottage. I halt at the bottom. Minutes go by. She emerges, throws something to the ground, stalks to the car, careens down the drive and is gone. Never saw me. The thought comes that I should kidnap Francesca. Drive up. A flicker at the window, hollow thumps from within. The door jerks open and there she is, in jeans and jumper, leaning on crutch, one leg bent but otherwise all intact.

- Saw you. I knew you'd come.

She hops forward, clings at my shoulder, searches my eyes, smiles a grand smile. Then pushes her lips into mine. Micro moment of tenderness. She backs off, surveys. Ruggy hair over polo neck falls to cupped breasts under a pink-white face. I'm queerly embarrassed. Her presence, beauty, shock me again. How did I forget?

- Nothing to say to me?
- So glad to see you
- I hope you are, my babe, because I've missed you.
My eyes throb. I want to kneel, rest my head in her navel. With a glint she says:
- Better come in... or have you escaped Lena?

Francesca Mars takes over as powerful girls might. I am installed in her little sitting room, and she leans on the door jamb and looks at me. I feel like a spare prick at someone's wedding. My gaze slips down her jean leg that ends in a tunnel. Look at her eyes... and there's the hint of a plea unvoiced, as if a wild skating rampage, then an upper-lip curl of irony that segues to a blush in her blossom cheek, then a far-off wide-eyed question I could never answer... until the brittle power gaze settles again. All this in five cavernous seconds. And I see how grief and rage, poverty and littleness and hopeless hope have furrowed the seas of her eyes these past weeks - grey waves, winter seas, hourly and momentarily in circus parade or stomping nightmare; all the turgid hours of loneliness. And how she'd have cried for someone to take it away from her if she weren't so sensible, but fears no-one will come; so, busily lest they see her grief, shrouds herself in sternness... which shrivels again like paper rice when absurd little hops and shuffles on her crutch betray her embarrassing living loss. Thus the eyes of Francesca Mars gleam out of the North like the Viking warrior god who crossed seas, laughed at storms, stared down horizon waves... yet somewhere in port a child stutters for the hand of kindness and the fatherly caress of peace.

- Didn't do your concert then?
And... I start to cry. Can't fathom it.
- My wrist is ruined... I wanted to play... for you I guess.

She pauses, seems to indulge me.

- Some other time then. Have you brought what I asked?

Please don't let it end here, god.

- Oh, sure I have. Right here.

I give it (a miserable token). Now I shall turn round and drive all the way back to the city.

But the girl of old who once had space for others sees my anguish. *Sit here with me. What happened to your wrist?* Mercy flickers in her face. I take her hand, she kisses mine. Her restlessness wells up.

- Go to that cabinet. There's a little pipe and lighter. We'll eat some heroin before Lena gets back. Then we'll get the fuck out.

Dirty Francesca is looming. I do as told. She sucks in the drug with greedy poise. Whatever she does is regnant, even low things. This stuff'll alienate us, make me lose her, make her lose herself. I give up. All this is worth but a ghost sonata. She slumps back in the couch hollow. I wait. *You*, she whispers. I'll have to do it. She wants a partner in her little shallow dream. I can't help sucking in the poison. We sit there side by side in the ticking room in the mountains on the last day of the world. I don't know the woman at all. Finally all we share is self-disgust.

- This is not for physical pain then?

- Whadda *you* think?

(Pause) - You called me and I came

- D'you love me more than your concert?

I don't answer. There are no answers.

Then she orders:

- Help me up. We're leaving before bitch gets back. I want to see the sea again. See that bag? Bring it. Put the drugs in. This bag's my clothes. Fucking crutches. D'you have money? Look in that drawer, there may be some. Box of food in the kitchen.

Now it's just mundane and morose. I do as told. And suddenly I feel for Lena. Shouldn't we wait for her? Are you insane? she says. But I scribble a note for Lena on a scrap of paper. It says nothing but that I was here and that we have gone towards the sea. Outside I find the packet she tossed.

Codeine. Obviously not to her lady's taste. We drive out. Francesca directs me through the village and beyond. Asks for music which I provide. She hums along distractedly. The day is mercifully blue, and soon we're cruising little roads in the stony mountains. Nature's wideness seems to restore her little by little. The edges soften and soon she's smiling at me again, in that empty way she's cultivated.

- It really was nice of you to come, darling
- Do you hate Lena?
- No no. But it's been pretty horrid. I don't blame if she hates me. I've learnt to abuse my friends.
(Take a punt) - You walk a tightrope
- What tightrope is that, darling?
- Between getting people to pity you and getting them to hate you
- Oh yes, I'm a master at that.
(Her irony threatens. Ignore it) - I mean, you've got to let us care for you without patronising you. So we can… feel like you're accessible
- Is that what you want - for me to be accessible?
- Not the right word
- Because I'm defined by no-one
- Defined by your need to not be defined?
- Ooh, that's deep
- I mean you're good at staying one step ahead, but maybe you can't any more. And maybe you don't want to. I'm sorry, that's not well said
- Life's *tough* for you, isn't it Nick?
- Easy now. I've been through things too. Including for you
- Funny, Lena said all this stuff. We've had all this *stuff*
- You've gotta deal with us. And besides, privilege let you indulge in the ugly and the sad. You were always a voyeur
- But now I'm *really* ugly and sad. And my happiness was a crime eh! To enjoy one's life was a crime. To help all the people was a crime. And to do it for my darling father was a *crime*
- Easy, Francesca. We're just talking. I want to be honest with you, not patronise
- Is this my therapy?

- No. Music's my therapy to you. I'll always play for you
- Good for you, Nicky.
(Frustration looms) - Let's stop, shall we?

There's a flat space, with a view. We can walk. I get the crutch. She hobbles with me to the edge of a bluff. We look down. The valley spreads out... a scattered homestead or two. The sounds of the world echo upward from far. Loneliness and beauty.

At that moment she buckles. The crutch falls. She is perilously near the edge.
- Help. Help me!
- Stop it Francesca.
I kneel down to her. She grabs me by the neck. *Help me daddy...* Now she pulls me on top. *Mmm, save me!* Her eyes glisten in mockery. She shovels my hand into her jeans. *You want me, wanna stick your dick in me. Everybody wants it. But I choose. I choose Peter Mars! No shame. He's my boy!*
- Fucking stop it!
And I'm shouting at her. She starts to writhe in a gross pantomime. We're too near the edge. And she fakes up an orgasm. *Ooouuugh! That's the real real thing! I choose 'em! I decide!* Her stump dangles. I grab at the leg. She shouts to the air and it scatters on the wind. She hollers again... screams at the ugly sky. I grip her. She flails me left and right but I hang on. Francesca Mars screeches till her lungs will burst. I cover my ears. Now the two year-old bangs her leg on the stones. Now the pain is physical. I grab her shoulders, drag her from the edge. Drag her like a sack in the grass. My wrist is killing. She's lolling her head. *Save me daddy! Save me daddy!* She spits at my face. *Look! Look, bastard!* Now she strains her crotch and pisses through her jeans. Bangs her head on the ground, over and over. Now, she slumps. Raucous breathing, in and out, and grinding noises. Then a pause... seems to recollect a thing... The face creases, the sobs begin... welts of them, staining the hills of her cheeks. The turning world is her bed of nails. The tears sickle down... fizzle little by little into moans, gulps. Her lake eyes glaze. She lies there... the sky absorbs. The

mountain wind whispers about. On the slopes and in the grasses the elves are disturbed. They're muttering.

Risk a trip to the car, find a blanket. Cover her up, sit in vigil. *Not one to do things by halves, our Francesca.* This with an almost-grin, when my heartbeat finally settles. I've been crying too.

Mountain and sky reign on, arcing the valley in autumn afternoon. I fear the winter's to come. No matter. I can't part from her. Every wound every insult, cements my need. She'll have no choice but to run from me; I've no dignity. Half an hour or so, and she opens her eyes. Looks up as if surprised to find me there. I help her sit, lean her against a rock. I've inspected the stump which has bled, and fetched bandages and ointments and clothes from the car. We slip her jeans and underwear off, replace them. She tells me what to do with the wound. It's all right, she says. I can't say I like the look of it.

We get to a bed and breakfast place. They're doing dinner. She's pretty subdued, no talk. Drinks five or six wines though. People glance at us with what I take to be pity. She wants a separate bed. None to be had. I creep into our room when she's tucked in, the intruder. She won't hold me, scant touch is all. Francesca sleeps. I lie there, trawl the day's events. Is she ashamed? The mind of Mars requires great and arduous journeys to heal. I'm pretty powerless: her outburst was pure sardonic hate. Can I afford to be insect-victim to her deadly world mockery? Can I cope with days like this? Past four. Depressed, I apparently fall asleep.

Perfect Day

Francesca must have got up without my hearing, and I wake to an empty space. She's sconced in the parlour with our proprietor.
- Lovely Mrs White served me breakfast.
Francesca offers a coy and cosy smile. The lovely Missus smiles too and says:
- Poor lass needs 'elp now she can't get about so good! She'll be needing her 'oosband. (Sit down dear, and I'll serve you) We cleaned her leg didn't

we dear, and dressed and bandaged it and now it'll be right as rain. Don't you worry, you're a strong wee thing. And so pretty: just look at them curls. Your 'oosband's a lucky lad.

Women are such naturals at propaganda. Mrs White proceeds to the kitchen.

- How's it feel to be my 'oosband, looky lad? whispers Francesca. We're in the cosy eighteenth century. Francesca likes a drama, even a domestic one.

- Feels weird. You slept then?

She smiles her liberating smile, as of old.

- I did, husband.

- What's on the menu?

- Hearty fare. Eat up. Will you take me to the sea?

- I'll take you anywhere you want, beauty. Except near a cliff

- I love you, truly I do. We'll have a nice day. Will you shave for me? I have no hangover! The gods are merciful

- You got a thing out of your system

- Quite possibly. And thank you.

Mrs White brings my breakfast. Francesca takes over, chops it up, feeds it in my mouth.

- See Mrs White, I'm a good wife.

The lady comes to my aid. - Let 'im be, dear. He's a grown boy.

Francesca wipes my lip with a napkin.

- Yes, a grown-up wee boy.

Next she shakes her great mane.

- Mmm, I need a stretch! But first I shall powder my nose.

She pivots on one leg, beauteous rump near my face. *No staring bad boy. Ruins yer digestion.* She plants a kiss on my offending eye. Even on a crutch, the sparkle and gravitas misfortune bestows, make her elegant.

Mrs White sits by. - Ooh, she had a little cry this morning. But we sorted her out we did. Keep a close eye, won't you mister?

- If I do she'll poke it out. She's independent

- Would I 've seen 'er on the tele by chance?

- Most likely. She blew her foot off in Africa

- Where's her family then?

- She's hiding out from 'em. I was lucky to find her

- Ooh, I don't know. People need people, that's for sure. There's a look in her eye. She's a clever one. But…

- She's reckless, I know. A hell ride in fact. Any advice?

- Hold her close, my boy. Give her time, give her time. She's a precious one, no mistake. She'll be popular then?

- Oh my god, on a bloody pedestal. But who are her actual friends? is what I say. We're not married by the way. She may be unattainable

- You don't say? Well, you know what? I'm not blind. If a girl is wonderful and beautiful in people's eyes, they'll still look for ways to bring her down for the sakes of their own dignity. Wonderfulness makes us feel useless, don't it? And she knows it. She almost wants to be brought down, back to earth like the rest of us. She may not let you marry 'er yet, but I can see you worship the ground she walks

- *Ahh.* I don't know what to do.

Tears start in my eyes. She squeezes my hand.

- She'll come round. If she knows what's good for her. And she does

- Thanks, Mrs White. Talking to you makes things feel real again.

Francesca is at the door, looking at us. Her eyes narrow just a bit.

- Ready? she says.

* * * *

(In the car) - Nice, Mrs White, isn't she?

- Sure is. We should go back there

- Oh I doubt it Nicky. She likes *you*

- You too. She told me

- I'm sure she did

- So you heard our little -

- 'Course I heard it. And it was all about me. Ooh, look at the view!

The road opens out and a silver wide sea spreads away before us. The day is clear again. An Indian autumn.

Why taunt with endless irony? Is Mrs White right that Francesca needs to fail, craves to be flawed and useless but doesn't know how? Needs to learn it? Ironic! Lesson One: how to become a lowly human. Get hated or pitied, but being human be sure to hate and pity in return. The goddess of Mars has trouble with love given, with compassion offered, trouble with other people in fact. Can dispense succour on a battlefield but can't accept it. Truly self-centred! And such a giver! How to solve the conundrum? Needs to walk into a *minefield,* lose her body, lose her divinity. And meanwhile the whole stupid venal jealous world gets to know about it. Perfect. Thus do we remain our unique superior self. In short: make partial sacrifice of self in order to elevate self. Just can't help being a genius and being lauded for it. But no! She planned a private death out there in the deserts of Eritrea. She's no fool. *Of course* attention-seeking is a child's game, and the true story is to die unheralded, unloved. But no mortal can abase herself that way, can't relinquish the core of herself. And Mars knows it… Welcome to Francesca's impossible romance.

But this is about me too. I want to save her. My struggle is to get her to value me. Right now I'm just getting in her way. What to do, what strategy? Yeah, emotional strategy is needed. Even when her heart says she is nothing but cold, strategy might warm her up again. But she's the world's bestest game player. I guess she invited me to play with her in her tragic little sandpit, to dance her little dance of self-pity. Test my limits. Flattering! But does she have the guts to carry it, this hero's tightrope walk? Can she be so sad and yet ruthless, so alone yet so dismissive? Her trouble is she has too many damned gifts, and though she invites them like vengeful beasts to trample her down they can't. She's a fucking conundrum wrapped in enigma. Boys like me can't get it. So Bright, use your 'feminine intuition', your 'artist's nose'! You want her on a pedestal because she promises you a wilder life. But you want to capture her. That's *mundane.* Do you have the guts to ask her to be part of your shit little life? Here we go, wallow in your *own* comfy myth. I'm too much in love with easeful failure, I'm no good at compassion, selfish artist yadda yadda. Fuck it! Perhaps she's a *snob* who cleverly exposes the snobbery in me. Listen to her taunting: 'do I have the guts to be good enough for her?' And more: 'do I have the guts to watch her fall to the basest bottom level, take her as filth and shit? Or the guts to let her be all things *she* wants to be: the great, the small, the unattainable?' Oh, whose conscience is *that,* hers or mine? Yeah, she knows nobody and nothing can contain her. But do you, Ms Francesca, have the grace to admit that someone on this planet might be good enough? Even the beautiful Luc was victim to your trickery of love. Dammit, I *am* good enough - because I confess you're the only person who ever shucked me out of my own complacent *superiority.* But we just can't have this conversation. Instead we need to play the game out. I'll force it out, sooner or later. Or she will.

- Let's go to the beach and feel the sand and the shallows, she says.

Ten minutes later we're parked at a field, and a path leads through dunes to a curling bay of glistening water. There's a headland with smooth rocks. Drifty seaweed bubbles in the heat of the sun. *Carry me,* she says. I piggyback her to the sand. She trails her crutches like a child.

- We need to live like it's our last day, she says.

We sit on muffly sand, the musical sort that squeaks. Intimate quiet, lapping of two-inch wavelets, fingernails on a board of glass ocean.

- When I was in Eritrea I saw how the only thing is to be free. The need to die to everything we are. And to everything others think we are. Now or later, it doesn't matter.

Her honey-voice, in the sunlight. I note how Francesca keeps her own metaphysic dialogue, an inner life beyond her role as social being. Metaphysics is her easeful place. At this level human interaction matters not a bit to her.
- I assume it will be *later*
- Of course, baby. But the future is now. This is eternity. What does it matter?
- Only the privileged may take such an attitude. Or understand it.
She smiles, squeezes my hand in a little conspiracy of privileged souls.
- I love Africa sooo much. I shall always go there in my mind. I shall always walk in the desert there
- Why did you step on the mine?

- I didn't know it was there, darling
- In a way you did
- God no! It was a bolt from the blue
- My theory goes like this: we're afraid of our perfection and so want to spoil it. Afraid to be happy, we need war. Witness your slaughterhouse speech at the RSPCA
- You think I'm afraid to love. To love *you* that is. But I do love. It's just that it's not static. It's here, it's there, it's shimmering, elusive. Not yours to own, Nicky
- I don't want to own you
- Oh yes you do
- I want to know you
- That means you want to own me. I can never be known. Not fully
- Well, neither can I then
- That's it. You played music for me: your way of saying it's hopeless, ineffable beyond our little human interactions, our tiny speech. Music was our best communication, you and me
- Don't say *was*. So what do we do?
- We play out our facets in eternity. Our numberless parts. We blithely forget them all. And repeat them in another life. We get brillianter and brillianter, closer and closer to gods, and then we… we come to a place where… oh we're so breathtakingly *little*. What does it matter? We'll disappear like ghosts in a dream
- Don't you dare, Francesca. And I do gloom better than you. Listen. Before I met you I used music, which I love, as escape. You're not a musician, so trust me. But you made me want to live. And so now you *owe me*. Can't turn your back on me. I'm everything to you. One person, right here. Deal with me
- You're very presumptuous
- No I'm not. I'm *here*. You can't avoid. Look, I know how generous you are, your big big heart. So I am going to reach you
- Lordy save us from reachy people!
- You're *lonely*. And you miss your dad. And you punish the world. You use Peter Mars, you say he's a great lay. And he is. In love with him? No way. You punish by all brilliant tricks. But me, I'm your test. (I'm taking

a *risk* here) Tempt me to hate you, pity you if you want. But don't try tempting me to love you. Don't try that one, Francesca. Because guess what? It's beyond your control. My love, my feelings, are beyond your control

- Think so, do you?

- And I'm as good as you. Otherwise I couldn't be *bothered* with you. (Fuck, I said it. Now I'm out of depth) But you make me want to live. You make me see what I am. I'm not ashamed, Francesca! Through you I'm finally good enough

- Sayonara, then!

- No. You can't wriggle away

- Yes I can

- A one-footed girl? Run then hey! The rules have changed. But I'll still be happy to take you home to mother. Yeah, you scale those dramatic heights and plumb those lowly depths. You're a master! But now you're going to investigate mediocre, average, normal, middling, domestic, undramatic, plain, silly, fucked-up, duhhh. With me. And I've never done it either. So shall we?

How will she cope with this? Silly silly me. Francesca commands the resource of an Empress.

- Anything you say, Captain *Boring.*

And save me. I'm embarrassed. I poured it all out and she's given me the finger. To think she's going to be impressed by all that!

- *Right.*

And I gather her up, like a bad actor, walk into the sea with her clinging to my neck and dump her. Then like boys do I shovel her head under, and once more for luck. She gurgles. *Unromantic bastard!* Yup! But she grabs my crotch and squeezes. - Try that! - *Oww!* She swims away, a one-footed fish. Sodding woman, always a step ahead. And water sticks to her shirt like sex itself. Nothing to do but dive after, despite stinging in balls area. The water's freezing. I pull her under but she attacks me back, and we squirm under till neither of us can take any more. Then she does it *again.* This time she's on top and pins me. I can't take it, have to fight, get rough, burst to surface. How romantic's that, romantic boy? *Good enough* are we? I'll help you live… underwater! We'll cut your goddam foot off. See how you deal! But she topples over, and her grin is from ear to ear. We stumble out, spreadeagle on the sand. No-one's about. I pull her jeans off, her panties too. She gazes up. Her pussy invites. Pulls a grotty face, lolls her tongue. I strip now, look down at her, blokey hands on hips, even turn up my nose despite her insane beauty, despite her stump. She farts deliberately and cackles at her own great joke. Yo sexy huh? You're all shrivelled, no use to me. Besides I'm Lezzo, Mister Tarzan. You ruined my penis, I say. Check it's in working order! She says okay, leans forward, bites it, screams with laughter and rolls away, sand all over her arse. I drop on one knee. It seriously hurts. She backs away down the beach like a childy spider. I try to follow, stub my toe on a protruding rock and yelp like an idiot. She thinks I'm fooling. I watch her dive in the sea fifty yards away. Mermaid. She crawls out, hops back down the beach… Francesca is fourteen. I lie watching her, sand in my ear. Blood seeps from my foot. She arrives, peers at it. - Ooh! 'E *is* wounded after all. Kneels close, blows hot breath in my ear, drops a gob of spit on my cheek, licks it all over. - Orr! Woife's ancient remedy forr fallen warrior! Then lies back, all indecent, shirt crumpled, sex open for the sky to ogle at. I sit up. My bloody foot stings. But she's up, leaning into me. Puts her vag in my face, claps a hand about my head, shoves her knee in my ribs. *Hurry up*, she says. Short sharp breaths. She's sandy-rough. It's tough for my back but I get in the swing. Luckily she comes quickly. And it's a good one. Better than champagne to suck the juice of Francesca Mars! She kisses my lips. Ooh! That's what I taste like? *Nectar*, I murmur. *All right, you're forgiven. Pax and all that. Don't expect me to reciprocate.* We look at each other. She pouts her lip in sympathy. Has to be lunchtime! she states. Do we have food? She spreads her leg outrageously. Wanna feed me some yoghurt? Harpie! Save it all for a rainy day, she says, when we're old and boringly mediocre and don't wanna live no more. So fun! So I dip my poor foot in the water. Sausage not shrivelled no more, she remarks. She studies me. Flicks sand about. Like a child.

I put on trousers, offer to get snacks from the car. When I'm back she's not there. A dot at the end of the beach. Follow the crutch holes. She's by the rocks, naked as the day. Do I like her wild, does it obliterate my male ego? Yeah, I can take it. I hope. So we eat. She butters things at random, shoves them in my mouth. I remark on her stump. Should it be cleaned? - Fuck the stump. Let it look out for itself! Which makes me appear worried. So she glares. Wanna be my nurse as well? No massa, you know best. *Sure do*, she says. The stump looks uneasy, naked. What if I were to cut my hair off? she says of a sudden. All of it. A dome. Would it suit me? I don't want to play but she persists: - Beauty's only skin-deep. What *am* I to you when I'm not in the room? Or when you're fast asleep? Or when I'm on the toilet? When I've got my period? When I fart in bed? *You're my fourteen year-old baby girl,* I say. This tickles her so she laughs and laughs (too much) and biscuit spits out of her mouth all over our tablecloth. Which makes me throw tuna at her in exasperation, which prompts her to pour orange juice over my sandwich. So I get a tomato and squish it at her face, and it's chaotic from then on and I almost get to have proper sex with her but she says no way it hurts there's sand up my bumcrack. You're too genteel Francesca, that's your trouble. We wash off in the sea, dress a bit, bury the food detritus and I piggyback her to the car. On the way she hums and bites my ear from time to time. I can feel her warm thighs, and her flood of hair over my neck.

So we lie in the field by the car for an hour or two, with music on the player. Bach's *Brandenburg Concerti,* her choice. Wagner's *Tristan and Isolde,* mine. We love the other's music; there's seriousness and understanding.

- You should've been a musician. Violin and piano. You'd be better than me
- Next life
- How did your daddy play?
- With heart on sleeve and foot in mouth! He was a funny funny man. Mummy never got it. Music was divine idiocy to him. Only a crazy fool could have invented it, he said. His favourite saying was: life's too too important to be taken seriously. Loved him to death though he was so self-centred. Like me, hey?
- No, you have a heart of gold. (She smiles to me) Why did you take the name of Mars, not your father's?

- You know the answer

- Do I?

- When I was fourteen I felt mummy abandoned me. I even felt my daddy abandoned me. I threw myself at Peter. He was a spunk anyway. He couldn't believe his luck, though I freaked him out at first. I thought I could beat my mother. Peter became my *habit*. Later I used his money and his position to help abandoned people. Simple huh?

- No regrets, no pain?

- Only a boy would ask that

- I'm sorry. Stupid question.

Wagner's *Liebestod* is happening. Anyone not affected by this piece isn't a human being.

- Doing your uttermost to win your *Isolde,* aren't you, my baby?

- If you say so

- Where will it lead to though?

- Don't ask.

* * * *

Late afternoon. Time to set off, she says. To where? Our village by the sea! And let me drive, it's an automatic. You know I won't be passive Nicky. So she has the wheel, and this time shoves on The Doors' *The End*. Oedipal Jim Morrison warns: *And he walks on down the hall... Father, I want to kill you... Mother, I want to - !* Screeching guitar echoes across the valley. Francesca shakes her mane with abandon. The car swings about on the high narrow road. Suddenly it occurs to me she snorted from the heroin stash when I wasn't looking. Looks like she had too bloody much. Now we're roaring down a straight under the hills, by stonewalled fields. I ain't happy. - Francesca, stop the car. I'll drive then you can freak out in comfort. *Bullshit*, she says. *Keep your hair on daddy.* There's a village ahead, the sea beyond. Red-sky sun splatters in our eyes. Surreal. I turn the music down, she ramps it up. I reach again but she snatches my hand and shoves it between her legs. Now she starts to nod her head, up down. *Francesca?* The drug! I shove her forehead up. Her foot lurches at the accelerator. The car surges. Fuck. I spot masts ahead. A harbour? The car funnels down a little cobbled hill. *Francesca, brake, fuck it!* My hands are on the wheel. She looks up like some death rider, clamps her hands to the wheel, stamps the accelerator! We clump across a quay, smack through a chain, suck out into space - and slam into water as if concrete. Every bone in my spine is crunched. She's slumped out. I nearly black out. The *Doors* are deceased. Blood is there. My window's open. Water surges. We're going under. My belt is jammed, fumble at *hers,* it clicks open. Come on! Gasping, shunt at the door. Wriggle out. My foot kick-shunts her head. Sick watery murk. Break surface. Car under me. Vague figures on the quayside. A shout. Someone leaps at the water! I gotta get her, get her. Swallow water, nearly black out. Can't help my girl. Up. A terrace... A head now breaks water, a man has her in his grip. Pulls her by the neck, shoves her at the terrace. People tumble down steps. He lays her out, turns her head. Kisses air in her. Pushes hard at the chest. *Call an ambulance!* Kisses her again, pumps her. Nothing. Ragamuffin scarecrow. Then she heaves, coughs, splutters, moans... She's back. *Gotcha!* he says. *Gotcha.* I'm leaning against the stone wall, head on chest. Can't take any more. Any more.

On the quayside I'm on a bench and the ambulance is there. She's awake. They slide her in, spirit her off. Our saviour, big blond feller, sits by. - I'm Tim by the way. We shake. Close one matey! Lucky I've been putting in the hours. At the pool I mean. Couldna picked a better spot to top yerself. She was drivin' eh? Pissed, or a bit of the old - ? (he gestures). Yeah right. Come to mine, I'll fix ya up no worries. What's with her foot? You two havin' a few issues?

Few issues, ha ha. Turns out he's an Aussie. Breezy hunk straight out of *Bondi Rescue.* He kits me out, drives us to the hospital. And there she is in a bed. There's a bandage across her forehead. Tim and me look down at her.

- Enjoy your ducking? he says.
- Yes thank you. And thank you for saving my life
- No sweat. Jump in again, I'll do it again
- I'll bear that in mind.

They look at each other. He grins and she smiles sheepishly. Lovely. Ten minutes of light chat then he gives his card, shakes our hands, drops us an invite for dinner then shoots through, as they say. Francesca is clearly impressed. And when F. is impressed by a boy, we know what happens.

No Worries

Five days we stayed in that little harbour town where Francesca almost got us killed. She seems remarkably nonchalant about it, which makes me grind my teeth. No actual apology offered. Aussie Tim feeds us up, drives us about, arranges the salvage (it was my car!) sweet-talks the cops, the works. No worries mate. Francesca is rather demure around him, plays up the salvaged cripple girl to his bluff hero. And on day three, guess who tools into the village? Had to happen, Lena Duvorchek is not a news bloodhound for nothing. She spots us at a pub bench on the quayside, ramps into a bloody speech to stir the village... till big Tim takes her in hand, sits her down, gets her a beer, tosses some redhead jokes at her. She shuts up and takes a good look at *him*. Later he says to me on the quiet: Where'd you pick these *chicks*, mate? I'll 'ave what you're having! Fancy we chuck Lena in the water as well? I'll let ya know, I say, but if you can turn her into a boy's girl I'll buy you ten beers. Oho! he says. Like that eh? I like a challenge. But, Francesca? She'd be *ahem* as well then? Oh shit hot. So where'd *you* fit in, mate?

Precisely.

These days are all too odd, and time is looming when we must get back to the city. The last night sees Tim and his Girlfriends headed for a club and proceeding to get plastered. Let 'em suck one last time on the Oz boy's uninvested careless liberties! I sit by the quay, stare at rainbow-coloured oil slicks on the water. No doubt big Tim'll have both his hands full tonight. What bothers me (more than bothers) is this: Did the Mars actually try to do me in - and herself - or we two together in a sweet suicide pact I didn't agree to? Her idea of commitment, or of testing it? There's a gutted feeling rising in me these days that says I'll never fathom this woman. But she's human isn't she? Oh yeesss, so much the human being. But then she isn't, she's a Goddess, with all the licence that brings. And you put her there and worshipped her there. Fool.

All our Investments

The weather has set in with rain and we're on the road from Snowdonia into England. Squat farmhouses drift by, curtain squalls drift in patchwork fields, mournful animals peer at us over jagged wetstone walls that seem to bar all ways, and heavy green-black trees lower over the roads. Lena drives at the edge of safety. On our foggy ride, gloomy realism impinges. The ways Francesca is in pain are hard to fathom. You, reader peering over my shoulder, witnessed some of them. What impact can such as me ever have on the psyche of a self-willed person? I talked of emotional strategy, but must bow to emotional *investment*. This is what turns us all into what we are. Emotional investment, a great ship that trundles by its own inertia which to turn around requires miles and miles of clear ocean, even if one wanted to, even if one knew how. We can say people are mercurial, that they blow where winds of circumstance blow, but they're not. We are the products of a billion invisible threads that tie us to a lifetime vision of ourselves, conjured and shaped and weighted and cloying like a long stifling dream. Who wants to lose anything: Francesca, Lena, me? We all invest everything in the great novel-saga of our lives. Investment in another soul is some powerful kind of giving, but every ego wants a return. *Is* there selfless giving? Can't be. Even self-sacrifice has its motive. We're players, we wrestle circumstance as if in a gymnasium, and hope for favour and gain. And displacement is the great law: whatever we do, whatever we gain, something someone somewhere will be lost. So, still young and with purportedly much to gain, Francesca and Lena and Nicky Bright share their foggy steel cage while the threads of their future separations shoot out invisible to the ends of the world. Ah, pessimism just crept in. Yeah we'll get Francesca her new foot and she'll learn to walk and will even eschew the walking stick (not a geriatric yet) and 'll even pursue her African dream - till the day it sputters, seems naïve and pointless when her contract with hope and helping bows to the fact that the sum of suffering never diminishes. All just a summer game for a young-old genius-gifted priestess, all that naivety and absurdity and rebellion. Such things were a refuge, a little holiday, here at the end of her cosmic road on earth.

The reader witnessed how the aloof Nick Bright uses music to scoff at the hollowness of art beside the crawling mundanity of the world's suffering. But he's desperate to participate, so gropes for a saving ideal: a cripple girl goddess, genius of high and low, artist of *life,* elite but real, lover and anarchist, Francesca Mars!

And Lena Duvorchek for her part has to dig dirt on all of us, be our reality check, our conscience. And she'll win her dour battle with her chosen country, her crusade to the establishment's heart epitomised by all the Francescas of Mars. What will she find there? *Herself:* steely vulnerable girl who changed her identity and her sexuality to feed a brave and vulgar belief in the great competition for 'Truth'. The battle for all the injustices of history, for the poor and downtrodden, for broken ancestries, for exile. She will drink her own dream of a better world where corruption is held to account, where the daily news no longer pump-primes itself on its own rabid importance but spills out its mini truths on the human condition, the social animal, the trends and struggles of quotidian civilisation, of man's lunging for light enough to pay off his mortgage, to feed his family, elect a saviour, create a nation, have dignity, solve the problem of living in comfort sufficient to oi-oi at the footy and slag off about immigrants and ogle at chicks in minis and get pissed and swear in freedom in a free country fit for sick bitches like Lena to live in. So I pity her, and I love her, but I will never change a thing about her. I guess she was my mate in a flat for a while, some time when we were young.

Carolyn and Peter Mars, like the Lady and her Macbeth, will cement their parental bourgie conspiracy and rein in their crippled half daughter, keep her on a leash while promising her the Future Everything, and will bit by bit with cloying and money try to drag her inward to the habitualness their middle class demands. And Carolyn will dessicate her life for philandering Mars who stole her daughter away (so she thinks) though she hadn't the wit or guts to cradle the precious girl herself or realise Leo Gorda was the love she should have cultivated, that though she understood not a whit about him he was her *adventure* and Francesca was their child - before the sheeting drizzle of money came down and sozzled her fear, enveloped her in security forever! And the day she'll leave Peter Mars will be too late. Francesca will be gone.

Do we see Francesca Mars living to ripe old age? Eternal goddesses cannot age, they just collect garments and throw them off again. Like the sadhu who awakens from trance to find they built a fucking temple round her, she will smile and entertain her scavengers and her devotees awhile… then one far day in the stillness of dawn when all are abed, she'll steal away, never to be coveted by mortal eyes again.

Ah. This gloomish weather's sucked me back - to the land of habituated invested pessimism.

We pull over in the border hills for a comfort stop, and the girls go their private ways. I stand in the road and listen to droplets of rain mist sputtering on its surface, under ghost trees in their rows that suffer the Atlantic drifts like ghoulish black mourners. An open gate and track lead away, perhaps to some anonymous farmhouse kitchen where a man and his wife stare out at the mist, nursing their tea, unaware of special travellers at their gate, who'll pass this way once and never again (they'd probably gladly welcome us). Lena stands by in her red coat and leather boots and natty red beret. I wipe a drop off her brow, trace a finger over her lip. *Love you,* I say. Fucking *cold,* she replies. We wait. Which way'd she go? Lena points to the gate. You better go look, she says. Tell-tale little holes lead off the farm track through a field and into trees. In a grey-green bower by a gnarly trunk in the sodden mist I spot her crouched, a crumply spidery figure with jutting stick beside. Her great hair's plastered and I see her pants are by her ankles. She turns at the sound of my step. *Sorry, couldn't get up…* There's mud about her feet and her stump is soiled. There's been crying. - Shall I lift you? *It's finished, Nicky. I'm finished.* Come on, I tell her. I lift her up to the tree, secure her jeans, pull her coat about.

- D'you know what? (I whisper it) You're the bravest beautifulest girl in the world, and the gods of the forest are rooting for you: gods of rain, winter and summer, gods of plenty and poverty all for you. All Francesca has to do is live and let love flow in her and be the divine beauty she is. Doesn't always have to be huge, she can do little things for a while. And appreciate her people who are there for her. We'll get her walking, get her a shiny new foot and she'll conquer again, all that she surveys. Mizz Francey with her frizzy river of hair and her wide eyes and her wit and her pouty arrogance that makes 'scavengers and devotees' like us want to die. (It's not about us) But she'll shine on 'cause she's forever... Jesus, miss muffet on your tuffet, you're soaking. (I lean in, kiss her up) Look, can't tell where is beautiful rain and where's beautiful tears...

She lets me lick her cheek. By and by, after more pouty gloom and tragic soul meditation in the dingy wet - which is seeping down my shirt - she slaps my chin and tells me to get orf. I am one sentimental loon. Half a smile for half a second. We take her crutches and she crawls on my back and we totter away across the grey field. For decorum's sake she gets down to walk before we reach the car.

Now the Welsh refuge and the soft borderlands give way to metallic rivers of motorway that rush headlong at the cities. By evening we're in the metropolis. The question rises: where to stay? The decision is our place in Chelsea. We get there, stiff and tired, and there's a note. Luc has been. Says Ayaan is with him and can he come back? *We have a problem.* I call. He's coming over. Straight away I regret: too many fragile egos right now. The girls are showering, doing their separate bits. My cellphone spits up livid messages from agent Brand. Mars as well: inevitable questions re. Francesca. He sounds oily. I sneak a look at Lena's texts. An editor seems keen to discuss a job prospect.

The doorbell. Luc steps in, shakes my hand, mutters apology. I manage to find him oddly reassuring. Outside stands the dusky Eritrean looking embarrassed and pouty by turns. I bring them to the lounge and we stand in no-man's land. Her eyes flicker to sounds down the hall. I tell them Francesca Mars is here... Luc recovers first. *Okay, it is meant to be.* What? Me, I'm tired, don't want messy business.

- Bouseri is sending Ayaan back to Eritrea. I have asked her to marry me. She is unsure. She is afraid. Basically we are hiding. Since when am I a criminal? We had no idea where Francesca was. Your phone does not respond. Is she all right? Mars will now counter-sue Bouseri for defamation. And Bouseri will try to punish me, since he knows I am involved with both Francesca and Ayaan. But Ayaan has lost faith in her father, I think.

And suddenly there is footless Francesca at the door. On a crutch. We all look at her. Luc steps forward.
- Cherie, how are -
- Don't come near. (To me) What are they doing here?
- I invited them… No, I mean they asked to come (Shit!)
- 'Lo there, bit of cocoa on the side. What's new with you?
Ayaan squirms, then glares.
- I will go.
Luc holds onto her.
- Wait! We have to discuss. Francesca, I am sorry. So sorry
- For what? Abandoning me? For leaving Nicky to look after me? Why are you not in Africa injecting poor people? Or did Peter stop your money? Or has that Bouseri accused me of whoring at him? Or has *she* been in your ear? Little Muslim girl with her hand in the till. What's the matter deary? Not enough richy clothes to wear? Guess what, he's too good for you. But not too good for me. Fuck *you*, all right!

At this point her crutch slips and she heads straight for the floor. Luc kneels to her. She starts to cry. He embraces. Apparently her wrist is strained. She holds it out to her big doctor. Their little tableau. I grab hold of Ayaan and pull her out the door, down to my studio. Lena sticks her head out of the bathroom. I point out Francesca and Luc. She screws her face up.

The Mars is victim to jealousy! Human, I like it. Ayaan starts to cry and I hold her wrists, sit her down. All this is too too much. In a foreign land, steamrolled by a madwoman. She wanna go home. And her doctor Luc is *engaged* to that Francesca! What a fool she 'ave been. But *daddy*, did he *really* have sex with her? I hate her. How shamed I am! But *daddy*?

Etcetera. Softly softly tone required.
- Come on, Ayaan. Time to wake up. Are you a child?
But Lena charges in.
- You want to criticise her? Get *fucked*.
The Serb shoves her off her feet. The whole neighbourhood will hear this.
- Get off your high horse, bitch. She blew her fucking leg off trying to help you people. Take your fucking nose out of the air. What did that watch cost? Those diamonds? Blood diamonds, bitch! And this (Lena grabs at her crotch) - hot black pussy good for everybody! Yeah, Big Daddy like to watch Frannie piss in bath - like village girl!
Ayaan is panting. She starts to shout. At this point I step in.
- Back, Lena. Stop it!
Luc comes running.
- What the hell is this? Get away from her, whore!
Lena turns on him.
- Whore? Mister Smoothie Frenchie? So smooth sooo kul-tuured. Want to mar-ee Fran-cescuh? Get real, Mars is real. Not like this - *gollywog cunt!*
Lena's turn of phrase is too amusing. Luc is speechless. He pulls Ayaan away. I hold onto Lena like a horse.
- Easy, girl. Shouldn't have let 'em come. Bad idea. We're all stressed. Hold yer temper.

I go after Luc. They're in the street. The girl is shaking. I apologise, hold her hand, tell her I'm embarrassed.
- We shouldn't be fighting over Francesca Mars, it's childish. Lena is loyal, shocked at her disability. Now listen Ayaan... listen to me, dammit. Do you wanna help Luc? Help yourself? Go to your father, use your power. Make him pull his head in, make him support any bloody programs Luc wants. You have the power, you're his golden girl. Make him do your bidding. Get off your chuff and do something for Africa. You'll feel better. Not feel like a hypocrite, right? Haven't got enough diamonds and clothes and all this decadent western shit? Be a proper Muslim. Help your people.

Luc will support to the hilt. And then the whole lot of us'll respect. You can be a heroine. You'll be a goddess!

I've no idea where this speech came from. But Luc is looking at me with… I think it's admiration. And Ayaan has gone very quiet. There's hiatus in the yellow dark street. She bows her elegant head, like an egret in a lake. Her earrings tinkle. Luc cradles her. Sweet tableau.

- We'll talk again. Thank you Nicky. Sorry. Sorry. Goodnight.
And the great white man and his long dark beauty fritter off down a Chelsea lane. I watch them go. Out of the shadows slips a silhouette. Francesca Mars seats herself on the bonnet of Lena's car.

- Heard all of that. Freaky speech Nicky Bright. You could do what I do. I'll coach you, for a fee. Then I can put my feet up. Or foot… (Silence) Has my Luc really gone? Can I lean on you? Lost my crutch, see.
- Nope. You can walk, on your own one foot.
She pouts. Which makes me relax.
- What would you be if you lost everything?
- I'd still be me, Nick
- Right answer. Now go and give your Lena a hug. We'll all go to bed. Tomorrow you'll apologise to Ayaan. And you'll start being nice to your mother. And you'll let poor Luc off the hook.
She rests her cheek on mine.
- Anything you say, Nicky nice boy music man
- And pay some bloody attention. I'll chop your other foot off
- I'll chop your balls first. You'll sing soprano, sweetie. And you'll play piano when I say. Private
- Deal. But if I'm knackerless you'll be all over Lena
- Might. Might not
- Make up your mind, cripple girl
- Why should I? I'm the goddess Francesca. Or did we forget already?
- Fuck no.

Four weeks later they fitted her with a prosthetic foot. Usual haughty complaints from the elevated one whose standards have dropped by a quarter of a degree. In honour of this she *shaves off her hair*. Every skerrick of red-gold mane down to half an inch. Presents herself one evening at my house. I am forced to gulp. D'you think it suits me, she asks. When I say yes she calls me a fucking liar and attacks, but it all ends on the couch, in disastrous beauty, since in the light of having recouped her pitiless attention-seeking mojo and my revealing several syrupy shades of irony re. the hair, the Mars is forced to admit my opinion might actually matter. And then she's in a quandary 'cause opinions don't matter, least of all boy ones. And anyway Lena will approve since it's more butch. But she's a bit conscious about that too, so is forced to allow me to peel her a grape and wait on her hand and (one) foot. And by way of reward she allows me to celebrate her physicality at close quarters, which she knows is important to me. And things on that occasion end happily when I fill her full of Chopin, or was it Schubert.

And Lena won't be jealous (yet) since she got a new job writing for some editor who red-carpets the ground she struts on and lets her write public scandal in exchange for further scandal at his office after hours. Told you Lena's gay thing was a pose. Francesca claims she's weaning herself off Peter Mars since nowadays he's a worse-than-ever poseur and snake-oil peddler of bogus third-world schemes. On the other hand she has to admit he *was* terribly anxious, poor thing, when she stood on that mine. Jury's still out, there. Besides, he keeps those nosy police away from me, darling. And mummy has cheered up because I'm seeing a bit more of *you*, Nicky. Though which bit of you she wants me to look at, I'm not too sure. More information on you and mummy please? (She wrinkles an eyebrow, but I'll have my secret) And if you like, we'll all go on a proper holiday to Wales one of these days, although I do have plans for a major little trip to Kenya in the spring… Oh no, *alone*, Nick. This life is far too short, and I must contemplate my subtle destiny. Seriously I mean. But am I a loser really? And did you see my pic in the Grauniad on Tuesday? I don't look like that anymore! D'you *really* appreciate my hair? Liar. Those media dickheads! They said I should leave Africa to the 'professionals', like them maybe! No, like Luc. He'll save us all. I've been seeing him by the way. Not his little Eritrean doll though. Oh you'll be happy. I was being drooled on by some bigwig the other day at the Purcell Room. I'm certain I'm going to get you some gigs there. Will you play for me today?

Too happy to, Francesca. During it, she sits up straight and listens with glorious unimpeachable intent. At the end she smiles the wide promissy glittery smile I like best of all. No irony.

And in that smile - though it shouldn't be so - is my whole wide world.

THE ELUSIVE

INNOCENCE

NICHOLAS FROST

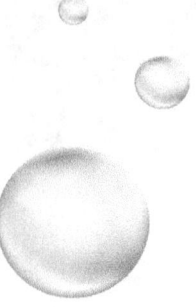

'll write in the great Book of Nothing, said Elizabeth Castro. Then they will know who I am. Who doesn't want innocence, no matter how obtuse the path? Dancer Libby Castro submits to demanding and needy people: Castro the director, Thiel the yogi, the lawyer Cortes, fatal Rosita, refugee Sophia, Omar the mute, Cross the analyst. Yet beyond her insouciant roles and lazy vacancies she'll be no-one's shadow: a straw, a girl unmarked, woman alone...

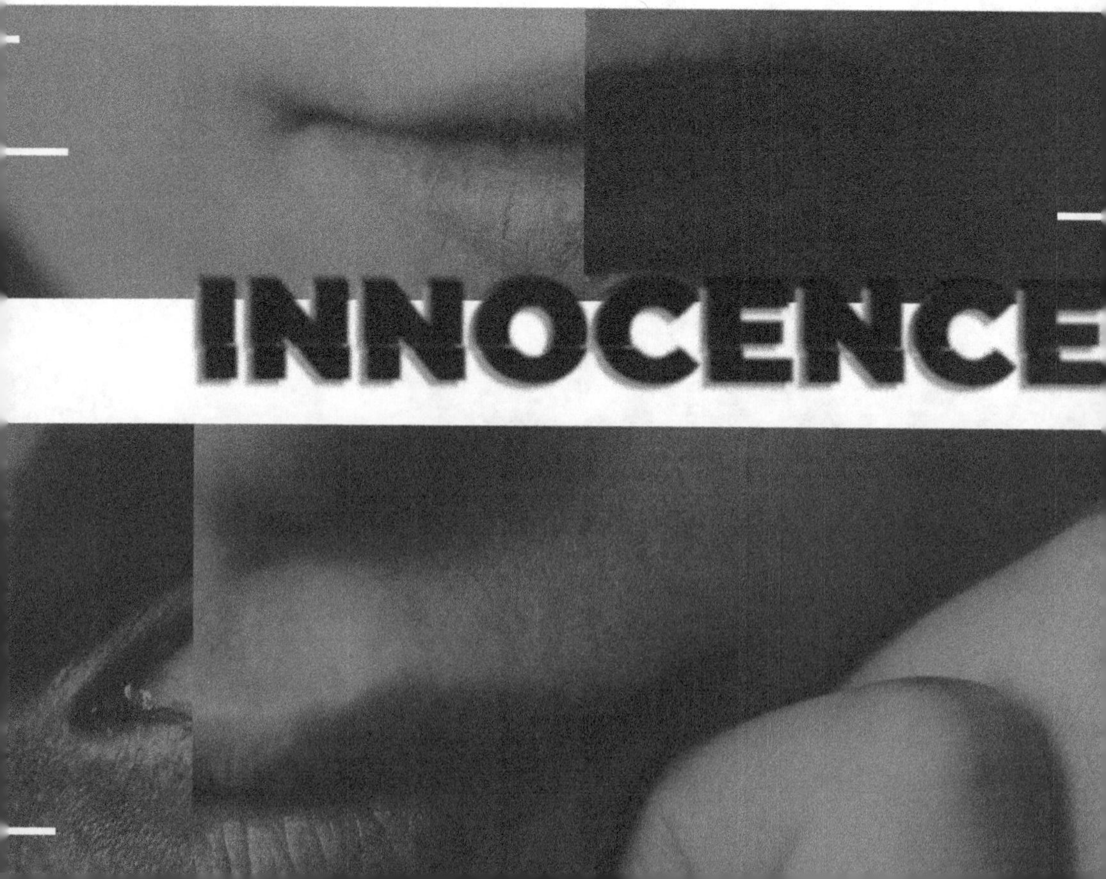

INNOCENCE

Innocence

Castro, My Husband

We begin in a theatre. The hour is late. Libby Castro the dancer steps onto a bare stage and awaits instructions. Lights glare in her eyes; a disembodied voice drawls out from the back.

- Elizabeth! I know it's midnight, but we require the scene to take form at least once according to how I conceived it, before our greedy audience tears it to pieces. We agree?
- Yes, darling husband
- Then do it, darling wife
- I thought my scene was to be blue
- It will be, just for you
- Is Bondy awake?
- Asleep. Right here. Now, if you please?
(Pause) - D'you really think the music is right?
(Pause) - The music is the music. But the dancer…
- Don't say it. The dancer is the *dance*
- Our little star forgets nothing. Lazlo - music!
Irony clunks in the dark. And Libby Castro wants to go home. There can be no art at midnight, only sleep, but Castro the director never sleeps. The cavernous wings yawn, concealing eyes. Libby collects body and soul and begins. Arvo Part's lugubrious cellos envelop the room; her choreography hangs like wet washing on her bones… yet the trance of night seems to lend abandon, and her body does things the mind can't think. The quasi-improvisation succeeds like never before. Even the master is surprised.
- *Good.*

Libby is relieved. But how will she remember what her body did? All I could think was how I'd like to pluck old Part's prickly beard. What's my dance then? The dance of body emptiness, I'll have to call it.

She stands there. - Thank you. Go home please. Take Bondy also. Now Nadia, I work with you. Gah, it is late.

Nadia steps from the shadows. Their paths cross, eyes meet. Smiles. Then Libby is gone, to the showers. After languishing in heat she collects Bondy and steps to the night street. Nadia's in there with Castro. Another hour you'd expect. Their little purple scene's all about sex, whereas mine is blue and melancholy. There's a green-tinged sequence with Nadia and me. Castro keeps his mouth shut about that... Nadia. She's taller, strong with dark hair, unlike me who's lighter and fair. We encounter each other in green luminous body suits. Hands buttocks necks... her eyes gleam when our navels meet. I quite enjoy that! Castro insists on scarily sensual. Has his ways. Nadia trusts him so he's demanding with her. Used to be that with me. We've moved on nowadays; now it's all irony, a sign of my maturing no doubt.

At home she tucks Bondy in, strokes his fair head. His round eyes drop away to pools of sleep... after which she goes to bed. In the dark she puts her lips to the pillow, touches herself for some moments. For Castro no doubt. Then it's forgotten, since she's asleep.

Next morning at ten she's at yoga. Here's Mister ('Yogi') Thiel - in charge today.

- Forward bend, assert the individual self. Backward bend, enter the stream, individual is gone. Forward, re-assert the individual. We make a posture, the universe makes its counterpoint. Thus, the dance. Libby Castro?

Libby is trying to twist herself like a pretzel just now. The dance. Castro would disapprove. Be present! he'd say. But I am present, where else could I be? What he really means is pay attention to where *he's* present, silly boy. Yogi Thiel's voice is gentle. A treat today, since he doesn't often take our class and since he's a meditation teacher. How d'you teach meditation, may one ask? Perhaps I should ask. Downward dog. Nose to floor and bum to sky. Mmm, who could be gazing? Oh look, lonely speck of dust on polished floor. What was its journey to my eyes? Serpent pose… ceiling far away, come again another day. Down dog again… There's the speck. Returned specially so I could gaze at it. Hold on… pain is good… why d'we twist ourselves in knots: is the world not as it is? I never used to ask, simply longed to be fit and slim and lovely. Then Bondy came, and maybe I see things differently. Maybe I'm just older.

Home for lunch, Libby scribbles in her diary as is her habit. Castro once suggested she record her dreams. She complied but now it's not just dreams, it's every bit of fluff, daydreams as well. Why not? Helps me sift and cope. When Bondy was born I wanted to write up everything. My little habit now. Sometimes I let Bondy draw all over it. My chattering mind! - not so intellectual. But dump it all in and I'm calm, not to say empty.

How will our new production go off? Castro's in his disgusted ironic phase. Right now all art is shit. He alone carries the burden of having to save us from ourselves since the critics will slaughter us. Bless him, we need him desperately. Yes, my husband is a strange intense man, but where would we be without him? This is the phase where he curses me left and right, but in the middle of the night he comes, takes my sweet backside and puts it exactly where he wants it. I'm actually happy when he does. And his beard tickles. He never waits for me, not nowadays.

When Bondy was on the way I stopped dancing. To be honest it was Castro's idea. Seemed to want the child so much, almost begged me in between his ordering me about. Behind every great man is a pliant woman no doubt. Was I indifferent? No - but I had to warm up to it, the bump and the weight and everything. When he was born I wanted to be such a good mother. Everyone gave advice but I wasn't sure what it meant. What's there to do? Let Bondy be what he wants, what he *is* I suppose. Who can interfere with what is?

At the birth Castro cancelled rehearsals for the whole day in our honour. Two weeks out from his biggest show ever. I guess I looked like I'd got in his way. He told me to stop being silly. Actually he'd choreographed pretty much everything from the big rubber balls which I failed to use, to the baroque chamber music. The birth itself confounded his directives but no matter, it all passed off with minimal fuss. No criticism from the critic! Despite all the pain. When Castro is helpless (not often) he looks at me with baleful eyes and touches his fingers together. This is the sweet moment... before the brow clouds to dismissive pessimistical irony (at all life's ineptitude). Me, I bask in it, the sweet moment that is. The birth put me on top for months. At home he'd fuss about and poke things and give orders that were totally useless. But I was useless too. So we'd once or twice actually look in each other's eyes and laugh, both sweetly embarrassed for different reasons. The thing is, Castro can't be reached. I can't do it anyway. And what about me? Maybe there are times when he wonders about me? I'm fairly sure there are.

Little Bondy was worrisome to me. How would he grow, how would we live? They say the divine holds us in her palm, but I seemed to gasp with vertigo... *with the unbearable lightness of being.* I read that phrase on a book cover. Seemed to be speaking to me.

Now my boy is six and I'm dancing semi-professionally again. But how do I know I'm any good? Castro's dance theatre allows no socially acceptable benchmarks. It's all infuriatingly avant-garde, and all sustained by his ego. Am I tired of it? No no, I love to dance, and I've been good at it. Just has ups and downs, that's all.

* * * *

It's Saturday. Libby and Bondy are at the line hanging washing. It's a dreamy day. Spring, in fact. Libby notes how Bondy likes to sit under the sheets and watch them billow and strain against the sky, as if sails on a great white ship. He's snug on deck with its warm caulked boards, and sailing into the blue South. Face buried in white, his hands clutching at cotton, he exclaims in excited confusion:

- After this, can I go play pirates with my friend Suzie La La?

Libby would let him go to heaven and back if he wanted, and reflects that one day she'll have to do it anyway.

- Sure you can, Bondy. Get your shoes. There are nettles by the footpath, and glass and muck in the lanes. I'll call Julie first.

Castro's barely there. But when he is he takes Bondy on his shoulders for a spin round the house before grunting and heading for his books and his texting. Bondy tends to wonder who this man might be; Libby can see it on his face. No matter, Bondy is self-contained. Blondy-headed little guy, the couple named him James. Later he heard about 'James Bond' and Libby called him Bondy, and Castro didn't object. He's quite plump, Libby reflects, but rather beautiful. Girls 'll like him. A mite too romantic though. Does he remind me of my father? The thing is to love and forbear, let him be free. What's there to lose by that? The dark life will grip him anyway, later.

Absence

Libby takes him to Suzie's. It's a sunny quiet walk through the lanes. What was *my* mother like doing this sort of thing? Libby thinks often on this. Since she has no role-models she'll have to invent them. Over time she has tricked together some pictures in her mind's eye.

Elizabeth! Her mannish mother used to call at her, ignoring the fact of her, instead sending a kind of unfulfilled challenge at everything about her. Tall, imperious, haughty, American - she took her tea and cigarette on the verandah, glared at the mundane, railed at the ordinary. Sudden speech, impatient gesture... did it cloak a fear of wasted existence, of amounting to nothing, of being un-special? Worrying behind windows at unfulfilled sex, at her obtuseness as a wife, at her lack of clothing sense. Bustling, arbitrary, all directed at nothing in particular... as if trying to wring meaning out of fierce panicked solitude. She was a tax manager or some such thing. Should never have got married. Should have been a bohemian or a lesbian or an aviator. Something! Mother always seemed to pass like a storm over Libby's head. And father died when she was eight.

He worked at a booksellers. She remembers *him*, placid in his chair in the garden, letting her flit about him and tickle his beard or stomach or his fair messy hair... She'd learn not a thing from his inset eyes, self-smile, passive quietude. He'd bask in the sun, doodle with his puzzles, put notes in the margin of a book. Nothing profoundly scholarly, just the tinkerings of one who noted life as it happened elsewhere. Perhaps he himself was a footnote in the margin of a book? She'd wonder if she might reach him, make him happy, get him to crawl with her on the grass in search of bugs. Once or twice she thinks he did, and those times she thinks he called her *Libby.* This is the name she likes. Better than Elizabeth.

Libby remembers she liked to flit about the garden, compose little dances under the hanging trees, sidestep daisies on the lawn and billow up her summer dress. Raising her face and arms to the sky, she'd twirl about till dizzy, till she could no more recognise a world reduced to mysterious colour, shapes, kaleidoscopes. Libby. *Libre.* Free... Later she'd run to her father or her mother, who were seldom together, and finding nothing much there would skitter off again like a bee in summer, and wonder what the other girls in other gardens did.

Sometimes she would stand in the house corridor in the depth of the night, without a night-dress, and listen for sounds in her parents' rooms. No-one ever suspected she was there. All her childhood she'd seemed to sense and see an *absence,* behind and between the things of the world. A bin standing in a corner waiting for its human family to come home and fill it with detritus; a tennis racket or wine-glass discarded; ghost reminder of activities done, not done... One time, the billow of sheets in sunlit wind in a yard; puffed reminders of lives slept, nights and dreams gone away. Or a frivolous magazine on the table, the exploits of beautiful and important youth, of young dancers. Once, the alarming rogue sea, its grey-dark mountains, no place for human beings. Another time, rows of poor chimneys, squat tenements, unknown kids in oily streets pantomiming play, as if life were a playground forever, tossing hours into the air to fall where they may, before some rain-squall sent them all inside to domestic prisons. She did not mix with any of them.

The Bug

Once the three of them went to Italy, and in their *pensione* she encountered a bug on a windowsill, trying to navigate the dusty glass. Ignorant of history civilisation wine or song - he was a bug in the sun, one feckless hour in eternity, seeking a path, feeling only the beating of his wings and the vibration of his heart - in a vault of yellow, amid a planet under a sun, below a mountain, behind glass in a dusty hanging noon. Hoped to meet and marry, have his child, die in the evening a contented thing, not cheated. In no place called Italy. Libby remembered the bug but little else. Except some similar bugs in a swimming pool deeper than a child. With her still, lazy gaze, she watched them wanting to live, desperate to fly to the sky over the forest, but they slopped instead inside this human sea. She wanted to scoop them out and dry them on the warmy stones. But *veneration* prevented her. It was absurd. They drowned. She never forgot it.

She read somewhere in an adulty book that the sands of time erase all things, that things are just sun-glitter on the sea without body or soul (whatever that could be). And she felt that nothing is ever known except by random eyes that happen to look there, who gaze with feckless nonchalance in that place... who scarce remember, unless they are entertained.

A single moment in a dateless afternoon, nowhere in summer, barely in Italy, long ago... Yellow-aproned flower-fields glide by in a car, parallel wires raked by poles under a cobalt sky, dust on a wind-screen clouding vagrant travellers' eyes; passing from unknown to unknown, place to name-forgotten place. In one such place a mute old woman looked at her, and Libby wondered if *she* cast her old mind back to a sometime when she played idly under the vault of heaven in a dusty noon by a roadside, in a parched land where feckless things passed before her eyes. Yellow-aproned flower-fields... wires... cobalt sky.

Oh! Here we are at Julie's place... Bondy likes to run ahead since he loves Suzie La La. She's part Italian, and a girl.

My past then. Great swathes of disconnection… tsunamis of forgetting… and some little jewelled things survive, that create a little world in which I wrap myself and take a meaning from. Little beads of meaning, little bubbles. How empty I am - one bug in the universe.

At the Feet of the Master

Ballet school was what dreamy unacademic Libby Castro did, and she enjoyed herself. When we say unacademic, we paint a picture of a girl who wanted to learn how to feel, and saw no point in analysing so-called 'facts' in a universe full of strangeness, surprise, melancholy, light. Only dance seemed to express a gesture and its result, without complication, outside time and circumstance. Libby once saw pictures of ballet girls by Degas in one of her father's books, and she'd wanted to be one of those girls, watched by her adoring father and mother, dressed prettily with sleek champagne thighs and blue make-up in a sweet theatrical world where the din outside the window didn't matter.

When ballet school finished she did some tours and a few musicals. She was rather good, but the whole thing 'tarried in a sort of existential vacuum' - so Castro told her the day after she met him. He was casting about for people for a new work 'in the method of Pina Bausch' (if that's possible), except that his strident political agendas were far from Pina's hands-off whispers to 'lift yourself up by your own hair'. He appeared to latch on to Libby in a vulnerably self-important, weightily humblified manner reserved for those he felt the need to impress with his genius. Libby said he found it 'amusing' when she turned up for their lunch with a little voice recorder - though one suspects he was touched but'd never show it. Things clearly had to proceed on the correct track, and Libby records many things (as you will see), since they'd otherwise have no weight or circumstance. Castro's speeches usually proceeded thus:

- Let me explain how things are, Elizabeth. When want-to-be artists come to me they're amateurish - unable to conceive of Art except as a bourgeois narrative-based reflection of bad art they already imbided. They think they can give what people think they want, and all will be well. Since art is entertainment and since artists want to be loved and famous, so they copy the Hollywood dream or what they imbibe on Youtube. And they're enslaved to the expectations of audiences who pay to see art – the mirror of capitalist values in which the artist is Salesman, Prostitute. Bourgeois society condescends to peruse our products of beauty, and buy them since it has money and wants to spend it on the beautiful. This is bourgeois success: to eschew the ugly and know that ugliness is banished from their world. Will their reaction be beautiful when they see the ugly products of my honesty? My dance is not the petty aesthetic of a ballet - it is the struggle of male-female, oppressor-oppressed, human-inhuman, rational-irrational, ugly-sweet. We seek no applause yet admit we are its slaves, ha ha! Here then is tension for us. We seek accolades yet spurn them, hate art yet are addicted. And can we live together as a true artist family - to challenge, reform, cleanse each other in a bond of trust? I shall (reluctantly) be mentor to such a family. I am criticised for what is called cruelty, for stripping to bone to find resistance, always resistance! and hold it up and ask my people to cast it off, to *submit*. (Cruelty is tradition. Have you not heard of Artaud?) I take no pleasure in exposing vague notions, cherished sentiments, wants. Am I a religious flagellant fuelled by self-hatred, exposing others' guilt? No, I anatomise the human soul. But my artists are no guinea pigs. They *resist,* and this is our little game. I may seem inflexible, but I have loved them though I am hard on them. Inwardly I suffer! I must generate the idea, intuit the possibility. This is lonely. It does not matter that it is me. People are same shit in different buckets! Ha, I am cynical no? Yet there is beauty - not in sentiment but in honesty. Some say I hate critics! To some extent this is slightly untrue. And I cannot be expected to show! It is for my artists to discover. I do not patronise by *telling*. Remember: there can be no democracy in theatre. Performer must submit to process, just as director must submit his vision to the performer's hand. Naturally I question. I only know that I do not know. I cast a question into the ether: at a certain point it must take shape. This is beyond control. I am not responsible for what comes. I have commitment only to truth as intuited. I cannot help if it must *dominate*. True, I am experienced but humble. I suffer: people do not see! And I am one of three most experienced directors on the planet. I have no huge international profile, but who craves this? We must work where we are, with what we have. We do the work, only the work. And I constantly doubt my own truth. Always doubt: this is my integrity. Our work is stupid and trivial often, but is our groping to *create*. I respect the artist who lays him or herself (especially herself) naked. Art is absurd, since we express stupidity, mundaneness in ourselves. And this is bravery. We are not original, we are fools. If beauty and dignity come by some miracle, let it be. I am accused of many things - misogynist, communist, fascist. I do not indulge. I love my people, my family. A family is what we are.'

And Libby felt she wanted to be part of something, something avant garde. Why not? Something strange weightless human beautiful ugly lovely lonely… maybe dance would lead her there, or Castro would. So began her real adventure in art - under the unforgiving eye of a self-appointed master.

Yang and Yin

No doubt, Libby the acolyte and ingenue has her insights. And did her man Castro have other acolytes? Oh, too many, and always female. Nadia is a new example. And did he appear to have friends? Of course not. Libby saw it straight away. Was he able to treat another as equal? Never. Could this inequal master-student coitus ever morph to up-grown equality? Never ever. Does he interest himself in others' work? Sure, in as far as he can mould or dissuade them from their decadent ignorant paths. Does he need? Oh yes, he is such a lonely pioneer. Libby felt it. But Libby is unaware in so many things, Castro does not fail to point out. What does she know? Maybe she has a 'strange skerrick of freedom' - and the consequences of this skerrick Castro would fail to note or wouldn't want to. Perhaps with her it's freedom from the burden of needing to prove herself, a difference between those who need to manipulate the world and those who don't. Great manipulators feel they are the lonely burdened ones, for without them nothing would be done, there'd be no analysis, no progress, no meaning to human struggle. Après moi le deluge! Insouciant blythe spirits like Libby who contribute nothing unless coerced by such as Castro - don't they see they are leaves blown on wind, grains in a sandstorm? Ah, but! Libby the nobody who chooses to not be somebody might wish to say: I harken to the unseen, to the Other, the Shadow Dancer... whose footprints appear in sands though no-one was ever seen to tread there... These mover-shaker types, they don't inhabit that universe. Libby from the start felt sorry for him. How can a small ingenue feel sorry for a big genius? He'd feel globally patronised if he found out. He must never find out, Libby knows.

We say that in the cosmic scheme we fulfil each other's lack since none are whole, and that all are born for a purpose: to discern their limitation, admit to it and willingly let another fulfil it. While controllers find this life a torturous episode, those like Libby who sense they can't control, are at an advantage. So she'll embrace the great Other in the form of a big hairy problem like Castro, and will love her other with a sort of quiet sorrowing pity. And she'll do her part as willing disciple, as the fool who must learn. And wonder of wonders, the Lord himself kneels at the feet of his silly disciple. Libby loves with humility under her petty complaints and discomforts and her self-sorry pricked pride. She believes in her Castro because he's a larger-than-life fiend with a heart, a precious prodigy who comes among us not often. And Castro himself was all huge humility when they got married. Libby believes this was one production in which he participated with an almost naïve belief that 'life as theatre' might offer some kind of little sweetness (but never 'meaning' of course), perhaps the sense of family he blindedly strove for in his dance theatre yet always stood back from as if it were too ironic for words. This cynic Castro when he stoops to join the human round, must imagine this simple sweetness as if an elysian romance, to be had once and never again. For to have more of it would be to enact the fool - to be fooled by a dream.

Libby was tickled by how he delighted in putting her in all possible positions in their lovemaking, and she herself participated with absorbed interest in the presence of this bear who just couldn't cram all the honey in his mouth at once. She assumed she'd be pregnant within a short time, and it was so. Did she have qualms? Of course, but what can one do? Truth be told, Libby can be so present and so pliant with him because... she is absent. What thereby is there to lose? Sometimes in the dead of the evening, after being happily mauled by her sweaty now sleeping mate, she would lie there alone, languishing and thinking… He is so absorbed in his own gothic soap opera, his own little play-pen, his ego-romance of great explorer, icon, genius, artist, playboy, eclectic, young turk, master, commander, jester, devil and steppenwolf and all the rest. And I am just a sweet little pussy and lips and limbs for him to play his tunes on. She knew the only kind of muse she could be to him was to be an amusement. No illusions there. Is this unfair? A bit. He did love in his self-centred way as well as he could. And well she knew. She took up smoking at this stage for a little while. Nothing serious, like a post-coital puff or two in the vein of 1950s moll. Again, it was a role. Libby is the insouciant type who can certainly play a role and toss it away. And she wore her blondy hair in a shortish bob since he liked the image of 1920s ingenue, or cotton slacks and horn-rimmed sunglasses in the 1960s style. All of these tickled him. In his hoary way he could commit to this worldly marriage, let it matter to him despite its lack of outrage and bohemian anarchy, as long as its irony was accomplished. Thus it would last. What were his terms? As long as her beauty was fresh to him she would be his only one.

But since beauty cannot ensnare us forever and must turn to ennui, she could not expect to always be his only one. Thus he explained this accomplished logic as if to a child. But a woman is no child; the man is the child. Libby did not complain at this. She had (she felt) the benefit of his honesty - a form of flattery. Still, the girl had no idea what her reaction would be if she found him with another. She needed to be special to him in some respect! She gave her sweet body to him after all. And she gave him a baby.

Guilt

Thus Libby well remembers the day she came upon Castro and Nadia in the back of the cavernous dressing room at the theatre, engaging in activities illicit but not un-theatrical in nature. How she watched them for a while as specimens of interest, even feeling some prickly heat before quietly closing the door and walking away. Then calling up Yogi Thiel and booking him for a private yoga class, a rigorous one. She said she felt her life as Castro's dancer was over… for good this time.

Sniffing behind Libby's evasive silence in the days that followed, Castro sought to initiate a kind of dissertation on the relative merits of his dancers. This prompted her to remark that, yes, Nadia certainly has a superb curve to her buttock (as she herself noted at first hand) and that in terms of breast and cunt size Nadia should undoubtedly be superior, for a man of his tastes anyway. When Elizabeth gets angry which she hardly ever does, she is fiendish. But Castro is not easily swayed from the logic of his acts! He is selfless in fact, since young Nadia requires his *commitment* to match her selfless commitment to his art. His is an act of necessity, no more, and Libby should at least grasp it, should see the irony. She certainly sees the irony of trying to open the eyes of a husband to his venality, and so is liberated from the need to care what happens next. She takes a kitchen knife and stabs him deep in the shoulder. She may have killed him if he'd not managed to kick her to the floor and she'd not struck her head in falling… At any rate, both of them lie on the floor for a while, and when Libby comes to and sees the blood and feels sorry and calls the ambulance and frets and wrings her hands and cries as he's taken away - she has forgotten completely her impulse to mortally stab him - as if it were a dream, a thought bubble. And thus she is his faithful wife again.

But then… she falls to recollecting what happened at Yogi Thiel's class, which puts a worser perspective on it all. How she submitted to his personal instruction which he administered with unusual care before she shoved herself on him and took him in hand. Sadly, he being very controlled she had to complete a job on herself, which he then assured her he enjoyed the spectacle of, which wasn't quite satisfactory since he seemed to smile in an ironic way that reminded her of someone else. Nevertheless he iterated that he liked her and cared about her, before sending her back to her husband. A subtle fellow! Now Libby wants a whole bigger bite of him but will be forced to deny it. Hence comes a raging guilt.

Suddenly cast adrift in a male-led soap opera, what's a girl to do? Shouldn't she run for help to her analyst – her trustable guardian?

Trust the Analyst

Reader, you may have been wondering how these details of Elizabeth Castro came to light. Autobiographic accounts always mix imagination, distortion, avoidance and wishful thinking. I as analyst (and your narrator, whose name is Cross) am regular witness to all of these. I see many souls, but few entrust me with their private diaries. 'Tis an intimacy that's tantalisingly elusive, since by handing over diaries the author clearly no longer values them. Elizabeth Castro came to me after the break with her husband. To my eye she seemed a person at once present and absent, aware and unaware, as if a ghost spoke cleverly on her behalf. Perhaps she was distracted. I knew I'd lower, even waive my fee: why profit from one capable of inspiring me, was my thought. The rewards of insight are superior to the filling of a bank account.

Castro lost no time in discovering our conversations and coming at me, warning on his wife's frailties and quirks. I found myself scrambling to evade a partisan role, since Libby's a girl who quietly inspires it. Scars from long wars to grasp my own prejudices alerted me to the prickly heat I felt every time Castro came calling. He didn't fail to remind that he was a wounded man but a compassionate one, since he 'told the hospital he fell on a blade after slipping in the kitchen'. And an indispensible one, since his wife couldn't hope to benefit from pseudo-professionals unaware of her permanent and delicate psychic state. 'A vacant ingenue in need of a mentor and parent, a naif in need of discipline!' Not to mention the issue of her child, her lack of responsibility to it, her directionless faith in its unsullied future (*her* child, *its* future). In short, a basket-case 'who worships him'. Such a *weight* on his shoulders, not measurable to 'outsiders'. I was forced to point out Libby was a free agent. He didn't like it.

After a lugubrious first hour in which she cried now and again, Libby Castro seemed to buck up and henceforward turned candid. As analyst, objectivity should sum up my usefulness, but Libby inspires the opposite. The elusiveness in her made me 'want to be more than a stranger'. I wanted to cradle, and to chastise if the truth be known; and she might have let me, if truth be known. Yes, I tended to glance at her dancer's legs a mite too often and fooled myself she didn't notice. She certainly noted that I'm not married. She informed me Castro 'would pay up for these sessions since he was the arsehole who fucked her up'. When I hinted at leniency on my fee, she remarked: let him think he's paying top dollar! and so quickly that I read it as a sign of conspiracy, which flattered me more than it should have. Mind you, she seemed to find it natural that I should lower my professional fee for *her*. Our talks quickly turned social: she'd want to clear out of my office and walk to the cafés or by the river. Sooner than decent she produced the diaries, as if she wanted rid of them. When I suggested she keep them, she insisted. What to do? Our little conspiracy. Guilty as charged.

At the cafe we'd have coffees and buns, her choice. We'll 'ave a tipple, she'd say. Safe and shareable chips too. No need to watch my weight now huh? She wasn't so delicate with the 'sauce' either - in fact Libby was frank about her husband's peccadilloes, including those in the sack. Too much information? Not for me. But she'd eye me up all the same, testing. There's nothing specific to heal in her really, I got to thinking. What do you offer a girl who appears to know nothing about what she wants, who writes it all down but doesn't care to read it? …Frequent asides about parents revealed variegated shades of confusion. Fodder for analysis? I couldn't possibly comment. I noted she dressed precisely for our sessions, or maybe she always did. Women are a mile ahead in the nuance stakes. She'd ask: 'How d'you like my outfit today?' On the plaisant neutrality of my reaction no doubt depended her opinion of me. Did I acquit myself? Nope. Instead, miraculously it dawned on me what I thought she needed… a change of partner. Fatal mistake of transference! I'm really not so skilled at this game: I failed to suggest 'no husband at all'. She wasn't impressed. 'Analysis is a fool's game, Cross! Don't you see it's karma? Some things have no rhyme or reason except as a result of something else which had no rhyme or reason except as a result of - etcetera forever. The rest is bullshit.' Should I explain to her she's hiding behind a defensive shield of thoughtlessness? No. And she didn't need to be cossetted or analysed or even advised, she said. Castro had done enough. She needed a *friend*. What do friends do? I guess they're just there, and they don't *exploit*. Gulp, mea culpa. And

Libby would pronounce: 'Why love a person so strongly? You only turn selfish and wallow in frustration when they don't love you enough back...' and she'd look at me with her wide eyes under that blondy hair. Nothing to say to that. Yep, I was out of depth, and once you lose objectivity you never get it back. Some will say that 'passively untouchable people' can only be exploited, not loved, that they seem to invite it - that this is why yours truly might offer something superior. Could I say it? No way. Happy to think it though.

- We only really exist or flourish in relation to each other. That's the drawback to unattachment, Libby. You end up alone. Unpartnered analysts for instance, are alone. Unpartnered dancers certainly are. Directors without acolytes are really so. The fiercest and cleverest of men like Castro need their *other* or they wither: that other who doesn't compete with them but 'just is'. That's you, there's power for you in that
- You're so right! Did he (that bastard) realise what a perfect partner he had? I didn't scorn him, didn't judge him
- Libby, listen. If we cease to identify with the other, we might claim to keep our identity. But a new danger is we might have no identity at all. Is this what we want?
No identity at all. Libby claimed she didn't know the answer to this curly question. But she does. Her emptiness scares me. It makes me chase. Her analyst is in a bind.

Glass Bead Games
It's a windy day. We're in our favoured café.
- Cross! I love the wind, it clears away everything. My hopes, memories, clinging, my identity. Oh! Yogi Thiel said something cool. Let me read. 'Who can entertain foolishness in a gale or storm? I stand as if on the foredeck of a ship at sea, feel the foamy gale flush out my eyes. Braids of bubbles career by, flung to oblivion. Here is our existence. Each is a bead of logic and belief, each is the substance of a dream. We are as nothing...' How cool is that? Next he says -
- Yogi Thiel? Who?

- Oh he's a guy I *really* like. Might even let him be my teacher. I need a new adventure. He laughs when I write down his quotes

- You need another teacher?

- Oh I see what you mean. But he's different, he's a bit like me. Not my *shadow*

(First sign of psycho-babble) - Er, maybe anyone significant is your shadow?

- Where'd you get that idea? A friend is not a shadow. You're spooky, Cross. You should get out more. Anyway, Thiel said (look, I wrote this too): 'It's never a physical place we inhabit, but only the glass beads of our vanity. These we inhabit as if in a dream, sustained by centuries of beetling belief. And one such bead is dependency. It's the root of others.' I see that in myself, dependency. But I do nothing about it. I'm reverential to a fault

- You're sensible. You appreciate people, that's all

- Ah Cross, I appreciate *you.* Gimme a proper hug.

I recall I gave her a proper hug, and then she kissed me next to the lips, which I took as some kind of signal.

- Look at this. Yogi said next (really, I only write stuff I like!) 'This is our glass bead game, all our little thought paradimes. All illusion is here, the mind's need to obsessively belong to ideas created by itself. All mesmerising, all so real. This belief is our dependency, demanding further belief. The beads get more and more 'real'...' Whaddya thinking, prof?

- Of a book by Hermann Hesse called *The Glass Bead Game.* Perhaps that's what he meant. And you spell paradigms wrong

- Don't say? You're a cute intellectual aren't ya, hiding in there

- Don't call me that. I want to be your friend

- Oh you can be my friend, no problem. Let's have 'anotherr tipple', shall we?

She affects a feckless Yankee style at these moments. Says 'anotherr' like 'motherr'. And I see that her mother is lost to her. At other moments she's like the self-effacing English who approves of booky types. Under all the games she's just a child. Can't get her out of my mind. (Should but don't want to.) But I forgot to say, Libby is truly friendly. I should appreciate this. And she listens to exploiter me. Untouchable as she is, at least I don't seek to impose paradigms on her unsullied mind. I pride myself on that.

A Dark Favour

In time Libby exits the family home for a small flat on Downer Street, taking Bondy with her. Castro calls continually - and appears to ask for mercy. Her excuse to him is that financial strain forced her to seek full-time work. So, after much humming and ha-ing of a theatrical nature he announces: *So be it.* Then ever-so-nonchalantly he makes a suggestion.

Two lonely weeks pass. One fine day she finds herself outside the premises of Daemon and Associates, a firm of lawyers. Sudden shift in milieu... from artist to mother to working girl in a business? One is bound to fail the interview. She is duly called to a corner office on the fifth floor with a view of the park. A continental-looking woman stands by a window. Libby notices: heels, dark business suit, late-thirties, tallish, straight dark hair at collar-length. She looks... formidable.

- Hello Elizabeth. I am Rula Cortes, Senior Associate. (She steps across. They corporately shake) Do sit. You have a resume? So you wish to be a PA. What do you know of our work?
- Not a great deal, I'm sorry. But keen to learn.
Rula regards her, studies the one-page resume. - Mmm. A dancer and a mother. Your husband is Castro the director? But I have seen his work. I cannot say I like it. You are surprised? Actually I make a point of patronising the arts. In our own work we see only degradation
- Degradation?
- People suffer in our world. Plaintiffs, criminals, refugees, prisoners, women, children. I have seen it, and I do not like
- But you save people?
Rula gazes at her. - Yes, Elizabeth. At times we do
- Excuse me, I'm a bit naïve. But I want to help.
(Rula scrutinises) - I'm sure you do. (Micro-pause) All right, I'm inclined to let you have a trial. I will train you, but I warn you it is demanding
- Don't you want to -

- Oh, I operate on impulse.

She smiles in a way that to Libby seems oddly familiar. Libby may have looked exposed, so Rula asks:
- Are you with him? Castro?
- Actually I left. For a while at least
- I see. Not a problem then. (Thinks Libby: Why's that not a problem?) Can you stay? I'll escort you through the ropes.
Libby has the vague feeling she's been favoured. People seem to do it. Let it be, then.

Exposure

Days pass and it's a Friday. Rula Cortes has invited Libby to her favoured bar. Other lawyers from the firm are there, young males included, and some of the boys crowd round Rula (since she has a reputation for entertaining in unconventional ways).
- Jerry, Carlos. Buy Elizabeth a drink! I've pushed and shoved her about this week. Darling?
- Tequila slammer?
- Jerry! So where's your little son?
- At my friend Julie's
- Aha. Now come close, it's noisy in here. How is Castro coping with your 'new life'?
- He calls every day
- You answer?
- Sometimes
- Do you forgive?
- Actually no
- And do you like me asking questions?
- That's fine, Rula
- Brave girl. I like you! So does Carlos. He is looking
- Tell him I'm lesbian
- Perhaps you are?
- Don't mind if I am
- I would like to help - since you are confused

- Is that why you gave me a job?
- Is it a crime? You look as if you need help
- Hmm. Well, I've been to an analyst actually
- Actually I know this
- What?
- Sorry. Don't be alarmed. I make it my business to know my people. The truth is: Castro calls your phone, I pick up, I tell him you are unavailable blaa, and he curses 'that analyst Cross' for 'encouraging this marital mess'. I put one and two together. And now you are upset
- Why shouldn't I be? You all know me better than I know myself
- Not true, darling. Come talk to Carlos.

The din in the room expands: zipped-up legal types letting off steam. Libby feels light-headed. A group repairs to booths at the back. It's hot. Several rounds later Carlos and Jerry have managed to touch her up a few times. Glittery-eyed Rula plays circus master.
- Back off you lot. Married woman
- Rula's divorced! confides Carlos. Rula slaps at him and Jerry laughs.
- I'd marry ya, Rula!
- Wouldn't last five minutes in the sack with me, baby boy
- Didn't he already? calls out Carlos. And the blades leap away before fierce Rula can slosh wine and ruin their shirts.
- Arseholes. But tell me, darling Lib. Why d'you still love your Castro-man?
Libby can feel her breath, and is required to note her cleavage. At length she answers.
- What'd Castro ever need me for? A girl he could dump on and call inadequate? 'Cause he married me for always. Doesn't bear thinking about. Guess I have to, though... Since when did he despise me?
- You think that?
- I remember when we met. He was so anxious to start his company. He called me an amateur and patted me. Did he want some kind of daughter? My ballet skills weren't enough. I liked Latin but never admitted it to him. And musicals, all the camaraderie. Sparks literally flew from him. Just a mysterious brilliant guy. Always discusses himself, that's his way. I don't

blame him, he's a genius-type. Self-centred beyond my imagining, but I suppose we all are. I'm sure I am

- Me too, my sweet

- Analysis is 'not my thing', Castro used to remind me. I s'pose that's why I need him. Put my head on a platter for him to examine. Our little game, he said. He was so clever he took pains to show me the *irony* of his dominance, the silliness of his need. Yet he always managed to promote himself through it, like: 'I'm a fool - but beyond normal conception of fool! You are sorry for me, yes? And zat may be your *mistake!*

- Tricky guy

- He'd say: Alas, we are human beings, and I in my turn feel for *you*. 'Abominably we are tied to one another.' Our 'ghoulish game': how shall we resolve it? I lay bare my faults but you are forced to love me, no? He counted on me thinking he was courageous. I did like him despite all his clutter and bluster. He needed to know I wanted him, and I did in my way. But never in that brutish way he wanted then *apologised* for wanting. I wasn't wedded to him like that. Then he blames me for 'not appreciating his lonely suffering'! I end up bound to him by my own *guilt*. I'm quite dutiful you know. Am I drunk?

- You're a beautiful girl. You and me are going to be a wonderful team.

And Rula kisses her lips, enough to make Libby suspect she may be a girl's girl. But Rula is canny and says she ain't. And who makes the goddam *rules?* Later the gang goes to another bar then another. Rula seems to have a cruelty thing with young Jerry; they exit stage right. Libby and Carlos end up in some alley, and he's keen and she belatedly discovers her panties are somewhere they shouldn't be, and he gets tangled in his fly after squashing her to the wall and she stops him just in time. None o' that; married woman me. She totters off into the night. Hours later she finds herself at Julie's.

Libby Castro dutifully relays all this to her analyst. 'Castro was drunk and ranting so I recorded him on my phone.' The girl seems keen to get to the bottom of this Husband. I confess I 'think it a little pathetic'. Does she want me as voyeur, accomplice? Saves solving a problem, to smudge it all about. Castro raves:

'...I don't need love, unlike my stupid performers! You try to love me and I will do the opposite, and you have to hate me! before I draw you back. Our little push-pull game. We are all sado-masochists at the bottom. To be punished and to punish! How can love be conducted otherwise? In marriage, where is love? There is only need. Where is respect? There is only desire to destroy. Do you think people are monogamous? Do you think I will submit to bourgeois-religious moral ethos? I will not be coerced! But I might be slapped and tickled! Ha, *you* will do it. We will create some rules for our game of power, for how you and I will fuck each other over. And we enjoy because we can't escape each other! Woman, you will always come back because you need! Because we are wretched souls... Aha, now you discover the self-flagellating religious man. I am attention-seeker, I admit it. I entertain my shadow. Do you admit I am *your* shadow? I will help you admit it. And yes, I secretly need to be loved. Inside my House of Art I dangle our relationship. Only there can we have courage! Not in little domestic house, Elizabeth. Don't try to argue, you are not intellectual, you are a little feeling person. I make you feel since I cannot feel! I am not jealous of your feeling, I am realistic. I need you and you always need me. Come here, fuck you!'

She snatches the phone.
- What comes next is not dignified
- Understood. Sorry
- Not for you to be sorry.

She has a cry, so I comfort. (That's all) I suggest she lie on my couch. She does. In time, she closes her eyes. It seems the job stress, little Bondy who's restless, daily calls from Castro, drinking bouts with Rula, lack of dance, that stressy liaison with the Yogi, draining sessions with me - have made her sleepy.

Helping the Needy

In my studio one drizzly day Libby idly lets it slip that Castro (despite all the tension) has asked her to befriend one Rosita, a former model known to him from one of his bizarrer shows. Can she help? A troubled

woman down on her luck, Castro says. (Bound to be trouble since Castro recommended her) He tells Libby to say 'it's she who needs a friend' - a clever stratagem, he proclaims, since it's Libby who'll do the helping. Does Libby refuse? Well, no. Couples are bound in arcane ways outsiders cannot fathom. (I've noted it too many times.) Castro doubtless wants to remind her he's a compassionate man - and Libby allows him to assert that possibility. Does Libby have a clue about the man's machinations? One delivers messages to her ears but the wind blows straight through the house. What could he want? Not her return I'm sure. Being a man I'd say he wants to downgrade her to 'ex-partner', replacing her with 'better women' while still holding onto her for when it suits. She'll see through that, I hope! Do we see how I'm skeptical of her? (I admit it since I care beyond the call of duty.) Yeah, I'll waive my fee but I want a result. Not getting one right now. So - (she informs) she'll meet with this Rosita.
- Wild goose chase?
- No way! Others in need can take us out of ourselves.
Others in need. Good one, Libby.

The Fundamentalist

The following scenes I feel compelled to report (at the risk of taxing your readerly patience) for the sake of Libby's therapy. A week later Rula Cortes, in a swank but noisome restaurant where she managed to lure Libby with the offer of booze and food, mounts her soapbox.

- Libby, time to come to grips with bloody Castro
- Don't care to
- Listen! He's a fundamentalist. Can't cope with anything outside his rigid emotional response. Anything alien creates fear, and fear is shaming. He needs to control the emotional response of others to reduce them to his own limits. He does this by violent aggression or some repressive system such as religion or art. Are you listening?
- I'm quite tired. I've indigestion actually
- Drink. See, at his core he needs to protect his ego - which is horrified at its own paucity in a vast cosmos. One big idea became his life-raft, his flag in the desert sand! And he nurtures this idea that explains all things,

becomes its own self-fulfilling prophecy, 'self-watering logic in a desert of meaning', perfectly explicable in its cool cruelty. And because this idea is the difference between life and oblivion he'll kill or die for it. Now it's safe to question no more. And once his value-system is entrenched we all get measured by its virtues. If he destroys your life it's because you contravened the immaculate laws of his system. You must be guilty, must be subversive

- Wow, you studied all this
- You bet. Since I have a Masters in psychology besides my Law degree
- It's not Castro, he's too subtle for all that. Maybe you're a 'feminist fundamentalist'
- No no, I've been in real relationships. Failed ones!
- Takes two to tango. I have to take responsibility
- Who said that?
- If you judge others you have to judge yourself. Yogi Thiel said
- Oh bloody hell! Yogi new-age fruity loop! I heard you two have a thing
- Don't scoff. I admit he's weirdly sexy. Can't help it if you must know
- That's why you're Castro's fool
- You seem mightily concerned about my husband
- Because I know him! …I mean, I know types like him
(Libby stares) - But you don't actually know *him*. He's unique after all. Isn't he?
- Sure is
(Pause) - Perhaps you met?
- Not that I know. I told you I saw his work
- Hmm. Wait, need the loo
- You mean you need to go to the *Women's Room*
- If you say so
- D'you get the analogy?
- Not really.

Libby's gone a while. Rula has several drinks. Libby sidles back.
- I called Julie. Bondy's upset and wants me. May have to go
- Okay, you go to Bondy, but listen: why did *Fidel* Castro, Che Lenin Trotsky Mao blaa blaa - create systems that murder individualism and

romance? It's about theft of individual rights, theft of ideas, freedom, self-esteem. Cult of leader sucking people dry. Bloodsuckers!

- You compare such men to my husband? You exaggerate

- No! Your Castro uses art to desecrate the artist. Strip 'em to their 'essence' in the name of a politico-artistic theory that'll deliver us from 'naivety'. Bondage to his choreographer's ego is all that matters! You have to beware, Libby. You have to be *critical*

- I am critical! But I have to be *fair.* We all have faults - and I'm sure you know yours… Anyway thank you. And I'll see you tomorrow. (She goes to leave)

- Fucking hell

- Don't be sad, or I will be

- Am I your friend?

- 'Course you are.

She kisses Rula but Rula's not happy. The boss watches her go then orders a gaggle of drinks. Has to pay the fat bill as well. Actually, Libby didn't call Julie in the women's room. She called her husband. Asked him 'if he knew Rula Cortes her employer'. Castro neglected to see what on earth she was talking about.

Christ Dressed in Black

Next time they meet in one of Rula's shouty bars, Libby has warmed slightly to Rula's theme. She's even scribbled her thoughts. Rula for her part has learned that Libby is not such a fool, and has resolved to be a shade more subtle. Fat chance.

- Castro's the demon on your back you can't shrug off, but you *can* hold him at a distance

- Oh yeah! And I was made to dance the 'daemon' in my work for him. I wrote down what he said: 'This daemon you can't escape is your shadow, your other half, that you must dance with and hate and love and bow to and curse and be fucked by, ruined by - until it turns into your bedfellow, then your husband then your offspring. Finally your soul mate.'

- Far out! He worms in and shatters your ego

- But he said his mission was 'to introduce the shadow'. To be a 'big shadow' himself
- He's Mephisto but he wants to be *Faust*
- Whaat? (they're bellowing)
- Faust! German weirdo
- Aah, don't really know that story. But he wanted it *all*: admiration, love. And get this: he wanted to be *hated*, despised like an insect, murdered in the mind of his artists and his public! So that the Killed One could be resurrected in our *pity*. Said he's like Christ dressed in black, come to remind us of our stupid narrowness. Smash us down so he can raise us up. Wants to be the masochist, suck us in his game of sadism, 'his lifelong embrace of beauteous grimness' (You wrote it down?!) so he could prove a cynical fact: that power is everything, that our 'only dance is with death', that our 'sweaty grapple of love and hate' is the only reason to live! Is there life before death? he'd say. 'A warlord must show no softness, the devil no goodness, the teacher no vulnerability. But you, my whores (!) must show your embarrassment and your hate. He'd say that. You're my performers, you do what I can't do. It is your privilege to be debased whereas I am helpless! Help me realise my dream: to help you heal yourselves
- Oh my fucking god
- So we danced up his big idea of 'self-abasement for betterment'. But he took it to a level we didn't predict. Now he'd tell us it was all *stupid and foolish*. Fools you are (he said) to embrace the idea! But I have pity and compassion, so I charm you and save you and draw you close - until next time I require you to slay yourselves! He invites us into his game and our conscience tells us to join in... Fuck. It's tiring to talk about.
But Rula's right there. - That shitty road of abasement never ends! Your ego never feels reward. Only Castro wins! You dance till you can dance no more. And your reward? To retire and die anonymous. But our Castro sits old and alone in his armchair on the hill - overlooking the 'grey uncertain sea' of his accomplishments and muttering to anyone who'll listen: 'You see I gave up everything for them and do they love me? They don't! This is my penance, my reward. But *never* pity me!' (Muttering laugh)
Libby starts to giggle. - That's him exactly. How'd you know?
- I know a lot of things, Libby. When our dark 'saver of souls' despises

people like you because of what you *are,* then he's just a fucking nobody who wanted to be a somebody. Despising you he's lost in darkness. He knows it but clings. Hasn't the guts to give up on power. So he despises himself. But here's his secret passion: he has to love not despise, but he can't! To despise oneself: is this not exquisite pain, the razor's edge where we experience TRUTH? He believes it. So he takes the role of puppeteer of innocent others, makes them dip their souls in the poisoned ink of their own death - before he ever has the guts to throw himself in

- Whoa, deep! But you're pissed off, Rula.

Rula tipples off her bar stool. Her eyes are green and wide.

- He knows the tightrope walk between love and power, this *sado-masochism.* He could never throw himself to the wind or drown, so he makes his devil's pact. Is he Faust? He has to doctor up and damn the souls of others. He's Mephisto! He's your soul's paedophile!

(The noise and jostle of the bar crowds in. Libby backs off a bit) - Come off it, Rula

- We're all addicts and losers. Castro knows. Who can die to their own failures? Not him, that's for sure. Only the *pure* can abase themselves at this level. Are any pure in heart? No, because they'd be beyond the equation, beyond this grubby need

- Calm down!

(Some people are looking over) - Sorry, sorry. Demon drink. I bore people easily

- No. But you're getting - complicated. Personal.

They pause. A noisy group exits; the decibel level drops slightly.

- But will I always be a product of Castro? Always tied, me and Bondy?

- What were you before you met him, Libby?

- There's a thought. A product of someone else?

- One day you'll have to give up his name

- I feel he's like my duty 'cause he's my shadow. He taught me to love my shadow. Sentimental things count for me. Funny, I can't think of him anymore without feeling sorry for him

- You who take the punishment are greater than the one who dishes it out. You don't believe it because you're self-effacing - when you want to be

- All people are great in their own ways
- You're annoying! Don't you see his limits?
- I see his greatness. What a clever clever man! I mentally bow to him. But as you say, I must wean myself off since I'm a sponge and so passive
- You love to play that little game
- Now now, Ms Analyst. I require you to be neutral
- Over my dead body.

Libby is feeling wrung out again. Some people have conversations, some deliver monologues. Why's Rula so full of it? Our Libby makes a weak excuse and leaves. This time the boss makes no objection.

Taking Responsibility

Witness then, Libby's therapeutic advancement. (Apologies offered) Now reader, if you'll allow, we'll delve into the subtleties of Yogi Thiel and see what he's made of, since Libby has put her soul in his orbit and can't keep her fingers off. Thiel at forty-six discourages the title *Yogi* when people offer it. He's called a subtle man but the truth is more human. The day he met Libby Castro he pretended not to notice her. Don't think of an elephant in the room, goes the injunction. But the mind is a subtle player of tricks, a noisome presenter of elephants even for one practised in studying and controlling it. In fact mind is more subtly devilish the more one claims dominion over it. It is obviously we who are responsible for our own mind, but on the journey called wisdom / mind control, there's a big irony and paradox: at first we think we can claim jurisdiction over the 'mad monkey', then later think it's hopeless, then realise at last we always had it… yet we don't! Paradox. To see the futility of control is the first real step towards it - at which point the controlling ego realises it is a fool and withdraws a little. But only a little. So, after myriad screw-ups we learn that Attitude alone matters, the appropriate attitude being one of respect or awe or utter neutrality. Thiel knows this irony, such is his level of development, but god knows (and this he laughs about) you can't control your desire to have sex with a sweet girl who trusts in you! Oh, the master shall bow to sweet desire, since he can put this event in his pocket and act as if it's divine will - and be ruefully ironic and thwarted and let it pan out as it wants! He can fob off the suspicion that he's failed after all these years to master the 'surges of life'. But it's harder to relinquish all that subtle ego-satisfaction that he's a seriously accomplished dude! Has one really gone to seed? All yogic struggle is moral struggle, or we'd not attempt it at all. We still need to do right and dodge the wrong, need to feel there's progress / evolving / betterment / result. Yet may one have at last left morality behind? Might Thiel, never married, be allowed to crave a sweet girlfriend? He knows the religions of the world tell him the flesh of woman is a risible side-show for a serious seeker, but after all these years what's 'seeking' anyway? The road has ended in a field, and all is relative, and there's nothing but the decision of the Person, and all is divine and not divine and there's nothing to do anyway. And there's such beauty in sex that the divine gave it freely! And with the right attitude, it makes no difference if you indulge or no. So here we are taking responsibility for the world and for our own decisions. Man does his thing, and if there's going to be clingy karma, let it be. For a man with the right attitude, no karma can hold. Attitude is king. Hooray.

So goes the theory.

When Libby came to him, Thiel saw how the universe had thrust him at her just as wholly as she'd enfolded herself in him, and he saw the futility of resisting. To avoid her would be to flee from Truth, so he let her happen. Dudes are primitive at the level of sex, he acknowledges, and he's relieved to have one primal instinct (a divine irony proving the rule of purity) that lets him admit to himself he's 'no master'. Now he can grovel at the feet of the common, holiday among the rough and beggarly. It was the divine who invented ignorance, afer all. Time to *really* submit, to wash his hands in fact. Long years of discipline (for an uncertain outcome) is tough work, and somewhere deep one resents it. Thiel admits he was made a snob by yoga, since he harbours a quiet hatred for the stupid world. Now he fears snobbery so wants to be made a fool again as penance; penance to hold up the middle finger to purity, to a life of self-imposed rules; to be the devil's disciple / anarchist / rebel / guttersnipe / idiot! Let the divine take care of it! Dump control, lose yourself, and take the (pleasurable) consequences. Ha ha. Ah, there's no end to the vanity of me, a little man called Thiel, who played his cosmic soap opera with jaundiced irony, who's seen the relativity of things, who knows all. And now for the big test at the end of the cosmic road: not to give a damn!

But now looms the unattractive part, the part that makes him just an ordinary prick - and he suspects with sudden dread that it's so - that Libby sees him as just that, not any kind of man of mystery. She wants to screw: never mind if he's a cultivated man. How to swallow that? Women toss erudition to the dogs, and there's the risk! Is it to be 'pearls before swine' with her? Don't fool yourself. The reward of yoga is to admit with certainty that you're nobody, nothing out of the ordinary, and that all your long and tortuous personal effort wasn't worth a gob of spit. Have the guts to admit to your vainglory a thousand times, and you might, just might have a chance to be fulfilled. There's definitely no glamour in it. Think you're superior and you're doomed. Thiel must take her as she is (and he doesn't know what she is) - and suddenly the accomplishment of a thousand lifetimes turns on how we handle the next little dob of shit in front of us! In short, he has to respect the little girl whether she respects him or not. Noblesse oblige? That ego again! Consider the other side: that since she only wants one thing, it would be silly to try to be magnanimous or lofty or chivalrous. But does the girl *care?* Ah, assassinated by emotion. Whichever way he turns Thiel can't win. That's his ironic reward for being a yogi: he must *fail* to master emotion. And what about intimacy and affection and friendship and all those sober things? He suspects she's but lightly wedded to those. But this too is his excuse, since if she were (wedded to them) he feels he'd be incapable of offering them. Lofty Thiel no longer stoops to the simple and intimate. His manner betrays him: 'faintly patronising and ironic' (and she knows it). He can't lie! The actress and bishop then? No! One's problem is, *to be used and not valued.* Here's a bigger blow to vanity than anything - the one thing that can't ever be erased by oodles of yoga. Vanity's our ego's raiment, and ego is imperishable. Be humble then! But the price of humility would be to believe that even a foolish little girl is better than you and all your works. *And you know it is not so.* Besides, women see through all this philosophy - the idea that moral effort and study can govern a life. Libby Castro is blissfully indifferent. Yes, she'll listen to your talks and love them as romance; she'll sit in awe at your feet then shove her fanny in your face. Confusion! Tension! How to be? What posture to take, Mister Thiel?

How about *Fuckasana*? This morning Libby is present at class, which by serendipity Thiel is there to take, though as everybody knows he normally wouldn't be. And then the slow unfolding pantomime: she'll be the last to leave, and she'll come to him, and will ask a question which he'll smilingly answer, and then she will lock the door, and his mouth will go bone dry and his detached irony will fall away like petal-showers in a spring wind, and he'll babble mentally some prayer or metaphysic or other to re-assert his precious film of self - before the girl kneels before him, quietly takes down his cotton breeches and with passionate intent sucks the papery identity out of him. Yet he, bemused by excess of yoga might *fail* in their passion, might fail to return to her what she craves - and she'll have to do all the work, there in the big yellow room above the teeming streets. And her wild-eyed blondeness, her absorption, her sweat... and her long serious aching climax - will be of a perfection beyond his reckoning, and he'll realise with horror that he is but a *spectator* in the joy of a sweet girl where he could've been a real participant - if he had the guts to be the nobody that god made him and just love this baby with gratitude and awe. So this is when he gets sad and wretched and feels sorry for himself, which is utterly lowering for an ascetic. Uh, emotion *hurts*. But he can't tell her, because she's already dressed and arranged herself and gone. He's alone. And he'll have to hope for a 'next time', so he can confess to her his issues. But really, will she want to know? Though she likes him and likes the idea of him, she wouldn't presume to get so involved with such a lofty man. In fact, irony of ironies, *her simple elusiveness* has slain him, the unworldly ascetic. Now comes his torture: remembering her sweet limbs, trembling before him on the mat. And the universe seems empty. How can he learn to love torture?

It's a complicated world, Mister Thiel.

Better Not Judge

Your psychoanalyst's version of what passes between the ascetic and his girl won't I hope lead to conclusions that I'm unreliably jealous, since their relationship can't compare with the honest intimacy Libby and I share. Maybe I really don't understand this guy. Perhaps I'm a cynic and a materialist. You choose. But at least she is real to me, not some sexy acolyte or dim ingenue; for what could be more bogus, more superficial?

Thus the analyst fools himself... Libby comes to me and she's agitated. And this is annoying since I have to skirt about because she has no clue what to do and doesn't grock how she habitually enslaves her psyche to invisible masters. So our analysis is hardly any fun. All I really wanna do is gaze at her pouty lips... which now reveal:

- Listen to my latest dream, Cross. 'I walk alone in a dusty hot canyon, assailed by voices, all in need, all calling at me, wanting to caress, cajoling at me. But I, the unjudgmental, walk on. Not concerned, not attached. And none of them can stand it!' Analyse that
- Well, if you cease to judge, you don't function as an individual. It's bogus. We need our ego. Anyway, when our investment in an idea gets tested we see how impregnable our beliefs are. Remember your 'glass beads'? We're lost without our good and evil, rights and wrongs, our self-image called 'Libby Castro'. Without our gossip and criticism and verbal assassinations and praise - what are we? These are the beads of our beliefs - and how hollow they are. But it's who we are, for better or worse.
She appears to swallow that. Then:
- But Yogi said to me: 'Non-judgement is an impossible but wondrous gift. It is the bravest thing to throw your worlds away for the sake of it. It costs you your history. *And freedom has no history.* You cease to be and yet you are. And no-one can tell you what you are! Not even you. Because it never did *matter.* You're boundless'
- That's not human. That's claptrap. That is a cop-out
- No. How can you say it is?
- Could *you* have thought all that?
- Maybe not, but I dreamed it so it's true. My unconscious says so

- Beware, Libby. Use your head. Don't parrot other people
- What's with you today? How dare you!
She's (irrationally) angry, and leaves soon after. Strangely, so am I.

Lost

Let's precipitately substitute an idyllic scene. 'Empty Libby Castro lies naked atop her yogi once more. She's reduced him to a fleshly man again. And it's her charming way to unburden her thoughts while spreadeagled across him with sex exchanged one minute ago and no withdrawal. Curious position for him, and well she knows it. But she's momentarily happy. He takes in her sweet breath, caresses her fair hair. The ingenue trills in earnest tones.

- I tell Cross my analyst every little thing I do! He's my *friend* by the way. But I want to say, Thiel: Nothing ever seems to really happen to me. Who does it happen to? I feel the world is 'just as it is'. I can't influence anything. My efforts just dissolve into things as they already are. My little will is just laughed at by the way things *are*. When I dance, 'little me' is like grappling with some huge Other. I'm like naked. Little me gets drowned. What do you say to that?

What would anyone say in such a post-fuck position filled with grace?
- You said it, better than I can. May I say how beautiful you are?
- You may, since I'm drowned in you… (tinkling laugh) But you have to answer
- Uh? Then I'll say: wanting to be a person is all our form and effort. Things come to being through desire. D'you understand *Samsara?* The endless absurd desire to express what is empty. Our dream of being a person is illusion… but we still have to accept responsibility! 'Libby' is and Libby isn't. Crazy, huh?
- Curly problem, prof. Did our orgasm happen? Our 'little death'? (She flutters her eyes, the tease) If our past's all gone, are we any of it? Or the future? What's now?

Thiel is too charmed. He barely wants to talk. But he's patient with his naughty nymph and neophyte.

- There never was a past. And there's never a present since it's always gone. Ergo no future, since it can never happen. (Vaguely embarrassing to say all this right now) Life is controlled ignorance: the effort to do a thing as if it means something when in fact it doesn't

- Mmm… not even fucking? (Her sparkly eyes mess with the man) D'you know I have an idea? My idea is… 'to have no idea at all'

- I think you're rather good at having no idea

- Don't interrupt, baby boy. My idea can't flourish in this city, with all its cloying invisible human strings. Only in a desert can it flourish. I wanna go to a desert, a faraway place. Refresh. Drink the nectar of forgetting. (D'you like my phrase? I'm writing lots of stuff) Wanna be naïve, lose myself. Then return - or never return. With Bondy my son. Hope he'll be happy to come. I see now I only exist in terms of relationships: to parents, husband, son, friends, therapist, you as teacher, Libby in my own diary. I never owned my life! But do I have to give it all up - in order to live?

- Er… yes. But no, really no. And I'm not your teacher. I'm your lover now.

Thiel always feels she's untouchably outside. It quietly panics him.

- You're my *guardian.* (She licks him) And my idol and my bad conscience. (She wriggles her loins) And you're keeping me from my husband

- Your fault

- Can't control it

- Why do you come to me?

- You're a wise man. I love to suck your dick (giggles)

- Which came first? Really, I wanna know

- Some things powerful boys must never know. Living with Castro taught me that

- And will you tell mister Analyst all that happened between us today?

- Ouch! Is he on your mind?

But he's yogically sad. So she'll try to preserve a little private space for him and her.

- Mmm… I want me and you… to exist always… in a place we don't even know - is forever!

And she's wriggled terribly close and breathed on him and enveloped him like a serpent in the garden. And so again for one eternal hour she reduces the man to aching flesh... before she quietly slips from his grasp and with a fond kiss, disappears. All problems solved. Again.'

Pain of Caring

Poor old Thiel is left alone wondering if anything in his life has prepared him for the vulnerability of becoming a lover. Years of training in contemplation and moral discipline, desperate negotiation with the soul, with ignorance, intransigence, selfishness, inertia, blind prejudice, conditioning; with glimpses into rare worlds scarcely intuited beyond the restricting sense-mind; in short, his long fumbling for the light - have prepared him not a whit for this strange aloneness... of *caring* more than his lover! Detachment always allowed him the luxury of pity. But how could he have ever trained himself to control emotion? Libby is the insouciant nymph who daubs his vacantness with her lipstick, whose love is lightly economical, who makes love with resolve and what seems like happiness... and who always goes away. Thiel is a feeling man despite his rarefaction, and his challenge is this: to care for her, all the while knowing his care has no consequence or resonance in her. He must hold on to care, for it is *integrity*. It must not be tossed away, it must be taken to heart though ephemeral, must be endured though inconsequential, must be loved though meaningless. Thiel is caught in the exquisite trap of this *Samsara*: you must care although there is nothing to have, nothing to keep, nothing to call your own. Ugh, the battle for innocence!

While I the psych feel qualified to speak of this man, I wouldn't presume to judge Libby's suffering or happiness, what she hides and what she shows, to Thiel or to me or to anyone. I suppose she cares for Thiel as much as she's able, which is not to say she's deficient in feeling, but touches the universe of feeling lightly. All will exploit her but none will touch her. All will use her, all will want her according to their ways. And yes, she'll fit their mould without thought or reflection, for she's a nymph and is like soft breezes... scarcely there. Libby Castro will never solve any problems; she gives herself wholeheartedly and then she goes away. *She is the girl who is gone, who will always be so...* At least that's my analysis, or my romance. And I know how Thiel feels her absence like a wound, but he mustn't complain, such is his karma. Or perhaps he should complain, perhaps he should cry out like a wounded lost inarticulate bull! T'would be something entirely new. And he'd be at the world's mercy then, oh yeah: what bravery that'd require! But instead Thiel gathers his spiritual sophistries and composes a new treatise - one to be admired by the metaphysically empty and hated by materialist fools. See how he compensates? See how he transcends the loneliness of love. Thus he prepares for his forthcoming Yoga retreat. Libby meanwhile has invited herself to this event. And she demands to be near him, especially during the nights. In fact she's barged in where angels fear to tread. He can't communicate to her how she's a problem, but she gets her way, and he's distracted. There's tension for the first time. When Thiel delivers his speech to the assembled multitude people remark that it's unusually caustic. Others note how close Libby sits to his feet, eyes fixed on him. Do these two inhabit the same universe? Does she love him, or he her? Judge for yourself. At any rate I take the liberty of reproducing bits of his transcript.

The Person is Empty

'What is a person? We begin with a white empty screen. We shall draw dots on it and call them particles. How to define a particle? Quantum physicists try to isolate particles to study their actual nature, only to discover they seem only to come into existence in relation to one another. How then did so-called Particle A get its 'identity'? Because of the so-called identity of so-called Particle B. Why bother to distinguish so-called material particles at all since they are 'co-dependent dancing ghosts'? We face the problem of the elusive. Things only appear to exist for extremely small amounts of time, and their properties are phantom: they are here and they are not. Heisenberg noted it. In his Uncertainty Principle, a so-called particle if it appears in time has no particular location, or if it has, its duration at that location cannot be measured. Now if a particle can't be located either in space or time with any certainty it clearly does not exist with any degree of reliability. Its existence relies on faith. What intangible force pushes the field to create these particles? It is the energy, the pulsation, the magnet, the relativity, the polarity. Some call it dissatisfaction and desire. But whose? Ladies and gentlemen, the Who is awareness, intelligence. The origin of the material object is in the relationship between the *observer and the observed*. I told you the factors in the observer-observed relationship only come into existence in terms of relationship, ie: they have no self-existence. Since the observer therefore cannot be proved to exist, he needs to find a *reason* to exist - hence he conceives an object that allows him to become the subject, or observer, of a relationship. This becomes his 'hypothesis', his 'narrative', his 'discourse'. Hypothesis leads to conclusion and he invests in it since it validates him. And now the observer can permanently exist as long as he permanently observes the so-called permanent objects he calls his own. These he can believe in, because, oh my god! without this relationship he can't exist. The objects become habitual. What materialist scientist wants to admit to this? Not one, because it would blow away his role, his status, his identity. So, out of this observer-observed relationship anything can be spun, as a spider spins the web out of itself. The *idea* of knowledge comes into being, idea of time and space, and atom, and hence science, and hence particle physics (which is nowadays the 'science' of trying to materially prove that which is not materially there). All our little worlds come into being like bubbles, like glass beads. We construct the world of matter out of ghostly particles, build concrete existence on non-concrete foundations. Can one build a house out of thin air? Apparently one can.

Who or what does exist then? We should understand *the idea* of relationship, idea of negation. Yin-yang, you-me, love-hate, good-bad, observer-observed. If a thing can't exist except in relation to something else, we have the following options: (1) neither exists at all (2) both exist, in which case they would have to be permanent and unchanging which clearly they are not (3) both are exactly the same thing, which clearly they can't be since there is a relationship between them, or finally (4): both are completely different, which they clearly can't be since neither exists prior to the other, ha ha. Under the paradigm we have set ourselves we must find an answer - any answer - or we will choke, or disappear up our own backsides. Or never fall in love again. Perhaps the Buddhists have it sussed when they say all is interconnected. But if everything be so, where is the boundary between any 'thing' and another? If interconnected, there could be no boundary, therefore no interconnection. Thereby it is one big soup, no particles at all, nothing individual. All is One. Therefore nothing happens. *Nothing ever happened.*

But the idea of observer and observed persists! If subject and object come into being as a result of one another, then both are phantoms; they dance a ghost-dance. Forever. And if forever, never. Listen: Conscious Being through the force of pure pulsating energy allows 'time' and 'space' and 'cause' to come into existence as the matrices of so-called 'events'. But if the event is nothing but the observer, then seer and seen are simultaneous and therefore beyond (invented) time and space. Thus we claim to measure in some matrix called time and space that which can't possibly be measured. And that which can't be measured can only be claimed to exist, it can't be proved. You choose your own paradigm, ladies and gents. We are seated in the power of powers, and what do we do with it? We let our judging intellect run rampant! And all our worlds will last forever, and we will struggle forever since we believe in them forever. Welcome to your own life-movie at 24 frames per second. We have no choice but to dwell in belief. Belief is what holds the worlds together. The Jew pops on his skullcap and lo, he is a Jew. The Islamist bangs you over the head with his Koran and lo, he is a Muslim. The Christian emotes over Jesus and lo, he is a Christian. The Communist invents a nice box for you to live in, the size of a coffin. The Capitalist expands it to the size of a house, with a bunch of expensive bling and a crippling mortgage. Some of us need to be loved, some need marriage, some sex, some religion… choose your cage! We all need cages and crutches, and that ultimate crutch, ultimate cage - is the need to exist as Person. How to appear to be a person? You have to believe it. How to believe it? Establish a relationship with something, someone. But what's the boundary between you and the other? Nil. You and it are a single dance. You don't believe this? Try living without air, without light, try living without body or love or sex. *Do I come into being because you are there?* I believe I do. And am I lonely? Yes, we are unborn and do not die. And we *are* eternal, timeless, spaceless, borderless – yet here we sit, listening to my pain-in-the-arse lecture. And here am I delivering it! This will be my last speech on this subject... A very good evening, and a very successful life, to you all.'

Poor plangent Libby is distracted by this diatribe on emptiness. Wants to assure herself his esoterical tone won't cancel their breathless love experience. It's a losing battle. Thiel is making an almighty effort to distance himself, and she has neither the commitment nor savvy to try to mend their issues. That Thiel did not look or smile at her as usual, upsets her, and he seemed sad at the end. She seeks him out. He's alone in his room.

- Thank you for the talk. It was... illuminating
- A talk only a man 'd give
- True, but a clever one all the same
- I don't wish to be clever. I wish to be true
- You said: 'Do I come into being because you are there? I believe I do.' Was this for me?
- I'll let you decide
- Have I upset you?
- In a way only a woman could
- How's that? Please tell
- Must I be your teacher? When your actions are the assured violations of a woman at ease with her ignorance?
- Beg your pardon?
- You're not interested in the content of my talk
- That's unfair! Listen to me. If a girl like me gives herself to you, then you should know that it is not nothing
- Does she give herself?
- Oh yes she does. She's your little 'particle', your little dust mote! And she wants to fulfill *you* in the only way she knows... Don't sneer at me, Thiel
- Are you 'devoted' to me then?
- Why not?
- I don't want devotees! I want you to care... about me. (Pause) And it costs me to say it
- But why?

- You know why. Because I'm in love with you
- Are you?
- You don't acknowledge feelings now?
- All right, you know best
- No Libby. But excuse me, I'm wrong. You don't acknowledge *men*. You're actually alone… Ha! Like me. I should appreciate it but strangely I don't. I want you like a child wants its… (he stops)
- Its mother. Sure. Castro wanted me to have his child and be his child. Where was his respect?
- Do you respect yourself, since you stayed with him?
- What would you know about my marriage?
- Teach me. No, I mean it, teach me
- Okay. All right. Take your finger out of your cosmic arse and show me you're a man
- Don't be primitive
- Show me, fucking saint on wheels!
- You'd sell yourself out?
- Fuck your famous purity. Come on! Come and get me - soft cock!

Bullseye. Thiel is overcome by the strangest feelings, ones he barely knew existed. He comes at her. Their eyes meet. He takes her by the hair; she gazes up at him. He slaps her with force. She gasps. He pushes her to the floor. He rips her cotton-candy dress. She's winded. He flings her limbs. Still no resistance! The woman is ruthless enough to know her man is truly out of control. She cries out only a little bit as he takes her from behind. While he's crying. She won't resist. Because now… they're one.

Minutes later, bundled in a corner, Libby finds she's bleeding slightly. She spies Thiel at the far end, bunched up with his head in his hands. She goes to him, puts her cheek to his, brushes his face with her lips. And for a long quiet time she empathises. Then she dresses herself, and steals away.

Wounded Confusion

The mystery girl hurries from Thiel's retreat to the house of her friend Julie. There, little Bondy is playing with Suzie La La. Julie minds her boy a lot, Libby knows, and she's careful around her. On this occasion Julie says nothing... 'But Julie's looking at me. Why does she always do that? Why does she have no husband, not even a man?' Under Julie's eyes Libby imagines the body of Thiel. 'Oh god but I will go back to him. I wish I had the guts to not. Don't want to think of my dark husband. The pressure's making me sick. I wanna prolong the delirious trance of sex. Even with violence. Thiel turned his gaze to me as if he needed me. Why would a man like that need me: can't he see what I am? Oh I can't ever analyse, can't grasp. Barely myself as it is. Vacant. Someone has to define me. I fulfill other people: am I their fool? When do they fulfill me? I'll let Julie wait on me. I know she wants it. Last time in her bedroom she put her arms about me. It was more than a hug. Our hearts were beating. She wanted... something. I can't respond the way she wants. She embarrasses me. She's hopeless! Like her child - Suzie La La? Who gives a kid a name like that? Oh yeah, Bondy did. Anyway Julie makes me lonely and sad, because I know the truth: she's like *me*. But I mustn't fail to care, and mustn't worry either. Worrying makes me suffer. Why should I suffer? Love is a curse... (She thinks of Thiel) To share, isn't that love's currency? Must share myself with others, mustn't be selfish. Mustn't be alone.'

Shadow Man Comes

So, fleeing from pillar to post, Libby wades into Rosita's world... Rosi the notorious, the model and actress formerly known to Castro.

On this drudgy Saturday Rosita is concocting a theme party at her flat. 'We'll trawl back in time: do gothy Eighties grunge, pills and cocktails, shiny lights, trance and greed! Gonna fake it like there's no tomorrow!' proclaims our lanky and lewd self-promoter. Rosi has her reasons and never says what they are. Her used and second-hand party people get it though: hanging in the strobey pulsing gloom her rent-amigos will get their rise from Rosi, taking bets on a doom-laden end - maybe spilling her guts in the white-tiled bathroom, or ending as a partnerless haggard figurine spreadeagled on a bed in the dead morning? *They* won't be there, having scuttled away, just as in the dark they crowded about. No worries! Right now all such denouements are postponed as rebel-slut Rosi tosses ecstasies and sneers and distorted love and heavy spaniard wine about the ego-vortex of herself. And Libby Castro just turned up. *Darling! We waited!* Solitary from night air and her gluey thoughts, Libby is startled by the pulsing grunt and sweat. The host parades her like a trophy-fish and the room consents to fete Rosi's special girlie. How will she swallow this latest blondy peachy compliant little paramour? Rosi's all bisexual liability - that embarrassy abandon we all like to suck on - but tomorrow we'll be sober and clean since there's 'such a thing as stability and order and being an adult'. Under the general glee, Libby has bruises that shout unsolved business with her yogi... And she suddenly sees: he got angry when I treated him like a child and didn't take him seriously. But really, I don't know *how*. Oh what a narcissist he is! Flint-eyed Rosita kisses our blondie's furrowed brow, and Libby laughs on cue and hates the sound of herself but pushes it off like all the other little issues in her life. Languid Lib can't fail to gulp the frothy cocktail, offer her tongue for the yellow pill, get fingered and breathed on by slender girls, get her sweaty tits kissed by stray men, cavort with jockeying strangers in homage to The Cure, Ramones, Duran Duran... all the while letting Rosita chew her up with looks across the room that whisper: *be mine.*

At length the crowd ghosts away. Libby knows she'll be last to leave, if at all. 'What of Bondy? Sweet Julie 'll feed him, since I'm not *there*. But Rosi needs me.' For Rosita's mood has turned. The girl has rings about her green eyes - a sunken vamp in red leather skirt and rougy-pouty lips that ever incense her male hordes. She's so sorry for herself.

- Libby Libby lie with me. Or gemme a drink. Some fuckin' party. My arse too fucking sexy, you reckon?
Her cellphone rings. It's three am. Libby picks up. Voice of a foreign man.
- This is not Rosita
- No, her friend Libby
- Hola, 'friend Libby'. Is the girl here?
- Hang on
- Did I say I want to speak with her?
- What's yer name then?
- Some kind of party? She threw a party?

(Rosita is staring) - Might've. You weren't invited

- Ha! That I care not about. Tell her 'Adios'. [CLICK]

- Adios, jackass.

(Libby sees she wants to hide, but too late) Sorry darling. I guessed he was -

- Lemme *guess*: some arsehole wants to repeat a pants-down episode but won't tell his name.

(Why would she lie to me? thinks Libby. But reader, why wouldn't she?) And Rosita turns up her nose, flings her legs askew on the couch.

- Come here darling, I need it.

So Libby obliges, gets smothered in alcoholic lips. They tangle bodily. But it's not actually fun. Libby slips away before dawn.

Cock Fight

In cock-eyed search for answers to her husband problem, neutered Libby asks Castro to 'meet up with Thiel and talk to him'. Castro obliges her - by inviting Thiel to his panel discussion at the city's upcoming Arts Festival. Libby is at first shocked at his presumption, then lets herself be persuaded that Castro's baneful ploy is in fact a clever idea. Deep inside her soul she wants her hairy husband to despise Yogi Thiel, though she doesn't see it.

The seminar is titled *The Spirit of Art*, and the room is more or less packed, chiefly with theatre and art students. The moderator, a tall miss in heels and horn-rim glasses is flanked by Wallen the bespectacled writer and Thiel, dressed in sober Indian-style shirt and slacks. He looks comely, contained. Not so, Castro. The beefy bear peers about, all beady eyes and twisty mouth. Libby confessed to me she felt a twinge of her old admiration for him... To begin, he tosses a spray to the room:

- Art defines existence. Existence is defined by struggle and art is the quintessence of creative struggle!

Thiel steps in, without hesitation. - If you think existence is anything but absurd, then my friend, you're asleep.

Ooh, good start. Thiel evidently decided on 'ambush'. Libby squirms, looks about - and suddenly spies Rula Cortes at the back. What's she doing here? Castro booms:

- You say asleep? My friend, I am not a bullshit-artist who dispenses soporific yogi claptrap to children desperate for someone to turn their eyes from ugly reality

- Oh, I merely ask them to accept themselves. I can't help it if *innocence* is beyond the sweaty human ego

- Forgive me for sweating, ladies and gents! No yogi is jealous or smelly, or petty or judgmental. He has no ego!

- Or he's human, and suffers what all people suffer. Perhaps you naively romanticise, never having understood souls who crave innocence?

(People are concentrating) - I understand myself and my shit and my lies. And my *ignorance* and my failure. I see brave ones who find ugliness and darkness and shadows within, and face these. And irony of ironies, they find beauty!

- Beware of beauty! Instead we must trade in sad unfulfillment. Like prostitutes, your artists will never be out of business

- And religion will never be out of business!

(Moderator) - Gentlemen, could I -

- Yoga has little to do with religion, Mister Castro

- That's a lie! And it is the artist who is the true modern seeker

- Yoga is no fad or fashion, though you apparently just stumbled on it

- I see it is your habit to patronise those who seek truth in unusual ways

- No, I applaud your struggle. A pity that it is littered with victims who serve your vision then form a carpet of bones on your personal march to notoriety

- Not so. I am as misunderstood and as obscure as I ever was. And proud to be so

- Proud is the word. A real teacher gives *respect*

- Does respect mean to pander to their ignorance, Mister Thiel?

- Not at all, but what of love? One day love might creep up and slay even you

- I will die for nothing - not even love!

And he grins to the audience. Who grin back. The pingpong-necked moderator is dying to get a word in, but this do-gooder out of her depth won't win here.

- Perhaps you are both influential teachers fulfilling the same need? Perhaps art and spirituality come from one source? Professor Wallen, would you comment?

Perhaps perhaps perhaps. Wallen takes refuge behind his glasses; he's no fool. Castro's just warming up.

- Mister Thiel, I am not accustomed to handing my wife to a charlatan who fills her mind with anodyne new-age bulldust, but who can't keep his cock in his trousers!

Thiel actually guffaws, and so does the crowd. The moderator gulps severally. But this is theatre and the punters seem to appreciate Castro's self-promoting righteous moralist turn, where everyone knows he's the opposite.

(Thiel) - And I am not accustomed to exploiting a string of young women (one of whom might be one's wife) in my onanistic masochism-quest using 'art'. I'm not interested in sado-masochism, Herr Director.

How could Thiel be so ready to dish the dirt? thinks Libby back in the tenth row. She vaguely wants to leave. But the audience is having a ball. Maybe there'll be a punch-up.

- Women are 'sacred' are they not, mister lapsed Yogi?
- They're certainly dispensable
- What? Are you mysogynist?
- You care for the feelings of no-one, Mister Castro, and that is the secret of your success - as much as you despise success
- Perhaps it's also the secret of yours?
- My 'success' is measured in loneliness and solitude
- Ladies and gentlemen, a handkerchief for the outcast! Come to my theatre. I'll have you crawling about in the dirt with the rest of us
- I wish I *could* dance. No, in fact I dance with the curmudgeon in myself. I am the fool and must admit to it a thousand times
- The fool is 'holier-than-thou' no doubt
- Dare you admit you're a fool?
- I foolishly admit you are one. Ha ha. In the 'cosmic' sense of course

- Come now, Castro. Should you not feel compassion for all the foolish ingenues and seekers who willingly serve your artistic vision?
- Have you seen my work?
- Perhaps
- Then you will see they are not foolish
- Why not? They do anything for you, I'm told. On or off stage. And perhaps a stage is a mere convention by which we dupe an audience. Like this one. But what happens in private is more interesting.
The moderator clearly wants to put a clamp on now. She flaps her notes, starts sentences and fails to end them. Castro has made his decision.
- What do you accuse me of, yogi?
- Ask your wife. She's right here in the audience
- You dare to speak of my wife?
- Ask her how she feels about her 'artistic experience'. Whether she felt nurtured - or betrayed.

Yo! Castro stands up. His sweaty bulk towers over Thiel. Thiel doesn't move but smiles instead. *Libby?* he says mildly, and looks Libby's way. Heads turn. Castro grabs Thiel by the shirt-front, pulls him to a standing position and head-butts him in the chin. Thiel buckles. The moderator totters on her heels, slaps out at Castro with her note pad. Student types at the front whoohoo and holler. Castro, heaving in his cream jacket, delivers an inflated bow and stomps to the exit, shoving the moderator's chair as he goes. Thiel is dazed. The poor woman flutters over him. Wallen stays schtum behind his glasses. Libby in the crowd sits knees jammed like she wants to pee. Rula Cortes comes down the aisle, squeezes into her row and pulls her out. People are laughing and ogling and pointing.
- Hey that's the wife of Castro! And isn't that his *girlfriend?* What a dude! Yo!

Honour Killing

As a proud and capable woman, Rula Cortes likes to wield influence, likes to publicly demonstrate her big heart. Libby has certainly sheltered under the umbrella of her capacious favours these last months. She notes that Rula has plenty of admirers, but where are her friends? Rula, no fool, has taken pains to explain to Libby 'how her competitive crusade against World Evil distances those who might love her, and how status and notoriety in law and politics exact their price'. But our Rula would 'have no qualms about paying, as long as someone special understood her sacrifice'. It appears this someone could be Libby, since nowadays she's Rula's intimate helper.

Libby's artist spirit lets her respond to the theatrical in Rula, though she senses that the woman is frustrated and brutish and vulgar beyond the pitying of it. It's a little thrilling though to sit in the eye of the hurricane, and Libby makes it her business to share the boss's joys and sorrows. She even suffers to be ministered to and patronised over her marriage failings (as we saw). Libby takes it all in with the subtle contempt the small unsullied people of the world have for the greatly tortured. True, Rula's big energies embarrass... but our Lib affects to love her for just those qualities. Besides, in these last months Rula's legal office has been a refuge from the troubling demands of men. Libby has to admit she's grateful despite her employer's gross demands, sweaty machinations, anti-fundamentalist rants; despite all the horror stories from Syria and Yemen and Libya and Ukraine, the voices and faces of asylum seekers, the noisy headlines, Zoom calls, shoutings down the line to lawyers and activists in far-flung places who don't speak English properly. Libby wonders how she'll endure all these peoples' suffering without being wounded in her heart. And oh when will she dance again? It's been exhausting... but no man-problems so far. Libby might yet wonder how and how much our hefty lawyer will reveal her inmost self to her arty little secretary. The answer lies in a Man.

One late evening, after a shambolic day in which Cortes has tried and failed to secure temporary asylum for some Jordanian woman, Libby finds her behind her desk, skirt shoved up, lipstick askew, bottle and glass in front, Radiohead gouging out the air. She spots Libby hovering by the door, ready for home.

- Not so fast, Secretary. Need your advice
- I have to pick up Bondy from -

- I already called up your 'Julie', no fuckin' worries. Made a few other calls as well. More on 'at later. Know what? Some women are so fucked over by men in this world they don't even wanna live. Wadda ya say to that?

Rula's spray is indeed the stance of the needy arrogant; she 'confides' in Libby but has no belief she'll get the point. Lib bides her time, turns down the music.

- Who're you referring to?

Rula stares (as if to say, don't you get the fucked-up extent of the world?).

- Had a few bevvies, so fucken what. There's a Jordanian girl coming 'ere by taxi right now. She's got nowhere. I'm having 'er at my place

- The girl who's running from -

- 'Course it fucken well is. You're on the *ball*. You'll be looking after her for the next days. Feed her, wash her stuff, get her about. She must have work, we'll find her work. Here's money. (She fumbles in a drawer) Shit, haven't got money. You pay, 'll pay ya later

- Rula, are you all right?

- No! Got a bone to pick. Just had freaking Castro - that's your husband

- on the line

- Why did he ring here?'

- 'Cause he knows I'm your employer and wants to use me to get to you. You slow?

- What'd he say?

- What didn't he say? Accuses me of all sorts of corruption and bullshit

- Like what?

- Use your 'magination! 'Zat the intercom? Go see. Fuck I need a drink

- I'd better get home

- To Bondee? To your little boy! Uh - where's *my* little boy? I don't have any little *boy*.

Exhaustion is curdling Lib's stomach. The doorbell rings. She peers at the street display: a scarfed figure in raincoat, five floors below. Libby pushes the button. Rula shouts through the door.

- Why'd the fuck you marry him anyway? Fucken sadist...

Libby hurries back in. - What? What? Rula?

- Don' look at me in that tone o' voice, sec'etry.

Libby stares at her as she slurps her drink. Then the lift-bell. The Jordanian

steps into the corridor. Libby watches. Under the headscarf, a severe expression. She peers about. Silence in the night office. She spots Libby.
- Hello? Is Miss Cortes here?
- Rula?
- Don't let her see me like this! Get her in your office.
Rula shovels bottle and glass in a drawer, attempts to stand. Libby ushers the girl down the corridor.   - Ms Cortes will meet you shortly.

Inside her office there's a silence. The girl is petite, good-looking. So here's another girl hiding from the world of men. She vaguely reminds Libby of someone. But now the refugee drops her head, starts to cry and tries to stifle it. We hear steps in the hall. Libby pulls the door to. Rula seems to be at the intercom. Her steps recede. The Jordanian glances about. Libby thinks of saying something but the lift-bell sounds. Now heavier footsteps go past, toward Rula's office. Her door slams. Libby peers out. There are voices, and one is male. She tiptoes to Rula's door. The heavy voice... *Oh my god. It's Castro.*

* * * *

- Has she gone?
- Ha ha! She is *here!* I fooled you again
- I don't believe you. Listen to me. She must not work here
- It was your shitty idea in the first place, so put up with it
- You don't need to punish me but you *like* to punish. Will it help you? Will it?
 There is a clumping and rustling sound. And a thump.
- Cunt! Don't you touch me! You think I'd ever give in to you?
- But you will, Rula. Because you want to. You always want to
- If I'd wanted your child I would have given it to you. You fool!
- Bitch! You took it. But you will not take away my wife
- Fuck you! I make my own decisions
- But you suffer! And you'll suffer always.

Another rustle, and this time a heavy crash. Several thumps and grunts.

Libby can feel her eye-sockets stretching. A creeping cold infests her waters. She can't move. Suddenly, the foreign girl appears in the hallway. She's swaying, comes toward Libby, grasps at her. Libby crumples, her hand clutches at the door handle. It flings open. She lurches inward into the room.

And Castro is there, towering over Rula who is spread over the desk, her legs flung wide. He grunts. His pants are undone. Libby stares like a possum in the headlights.
- Elizabeth! So your boss *lies*. I thought you were not here. (He zips his fly) At least you see the truth. Rula has betrayed me. She also betrayed *you*. It is regrettable as you see... Who is that person?

It's a measure of the bastard that he can divert attention from himself at moments like these. And now the slut Rula who was frozen *in flagrante* adjusts her skirt, strides past Libby, peers stonily at the girl.
- She fainted. Nobody fed her. Bring her in.
So Libby and her husband manhandle the Jordanian onto a sofa.
- Elizabeth will make tea. Castro, go to the night-supermarket and buy food. Do you think you can manage that?
- I will go. Yes. Yes.
And he does. And Libby totters off and brings tea. And sexual Rula meantime has re-done her make-up. The girl sips the tea, clutches the cup. Castro lumbers in.
- Ham sandwiches, some pies, not halal I suppose. But let her eat. What is her name?
- My name is Sophia... Sophia Zohran. I am the refugee
- She speaks English. What's she doing here?
- Her father and brothers want to kill her because she'll marry a film-maker. I try to get asylum.
Castro grunts and peers at her. - What does she do?
- I am an artist. I make designs. Miss Cortes will look after me.
- Hmm... (He speaks as if to a pet hamster) Listen to me. We are going to save you. Eat the food. The food. Where will she stay?
- At my apartment I assume

- Or... she can come to me. She can stay at my house. This is better. Sophia: all right?

Sophia gazes at Rula. Rula appears to 'think hard', then says: Yes, go to this man's house. This is better. You can trust him. I will visit. Don't worry. Everything will be all right.

Castro beams. - Okay okay. Good good. And Elizabeth. You will help me take her there...

But Libby is not to be found, by anyone.

* * * *

Libby Castro wraps her arms about her in the night street. Those snarling voices behind the door! It makes her shiver... Yet there are things in this life she absorbs with minimum explanation. 'So Rula's one of Castro's girls. Should have known. Got her pregnant. (He likes offspring, wherever they come from) And she aborted it and he's angry. She wants him angry. She wanted that baby. But she cut it off to spite his face. And she hates him but wants him back. *For a repeat.* Why latch onto me then? Ah, to get near to him and avenge herself. And she's jealous of my Bondy. Well that's that. And no more job. The Arab gets my job now. And abuse that goes with it! That Rula's out of control. How should I react? *Stab the fucking whore in the neck.* No - no honour in that. I'll go away, go away. I'm a dupe. Deserve it. Left my husband, lose my rights. That's moral. Anyway I'm sort of free now. And Rula isn't. Nor him, silly fool. But who can I talk to? Cross... would he get it? Maybe Thiel. *Poor* Thiel. Or Rosita? God no. Go to Julie. She wants to be close to me... but I just *can't.* Perhaps I should go face my husband. Oh that Rula really lowered me. (She starts to sob) I don't like any people. Not in the whole shitting world.' Libby Castro ends up in an alleyway somewhere. She rubs something out, painfully, behind a skip bin.

Girl in a Corridor

Your narrator this morning got a call from Libby's loyal friend Julie, describing how she found Lib alone in the corridor of her apartment block in the small hours, semi-clothed and shivering. Julie is breathless and alarmed, doesn't know what to do, fears Bondy will see his mother like that. I empathise. But why call me? At our next session Libby has nothing to say about Julie's embarrassing find. Instead she prattles zestfully about the Castro vs. Thiel debacle. In fact she babbles. I never pretend our analysis offers formal healing: I crave her company though I tell myself I don't. And she whose instincts in that quarter are as tuned as ever, lets me wallow in my Elizabeth Complex. No doubt it flatters. Still, I protest that she's been typically muddled and lazy in her effort to solve the Castro problem. She takes this medicine with a sort of doe-eyed irony before giggling like a girl and returning to her juicy topic.

- Did I say I crept through Castro's window on the night after the conference and rewarded him in the dark with all his favourites including a face fuck?
- Er, you didn't
- I had to let him have it, since I'm leaving him for good. I think it's best
- For good?
- But I won't be running to Thiel! I'm going back to discipline
- Oh. You'll dance again?
- Oh yes! (Pause) Well, maybe... oh, how will I do it?
- Are you still at the lawyers?
- Umm... (Pause) That Rula wants to rule me! We won't talk about that
- Why not?
- 'Cause I'm seeing sweet Rosi. (I fail to get the segue) And I'm learning that my evil husband knew Rosi extremely well
- Yeah?
- It's not what you think. Rosita needs my help
- Right. Now, this 'war' at the conference. Surely it struck you as sad?
- 'S not my problem
- I recall you were shocked
- Well I'm over it
- Just like that
(Suddenly) - No! Not 'just like that'. It cost me! Everything costs me, mister analyst (She glares)

- Have it your way
- Who's jealous! The thing with you is that I tell you things I tell nobody. And that's why *you* should be happy round me. ...Oh come here, idiot.
And she kisses me on the mouth. Her mood's weird today.
- Lighten up, Cross-patch! Now listen, I have to tell about Rosita. I've kept up my diary. Listen...
But sadly, her analyst is fed up with contradictions and diversions.
- Julie's upset about you standing half naked in her corridor in the night. There's a pause. - So she blabs it to you
- I was surprised. That she called me I mean. (Silence) I don't judge you, you know
- Is it any business of yours?
- No.
She glares, then the eyes soften. - I was going to talk to you about it
- Do what you like, Libby. No-one owns you. Or perhaps you feel people do. They certainly fight over you.
She looks away. Her pause is so long I start to lose heart.
- Listen to this. Once I worked as a chambermaid in a city hotel. I had to go into all the rooms. Used to serve rich people. Despised 'em. Sometimes I'd lock the door and strip off all my clothes and kneel by their bed, and do it. Used to linger - with my finger. Just for the danger. Then I'd take a shower and use their soap. Ha! And then I'd do my work. I never needed anyone, see. It was more fun alone.
(Her stories are always slightly theatrical) - Should I believe it when you claim it was more fun alone?
- You think I'm afraid to need someone
- Oh but you are, so you guiltily compensate. You get 'involved' (get married) because you think you should be dutiful. But a part of you doesn't give a damn. You might even rely on violence.
The violence bit was dishonest, but I'm inclined to shake her up.
- I should hate you, Cross
- Don't. Because I'm honest with you at the end of the day
- Love to believe it
- It is hard to reveal yourself
- You think my little jerk-off story was hard?

- No. It's just hard for you to admit to *why* you do it
- Careful, mister analyst
- I have nothing to lose. *You* do
- You're more fucking stupid than I thought.

Ugh. Flying blind here.

- Why? 'Cause I'm in love with you - is that what you want me to admit?
- Listen, you cunt! I come here over and over, I talk to you, tell you *everything*. I may not be an intellectual, but when did *you* put yourself on the stand, on a stage to be looked at and fingered and analysed and abused and duped and fucking shitting well manhandled? What do you do in your poky little office? Jerk off when I'm out the door? If I say I like to be alone, then I fucking well like to be alone!

(I never saw her like this) - People inhabit strange and different rooms, Libby. But you sort of 'creep down the corridor past their doors'. Where's the exit? Is there one?

- Whaaaat? *Uuugghh!*

Her little mouth-scream makes me shrink. Too far! Amateur. Pompous bastard. The naked nymph fingering herself in the rooms of strangers *replaces* the lonely girl standing in the corridor.

- *Analyse this!* She looms over my desk and shoves half its contents to the floor. I fail to move. She leans over, parts legs, shakes her arse, lolls her tongue and puts a finger in her crotch. Is she wanting me to improvise? Now she grabs my lapel, twists me over my desk, splatters a leg across me. Never been this close! Libby? She makes pained moaning sounds. Then a big sigh. - Ooh look daddy I pissed my pants. All wet! (It isn't) I want to shove her off but she clings and pushes her crotch at me. Little frowning ragdoll intent on her work!

- Don't fuck with me, Libby
- No really, I do it for you, sexy analyst!

But she loses heart, and slithers to the floor. Oh, you wanna be sorry for yourself. Precious artist and your stage emotions. Where's any outlet for *my* anger? Oh that's the point: there's no outlet for her. Don't interfere with a patient! Elizabeth Castro's my patient - slumped to a foetal ball. I sidle out the door. What's an analyst to do with himself? Meander, stand like a lump, stare at a mother in the street with a toddler on a leash, stare at all the world's strange ordinariness. Shit it - back we go. She's sitting up like the mermaid of Copenhagen. I kneel to her in my crinkled suit. Suddenly feel a need to cry. She's like limp, vacant. I hug her a while. She lets me. At length she shrugs me off, straightens herself, walks out. I hurry to follow, down the path.

- Libby?

She sighs, turns wearily at the gate. I'm an extra in her snuff movie.

- Don't worry about me. I'll see you. I'll call, all right?

I tell her all right. And watch, as she walks off vaguely down the street-corridor.

Oblivion

When she did call two long weeks later, I let her know it felt bad to be the butt of her generalised men-hatred. But she demurred, seeming keen to defuse it all like everything else horrid that happens to her. Anyway, she comes on over, and seeing my discomfort offers a hug which I formally accept. I grab at our safety valve of talk - but she seems intent on her latest sodding episode with Rosita. By contrast, the Rula-Castro affair costs me polite agonies to prise from her. When she wants to evade, Libby bungs on the charm and flutters her sexy eyes. (Tells it all eventually though, since she's a good girl) Would any of it explain our little scene over my desk? Nope, dark corridor there. But! At least she bounces back. Though some people never learn: there are powerful things they've no resistance to. Such a one is the lurid Rozzitaaa! Now here's a real master of hysteric scenography.

Presumably (the theory goes) if we feel and express ourselves truly madly deeply in this life we'll amount to something profound. Our hysteric Rosita is head-hunting a thing that doesn't want to occur: justice from a man. Don't even mention being happy; happiness lost is dead and buried. Why do women never get it? I may be a mediocre shrink (prejudiced, pompous etc) but at least I think. Sado-masochist games are contagious and that's the beauty of them: you hang out sadly for the sadist and he never lets on he gives a damn. You'll do anything to prick his conscience, make him look at you - but above all you have to spite him, punish him. Why? 'Cause you gotta win him back. And all your other fucked-up philandering is for him as well. Here's the twist: it doesn't really matter who he is; any man will do if your name's Rosita and you're lost in the chaos of yourself. Might even kill yourself for selfish love. Meanwhile other acolytes are there to be impressed. Libby sure is. Rosita is a legend to all her friends, but (as we've learned) none of them will touch her with a metaphoric pole. They've seen it all, heard the speeches: 'People! If you've a problem, screw it! Welcome to my cult of destruction. Die free. Oblivionne!' But now Libby is around so it's: 'Are you scared, are you bourgeois? Men are bastards (except your Castro). Shall we show 'em? Shall we fecking show them?' Yep, every sodding weekend, Libby trawls with Rosi through her bars, parties, nefarious clubs. And Libby's conscience says it spells the death of discipline - which nags at her. Always feels she wants discipline, wants to be dominated by it. 'Dance, yoga, stern tellings-off, all that... someone has to impose it, a Thiel or a Castro; they always did it to me. But will Rosita? And will I put on weight and will my looks fade? Don't laugh at me, I need my vanity, it's part of me.' Rosita spits in the face of vanity and discipline, but it takes discipline and vanity to be so systematically dissipated, especially when you've a spite-filled goal in mind. Rosi's problem is she needs people to believe she's a scandalised victim, but still has to be nasty-naughty enough to punish the evil guy. People end as collateral damage. Her ever-shrinking corral of amigos proves it. Catch 22. Libby realises she's the end of the line - or perhaps Rosita flourishes permanently in the ante-rooms of Doom.

Tonight (as Libby tells it) we're in the Glue Bar, which happens to be a haunt of *Raul,* the hated one. Rosita is in the ladies room pissing money against a wall or vomiting it down a hole, one of the two. And suddenly there he is, Raul, the man himself. Libby knows him from his photograph which Rosi once theatrically ate in front of her. Oh what to do? This should be the big moment: shoot-out at not-ok corral. But he looks smaller than the meta-monster Rosi has created in Libby's porous mind. A young stud alone in a bar... younger than her actually. God! Libby does not much premeditate at the best of times - so she steps over, holds out a hand and says:

- I'm Libby Castro, Rosita's friend.

Dark eyes stare from a handsome face. - Is she here?

- Yes, but -

He heads for the door.

- Wait! Libby finds herself in the street, and he's walking away.

- I just thought -

He rests his dusky eyes on her. - Thought what?

- Er, wanted to know - who you were... because -

- Because you have heard so much. (He steps close) All of it is lies.

Blond Libby in her strap-heels and blue-tight dress smells truth in his perfume. She glances at the pub door and so does he. And he shrugs. - Walk with me then.

Loyalty challenge! Oh well, I'm no use to Rosi if I never met the guy! I can talk to him, find out er... things. She follows Raul. Suddenly she sees she hasn't thought about anything much these weeks - like why she's with Rosi at all. Just kind of jumped in a big hole of drinks and drugs and babble and... the other thing. This guy's fitted shirt and ball-hugging slacks... he looks *fit*. Ah I know: entry point.

- I talked to you on the phone after Rosi's party. Remember?

He doesn't, or says he doesn't. No matter, start fresh.

- So where... will we go?

He smiles, looks at her. She sways in front of him, handbag dangling from a finger. *This way.* He's brisk, she skips along. One block, then a door. Oh. He steps into a passage, she follows, he clicks the door. Now she's against a wall. Surprise. Her panties go down in a single thrust. His fly expertly opens, he pulls her leg about him, crushes her up the wall. They mouth-breathe. She gags under his tongue. Hushed and rushed seconds. He fills her in. Sweet Jesus! But Libby's not a novice. She wants to slow him, get to where she wants. But it all rushes up at once and she cries out loud. Stinging beautiful fuck. The breath's sucked out of her. He steps back, does up his fly. Actually takes a look. She languishes... tilts her head, curls a finger about her pussy. Whore's parade.

- Okay. Come tomorrow - nine at night. First floor. We'll have wine. Dress sexy.

And he steps away.

Next evening Libby's there, dressed sexy. She made excuses to Rosita, who didn't like Libby's sudden exit (nor sudden return) last night. There's dark intuition about Rosita. Libby quails a bit. Screw it, it's research. Raul lets her in. No chance for wine or niceties. Libby loses her skimpiest panties in seconds (didn't need 'em anyway), cutesy skirt twists about and her heels cut holes in the sheets. Full hour of lushy heat, and he swallows the whole menu. Libby is wrung like a rag doll. After, Raul seems impressed, solicitous even. Brings her wine and snacks. They lie about, and he actually talks.

- You are loyal to your fucked up friend
- Am I?
- Don't get me wrong. You are beautiful. I like blonde: cunt and arse. Rosita is smart to send you hey? She knows me: you are tempting for how do you say - practice for real thing. Please drink, eat. We can repeat. Rosi is clever, hey!
Libby starts to get a creepy feeling.
- So with me you imagine you're -
- With Rosita! What do you think, that I fall for you? Our relation is unbreakable! But you take risk. I congratulate.

At this, Libby (she told me every bit) slides into a bit of a dream. Situation strange. Doesn't know what to feel. 'Void' is a word that comes. Or, Stupid Betrayed Smaller Lesser Hung Out To Dry?
- All those? You're an *adult*
- I'm a fucking child. That is, a child who fucks. Did Rosi plan it? To be the pawn in her grungy game! I mean this guy's a bastard (sexy one, mind) and cleverer than me. Both are. That smug world of his: I walked right in and opened myself to that! Even then I got drunk with him. What else could I do? His wine was expensive. After? Didn't care what happened. Deep throat roll over. So I'm skewered with his cock in my arse round

dawn and he says: 'Don't believe her if she says I stole money from her. It was the other way round.' Why would he say that? I was intrigued. Next night I went to Rosita and told her everything - or most of it. I'm not clever: she pulled me off the bar stool, wanted to throttle me on the floor. Bar staff kicked us out. Later she apologised. I accepted it. She was strung out. Next she comes on to me in a back street. I was too tired; told her. (Oh I was firm, Cross.) Later at her place she suggested we both go to Raul. I asked if they were on speaking terms. Are you stupid? she said. I said I wasn't, but I said okay. I thought if I refused, their relationship'd never be healed. Am I a dimwit? But we were always drunk or stoned, see. She's got a mind like a steel trap even when she's loaded. We went, he opens the door and his eyes go wide! We stayed, drank his plonk. They went in his room. Then she started shouting. There was violence. Ugh, I just left. I was tired. Besides, Julie me called three times, complaining, so I had to take Bondy from her place to my old flat. Rosi called me next day, wanted me to come. I took Bondy to school. He's unruly, poor kid. I went to her. She had a new plan, even though she had cuts and bruises in places I didn't wanna see. All about whips and knives. I told her I 'felt a bit used'. She embraced me and said it'd 'be all right'. Whispered and purred. She can be sweet like that. She's a very hot lover. I'm usually pliant after she's worked on me. She even tried a trick on me with a blade. It was scary but hot. We went to Raul's that afternoon. They both got in a bad state. Drugged out. She was tied. There was even blood. I wanted to leave but they wouldn't let me. Dosed me with some shit I didn't want. I ended up in a bad way, tied up by them both. It hurt - and no come even. Sick. This went on more times next day. In the end I excused myself. Neither of 'em seemed sad to see me go. But they kept calling me up - like five times a day. I showed discipline not going there again. Besides, Bondy had flu. I knew they hated each other and couldn't part. Weird. But after, I actually felt kind of... left out! I got sad. But I feel superior now. Got away with it! Never really fell for it, you understand. Apart from at the start. On reflection he was the best bit, on his own the first few times. I won't see Rosi again. Unless she reforms herself. But I've a suspicion she'll always be like that. It's her identity, little *snake*. I've still got a soft spot for her. She knew where to put her tongue... Good story, eh Cross?

- Excellent. (I murmur) And what have we learnt?
- Just told ya. Keep out of other people's business
- Hmm. Castro sent you to her, right?
- So what? I'm a grown-up
- You said you were a child

(Silence) - Okay yeah. Castro 'll come prying and he'll ask questions and laugh and wag his finger, and he won't say it like you did (he's too subtle for that) but he'll imply: 'what have I learnt?' and I s'pose I'll have to thank him for it

- Quite so. And your performance in my office the other day?
- I was on drugs. (Pause) Cross, didn't you get that?
- Okay, I believe you. (She scrutinises me) I really believe you.

Libby gives her sweet yankee smile and leans in close.

- The things I tell you mister analyst, nobody ever hears. So you'll believe whatever I goddam want. Are we understood?
- We're understood.

The Cynic

Libby Castro: manipulator. Cross the analyst defers to your attention-seeking games. I know you 'compensate for lack of worth in your other relationships, for slave-loyalty to all the exploiters, for loss of your parents blaaa'. I'm your shrink (and you definitely cure *my* shrinkage). You manipulate me like no-one else, and I know you like me: who else gets all the sex-gossip and tittle-tattle? Yep, romantic creature, you're empty and charming enough with me but I guess you laugh when I act like I'm special in your eyes. So let me tell *you* a dream: 'I'm stepping down a brilliantly-lit hallway. Doorway after doorway leads on and on into the light. In one room my attention is caught by a low, dark cupboard. I open it and poke my face in. Suddenly I'm struck on the forehead by a massive blow! And I wake up thrown ten feet from the bed, on the floor, startled and bruised...' We analysts obsess about 'capturing the complexity of human wiring': we poke our noses in nooks and hideaways, want to pin it all down. But be careful what you wish for! The more you take a thing apart the more you'll loathe it. The more we hear of people's ways the more jaundiced we get. And while we pluck the low-hanging fruit of human analysis - banal simplistic mechanical childish puerile ignorant immature undignified foolish absurd - just when we think we know about all of these, a ghostly voice whispers: 'You don't, you don't, there's a ghost in the machine!' Because we analysts never *participate*. That's why I never forgot my cupboard dream. I forgot the *innocence*. I forgot wonder and awe. Innocence somehow withered away from me like a dew in summer. Some say naivety is balm for the spirit, is faith in life itself. But for me, naïve people were always ignorant. Especially the ones wrapped in bliss who admit no conundrums, who cling to passivity, avoidance, childishness like petrified creatures in a bushfire. Who can leave these people alone? I have to shake them, have to re-arrange them. Thus, I embrace the cynic. Only cynics know how to live, I always said. But this bred a fear, that blew into my garden from the world's rough edges - because secretly I always dreamed about innocence at the end of my journey into dark cupboards of the mind. Let me fail to sniff out truth, let naïve souls have their peace... I return to the diaries of Libby Castro in order to re-arrange her in my mind. Why are there so many amusing doodles and scribbles in her margins? No matter, I take the following entry to be a welcome sign of cynicism.

'So I wake up again. What to do? Oh first I must attend to the body: have to wash it, feed it, give it some clothes and show it off. And then take note like a concerned mother when it has its aches and gripes and sores. And I trudge about... not dancing at all! And this day I have to keep my feelings under control - make sure they don't lurch all over the place, since my mentality must impose some kind of silly order, satisfy itself the world makes *sense*. Necessary connections shall be made with community and people and places and relationships. All that papery meaningfulness. This'll take some hours. Not to mention the fickle intellect needs to know it isn't bored, that there's 'meaning', that life is not a waste. So we have to catch up on the TV news, and be sure to observe some clever programs concerning atoms and economics and art... I don't even mention Bondy's little world. Oh why do kids' lives seem so wasted? All those years spent trying to grasp a thing that's perfectly obvious to an adult. Scrub about in their little bead-games, all oblivious to struggles and traumas to come -

and repeat what's been discovered and done a billion times before in other finished lives in a million other centuries on endless planet worlds. Who cares eh? It'll all end in shit and crying and misunderstanding anyway. What's the right word for my sad case? *Repetition.* All I do is copy. I don't think. In a crisis I just have sex or stand naked in corridors or get drunk and stoned. No more crisis, please god! Please. PS: I wonder what on earth happened to that little Jordanian girl?'

Exit

Libby can't bring herself to return to the legal office, but she must find shelter. Turns up one day at the Yoga centre. It's near-deserted. Asks for Yogi Thiel. Bossa, a senior student, informs her 'the Yogi cannot be corporeally located at this time'. Turns out no-one has a clue where he is. Perhaps he's in private retreat? Bossa is cool with her; she feels something's wrong. Suddenly she wants her Man - a wild unruly feeling! A wave flushes over her and she turns red. He turns away with a faint smile. She assaults his back.

- I know him better than you. He won't talk to you but he will talk to me! Her voice appals the reverent air. Bossa stops; his ascetic frame bends from a height.
- You disturbed him and now everyone suffers for it. I also know him
- But he's a grown man. I have a right -
- You - have no right.

He showed his contempt! Libby is startled to discover there are others who seem to be involved with her Yogi. (Ashrams don't register with her) Right here is a self-centredness she has no idea of. 'I *am* special to him, that's his problem. But these men erect defences. I could hate them. I have a right to see him! ...but he wouldn't see me. Oh, I'm a fool. I'll go home.'

She trails away chastised. And ends up, with Bondy in tow, at her old house… where Castro resides with his new protégé: the waif from Jordan. Rula didn't actually fire Libby, but to resign was the dignified thing. Also dignified, to return to Castro? For Bondy's sake, she tells herself. She finds the girl Sophia encamped in her own ex-bedroom. 'Mister Castro is out casting his new production,' she is told. One that Sophia will certainly be a part of. Sophia with new-found confidence basks in Castro's hyper-attentions - but takes care to recall her 'plight', such is her status in this refuge-country. She is thus coy with Libby, or affects empathy for the embarrassing plight of a rejected wife. Can we be friends? says she, taking Libby's hand. Lib is a sucker to charm at the worst of times, and Sophia perceives: here's a hollow soul in need of a friend.

Sweet Sophia Zohran, it turns out, sees many things that might advantage her. One was to try to marry an educated man of better caste, a match opposed by a religious father and hot-headed brothers. These men are currently painted as villains in a soap-opera of feminist struggles played out on the international stage. Sophia (being a woman) is something of an actress - specialising in this case in virtue - and her only crime (so she tearfully explained to Rula Cortes) was 'to feel and to fall in love'. To be victim to male injustice is a pregnant role, especially in these woke western climes.

Our friendly Libby meanwhile, having experience of Castro, feels the need to help her. And it helps there's a dash of romance since Sophia hails from a far desert country. Libby is drawn to victims. It is the insight of a naïf to see the victim's need, their festering wound, and to tend to it with love. Which the (cynical) victim can only soak up, being in need of love after all. Castro himself, ruefully noting the truism that in Muslim culture women are downtrodden, must also lavish compassion therein; that's his scheme anyway. Should we say that Castro is naïve? (Yes, he and Libby were always partners in this.) And yes, because he never admits that when he replaces women he simply refreshes his own need to be needed. The hairy one at intervals needs to cleanse himself. In fact, Sophia could be the harbinger to something new: after feckless Elizabeth, rough Rula, disappointing Nadia. A narcissist can only blindly project himself, flattering others for his own ends (in this case through art), and people and things must serve those ends, alas. Of course, our waif Sophia knows all this.

The two girls lunch together in the kitchen, and Sophia tells her sad story. (She's practised at vulnerability.) It seems her lover is a filmmaker, and a controversial one, and she followed him to this country where he shot a film, and when he went back he was arrested for being un-Islamic. But she failed to return there to support him, fearing the retribution of her family of males who made it plain their honour had been compromised. Now *there's* a story, thinks Libby, to put one's own troubles in the shade. And when sad Sophia lightly enquires about Libby and Castro, Libby is impressed with her delicate empathy.

Castro returns at this point, and is consternated to find them together. But he hides it, magnanimous fellow that he is. He even joins them in a drink. Presently he sees that the women's camaraderie might save him quite some effort. And he is extra nice to Bondy, who allows himself to be engulfed by the big hairy guy for a moment before bounding off to examine the familiar house. But, the situation for these adults is too too precarious, in ways we will now describe.

- Elizabeth, you will be interested to know my new work concerns the effect of bourgeois social structures on Islamic fundamentalism, specifically comparing marriage and family, east and west. It is serendipitous, yes? that Sophia has come at this time. Hence Sophia will advise us, visually and choreographically. Under my direction naturally. You have no further interest in dance, I assume.

Apparently this is Libby's self-inflicted crime. It is hard to describe the loneliness of a dancer who is lost to dance, and bloated Castro is ignorant of her loss. But Libby only murmurs that this is 'all very nice'.
- Nice? Actually it is far from that. We are faced with the prospect of east-west conflagration - unless we artists effect the necessary meeting of minds. Actually this is one of the reasons I became... emphatic... during my discussion with the Yogi Thiel. His watered-down eastern dogmas seemed to me a disturbing incursion on weak minds. Actually, have you seen this yogi?
- Why ask me?

- I suppose I am forced to feel guilty at my perhaps foolish behaviour (He actually winks at Sophia)
- Oh well, apologise to him then
- I hope you might do that for me.
And Libby, the fool, actually allows herself to entertain the possibility.
Says Castro: - I can hardly meet him myself. Naturally I would be beaten up!
The spell is broken. Libby is angry: she wants to laugh out loud. (But keep it *civilised*. Sophia is here)
- Thiel is a pacifist. Myself, I never saw him get upset, ever
- I expect that is another myth. Have you observed him at close quarters? (Slight pause) - Close enough.

There's an evil nuance in her phrase he doesn't like. Castro suffers bad claustrophobia around humans, and now he starts to bristle.

- Actually Sophia, my wife ran off to see a holy man since reality is too hard to deal with! And we have to explain to her that things are not usually as *romantic* as they seem. Perhaps your own romantic experiences confirm it?
Sophia badly wants to not be the butt of a marriage war.
- I also am inexperienced in love. But, I must follow my heart. Women cannot always make their own choices. And men must learn respect.
This is fine conciliatory prattle, to be swept away forthwith.
It is the hardest thing for the cossetted naïf to give up her world, with all its self-justifying love and obeisance (and secret pity) for the suffering beings around her. But Libby Castro is beginning to have no choice. (Perhaps my own prodding contributed.) Abandoned by Castro and by Thiel and by Rula - and facing substitution by Sophia (the new, purer version of her and Castro), she suddenly sees for a moment in time - that it is a great *refuge* to be a cynic and a hater and a non-carer and a wild selfish unruly fucker who contributes nothing to the sum of human happiness! And as I told you, Libby seldom gets mad but when she does, it is as if another being has descended from the stratosphere. The issue now is, after Libby's alien double has murdered and passed on, will she regret? Oh, how I hope she does not! We all love you, naïve one, and we'll always feed on you and

use you and laugh at you and will all be contrite and sorry, but our childish crap will never end, never. I, Cross the analyst shouted this at you but you never heard. Yet now in a moment of piercing vision you'll assassinate! Like a sniper you've seen the possibility; you're better at it than all the cynics. And wonder of wonders, you always saw cold controlling mastery in others but never cared for it. Just unimpressed. Supreme innocence! to be unimpressed with the temptation of mastery. You go, girl. Thank God for people like you.

- Castro just wants to fuck you up the arse, Sophia. You know that, don't you?
Followed by bare astonished silence in the family kitchen.
- But you won't let him, will you? Being deeply in love with another man and all that. It'd be so bad - for dignity, for your position. Dishonourable, suicidal. Though I don't wear a hijab I'm really quite wise. Everyone sees me as a silly blonde. You mustn't trust blondes. They ruin men!

The end bit was a bit off the rails, but no matter. The knife's gone in. Loyalty just died. Castro loses. Sophia peers into a pit of shame. Does she see Libby has told the truth?

And Castro, the fucking jackass, is too thick to see what his wife just did.

She just left him.

Despite the cost, despite the loss, despite his wondrous cleverness, despite the fact she'll never dance again, despite how she kind of loves him, or would've if he'd let her, if he'd given her room - that loyal girl. Despite her running to Thiel. Couldn't take Thiel could you, you jealous ignoramus. And Castro will grock it eventually, and he'll seek revenge and guess how? By trying to get her back. But she won't ever be there.

This stupid scene starts to recede from her eyes. She starts to see her family as a dry little grain in a beached world of families, all living and struggling and dying in the world. She wants to go away. She plucks Bondy from the garden and hastens through the gate. The four winds of the world blow in. There are tears… At the bus stop there's no bus. She and Bondy wait. She grips his hand. Presently she notices a figure in pale blue silk and a hood hurrying down the street. Sophia. She comes up close. Bondy gazes up at her. Libby notices her curves and breast inside the fitted robe.

- I am so sorry. It was too awful for you. Myself, I will not stay there. (It seems she might cry) Will you come back? The man who will be my husband is in jail. Oh I miss him! What shall I do? Why did Cortes let me come to this house? I am shamed. I feel for you, truly. We are so powerless. Let me be your friend. Tell me what I can do.

Libby is exhausted. And she doesn't see the truth - that Castro just ordered Sophia to follow her, on pain of expulsion. It doesn't matter; she has to run. Julie's house is her last option. She offers to Sophia to come there, so that Sophia is placed by Libby in a delicate bind, requiring all her skill to manage.
- Oh yes. Thank you. I must not burden you. I will try to come. What is the address?
- Twenty-two Beach Road. Not far from here.

There is a pause. Now Libby must let go, because the bus has arrived. Through the window she sees Sophia stand, fretting and alone, on a pavement in a foreign country. As the scene recedes, she thinks she sees the enrobed girl walk hesitantly off… back to the house of Castro.

Nothing Girl

In the end, Libby Castro cleared out.

She and Bondy took a ship, across the pearly Aegean. During the days she sat at the stern languishing in a deck chair as the ship carved its slew of white over the sea, and birds drifted at the masthead, suspended in the sky. She sprawled by the hour, with sparkling juices always within reach, presented no doubt by some swarthy waiter who lightly fancied his chance. Bondy played about the deck, and sometimes he'd roll on his back, let his face nestle in the sun like a cub in the African savannah, and she saw that he cared nothing for this life at all. Just as well. Every mile to her was lost and gone; this ship would never return but would sail to the end of the world. Who needs anything? We are dust and sunlight, we drink in the winds of the warm south, we are ghosts of the yellow days. We'll never come back.

A thin shadow crosses her sun. Oh, it's the swarthy waiter boy. Does he want to fill my drink - or drink my fill? Libby experiences a cool tingling in several parts; the knees outside her frock languish. What's to be done? Will you help me with a little thing, she says. My cabin is this way. Bondy squints up at them as they cross the warm deck. The whole world knows but looks the other way. In her little cabin she pulls him into her, gets filled to the gunwhales with all the muscle and blood she can take. He knows the ritual (she can see it in his pool-dark eyes) and nothing is said, only the brutal exchange of breath and fluid. This is where Bondy came from, she thinks. His tongue lolls in her gaping mouth and for aching seconds she shakes uncontrollably and so does he. Then, there's only the slow slowing of their heartbeats, and the heavy slow roll of the ship under her back. After he has left, without a word of Greek, she lies there... fingering the semen and sweat and juice on her legs... and swims in the hot nothingness. Saves me performing it myself, she thinks. Love is simple, the universe is nothing but sex and death. Our sly language of life is thus uttered, and we go our ways. Perfect.

Later she's back in her deck chair, the hedonist in love with Nothing. Bondy wants to go in the pool. She takes him. He flutters in the shallows like a little bug and smiles up at the woman, his simple benefactor. She's not ashamed, not a bit. Libby in her cotton frock looks out to sea. Whatever I do, the great silent world rolls on. Nothing ever happens. Nothing ever happened. Look up at that great blue field of endless sky, that legendary sunlight glittering on a glass ocean. Why do we live, why *do* things, why strive like we do? Only a human is made to ask outrageous questions. But we ask. It's our metaphysic torture. Only drowning in the pool of sex can salve it, fix it. That's what I do anyway.

The ship sails on. She falls asleep in the sun and has her simple dream. In the dream all is fresh and dewy like a lingering morning in the garden of god. Our past is gone, we're oblivious on a journey to our end. *Freedom has no history.* She heard someone say that. We are transparent, a straw in the wind, a circumstance, a clamour, a whisper of a time that never was. Always alone: not lonely but somehow cradled. Lazy. Easy. Easy.

Ties That Blind

Yet voices in the complicated cities gather and mutter. Where Libby creates a vacuum, busy egos rush in with their moral clamour, their outrage. Blondy girl lost in the big world: you can't just run away like that! There are duties, ties that bind, relations, hidden histories. We your people (who use you but need you): have we no rights? But Libby seems to have distributed her intimacies so that each feels the *ambiguity* of loss. And no-one can stand that spaceless weightless quality: how she appears to have no agenda, no special definition, no particular footprint, no anchorage, no result-driven self-involved time-constrained learned planned left-brained goal-oriented *purpose.* Controllers of the world can't stand it.

Castro has called up your analyst, and Rula Cortes too. They seem to constitute a ghastly team. Are they suspicious and jealous that I know inner things about The Girl? They mention the child as well (though they barely noted him before) as a 'catalyst for urgent action'. Now little Bondy is Property and a scapegoat. We must get the child, they say. But what would I know that they don't?

Ah. Her whereabouts.

Call me a hypocrite but I'd like to have her back. It's hard to construct her from afar. She distracts my mind, whether I'm alone or with my clients. I drift away to ships and to far countries… her slender hand holds her son, blondy hair frames her cheek, her curvy figure basks on a beach… I admit I want to own her - and tell myself I fear for her sanity, for her coping, her child. I'm in the corral with Castro and Rula and Thiel and Rosita and Julie and the rest. I'm ashamed of us all. We clutch at straws in the wind.

So I'm obliged to contact her, tell her. Castro has served a writ for divorce. And he wants permanent custody of his boy.

The Child

There's a big silence from her end. Finally she messages saying the news has taken the wind from her sails. She was at peace on her little pilgrimage to shrines in Armenia… One day she slips back into the country and turns up at Julie's. But Julie is not welcoming. What has happened? Libby has no right to demand, except to hope that her fall-girl will do as she always did. But you can't be lazy with people and relationships. People have feelings, and weaknesses. Libby tries to embrace Julie and there's a scene. Suzie La La cries and Bondy clings to Suzie: all they want is to play in their little sandpit. It's about to get bigger and more complicated.

- What have I done to you?
- What have you not?
- Oh no, Julie. I'm a married woman
- Not for long it seems
- Oh! And you'd punish me because I'm not entirely gay? Don't you want a friend?
- I don't need you. Take Bondy and go
- He doesn't want to go. He loves Suzie.
It's true. Every day on holiday he asked for Suzie. It bothered her but she did nothing about it. Now too late, Libby starts to cry. It's a bit pathetic.
- Don't fall in love with a person like me, Julie
- Get out of my house.
Libby does. And through the window, she sees that Julie is crying too.

* * * *

Castro did his dirty work, and Julie was easy: he simply let slip that Libby was entwined with Rosita. Benign Castro never acts without reference to his own interest. Because? Those who entour him in this sandpit of a world are in need of correction. Yogi Thiel mind you, did not assent to such correction. Castro would not associate with anyone estimable enough not to need his guidance. That person would then constitute a rival: their proximity would discomfit him. If he does associate with you, be sure he regards you as safely inferior. What then if he were to *dissociate*… from

426

his wife for example. Could he use boredom as an excuse? No, truth be told, Libby has 'depended on him too long', and 'her influence on his boy is negative' (another irony since neither of them ever particularly engaged with Bondy except as a point of convergence). The answer is to punish. He can't ever admit he needs any soul except on the 'artistic terms' of controlled vulnerability he likes to set himself. Castro therefore writes a letter to his wife. And typically he spreads the news about to significant (or insignificant) others he thinks he controls, including your analyst.

'My dear Elizabeth, it is my sad intention to file for divorce and to take guardianship of our son James. Naturally under such circumstances you would be able to see him from time to time. My decision depends on the following: Your recent prolonged liaison with Rosita Caro has proved beyond doubt, to me at least, that you lack the discipline and clean living necessary to be a proper guardian to our son. Your friend Julie has been kind to inform me of certain details amounting to continual neglect of parental responsibility. I know personally how you always struggled to achieve the necessary focus to be a serious artist, and this is sadly reflected in your laisser-faire approach to parenting, the result of which is our son affects to be completely emotionally disengaged. I myself am a victim of this. Your recent decision to sever steady employment with Daemon and Associates and instead take a 'holiday' with a six-year-old child in frankly obscure locations while informing no-one, was irresponsible; and your lack of communication was a source of anxiety to me, affecting my professional work at a critical juncture. Not to mention that the boy has been out of school. Your employer Rula Cortes has also been deeply inconvenienced. I have apologised to her personally. Further, your liaison with the yoga teacher Thiel was a breach of filial duty and a further example of waywardness, callousness and indiscipline. My recent anger at this, resulting in a public fracas, is to be regretted, but I am confident any reasonable member of the public will see that I was systematically provoked. And I note you did not 'cheer for me' at all... I have also taken the decision to re-open the facts on an incident of violence perpetrated by you on my person some months ago involving a weapon. I note that I have not recovered the full use of my shoulder, and it is causing pain and distress... I take no pleasure whatever in these actions, but see no alternative - for the good of all members of our erstwhile family. I send you, despite all, my warm best wishes. Castro. PS: I have no objection to your returning to the family home for the present.'

Behold the handiwork of a narcissist (he gets professionals to write his letters): cynic mastery of the politics of righteousness, coward's calculation of psychology, brazen eye to publicity. We shouldn't judge the man though; we should *stab* him (figuratively speaking). I'd advise Lib to fight but I've the old hollow sense that she can't or won't do it. To my mind this is her tragedy. Still, I offer for she and little Bondy to stay with me awhile. She won't. Takes a low-rent room instead.

Rula Cortes, confirming that the best form of self-righteousness is attack, ferrets her out. Rula is made in the breed of Castro; to wit, she does not regard mistakes or callous actions as any reason for regret or guilt. To the contrary, when the going gets tough the tough get going. Too many people suffer in this world for little transgressions to be bothered with, blaaaa. Like Castro she is a mover and shaker, and status affords her certain rights...

- Elizabeth. I am going to explain to you that the preposterous scene at my office that night was over a child who was never born. And why was it never born? Because I failed to grasp that to seek the favours of a man is no reason to conceive a child. A child was aborted as a form of ransom and punishment. And Castro has suffered. I did not see how he has suffered. And I see now that I was callous and made a mistake. I did not show respect. Naturally he is a chauvinist and manipulator and all other things I have patiently explained to you, but he has a heart and I do not think him a bully and he did not deserve to be blackmailed. I have softened therefore. I will not descend to that place again. And that is why I say to you: you must not use your child as a bargaining counter, as a touchstone for rivalry or hatred. You must let it go if he asks for it. Do you understand?

Rula's arrogance and narcissism suck Libby's breath away. She merely remarks:

- At least I had his child. I'll do what is best for Bondy.

Lack of engagement with Rula's ego prompts the didact in her.

- Do you know what the child represents? The child is *oneself*. Has your so-called analyst Cross not explained? He's a fool then. The child is the one who runs away, who does not face responsibility, who puts herself in another's hands, who lets the other make decisions for her. The one who allows everything to occur then complains bitterly. The passive-aggressive! This child is the one who succumbs to mental and intellectual laziness, thinking the world will put itself to rights. And this child is the vain attention-seeker who'll use charm, insouciant sexuality, to get the experiences she wants

- I seem to recall you came on to me once or twice

- I'm revealing myself to you, Libby

- I have a sense you're using me. As you did all along

- I care about you! I employed you! Qualified women would kill for that job. And I confess now to you, not to him, my abortion mistake

- Thank you. No doubt it hurt

- Have you any idea how it hurt?

- You'll say I don't

- He's *your* husband, Libby. Take responsibility

- Me?

- You don't want to feel at all, do you?

- Perhaps I'm just a dunce

- Don't be passive! (Pause) He and I were before your time anyway

- All past tense. I get it

- You're impossible. Why do I risk so much to help...

- Because I'm a hopeless little child, Rula! Need to be looked after by the grown-ups! But it's not all bad. I'm good at spontaneous. I just left Castro! Even the big genius doesn't get it with all his agendas in his big head. I left your stupid job too. I went away on a ship. I was in Armenia and I saw so many things. There was friendliness, people being nice, joy and fun. And even wonder. And what is wrong with sex? Don't be a hypocrite Rula, you're a bit blind to yourself. Why take up all the space with your big self-agenda? So you had an abortion. My god, what a fuss

- Fuss. What the fuck do you know?
- Nothing. That's my point
- Wake up, girl. (Pause) He will marry that refugee
- What, Sophia?
- Join the club, Libby... join the yesterday girls.

Libby is embarrassed. The bathos! But Rula wants to sustain her noble vulnerableness, and ruminates aloud.

- Castro will hate me for this... but he can't stand the fact that he needs you. He fears it. So to be elusive - may be your best option. (Libby gazes) You see, again I've helped you
- You mean this is his way of hanging on to me?
- Don't you get it?
- But for what?
- For his fragile ego, darling

(Silence. Libby pretends to think about this) - Did it work in your case? Rula's eyes are hollow. - I just confessed to you. Yes.

- Mmm, I'd better run a mile then
- No! I mean... no, you should *fight* him. You'll at least keep your dignity
- Don't care for dignity
- Oh you will. You *will*, Libby.

With this portentous phrase, Rula leaves, her dignity and her agenda intact.

A Spiritual Letter

Soon after, another dark wind invades the withering garden of Libby Castro. She is suddenly lonely, so goes once more to find her Yogi, assuming he'll be there as in former days. Yet truly he is gone. All she encounters is silence and the hermetic circle of Thiel's people. They look through her as if she's an alien and send her off; but she returns, and returns again, clinging like a waif. Finally a young fellow (not the aloof Bossa) hands her a letter. She recognises the elegant hand of the teacher, her former paramour. So - the only person Yogi Thiel actually wrote to before he disappeared without trace or shadow was Libby Castro. What does it signify, that she was so important? Libby did read his letter (printed below), then passed it to me. She explained she dislikes encumbrances, emotional ones. No surprise there. And she claimed this was just as true for Thiel.

'Hello Libby. I intend to go away for a while - but not to any physical address. At the end of a long road there is only 'where we are'. At this moment you are where I am. Are you flattered? Best not to be, though you are far from incidental. Should I bow to you because of what you 'signify' or because you are you? You are not just a symbol for love, but a girl I love. I was led to detach even from the affairs of the heart, but now I know that the heart is all there is. I kind of knew it but didn't. I saw how the simplicity of your smile and your refusal to be anywhere but here with me, or anything but simple with me, was a *gift*. I am as demanding and as possessive as anyone. Like your Castro, I suppose many people want to possess you, but you don't let them. And this is coldly cruel but also kind. It helps me. Because I can care for you and not have to turn it into anything else. This fact should suit me. Most men can't cope with detachment, they fall for women. Hence I am a brave man! I run off instead.

All people want a big slice of life, and come to this physical realm in order to validate their needs. I am getting bored, not with life but with myself, my constructed self, the endless round of emotional insecurities and petty thoughts (not you). Best to go and sit still in a desert somewhere. I gave it all a red hot go and I've had enough. For now. I await my 'return' in a life to come. It is all fading already. Do you know how when we go to a foreign country, the old place ceases to exist because we fail to think of it? Our life is the little bubble in front of our eyes, your bubble and mine. Who needs it? I will be called back to this world no doubt, having failed to summon the energy to go deeper into the light. It takes guts to go on when you see it's but a great prison of repetition. I give up.

But I remember you! Your curvy body and your blondy locks and your faithful eyes that asked for nothing from me except to be there. Am I naïve? I don't care. You gave simply and lightly, to me. You are better than you know. All power to you, and all love. *Thiel.*'

No Footprint

Weeks have passed. This analyst is vaguely haunted by Thiel's journey. To care or not to care, that is the question. Did he really engage in this sea of troubles, or spit it right out? Was he right in taking his own life, as we now assume he did? Logically yes, since it makes no difference whether he inhabited a body or not (where is his body now?) and logically no, since life is never his to take. There are no rights or wrongs, unless we indulge in moralising. Still, all suicides seek attention. He will claim he was no suicide. I suspect his 'death' (and therefore his life) made no difference at all. And I'm sure that's why he did it... so that he could swallow that little fact himself. Brave man. Here, found in his personal papers, is one more passage he may have spoken. I swallow my pride and print it here.

Enjoy your Delusion Paradigm! 'They say this world is flux, continual change. But if change is continual, what changes into what? Observe the flaw in this vision. If a 'thing' is constantly changing then the 'thing' is never what it is. Thus we cannot say a thing changes, since it is not a thing. No things, no change, no birth, no death: welcome to *Samsara*. Samsara has no self-nature! There is only borderless self-existent *awareness*. Its state is eternal bliss, absorbed, self-aware, without fault or illusion. This awareness must be solely present if there's to be *any* point of focus, limitation, object, world. Yet here is this crazy infinite world of 'things'! We may say that the seer only comes into being with the object. But the ego automatically creates the 'delusional state', where subject and object appear to occur, so that all transaction depends forever on that. Yet there must be a reality beyond delusion, otherwise delusion would not be known for what it is. The Seer is not confined to any tiny ego! This then is the self: self-existent, utterly aware, in bliss – and it delights in 'assuming form, choosing form'. The sages have said it: there is a mysterious power arising in and as ourselves that conjures dreams and hopes and sorrows and beliefs, our loves and hates, our passions, attachments. Yet we ever *witness* it... Please understand. Take responsibility. *Be as you are.* And let there be peace upon you all.'

People with Guts

I the bald analyst feel exposed by such a text. Delusion and attachment. You'll note by now that I am a semi-unreliable narrator with a disturbing agenda. I filter people through my self-interest and self-awareness, or lack of. Do you see how I tend to denigrate those who appear too much like me? This points alas, to one's insecurity. You have met power-people who are attached to this idiotic life, committed to their footprint: passionate mover-shakers who sacrifice and thus are heroic. Should we laud them? Castro, for his attachment to art, his histrionic posturing in the great Sandpit, his 'challenge to us all'... or Rula, for her gruesome war for independence? Or Rosita for her ferocious devotion to self-destruction... or Thiel for his pitiless attachment to non-attachment? I have to admit: at least these people have guts. Yet, which of them does not seek peace or connection or happiness or love or approval... which all are *innocence* by another name? And what if a person has no agenda, no particular footprint, no anchorage, no specifical definability? This'd haunt the analyst! No wilful result-driven self-focused time-constrained learned planned-out left-brained goal-oriented purpose! Better not laud Libby Castro then, who seems barely attached to any freaking thing... well, to 'this and that'. A dream of dancing. Dabble with wifehood, tinker with motherhood. Bit of yoga. Trips away. Shopping. Duty. Loyalty to teachers. Doses of love by and by... no, the girl has no guts - and those little doses weren't even her fault since she has a body, a sexy one, into whose little panties our esteemed Yogi like unto the gates of heaven gained entry. I have to admit it's more than I will do. He's possibly a legend.

One other thing. There was no actual funeral since Thiel's physical person was never found. Some of his students got together and meditated. Did he leave them in the dark? They'll need to figure that out. There was no ceremony, no fuss, nothing at all really. Fitting, except that one student created a nice message and put it on a wall. 'We feel it all, so we are saved. What we did never was, where we are is passing, gone, and where we'll go and what we're doing is our ghost-dance of eternal emptiness. But we *feel* it all. We must feel it! Every moment, every un-moment... Thank you Mister Thiel.'

Girl in a City

So much for stories of Libby Castro and her mysterious lover. Where are her friends, and where are women when she needs them? (Her distant tortured mother comes to mind.) I worry. A day ago, sweetly dressed, she dropped in at my office. She didn't know what really to say, so she left. And I followed. Sneaked behind her through the city market. Absurd to want to invade her private world. And spoilt too, since she confided in me. Libby is elusive.

This day she's in a little stripey tank-top, and her bob is clipped back like a teenager's. In the sun her shoulders glisten as she lingers, pores over the knick-knacks in the stalls. Her moves are graceful but transparently routine. Has a way of turning her head and standing as if there were somewhere to go, something really to do... she who might be at home in an eastern bazaar where no-one knows her, where there's no special reason for being. Weightless girl. Through the window of a bookshop her neck is arched... over what book? Landscapes - far countries - recipes - body love - a romance? Sun on the street outside. She wanders, stops at a café, peers at a menu. Waits for something, anything. Enters and sits by a window. Speaks to a man who turns away. We wait. He comes with a glass. She sips, sets it down. Her hands are folded. The turn of her neck. She stares outward, in my direction, doesn't see me. Somewhere in the universe... a little bar, and a blonde girl called Libby, lingering over a glass.

Sophia's Choice

I now indulge my imagination, not having any first-hand report, in order to set the scene for a pivotal event.

Educated and studiedly naive middle-eastern girl Sophia Zohran is used to deferring to men in order to secure things in her life. True, she rebelled against institutional family bullying, but it was weak-hearted, and even now she feels the guilt. Refuge in an alien country far from family is a huge step, as Allah is her witness, and now she is experiencing slow panic. Should she pursue her filmmaker lover back to Jordan? Where is he anyway, and will it help, and is he really radical as people say? Will my life turn well if I stay here? This Castro said he will sponsor me. No, I must support this odd hairy man. For now. But he is disturbed! And how to disentangle him from his wife! I see she wants to leave him. Ah, her sexual insult to me... not even my brothers spoke in such a way. I agreed to befriend her but now I see she is a spoiled little western girl and uneducated. God help me for saying this but she is a bitch. Castro tries to help because she is helpless, and he is actually kind under his gruff (I do not say ugly) exterior. I understand men, this is how they are. And where has Cortes gone? I did not like her. Did she feed me when I needed food? I was a trophy to her, an item for her resume. And ugh she drinks, not to say her unruly sexual talk. Why such talk? Still I must be polite, which my father said will bring us closer to God. And should a woman be weak and hysterical? Never.

Unless it gets her where she wants to go.

Since his letter to Libby was met with unaccountable silence, Castro has apparently been displaying worrying signs of emotional honesty. He wants to summon her to his house, talk her round, demand to keep Bondy. This is unclever; such boisterous acts show no respect for process of law. But he doesn't care, he's a free spirit. Sophia sees the danger in this for all parties including herself. She hovers about him now, testing the limits of her influence. Should she bravely stand up and be counted, or like traditional women seek to gain by subterfuge? Over the weeks she's made sure to cook his meals, introduce tantalising mid-eastern tastes, wear her fashionable robes when he's present. And she is careful to pay attention at rehearsals - which if truth be told mystify her. She sleeps alone, notwithstanding her array of graceful goodnight glances to him before letting the forbidden door kiss itself shut. To be in such a bind merely unleashes the player in Castro. He tests her, pressing in every way at the irony of her position. Will she continue to play pliant sweet arab girl or be forced into vulgar western feminisation? Things can't go on like this. At last she 'confesses' that she cannot comprehend 'his manner or his method'. To which he replies, 'Welcome to my theatre, Sophia!' She is silenced by that. And soon he starts to lose patience with her. As hard weeks go by she starts to see: Libby Castro is not such a bitch after all, despite the terrible arse-fuck insult… which remark amplifies itself day by day; and she broods and broods on the horror of it in the deep of solitary nights in her dark room. How can it be that a little blonde girl can say that to her husband, and to *her*. And she notices with dismay… there is heat in her body. There is dryness in her mouth, her heart flutters, she can't get the actual possible image out of her mind. Sophia is forced to admit… she wants to *see* her, see the blond girl. And the need grows and grows. 'I shall call on her, ask her to come. Why does Castro not call her? And I am alone with him!' Castro watches. One night in the dark he enters her room. The game is up. She is violated in her own bed. From behind, unfortunately. But it is perfectly fitting considering her role. And where is her protest? She is speechless.

Days pass… and she starts to hate herself. She is inwardly distraught. Castro carefully forebears in not repeating his midnight act. He even attends to her with tenderness, mingled with a modicum of paternal sternness. Sophia! He will tell you he cherishes your Arab-girl naivety, that he must get near to you to nurture your sweet quality - while getting you inured to his ways, piece by piece. He has a big plan for you. He cares. You will see.

And it is not the case that Castro has neglected his wife, though she insulted him. He is merely being circumspect. Emotional patience is never his forte, yet strategic patience is. Eventually everyone comes to him since he is the sun around which little planets revolve… And lo, he gets a call from Rula Cortes – who after all is Sophia's case lawyer. She visits the house and there is discussion, and Sophia hears that her asylum case 'hangs in the balance' but Inshallah and with Rula's and Castro's strenuous help it 'may yet succeed'. Castro invites Rula to dinner and she, surprised, agrees. It's all very jolly. What is going on? Whatever it is, Sophia must cook delicacies for them all.

But next day Sophia slips away and finds the house at twenty-two Beach Road, and meeting Julie discovers that Libby is long gone. Sophia is half afraid, and the mere sight of the Arab girl says to Julie that the girl badly wants Libby Castro. Julie will be forced to pass that information on, since women do their duty out of love and guilt, and where the road to hell is paved with good intentions. Libby gets the message and goes to the house of Castro next day. With her boy Bondy.

Could Libby ever actually give up the child? She hasn't thought about it. She supposes Castro has some rights, though a court hearing would be upsetting. But what about this Sophia: who can believe she will be content with Castro? Sophia answers the door. Her blush lets Libby see in an instant that something has changed. Castro appears. His little eyes show triumph, yet he kindly puts his glee aside and kisses his wife. There is a silence. Sophia clasps her hands together, looks furtively at the wife and slips away. Libby enters the dining room. Where's the lady gone? Bondy says, and runs ahead, down a flight of steps into the lounge beyond. Allow me to make a call, says Castro. He steps out, returns a minute later.

- So you finally come. I assume to discuss the terms of my letter
- Don't you want to welcome Bondy?
- It can wait. But you, are you well? I am sorry to do what I do but you leave me no choice
- I am his mother
- But are you a proper one? You run amok with Rosita when I ask you to help her. You steal away on a ship so I cannot see my son. His education suffers at this critical time. You get tangled with a celibate yogi! Is it fair on him? And where is he now? Your employer is left in the lurch and she must prepare the case for Sophia! The list goes on. And I have to say you are capable of great violence. Look at my shoulder. Has it healed? It has not.
Libby withers before the mountain of her husband's ego. Why did she come?
- And you and Nadia?
- What! This was a trifle. I told you I was required to humour her. She is young and stupid! And she 'compromised me to seek favours'.
He has chosen outrage as opening gambit.
- But why would you take me to court?
- Do you listen to me, Elizabeth? Did you read my letter?

- You can see Bondy when you want
- Aha. So you *want* a divorce.
At this juncture, Sophia Zohran enters.
- My wife and I are busy. Please leave us alone
- But I have a feeling I should hear this discussion. Since it concerns my future…
Both of them stare at her, but Castro senses something. Ah! Too late.
- Elizabeth, your husband has *claimed me as his own.* Is this for better or worse? I cannot yet tell
- I beg your pardon?
- Get out of the room, woman!
- One week ago. As you predicted. He filled all the holes in my body. It was very dark, but he did the job.

A very guttering silence. Libby turns to him. There is a sort of sneering self-pity on his face.
- He must marry me now. He has no choice. Or my brothers will hunt him down and cut his throat out.
Castro's eyes bulge for a moment. Yet he is insulated by arrogance.
- She's lying
- About what? Your being killed or your being a rapist?
Libby has woken up. Sophia takes her hand, whispers.
- I am sorry. I am really sorry.

In a strange simultaneity, they turn like sisters to face the rapist Castro.

The Fall of Castro

At that moment Bondy runs in, sees the adults in their incomprehensible big world, looks to his mother, grimaces at his father. What happened next is all conjecture. It may have been that Castro snatches at Bondy but Bondy runs down the steps. Libby will have protested and Castro may have pushed her roughly back. It is possible she actually picked up a chair and swung it at his head, but it may have collided with the door, which definitely hit him in the side of the head… and there's reason to believe he swayed backward through the doorway into the body of Sophia, and it is possible she let him fall so that he likely toppled down the short flight of steps beyond, and split his head open and fell into black unconsciousness.

One thing is clear. Libby and Sophia have no plan for what to do next. Bondy is bundled upstairs. Numbed minutes go by. And like magic, Rula Cortes is there. She hurries into the room, sees the body.

- What the fuck is this?

She stares; they don't move. - Ugh. His head's bleeding. Get an ambulance. Call the fucking police.

But Sophia Zohran knows how to throw a fit. And she does it now.

- He's dead! He's dead! It was not me who let him fall. He hit his head on the door! The door! It wasn't her. Not Elizabeth! But what are you doing here? How did you know? What do you want?

Rula sneers: *He called me.* She steps away, stabs at her phone. But Sophia grabs at Rula's mobile, flings it.

- It was you who hit him. You! I saw you

- Stop it, Sophia! (Libby finally speaks) Yes, call the ambulance. Use the house phone

- No! He raped me, he should die! *I am pregnant.* With the child of that man. That man!

Libby stares at her. - Are you?

Sophia glares at her furiously. - Of course I am! Let him die. I don't care.

- Oh. I see. Yes. Yes.

Rula looks from one to the other. - What sort of fucking scheme are you two concocting?

Three women hover over a still man's body.

- Same game as you maybe

- He's your goddam husband!

- Not any more

- This is *bullshit.*

Rula barges for the door. Sophia bars the way. She grabs at Rula's neck. There's a hideous scuffle. Libby comes from behind with a big vase in her hand. She swings it and Rula is pole-axed, down, gone like Castro. The assassin drops her weapon and it cracks. Silence. They look at each other. Bondy peers in. The women regard him vaguely. He skitters across to the bodies. Looks down, looks up. His mother's eyes hold mysteries he can't explain. Are they dead? he says.

The arab women is prattling. - This was my choice. I believe in you, I care for you! He is a bastard but he is your husband. I am sorry. Yes, it is my own interest. Women are so dependent, we can only manipulate! But I am also a Muslim. Should I forgive? I must forgive but I will not deny my anger

- Shouldn't we blame Rula for all of it? We'll say she attacked him because the two of them fought over the baby who died

- What is this?

- She aborted his child. They were going to have another one! Until *you* came along

- I knew she was the devil

- So I came upon them together - and I hit her. Out of anger

- Wait. No… it was me. I did it. Me. For your sake, Libby.

And Libby bows her head.

- If you say so, Sophia

- Come here. My poor poor girl.

Sophia takes Libby about the neck and hugs her. She kisses her lips. Libby feels her lips. And there's heat below. For both. Sophia slips fingers into Libby's blonde hair. Bondy watches them. Clinging together, they ignore the child. He tiptoes away, out of the house, onto the street.

Their faces are close, and their breath mingles. There are tears.

- We'll run away from here

- Yes… no. No, I must stay here. I must face your police. You will go. You can go to my country!

- Are you serious?

- What choice do I have now? Either I survive this or I am finished, dead. Now we must call the ambulance

- I will not walk out on you! …But wait. I need to take Bondy… Bondy!

Suddenly he's not there. Libby runs through the house, and out into the street, and into surrounding streets. She totters back to the house. But now an ambulance has come. And a police car. Sophia stands in the doorway. She stares out.

Libby backs away. Away from them all. From it all.

Freedom Has No History

Let me explain how we can erase things, and why we must erase. There is no such thing as history, except history invented for the convenience of propagandists and politicians, for the delectation of scholars, for the solace of sentimentalists. There are no time-lines, no consequences, no significances beyond the fancies of you and me. For where is the history of the voiceless, the forgotten, the unknown, the unspeakable little people, the used-up animals, insects, bacteria, flotsam and jetsam who lived and passed away yet felt all things and documented nothing except that their very breath was a document of truth cast in the bright air and lost to millennial sky… These are never summoned by the denizens of the future, who concoct and finger history only to serve themselves. History is our own story, manufactured for our own business, serving our agendas… And all the selfish-stupid powers that be will try to summon Libby Castro back for her crimes. And she'll never return. For without history there is no guilt. And without guilt there is freedom. And freedom has no history.

Exile

Libby is far gone. I, Cross, arbiter of all fact and fancy in this narrative, am the sole conduit for the confessions (true and false) which make up the history of Libby Castro. Her texts to me resemble the tracts of a compulsive diarist: scatty but strangely coherent, off-hand but quietly self-eviscerating. Out of them all, for my own purposes, I piece together her final story.

'…Weeks of journeying through Anatolia and Kurdistan by bus and lorry. Country unknown, country unspoken. Don't care to be traced. Taking responsibility for the whole of myself. I wear the hijab. No-one sees my fatal blond hair. I clutch at safety inside my robes, all my secrets. And Cross, I found a village under the blue sky. The name sounded like *Nektar*.

I adopted it. Do you like? Bare hills and stones. Little houses, chalk walls, white and magenta blossom, dust. It's too hot. The biblical scrub-desert sears my sinner's eyes. Please tell Sophia she fills my thoughts. I feel as if I should be her. In exile from men, in her own desert country. I might go to her family one day, explain to them that she's a kind of heroine. Am I a fool to copy her like this? Analyse me Cross, if you dare.

Everything Is Simple.

I found a stony hilltop beyond *Nektar* - and there I sit, garbed in my white. The view is stupendous! Desert and sky collude, and behind my closed eyes I become the silence. In the silence there's no place for human beings. Life becomes simple. Nothing is, or could ever be, out of place: everything just as it is. It's not human. Why should I worry or strive? But I fear that Thiel may have missed something. *Everything as it is.* He lectured about *maya*, the illusion of illusion… but I am not so dull, I have a mind. I just do it quietly, wait for insights to come. I don't write books and strive for complexity or want to control every nuance. Things come to me, and quietness and simplicity gather about me often. But I never spoke of it since there was no space to, and because people were not interested. I am the type who never gets recognition, and in fact I am misunderstood. Up to a point I don't mind, but it can get on my nerves. Noisy Castro gets on my nerves because he won't let me be his partner. Do you think I enjoyed leaving him? He is such a hopeless helpless fellow behind all that brain. Now I patronise him, just as he did me. Is he all right? I hope he is.

I have my insights. And words don't do them justice. I see this *maya*-world is the invention of my dissatisfaction and my desire. When I strive and want and complain and get confused, *maya* is there like a sandstorm whipped up by the agitation of my mind. But when I relax, and I seem to disappear, *maya* veils its face… and there is just the soft dance of simplicity. The thing as it is, the act as it is. And even if I must tend to the body and think and work and do so many things, these are not a problem. It's just simple activity. What do you say Cross, not bad eh? Am I the Girl or not? Not so stupid! You should come to the desert. No neurotics here. Not that I mean you're one. You're just complicated. Are you a cynic by any chance? Do you remember my dream? I walked alone in a canyon assailed by voices, all in need, all calling at me, wanting to caress, cajoling at me. But I the un-judgmental, walked on, not concerned or attached. Remember how none of you could stand it? Cross?

I don't need anything now.

And when I got furious (not often as you know) it all came like a strange alien - then passed away as if it never was. I forget it all, the violence. I suppose I should ask where it comes from but I don't or can't. I don't recall my acts at all. Thank god for forgetting. Should I worry? Maybe it's the other fool's problem since they provoked me? Maybe my rage is divine justice, the sword of correction delivered by me. Oh my, how Islamic, how philosophical.

...I have the vague recollection that Castro fell to the floor. I don't know how. Maybe I shouldn't talk about this; the law might want to know. You'll explain to everyone won't you? You know me best. I'm basically a good girl, not evil or vindictive or nasty or mad. And I do care for people and try to be dutiful. I guess I'm a sinner, but who isn't? I can't control everything. Poor old me eh. Can you check he's all right? Castro, I mean. And Sophia. And my little Bondy. And Rula too. And text me. You'll help me Cross, won't you?'

* * * *

Violence, her 'strange alien', the dark flip-side of her failure to engage. The shadow! If she did swing that chair at him she might yet have killed him. Killed her husband Castro. Question is, has she blocked it out for good? I'd say not. And will she lie to me now? I hesitate to tell her that Castro's in a deep coma. Will she continue to write? I really am selfish. I'm her lifeline now. I must take care to keep it that way. But I'm sure she'll do violence on herself, abuse on herself, out of guilt. Stay with us Lib, let me be your samaritan... since you will be my suicide.

* * * *

Later. '...*Cross, I guess he did fall down*. And heavily. I can't piece it together. Sophia was there, Rula was there, and Bondy ran away. Tell me they're all right! And what about Castro? You're not telling me! L.'

Devil's Pact

I ought to tell you, reader (since Libby won't) that at the house of Castro, Rula Cortes sustained major concussion from a mystery blow from behind. Nasty cuts too. Who was it tried to thwart Rula in her odyssey to tame or destroy the mendacious Castro? Only his wife! What foolishness. Despite Rula's power struggle with the father of her dead child, her altruistic side as a champion of downtrodden women will let her *pity* Libby Castro and Sophia Zohran as dupes of a man she never gave in to. But it was a grotesque pact, to help Castro commandeer his son Bondy back in exchange for giving Rula a new love-child. One she'd keep this time. It's for this reason that she now ruefully tells the police that Castro 'slipped and fell' - a tale that strangely tallies with that of the refugee Sophia. Oh, there's still mileage to be got for an immigrant lawyer 'protecting innocents from male oppression'. Meanwhile Rula blithely broadcasts to all who'll listen, in a voice both rueful and warning, that Castro will certainly wake from his 'little coma' and return to the old self we know and love to hate. But in her dark hours alone with the bottle, we know our female dragonette fingers her wounds, grits her teeth and prays (between curses)... for him. Even though he's a raper of women. Uh-huh, uh-huh, a raper. Mmmm... Oh yes oh yeeaahh.

The Coming of Omar

'...Cross, there's a strange boy in my village of *Nektar*. They tell me his name is Omar and that he's mute but not deaf. He followed me in the market and in the street. Kept his distance but I knew he was watching. I thought he'd never seen a western girl! No-one seems to know about him; he has no history. People whisper like he's the village idiot, but I know he's not. He plays his roles just for them. And he likes me, I can tell. I invite him to come to my room. He's pitilessly silent - and every little thing with him is 'significant'. His silence is addictive, like a drug. We watch the battle-ants march in columns across my ceiling... or lie there while the desert breezes flap my curtains in significant slow motion. He is elusive, an enigma like nobody I ever knew. I feel so floaty. Nothing here under the sky has any *result*. I'm a dust mote here, a particle with no particle to love or hate. Except Omar. I love enigmas, Cross.

And Omar got his hands on my phone camera and he points it at everything. At me most of all. He spots all my moods, my quirks, and he doesn't put up with much either. I pose for him, expose myself bit by bit. I confess we've been lying together at night. He likes to finger my blond hair. But he's disciplined. No sex! What has he to lose, I ask myself. Nice willing white girl. He's quite beyond me in that way. I hint I'm ready even though I'm shy with him, but he mysteriously keeps me at bay. It's not so easy for me! But if I think about it, he's right. There's a purity between us. He seems to be concerned for me, and I feel precious with him. Real, not patronised. We're almost a couple, a strange one! And he's a 'teacher' I think. I *feel* all things he does, I read him like a crystal... but learn no facts. Instead, moods creep over his face with incredible quietness. I watch them pass like clouds over the desert days. We smile at each other and I'm content. He is even blushing or bashful at times, especially if I dance for him! I mock up a version of Dance of the Seven Veils and he thinks it's hilarious mockery. After, his brow turns serious and he sits still and he thinks. I cover myself up out of respect. I'm never naked now. A chaste girl at last. I cover all things up, Cross! But my gaze at him is naked whether he sees me or not. Then he turns his liquid eyes on me in the most solicitous way, and wonder of wonders, he sheds a tear! I assume it is for me. Or perhaps for things in himself I can't ever know. I believe he's seen horrific war. Maybe he never had a love affair and he wants us to be sacred. Perhaps he's a pure boy. I submit to him in all ways - and trust he knows more about me than I do myself. Come to think, that wouldn't be too hard since I am a cipher, a dupe, a dunce in that way. And I don't mean to be sorry for myself. I'm like the blank page people write on. I don't mind. Some of us must be pages. Let me just be happy. For as long as love will allow.

Oh but we have our 'conversations'! He's like a trickster making mysterical signs! Loves games, and mimes (all about me) which have me in stitches. You and Castro would appreciate this boy, he uncovers our deceptions! My role in our game is to guess his intentions and call out. Something like this:

He acts out 'insanity', laughs hysterically, points at me and at his head. - *Thinking makes us crazy?* I say. He reaches at the air and crowns himself. - *People want control!* Then he strangles and shoots and stabs himself! This bit is exaggerated but he's a great actor. - *Power kills!* (Cross, maybe he hints at my hidden violence?) Then he stares at me, flips an invisible coin. - *We have choice?* Then he jumps on me like he wants you-know-what and pulls me on top. I tell you Cross, he's gazing close! - *What!* I'm forced to say. Ah, he hints I use sex to shield myself. (Not with you, Omar!) Now he's very heavy and weird. - *I submit!* I gasp. And he prostrates before me. Then he taps my head. Sternly. Yes, I'm a sucker for power-seeking intellectuals - all passive and naïve. But then he cowers in a corner and whacks himself till I have to stop him! He means I'm a masochist and a coward and a runaway. Now he struts with his nose in the air. This is me being inflated. So he pouts, pores over some little ant. He thinks I pity him and patronise him. Then he crosses his eyes, lolls his tongue. This says I'm confused and lazy. Then he's quizzical, stands on a chair and gazes to heaven. *We all must go beyond this silly world.* He's right about that. But then he takes my face and squeezes and slaps it. I think he means I have to 'face it all'. Then he caresses (that's the best bit) then steps away and beckons coyly. *So I'm a tease!* Jesus, if he knew. Then he waves bye bye. I don't get it at first. He walks away, out the door. I feel a chill, but it's true: *I'm so unattached - and in an ignorant way.* Thiel already woke me up to that. D'you like our games? But Cross, the thing Omar really doesn't know about me is that I'm *violent*. It eats at me and I won't ever tell him. What do you say, psychoanalyst who loathes theatricals? (See, I wrote all this out just for you) Got me sussed, ain't he? But is he going to take me? God, I'm praying for it. I'm no celibate.'

* * * *

446

Crikey, she can scribble. But there's beauty in it. What to think of this Omar: can a killer of speech be trusted? She says he's a war victim but what's hidden there… Ugh, the pain of distance. I miss her. And now she's taken on her 'violence' like a little fetish. I say nothing to the authorities about her whereabouts, but by this stage I've hinted to her that her husband is in a coma. I take care to say the signs are 'hopeful'. There's a silence… but then she writes again.

The Edge

'…*I remember it now. What happened.* Cross, it doesn't matter any more who knows it. It was me who picked up the chair and tried to kill my husband. I tried to kill my father and my shadow. But that door got in the way. He went down, whichever way. I have surprising strength when I want to show my displeasure. You've seen it Cross, in your office. Why do you think it happens, even once in a while? I guess you say I'm too lazy to put my needs consistently. Yeah yeah. But I feel sorry for the world and want to please people, and I think I'm enthusiastic and optimistic and suddenly realise I'm being abused. I stabbed Castro once, as you know. I was sorry that time too, but as soon as it happened it seemed not to matter! He used that little lapse against me. It occurs to me I don't face things too well. I hide. True, I get involved with other people's affairs (think of poor Rosita) but I don't really want to. I don't want to be involved with my *own* affairs. I wear this world too lightly. It's so empty, don't you think? And then I'm disgusted at my own selfishness. I'm aloof then try to compensate by taking an interest. So I always want to hang round the interesting people but they all take me for a fool. *You* didn't, Cross… or did you? Oddly, I was never really afraid of anyone.

The desert kills memories. Everything seems lost as if it never happened. One ghostly thing replaces another. There's no history, no karma. Who needs people now? I don't even need art. Don't need anything. Am I depressed? Would you say I am? I'm getting rid of things. They all seem small now. Here I am on my little hill outside the world. I bought a little string of glass beads at a market. I call them my Thiel beads. Omar liked them! He saw the point straight away. He placed them round my neck. Like a wreath.

Did I run away, Cross? They won't find me. Can we ever deal with anything? I'd say no. In the past I've been dutiful and naïve (naïve might be good) and self-serving and attention-seeking. And demanding. And uninterested. And a fairly hopeless mother. And selfish. What else? What other shite can I beat myself up with! All that manipulative ego and fear and calculation and power... uuuuugh. But that's other people. I don't think they're me... but with me there's this guilt.

Cross - what do you think innocence is?

* * * *

...Now people in uniform are looking for us. We had to run away from Nektar. I don't know where but Omar knows. One day we camped out near some ancient columns and stones in the hills. They had scrabbly signatures of the dead like graffiti. Those people, where are they now? The girls, the children, the old ones, warriors and wives, minstrels, lovers, the wise. Omar and I chalked our little names in the stones. Our silent ritual. I felt sad all that day. As if I sensed there was possibility beyond my imagining... that would have to wait till another life. I held him. And he knew, knew exactly how it was for me, how it was for us. We are inseparable now. That saying: we only have it all when we know it'll be gone. This was Thiel's razor's edge. I get it now, and he's gone. And I know Castro saw the same conundrum. Thiel was incredible the way he sensed the impossible contradiction of our lives, that we are ghosts who walk. But I also loved the way Castro milked this irony to the bitterest degree! He was like a furnace that refused to die to ashes. What do I feel about my husband? He's naïve like me. Does he know? I believe he wanted to be a kind of child, yet he always rode the tiger of cynicism. Right to the edge of a cliff. And how he risked falling off that cliff. He wanted to see if innocence was possible at all. And he even married silly me.

…But I will end up helping him. You'll see, Cross. I am not such a fool after all.

So here I am. Everything is all right. This is me. It's all simple. Omar has lots of good photos of me. Thank you Cross. You're my pal.'

* * * *

The texts dried up. The above was an extract from her last. Days later a report appeared in a newspaper that police were still searching for her. Then nothing. Until a new story, on news channels and in several papers. It is not possible for me to dramatise Libby's passing.

Somewhere near the border of Armenia and Azerbaijan, the body of a girl is found in a canyon at the base of a cliff. It is identified as Elizabeth Castro, wife of the noted director. A local boy apparently alerted the police. One assumes this was Omar. One assumes he did not care whether he was under suspicion or not. According to his story (I guess he mimed it) Libby fell by accident. Possibly she stepped backwards while posing for a photo that he himself was taking.

A photograph was actually published, presumably taken just before the fall from the cliff. We see her in a robe with her blond hair showing, since the headscarf is tossed back a little. She is depicted smiling sweetly, and does not appear to be troubled at all.

This is me, the face seems to say. *Here I am. In the nothingness. No drum-roll. Just a photo-moment. Everything is simple. In a minute I'll be gone.*

I shall write in the great Book of Nothing, says Libby Castro. And then they will know who I am.

* * * *

A simple fall: the ultimate do-nothing thing. Naturally she was depressed. But she seemed at the end to be cosily in love, with an unreachable boy who never spoke of it. Did this Omar push her to her death for some ironic end known only to a mystic? Or for the sake of his honour, or for *her* honour? Or for love? I hope he cried for her. And who knows what he was… a wounded and wounding innocent, or just another manipulator? No doubt he had his mute agendas, like all of us. And here's an innocent question: should we live by agendas? What should I say (or invent) about a girl who seems so defined by the egos around her? Must she always be our 'victim'? No human being is simple, and anyone who asks what innocence is (as Libby did to me) may well be innocent, but not simple. Apparent simplicity (I hope I have shown) is not simple at all. I saw her quiet elusiveness and her child-like self-regard. And her naïve and friendly optimism, a quality exploited by all. I showed you how she met exploitation with pity or passivity, or the ducking and weaving of denial. And how she turned to stuttering violence, to self-violence, rebellion and flight. I showed her regret and her guilt, and how her seeping depression segued to loneliness, and how this turned to a delusion of fulfillment by means of emptiness, or new love, or holiness. And at the last we saw the serendipitous accident. The serendipitous suicide.

As her chronicler I tend to construe the facts of her death to signify illness and failure… when I'm sad and miss her that is. But then I remember we make things up to suit ourselves. *Perhaps she serendipitously stepped into space - walked on air - floated in the ether-wind - settled lightly like a bug in the dust of a quiet canyon… as one does in a dream.* She was very elusive! We'll never know for sure. You and I concoct our little bubble universes, furnish and inhabit them with clinging fear or lazy habit or staunch ignorance or rabid belief. But there comes a time when every one of our bubbles turns meaningless. Should we try to replace them with other more subtle moves in our glass-bead game? Let's say all girls like Libby Castro have endured, in their painful innocence, in a million lives, in finer and finer expressions of an unfolding gyre, until one day… we are able to say that Libby Castro sensed (she's not intellectual thank god) that if you suffer the disease of innocence then it's better to be an empty woman, who is gone. Not to be someone's shadow, not to be a little planet revolving about someone else's sun. Just to do and to be nothing at all. Or at least nothing much. To be somehow cradled and not lonely;

light, insouciant, *libre*, free. Libby Castro took refuge, and became a girl unmarked, a straw, a suggestion, a circumstance, a desert spirit, glint in the wind, flicker in sunlight, breath unheralded, woman alone…

Now maybe we should do her the ultimate service - and forget about her altogether.

All the Survivors

Reader, I should wrap up a few loose ends according to the little sado-masochism, perpetrator-victim side of our drama. My character-list of aggressive mover-shakers badly needed their victims. Victims in their turn accept the role of prey since they don't know what they want, while they dimly struggle toward some hope of power. But can any of us get past this great push-pull karma game, can any of us win through to innocence?

As Libby's analyst I retain a piece of her that no-one else could. She imposed on me with her teasy roles, her lazy vacancies, her insouciant gossip, her scribbles. But she was honest with me in her way, and despite the baby-lies she laid herself bare. The unthinking dull clingy dutiful lazy here-today-gone-tomorrow games - she played these like she did with her other vampires. Yet with me she was cool and circumspect, though she knew I craved to be her husband. For me it was hard, but that distance I took as a mark of her clarity, of her respect.

Rosita Caro, rampant but brittle, user and abuser, stayed alive despite the knives and now has her hooks into a generous boy with a pot of money. Despite playing nice this time, we fear our fatal girl will spend it all and move right along. Viva Rosita, survivor. She'll find her 'innocence' one day along her dark paths, since either love or death will leap out at her. Then she'll have everything she ever wanted.

Sophia Zohran got packed off home to Jordan. She will face up to the ignorant males she finds there, now that she has resolved to get truly independent. I suspect she'll stay in one piece. And Rula Cortes, who really can't stand to lose a trick, is lobbying to get her back to the 'safety of the west'. And will succeed, without a doubt.

Little Bondy lives with Julie, who thus holds onto a piece of Libby Castro. The boy in his turn clings to Suzie La La. One can only assume he misses his mum. Day by day he'll begin to build a mythology about her. Good luck with that, little Bondy.

And Castro did wake up, though he hasn't been exactly himself lately. 'Subdued' is a word being bandied in the backrooms. Rula keeps an eagle eye on him meanwhile. She has her big plans - which haven't been born yet. And if Castro does come back to his completed hairy self - as I'm sure he will, being a force of nature - he might fall to reflecting a little on his wife. On the sunny shadowy empty girl who took his name and kept it. We'll watch him sweatily construct his Artist's Version of their truth together, for his own self-sorry benefit. Naturally it will be bittersweet and ironic and complex and absurd etcetera etcetera. The great director might even contemplate composing a new and beautiful artwork. In honour of, not in exploitation of, his sweet Libby Castro.

Just like I did.